1

Victoria found herself both mortified by the depth of her lies and exhilarated by the experience of having just made more money for "nothing" as the final buzzer went off in the New Orleans Pelicans basketball game on January 30, 2019. Mail and wire fraud had become an unknowing habit of Tori, as she was known to her friends and victims. Innocent in some ways to a fault, Victoria Blair used her real name when robbing men and was clueless about the legal significance of her now occupation.

She would not call it criminal or prostitution. No no, Tori was taking advantage of men who deserved it; mostly middle aged, married men who frequented Seeking Arrangements looking for young women to share discreet liaisons with on occasion. Tori was hesitant at first to dip her toe into the rationalization pond when her friend Brit mentioned it to their group of friends in the fall of 2016.

Brit, the self-appointed leader of the Fabulous Five as they called themselves, was a senior at Louisiana State University. She fashioned herself as the new Gloria Steinman, yet her thinking was more geared towards taking vengeance on men for their rule of the patriarchal society. In Brit's world, full of studying business and engineering as a foundation to pierce the glass ceiling holding back women executives, many 18- to 22-year-olds were meeting older men through social media and having sex for money. Disgusted by the thought of having sex with older men and viewing this as a continuation of male dominance over women, Brit decided to pull together her squad and claim vengeance on this class of men all the while making a few bucks.

Brit's rationalizations were endless, it seemed to Tori at first. "Men have and do dominate the world," Brit would say. "It's about time that women use their power to equalize the situation." These words came from Brit's mouth constantly. Brit's idea was that women should use the power men give them in being sexual objects to take what they need to succeed. Not a novel concept and, in Brit's mind, it was helpful and justified getting men to fund women's advancement.

Another theme from Brit included rich men taking advantage and using women sexually, so the women might as well use the men. The two wrongs make a right approach also shined forth in other ideas, such as the men were deviants sexually praying on young innocent girls, and also that they were in large part cheaters to begin with. Brit's rationale was Robin Hood-esque.

One night when the Fab Five were having drinks and commiserating about how little money they each had to pursue their hobbies as well as how hard some of them had to work to just pay for school, Brit suggested that older men on the Seeking Arrangements website could fund their adventures and education. Seeking Arrangements, or SA as it was called, was a social media platform available for men and women looking to establish "arrangements" similar to mistress style relationships. In truth, SA was used, particularly after the demise of Back Page, a prostitution webpage, for a variety of reasons from a pay per meet venue all the way up to a place to become a trophy wife and everywhere in between.

A significant number of girls at LSU talked about SA. The Fab Five were not in sororities; less than 25 percent of the students are Greek at LSU. Nonetheless, girls tended to congregate near each other in classes and openly discussed SA. Starting when Brit was a Freshman from Alexandria, a small town located in the middle of Louisiana, Brit would hear repeatedly in class girls talk about this website where college girls were not only inundated by middle age men from whom they could choose but the money and fun times available. It seemed so attractive, the money and fun; although Brit was disgusted by the older men.

Alexandria was a small, conservative town with many Bible belt influences. Brit was raised in the evangelical fashion. A stunning beauty with long brown hair, which could easily be put in girlish pigtails, Brit had sky blue eyes. She was used to older men looking at her everywhere she went. Teachers, coaches, and parents' friends were from a very early age looking at her in a way that pierced innocence. Her earliest encounter was with the chaperones at a church weekend. John and Simon, young adults from the Church of Christ who were both married, flirted so much playing with the 12-year-old Brit by tickling and chasing her around. When they would catch Brit, she could feel something uneasy about them placing her on their laps and hugging her. This occurred while John and Simon's wives were in the church's main room cooking for the group.

Brit's father was a stern man who insisted on strict discipline. Ralph Simpson was more of a "do what I say, not what I do parent." Brit knew Daddy, as she called him in the deep Southern way, was a drinker. Since she could remember Daddy, a banker with significant respect among his peers in town especially at church, always had a drink after work and several with dinner. As Brit got older, she knew her Daddy was a man who many depended on in town. The more he drank, the more he talked. Ralph would have business discussions at dinner with friends and after dinner in his den with clients. From what Brit could pick up on, her dad was condescending and quite judgmental.

It wasn't until Brit was 16 that she found out Daddy was unfaithful to Virginia, his wife of 25 years. Brit had two younger sisters and an older brother. It was a Saturday morning when Ralph had been out all night that Virginia just couldn't cover for him anymore. Perhaps it was Virginia's boiling point; she waited until Ralph was in their room to let go completely. A diatribe about the mistress and many before her spilled forth, including words Brit will never forget: "She's as young as your son!"

Peter, Brit's brother, was 20.

Crystal, Brit's best friend, would never mention the explosion and neither would Brit. Ralph said nothing on the subject and, as far as Brit could tell, the entire Alexandria community thought the world of her dad. Brit did too, sort of. The drinking and affairs stuck in her head, way back in the place that influences decisions and actions, yet we do not understand. Consciously, she chose to study business and engineering. Business to follow specifically in her dad's footsteps and engineering as she was always advanced as a math student.

It's hard to know just how influenced by Ralph's conduct Brit's reaction to the girls in her freshman algebra class was when she heard about SA. Brit knew this, a chance to get money, was available, and she was going to see what it was all about. After listening to girls in algebra, one October night in 2016, Brit signed on to SA.

Creating a profile was easy and free for women. There were literally stars for girls who were in college. How would she describe herself and what she was looking for, Brit pondered. On herself, Brit didn't want to give too much away. She decided right off to pick a fake name, Sally. It seemed simple and homely, like a middle age man might want in a young college girl she thought. That thought shaped her description, "Young, first time user, smart, cute, fun and lover of the world." This would cover everything Brit decided—short and sweet.

As for what she was looking for, Brit simply stated, "Generous and kind man for companionship and support." Again, simple and calculated to attract most middle age men by playing to their ego. What man wouldn't think he was generous and kind?

Now it came time to attach a picture. Brit didn't have to think long on this one. No way she would put her face out in public. Brit chose the no picture option. She didn't hesitate to press the accept button where the terms and conditions, which Brit was too anxious to read, were contained in very small, single spaced print. Quick came up a message, "Your profile is under review and will be published as soon as we determine it meets our standards."

Not a day later, Brit was online and available to all the men as well as able to search and send messages. What a new adventure; she had no idea how intoxicating the searching would become once she started. The first night, she barely slept. Her in box was inundated with requests to see a picture and other propositions. Right off the bat, men requested she send pictures naked or performing sex acts for money. *Never*, Brit thought. Others wanted to talk and find out as much as they could to access if an arrangement was possible. Messaging with these men went on endlessly that first night.

Brit closed her laptop around 4:00 AM having numerous men as potential. *What were her intentions?* she thought as she started her morning run the next day. Brit's alarm went off painstakingly early that Wednesday morning in October. Not too cold, Baton Rouge Louisiana could be 35 to 85 degrees in October, and this morning it was a nice 60 degrees for her run. A cross country runner and track team member in high school, Brit tried to run five days a week at least. She was quite disciplined for a college freshman, and today found her up as usual at 6:00 AM, only two hours of sleep. It took her awhile for her mind to get firing.

What would she do with all of these would be suitors and various proposals? All of the interested men wanted pictures of her except a few. Brit was talking to a few men who just wanted sex for money and did not seem to care about her looks, or at least they did not persist in asking for pictures. There were also a few quite older—in their 60s and 70s. The idea of even having coffee with a man 40 to 50 years older than she repulsed her. Of course, Brit thought, they did not care much about what she looked like. Brit decided to eliminate these categories of men.

Still not knowing what her intentions were, Brit decided to proceed cautiously, or so she thought. She would continue to talk to men and see which ones would understand she could not share her pictures. This strategy was employed during her first class. All of her classmates carried laptops and, in class, it was common for the laptops to be on your desk for notes or research. In reality, almost everyone in Brit's 8:00 AM political science class seemed to her to be texting, on non-class related websites, or on their social media. In order to hide texting and social media participation in class, many students used their computer to make it look like they were paying attention and taking notes. Some were bold and used their phones outright.

Brit's inbox had 17 messages. Just between the 4:00 AM and 8:00 AM time, Brit received messages from nine new men and eight messages from men she was already talking to when she went to sleep. When the one-hour lecture ended, Brit realized she had not heard a thing. Even though she was a serious student and determined to succeed, this day would be full of messaging on SA, no matter where she was or where she went. Even at the gym, Brit was on the bike and elliptical using her phone to message.

Brit had succeeded in getting some men to share their pictures with her without her sharing. A few were offering her money just to meet in a public place for coffee or a meal. Why not? Brit excitedly daydreamed of meeting men for money. Her first taste of the sweet addiction that was developing. Musing in her manic mind, Brit thought, *If I can get $100 to meet a man and, if I meet two men a week, that's $800 per month.* This would be enough for Brit to pay rent and bills in an apartment next year after she moved out of the dorm.

Brit's roommate in the dorm was Valarie. The two of them lived in a suite with two other girls who shared a living room. By all standards, it was one of the best dorms on campus because of the common living room. Of course, the bathrooms were down the hall, but the dorm was all girls, so there wasn't much concern about boys when she went down the hall. Valarie was from Baton Rouge and a cheerleader in high school. Also in the suite were Colette and Cassidy, who were both from Lafayette, Louisiana, a town an hour drive from Baton Rouge. The four suite mates were the closest of friends by October, just two months after starting their Freshman year. Not in a sorority, the girls did everything together.

Brit was hesitant to tell her friends about SA and, after a day or two of messaging, keeping it a secret made her feel special. She certainly felt wanted from the messaging. Brit was ready to start meeting men for money. She planned to save everything she made. Her parents were paying for her school, living expenses, and were generous enough to give her a monthly spending money allowance. She would save for the apartment and special occasions, she thought.

Frank, as he called himself, was a doctor in Baton Rouge. Married with kids, he asked Brit (Sally) to meet him at Glazed, a small donut and coffee shop near Our Lady of the Lake Hospital where he worked. Frank was an ER doctor who worked 12-hour shifts starting at 6:00 AM. Since Glazed was open 24 hours, Frank offered to meet Sally before a shift. Glazed was seldom crowded before 7:00 AM and had a few very small tables in a corner. This was a perfect out of the way place for both to keep their rendezvous a secret.

Frank waited patiently at the small table nestled in the far corner of Glazed's rectangle shaped room. Slowly sipping on his coffee while he checked his messages, 5:00 AM passed. Brit had no trouble waking up to see Frank. She barely slept at all the night before. She did, however, have a difficult time pulling into the small, five-car lot and facing the meeting. Not so much worried about her safety or even about her identity, Brit found herself nervous as to whether Frank would like her. He hadn't seen a picture, and what if he didn't adore her? This was, of course, a preposterous thought, given her natural, young beauty and fit body.

Finally, Brit pulled in at ten after 5:00. It was not in her nature to be late. As a matter of practice, she never was late. Now Brit was concerned about that, too. Regardless, she exited her car and could see Frank as she approached the window. He was cute.

Brit was more than a little surprised as to how much she was attracted to Frank. Stumbling as she opened the door, Brit started to walk towards him. Her feet felt different and she felt weird hearing herself say hello. Brit finally sat down. An awkwardness came over Brit as the small talk began, prompted by Frank passing her the $100 agreed to in a tightly folded single bill. The bill was folded, so he could place it in his hands and shake hers to hand it off. The uneasy feeling continued as they stumbled to communicate at first. Adrenaline pulled the two through and, before long, Brit has shared her real name and many personal details as they flirted.

After 20 minutes the conversation got serious.

"How much money per month would you want as an allowance to see me 3-4 times per week?" Frank asked.

Brit, not having prepared for these questions, said $800, as that was what she intended to make from her first thoughts about an arrangement.

Frank giggled slightly and replied, "Well, okay, let's do this."

Brit knew she had said the wrong thing as soon as Frank giggled. It was that instinctual way people get an uneasy feeling from a situation they know little about.

"Are you free tonight when I get off?" Frank asked.

Oh my, Brit thought, *the reality of this is now.*

"It depends," Brit said, "what do you have in mind?"

Frank replied, "I have an apartment nearby I keep for my arrangements."

Brit nervously said, "Yes."

Frank had just explained to Brit that he'd been doing arrangements since 2011. Five years into the lifestyle, Frank had many meetings; some one-time meets and, with two women, two long-term relationships. Frank explained to Brit that he was looking for something long term and significant; that he had done it before; and that he would be there to support Brit. "Support," Brit didn't understand.

As 6:00 AM approached, Frank got up to leave for work and pulled out his phone.

"What's your cell?" he asked. Having the number, he then asked, "Would you prefer cash or PayPal?"

Brit replied, "Do you have Venmo?" while thinking about how quickly she responded. As if a friend was giving her money for a share of dinner, Frank asked what the Venmo name was and, in a flash, had sent the $800.

"I'll make sure this happens on the twenty-sixth day of every month we're together."

Brit rushed home, changed into her running gear and took off running with a face mostly full of makeup. The excitement and terror were building. She had only had sex with a couple of boys, and both of those were serious boyfriends or as serious as they could be in high school. The last encounter was right after school started, Sean, Brit's boyfriend senior year, was going into the military. Brit went back to Alexandria to see him right before he shipped off in September. The two agreed to stay friends and that dating from a distance didn't make sense. Brit was always very practical, she thought.

Later on, in algebra, Brit couldn't resist getting on SA. Even though she had agreed with Frank to an arrangement or, so it seemed, the parameters were unclear, and she could not resist the temptation. The thrill was intoxicating.

When the class was over, Brit stopped an acquaintance who she'd heard talking about SA previously and timidly said, "Do you have time for coffee?"

Maria Lesson, an outgoing beauty from Chicago, replied, "No, but I've got 10 minutes before my next class, shoot."

Shoot, Brit thought. Obviously, Maria could sense Brit had questions about something.

"I've heard you talking in class about seeking," Brit said, stuttering a little, "arrangements."

"Yes?" Maria paused. "What do you want to know?"

"How should I approach men?" Brit asked.

Maria responded, "Don't have sex for less than $500 per time; you need to know the value of your time and your worth."

Shocked Brit couldn't think of anything else to ask and replied, "Thanks."

Later in the day, Brit was with Colette at lunch when Colette asked a friend to join them.

"Tori, please come sit with us," Colette said. Brit was conflicted about talking to Colette about her experience, and it certainly wouldn't happen now Tori was at the table.

The three chatted for 45 minutes, during which time Brit learned Tori was from Gonzales, a small town outside of Baton Rouge. Tori was so sweet and innocent. She spoke in a high voice and her eyes bubbled the way young girls new to a situation did. Tori was filled with joy. Tori wanted to study psychology. Her dad was in real estate, very successful, and Tori was an only child. Interestingly, Tori's dad was 78, meaning he'd had Tori when he was 59, and Tori's mom was now 41. Brit did the math in her head—Tori was 19, must have stayed back a year in school, and there was a 37-year difference in her parents' ages.

Colette and Tori had met in sociology class, and Colette clearly liked Tori a lot. In some ways, Brit was jealous already. But, Brit couldn't help being attracted to Tori's enthusiasm. The three decided Tori would come by the dorm tonight after dinner to hang out. That night, October 26, 2016, would end up being the start of the Fabulous Five.

Tori was immediately "loved," they all proclaimed that night, by Brit, Colette, Valarie and Cassidy. From this day forward, the five would be inseparable.

2

Place du Plantier was an inexpensive, clean apartment complex near Frank's work. He had acquired the apartment two years earlier when he was in a serious relationship with a prior arrangement. Katherine liked the place and moved in not long after she and Frank met. Getting Katherine to leave, however, had been quite a chore after Frank caught her lying.

Even though Frank was married with two young girls, he insisted his arrangements not see anyone else. It became apparent to Frank that Katherine was not abiding by her monogamy promise one day when he showed up at the apartment and saw a condom in the trash can near the corner of the bedroom. Stunned, Frank didn't know what to say. While Frank and Katherine did use condoms, Frank always wrapped his in toilet paper and left the bundle in the bathroom trash can. The amount of the condom unrolled was also a giveaway that it wasn't Frank's. Seeing the condom made Frank quite uneasy.

As Frank and Katherine approached the bed, Frank asked, "Did you see someone else here since the last time we were here?" Frank motioned slightly with his eyes to the trash can.

Katherine replied, "Yes, I mean, we're not exclusive, are we?"

Stupid! Frank thought. *Does she think I'm stupid?* Frank replied calmly and with a firm tone, "You know we agreed you wouldn't see anyone else."

Katherine at first denied remembering any agreement as such and, then, when Frank pushed her, she did the common pivot and attack move.

"Well, you're married, and I'm all alone here. At least I'm not cheating on my wife," Katherine said.

Intending to make Frank feel guilty worked. The two continued the discussion, and eventually, Katherine cried, explaining all she needed was to see Frank more often. Playing to Frank's ego worked, and they were back together in a flash, albeit temporarily. It wouldn't be a week before Katherine was asking for money and, insinuating that without it, she would seek other arrangements. Frank, left feeling like an ATM and realizing she would always lie, asked Katherine to move out. Attempting to be kind, Frank gave her two months of their agreed to payments and asked Katherine to be out before the end of July.

When August 1 came, Frank stopped by the apartment and, while Katherine was not there, it was obvious she had been living there, and had friends there, too. The apartment was littered with dirty towels, sheets, food containers, and Katherine's pipes. Katherine was a weed smoker; for her anxiety, she said.

Frank texted Katherine, "You were to be out today. I'm at the apartment."

Katherine responded, "I don't have anywhere to go, Frank."

Frank asked, "What happened to the $5,000 I gave you? It was for a new start."

Katherine replied, "what do you expect me to do?" not answering Frank's question.

Frank replied, "Please be out by the third."

Katherine said nothing.

On the fourth of August on his way to work, Frank drove by, saw Katherine's car, and texted her, "Are you out of the apartment?" No response came to that text by the time he got off work, so he drove by again. Katherine's car, a beat-up, grey Mazda with many dents, was still there. Frank searched his brain for what to do and recalled a private investigator who had worked for him a few years back to uncover a credit card theft. The investigator was hired by Frank's credit card company to investigate multiple charges at a strip club Frank frequented, but on a day Frank was not there.

Frank called P.J., who recommended they put her out. Not wanting any attention, Frank arranged to pay P.J. to do the dirty work. Frank always scurried quickly in and out of the apartment complex, which was off of the beaten path of anyone he would usually know. He always parked behind the building where a back entrance was, so no one could see his car if they drove in front of the main entrance.

P.J. recommended the eviction be done sooner rather than later, and early in the morning. So bright and early the next day, P.J. entered the apartment with Frank's key and woke up Katherine.

P.J. said sternly, "I'm moving all of the things in here that belong to you out right now unless you get them first and will have the locks changed in less than an hour."

P.J. was prepared; he had a helper and a locksmith with him.

Katherine went absolutely nuts, first threatening P.J. with a law suit and, then, threatening to call the police for breaking and entering.

P.J. dialed the Baton Rouge police department's general number and said, "Hi, my name is P.J. Williams, and I have someone who needs to talk to you."

Katherine hung up the phone right after P.J. handed it to her. She picked up her phone to call Frank. Frank didn't answer, just as P.J. had requested. Dejected, Kartherine groused at P.J. and started to get her clothes. P.J. started putting toiletries and such into trash bags and moving them to the parking lot outside.

Frank paid $1,250 for the experience, and Frank had to explain to the apartment manager why he changed the lock. A white lie of course; he lent the place to a friend who lost the key, and he didn't want to bother the manager since it was his fault. Frank hoped the manager wasn't aware of Katherine's things she didn't take when she drove out mad. Katherine had come back to get the items she left on the walkway near the parking lot the next day. A few items were remaining from what hadn't been picked up by others. Regardless, Frank was free of Katherine, and he already had been searching for his next lover.

Brit had so many questions when she walked into the apartment. Frank had worked "half a double," meaning he worked 18 hours and got off at midnight. It was 12:30 AM when Brit walked in. Frank had a maid thoroughly clean the apartment after Katherine left, although he still used the same linens. And there had been a few girls there since the cleaning—pay per meet types who Frank had seen in the interim. Pay per meets were girls Frank thought for the most part were prostitutes. Although they didn't call themselves such and would never admit it, these girls didn't stay long, had no interest in an emotional connection, and got paid in cash mostly in advance first thing when the meeting started. How far off from being a prostitute was Brit or Katherine, the thought had not crossed Frank's mind. Brit hadn't gone there either mentally.

Brit started with her questions right off, fueled by the nervousness of the sex she knew he expected since he had already sent her the month's $800. Money was something she wanted to talk about, though Brit didn't want to give the impression she was going back on her word.

"Have you ever met girls here before?" Brit asked, knowing the answer, yet trying to use it as an introduction for the money topic.

"Yes," Frank replied.

"What was your arrangement with them?" Brit approached the topic.

Frank tried to be coy, replying, "Various, it all depended on the situation."

Brit pushed, "I'd like to know the different types, if you don't mind sharing, as I'm so new to this."

In his mind, Frank didn't consider himself one to lie elaborately, and he also was ready to make Brit pleased enough for sex. Frank stated, "Sometimes the meetings were casual and range from $300-700, and some were allowances which are traditionally less being based on needs and not time as well as being more consistent."

Brit now knew Maria was right on with the money and, wanting to know more, she asked, "Your last arrangement, who was it with, and what was the allowance?"

Frank, not wanting to answer truthfully for fear of upsetting Brit, did exactly what he feared. Frank made Brit feel cheap and not valued when he said, "I gave $2,500 per month to Katherine."

Brit didn't really know what to do next. She felt used already and nothing sexual had occurred. She looked toward the floor sheepishly as Frank blurted out, "I'd be happy to do a $2,500 a month allowance for you, too." He explained, "I just agreed to what you asked for and can tell you feel you made a mistake."

Brit was amazed at Frank's thoughtfulness, generosity, and insightful nature. Now she felt connected to Frank on a level deeper than pheromone chemistry.

Frank couldn't have been more of a gentleman after Brit gave him a huge hug and said thank you. Frank asked, "May I kiss you, please?"

Brit nodded her head and the two kissed. Brit hadn't kissed so passionately in her life. It was intimate, slow, and gentle. Frank ran his fingers through her long brown hair and on her arm. The two hugged and kissed for 10 minutes, getting to know each other's energy.

Frank took Brit by the hand and slowly they walked to the bedroom. It wasn't decorated much; a mirror, dresser, bedside table with a lamp. Brit was amazed at how much she enjoyed the interaction. A fantastic experience, totally, Brit reflected as she lay in his arms while he stroked her hair, both of them silent. After 10 minutes, Frank kissed Brit on the head and said "Wow, I could get used to this." Brit smiled.

The moment didn't last too long as Frank was up and in the shower almost immediately. Brit took Frank's lead and got dressed. The two made their next meeting date before they left and, before Brit had pulled out of the parking lot, her iPhone pinged. She looked down and read a message from Venmo: "$1,700 received from Frank Trotter."

Brit so wanted to tell someone and, still, the fact it was a secret excited her. Back home, Brit couldn't sleep. On the computer right away, this time she googled him. Frank Trotter, 46, Tulane Medical School graduate cum laude '96 and University of New Orleans, undergraduate Biology '92. Married to Samantha, a member of the junior league of Baton Rouge and very active socially from the internet searches. Samantha was pretty from her recent picture in the Baton Rouge Advocate taken with the Chief of Staff at Our Lady of the Lake Hospital during the annual fundraiser Samantha helped host. Samantha seemed smart, nice and pretty. Why did Frank cheat with Brit though?

Over the next several weeks, Brit and Frank would meet as many as six times a week and never less than three. Frank declared his love for Brit right from the start. Brit knew she was in love yet didn't dare say it. She was so afraid. Tori had been turning Brit onto Fleetwood Mac. One day just into the relationship with Frank, Brit recalled an obscure angry Fleetwood Mac song "I'm So Afraid." It made her jerk and flinch.

Brit, an amateur artist, decided to paint about it. Frank's hobby and love was music, so she picked her favorite song, "Somewhere Over the Rainbow," and used it for her theme by painting a gigantic rainbow on a small 11 x 17 canvas. *Something to hang in their apartment*, Brit thought. On the back she painted the words, "I love you, too."

The rocket ship romance got a turbo boost that day in November when Brit gave the painting to Frank as a Thanksgiving present. Frank had not lied to Brit about Samantha. He loved her and their two girls. Frank was not monogamous. While Samantha didn't understand, Frank wanted to pursue multiple loves at the same time. Samantha, having been informed of the truth at a time in their family's life where she believed leaving was not a solution, reluctantly accepted Frank. Besides, she adored Frank, and he'd change eventually, she thought.

Brit and Frank would see each other for nine months before trouble started. Frank saw other girls. At first, Brit didn't want to believe it. There were tales of strip clubs, friends, and way too much to drink. *Harmless*, Brit thought. Brit grew up in the age of porn on the phone/computer and strippers being commonplace; even girls her age routinely went to strip clubs, sometimes with fake IDs. Brit would get more and more hints over the months of Frank's sexual liaisons, and she didn't like the fact Frank had others. His wife was fine, but others. This had not been discussed.

One mid-August day, right after Brit started her second year, she asked Frank point blank, "Are you seeing other girls?"

"Yes," Frank replied. After a moment of silence, he added, "I'm not monogamous, we discussed this in the beginning."

Brit pushed, "I know, but we're in love, and you spoil me so. Aren't I everything you need and more? You're always telling me how I'm your everything."

Frank acknowledged Brit's feelings and added, "This is who I am. I'm polyamorous. I love you and my wife, and want to see and enjoy others, too. It doesn't take away from my care for you in any way."

Brit didn't understand. She would never understand. How could this be true?

Brit accepted and supported Frank's marriage and relationship with Samantha. It was part of the agreement. Brit never complained about Frank spending time with or money on Samantha. In fact, Brit suggested things to help their relationship, like the time she asked Frank to get Samantha a gardener to come weekly after finding out how much Samantha liked fresh flowers in the front yard of the house. And Samantha did love the gesture. Brit did not and could not think of supporting relationships with women other than she and Samantha.

"I don't want you to see anyone else but me and Samantha," Brit announced.

Frank replied, "I'm sorry, dear, but that's not going to be possible."

Their first major struggle boiled. Frank and Brit had been on vacations, seen each other almost daily, and been as intimate as any couple without kids. There had been no major flare ups to date. Yes, some disagreements, and even arguments, but never to a relationship-threatening point.

This disagreement would tear Frank and Brit apart slowly. The youthful trust Brit had for her first true love diminished as she started to see Frank as a user and a creep. As Brit asked and Frank told her about his other girls, Brit felt used, like a sex object. Even though she knew in her deepest heart, Frank loved her, the negative feelings and fear pervaded. These emotions were ignited over and over again when Frank would have unexplained time or outright admit to what he was doing.

One night, when Frank was working, Brit went to the apartment just to get away from her roommates and have some peace. Brit missed Frank terribly when he wasn't there and, at the apartment, she could wrap herself in his scrubs, so she could smell him and be close. This practice was something Brit didn't share with Frank, as now Brit thought it made her look weak. When Brit arrived the lights were on. Brit didn't know what to do, pacing outside for a few minutes, she decided they had been left on and went in. When Brit opened the door, she saw two wine glasses partly full and a joint mostly smoked on the table. Brit sat quietly on the sofa and waited. She could hear lovemaking through the not-so-thick walls. Eventually, a woman opened the bedroom door and came out. It was Samantha.

"Are you Brit?" Samatha said.

Timidly, Brit replied "yes, I am." Samantha shut the door as she whispered into the bedroom, "I'll be right back, honey," and sat down in the chair across from Brit.

"What are you doing here, Brit?" Samantha asked.

Brit replied, "You know about me?"

Samantha followed, "Yes, Brit, Frank has told me about you recently. I knew there was someone he was in love with and pushed him for details. He told me about you and this apartment. I had to see the apartment for myself. And now you. I'm glad to meet you."

Glad! Brit thought. Brit could think of many emotions for the current situation, and "glad" was nowhere among them.

"I'll leave," Brit exclaimed.

"Please do," Samantha followed, "but please know that he'll never leave me for you, and you're temporary. I wouldn't want to see you get too involved and hurt. Frank is a sex addict. A love addict, if you will. Or at least, he thinks it's love. He will tire of you, want someone new or many new and, then you will be left emotionally, if not physically. I've asked him for years to get help with his drinking and sex addiction. Frank just says he has a stressful job and needs his outlets. He also rationalizes his sex addiction with polyamory. I'm sure you've heard it."

Speechless, Brit picked up her book bag, which now seemed to weigh 1,000 pounds and hit the door. Driving home, Brit tried to process what she heard. While the thoughts from Samantha's statements rang true, did Samantha just not understand Frank? Not too long into the ride, Brit's phone pinged. She looked down. A text from Frank read, "I understand you and Samantha talked. I won't be able to see you for a while. I'll be in touch."

"What?" Brit replied. "When?" she texted again. "I need to know," a third text. "Don't ghost me," a fourth text.

Ghosting is the practice of not responding to texts or social media messages. To make matters worse, Frank and Brit had iPhones with read receipts on, so she knew he read the four texts and didn't respond. This is called "left on read." It's a horrible feeling, and Brit was amazed Frank did this to her.

Ghosting developed in the social media age. It's customarily been taught to return letters and calls; even with email, it's custom to always reply in an appropriate amount of time. Somehow, young people in society now found it acceptable not to respond to a text which clearly calls for a response. It's a practice Frank had many times abhorred when Frank and Brit talked about generational differences. Brit kind of agreed. It was rude, selfish, and uncaring to others to get into a conversation and leave it without wrapping up. *A terrible thing to do,* Brit now thought.

Brit would text Frank five more times later that night and the next morning. Upset and frustrated, Brit instinctively knew, somehow, she could turn to SA to feel better. There was always a train of endless men wanting Brit on SA to make her feel good about herself. This time, however, the messaging had a different flair, and Brit could sense it. She was mad, angry, and it showed in her messaging. Brit was demanding, looking for top dollar and only answered questions she wanted. She would get deep into conversations and just leave the man hanging for no explained reason. Days and days of this messaging occurred, and it kept her from messaging Frank, which she thought was a good thing.

Brit almost had begun to think she'd never hear from Frank when her phone went off on August 26th, Venmo message, "$2,500 from Frank Trotter". Brit's body filled with a rush of excitement. She responded to the Venmo message, "When can I see you?"

Frank next sent a text, "Please meet me at the Fairfield Inn and Suites Monday morning at 5:00 AM."

Brit didn't hesitate.

"I'll be there." She continued, "What happened?"

Frank answered, "It is best if we don't communicate until Monday."

Monday seemed an eternity away although it was less than two full days. Brit had an SA date that Saturday night. She had been going on dates charging $200 apiece and acting like a huge bitch; sometimes getting paid in advance through a blind PayPal account she set up and then not showing. Brit's anger was apparent and no man, regardless of how persuasive, had convinced her to take the situation further than a first meeting. There had been no sex, much less even a kiss. Brit was starting to enjoy the money, however. Between what Frank gave her and the couple of weeks taping the endless line of SA men willing to pay for her pain, Brit had bought a new car, many clothes, and accessories. Brit was interested in and had started going to see EDM shows with the Fab Five. Brit even had a few bucks put away for the apartment the Fab Five moved into August 1.

Frank had helped Brit get a car. As a matter of fact, dependent on the allowance when she bought the car, Brit wouldn't be able to make the monthly note or insurance had Frank left her. The last several weeks had been difficult, thinking about what she would do about the car when her savings ran out and if the trail of men on SA disappeared; not wanting her credit scarred if she couldn't make the payments on the four-door Black Cadillac, Brit had lied to her parents telling them the car was a deal from a friend's father who ran a car lot where she had a job. Brit had convinced herself completely over the last several weeks that her SA fueled approach to funding her life was justified because bad credit would ruin her chances of a great business career.

Brit stayed on SA until Monday morning.

When she approached the hotel, Brit got a text.

"Room 215."

Brit responded, "Almost there." She walked in, and Frank was already in bed. *How presumptuous*, Brit thought while at the same time being pulled like a magnet to him. Brit stripped off her clothes and jumped in bed embracing Frank. Frank loved the way Brit looked in tights and a small running top. These were not easy to rip off, but Brit managed nicely, and Frank enjoyed watching.

After the heaviest passion the two had encountered to date, Frank said to Brit, "I'm so sorry. I hope you knew I'd be back. Samantha has been monitoring my phone, made me get rid of my apartment, and threatened to leave if I ever saw you or anyone else."

Brit responded, "But she knows you are not monogamous and have not been. She told me so herself."

Frank continued, "Samantha is very threatened by you. She said my life is over if I don't leave you and stop all activity. She's threatening to leave and take the kids."

Brit raised her voice, "Take the kids?"

"Yes," Frank said anxiously, raising his voice, too, the way volume escalates in conversations when people get excited. "But I've talked to a lawyer who said unequivocally that she can't keep me from the kids if we split and cannot move them from Baton Rouge. The law presumes 50/50 joint custody, regardless of having an affair," Frank said.

Not knowing where Frank was going with the conversation, Brit replied, "Great! I know how much the kids mean to you."

Frank and Brit talked for 30 minutes about how Samantha didn't understand him anymore. How Samantha didn't care about Frank's stress or feelings and how Frank could not live his life with just one woman. Brit adored how intimate Frank was with her and how she understood him. All of a sudden, Brit realized where Frank was going or might go. Now the other women issue didn't seem as big of a deal given she, not Samantha, was the one Frank could relate to, confide in and depend on.

When Frank got up to leave, Brit blurted out, "Leave her."

Frank looked back shocked.

Brit continued, "I understand you, and we can be happy together."

Frank with almost a sad face approached Brit and hugged her, saying, "Thank you, princess, but you're too young."

Brit insisted "I'm in love and know what I'm doing. This can work and will."

Brit insisted Frank think about it, to which Frank agreed before darting off to work. The two agreed Frank would get another cell phone to communicate with Brit, and they made another date for the next morning at the same time.

Brit went home and started her morning run. Up to five miles now six days a week, she pounded this run out with the fury of makeup sex and anger towards Samantha for hurting Frank. There was no doubt in her mind she and Frank could be free. Somehow, the negative thoughts of Frank with other women had mysteriously vanished. It never crossed Brit's mind, if Frank would leave Samantha for her, would Frank easily do the same to her?

Brit may not have been so bold about the connection with Frank if she had not gotten to know Tori and her family well. Over freshman year, the two had become close friends. Tori was submissive, and Brit dominant. Tori was almost like Brit's minion, in a way. Tori regaled her father as her best friend and frequently spoke happily about the wonderful relationship her parents had. They were 37 years apart in age.

Brit, fueled by this example of success with a major generational gap and knowing her father, too, had love affairs with younger women, started to daydream during the run about mothering Frank's children. Frank's children, 10 and 12 years old, were spitting distance from her age. Brit could relate. She could be the stepmother/big sister type. A best friend, if you will.

Frank, meanwhile, was disgusted with Samantha and did not want to give up Brit or other women. He daydreamed, too. With a woman who understood him, Frank reasoned he could have more freedom. Frank's daydreams included sleeping next to Brit at night. Her nice, toned, almost-20 body pressed up against his, cuddling.

Frank's ego swelled from being wanted by Brit, and he started to think divorce was a viable option. He called and discussed the matter with his lawyer, who explained custody was not the real issue, but splitting the property and child support could be problematic. The Trotters didn't have much in the way of property other than a house and a 401K plan. The 401K would be divided equally and the house would have to be sold. Neither Trotter could afford the note and upkeep of the house if they separated. Samantha would be able to stay there for a year, but that was about it, Frank's lawyer explained.

Frank and Brit planned the move over the next several weeks. Once the kids were back settled in school, perhaps early October, and Frank and Brit had a place to live arranged, Frank decided he would tell Samantha and move. Frank had not mentioned to his lawyer he had a college sophomore girlfriend he wanted the kids to live with when the separation occurred. This turned out to be a big mistake.

After Frank rented a house and mostly moved Brit in, he told Samantha. Almost immediately, Samantha filed an emergency motion with a divorce proceeding, insisting that Frank could not have the kids live with him and his girlfriend. When Frank was served at work with the papers, he remembered Samantha telling him as he left the family home, "You're not going to get away with this, you fool. Do you realize what you're doing at all?"

Frank called his lawyer and read the papers to him from a closed patient room, so the ER employees could not hear or see. Frank's lawyer, Ted, told him Samantha had a decent argument.

"No judge is going to look favorably on you moving out and your 10- and 13-year-old girls in with a college sophomore," Ted said.

Frank panicked.

"What am I to do?" he asked Ted.

Ted replied, "You can take the risk you'll not get much custody, move Brit out, and not ever have her sleep there when the kids are there, or go home."

Going home resonated with Frank. Why had he not thought this through or given Ted all the facts? *Frank was a smart man*, Ted thought, and, here, Frank immediately seemed to now know he acted too fast and thoughtlessly. Terrified to lose contact with his kids and with the same knee jerk intuition he had decided to move out, Frank called Samantha and pleaded, "Please take me back. I'm a fool."

3

Brit was given a check for $5,000 and her car paid off. There were no goodbyes, and the entire transaction was handled by Ted, Frank's lawyer. When Frank asked her to move out, he told Brit she would be well cared for in the transition. Fortunately, Brit had not told the rest of the Fab Five, and she had kept her room and some clothes at the apartment. Brit didn't want money; she wanted Frank. He wouldn't listen or even talk. It was quick and decisive.

Ted indicated to Brit how much would be paid if Brit signed a confidentiality agreement preventing her from disclosing anything about the relationship. When Ted emailed the agreement to Brit, she noticed it penalized her on breach with $20,000 per infraction. She refused to sign, telling Ted she didn't want to have anything in writing evidencing the relationship at all. Frank, through Ted, paid anyway.

Brit decided right there and then men of this kind, all men from that age group, needed to be exploited before they did it to others. Every good idea and leader needing a team, Brit started to recruit her four besties into the cause. Her first step was at a night of drinking. These nights happened at least once a week when their schedules from school, work, and clubs could be managed for a little girl fun. On this night in particular, the conversation turned to boys their age and, as usual, more than a few complaints flew as to how much they were users, didn't value sex or relationships, and could not be depended upon. Brit thought about Frank and her dad. Not much different absent the money and slower play to intimacy. Yes, the Fab

Five agreed that late teen and early twenties boys were not worth the time. That's when Brit introduced SA.

"Have y'all ever heard of Seeking Arrangements?" Brit asked. All of the Fab Five were well on their way to being drunk. Tonight, they were at home. A four-bedroom, single family house near campus. Only Brit, Colette, and Tori had their own rooms. The other girls, Valarie and Cassidy, shared a room. The house had a nice kitchen, living/dining combo which looked out with picture windows into the back yard; typical for a renovated 50s-style ranch home in Baton Rouge. The girls enjoyed hanging out together in the main room and were there in some form or fashion all the time anyone was home.

"No," Tori replied to Brit first. Tori was by far the most conservative and naïve of the group. The other three had heard girls talk about arrangements and sugar daddies at school, but none were familiar with the specifics other than young girls being paid to hang out with men for fun and sex. All the girls seemed very interested in the topic and at the same time reluctant of older men, except Tori. Having a dad so much older than her mom, it was "in her DNA to be attracted to older men," she told the girls. The rest of the Fab Five were intrigued, not having known much about Tori's attraction to older men.

Brit started in.

"I've done it before," she told the girls.

Amazingly excited and talking all at the same time like young women sometimes do, the questions flew at Brit.

"When?" Colette asked.

"With who?" Cassidy chimed in.

And, "How much money was involved?" Valarie wanted to know.

Tori questioned, "Isn't it prostitution?"

Everyone was quiet, likely because this was more of a rhetorical question than Tori intended. After a sobering silence, Brit responded, "No, prostitutes sell their body for money. In an arrangement, a girl gets an allowance for her companionship and time with a man that wants an emotional connection, not just sex." Brit was amazed this flowed so freely and without significant thought. She continued, "We have something of value; our youthful nature and time. Older men desire for us to share this with them, so they too can feel young. It's nothing like getting paid for sex."

Brit had the power of persuasion for sure with the group, as they all were convinced before Brit finished and wanted to know more. Brit told the story of Frank to the group.

"I spent a considerable amount of time over the past year with a man who adored me. He gave me $2,500 per month and recently paid off my car. His name is Frank, and he taught me many lessons; a mentor if you will. He taught me how to work Seeking Arrangements', SA it's called, webpage for mutual benefit. He taught me not to rely so much on what men say, but the fact that they desire young women, we need to know our value and get paid for our time. We are good girls, smart, young, and pretty. Frank taught me men don't need to know the truth or even really deal in the truth. It's okay to lead them on and play games with them; they like the torture."

Brit's girls were stunned.

"We had no idea," Colette said.

"I want to try it," Valarie added.

Tori was more contemplative. She always agreed with Brit and followed submissively, yet something seemed a little off here. Perhaps Tori picked up intuitively that Brit was not sharing the whole story of Frank. Tori didn't dare ask what became of Frank and, surprisingly, no one else did either. Everyone wanted to see SA in action and get some money. Even Tori was starting to see the value in her as a sugar baby, for her mom was essentially one under Brit's description.

Tori's mom, Ashley, was a waitress at the Starlight diner in Gonzales and a student at River Parishes Community College when she met Harold. She was 22 at the time. Originally from Shreveport, Harold Rosenblum moved to Baton Rouge to pursue his ever-growing real estate and video poker business in 1996. Harold was a bachelor who was raised by his mother in Shreveport on oil and timber money. Prep school educated prior to his time at LSU, Harold excelled at running the family business under the close watch of his strong-willed mother, Betsy.

Betsy inherited significant money and investments from her husband, Johnathan Rosenblum. Mr. Rosie, as he was affectionately referred to by his drinking buddies in Bossier City, made a killing buying property in the Great Depression with cash he had saved running and, later owning, a timber mill. These real estate investments, some would say property stolen from owners who couldn't even pay the taxes for prices so much less than what the properties had been or would be worth, turned out to have lucrative oil and timber. Later in the 40s and 50s, the money really started to flow. Betsy and Johnathan had Harold in 1938 and, not much later in 1941, Mr. Rosie would die in a bar room brawl over either a poker game gone wrong or a woman; could have been both. Mr. Rosie was a popular, successful man during a difficult time, and the varying tales of his life and death were local lore.

Betsy took the small fortune left her and grew it into major holdings, not depending on or trusting in any man after her Johnathan's passing. Betsy was no fool. She knew what type of man Johnathan was; the habits he had and company he kept. Although she was always after him about the lack of substance in that part of his life, Betsy respected Johnathan. He was a good provider, and cared for her dearly. Through Harold's early life, Betsy was hard on Harold. Constantly pushing Harold in education and sports while providing for him a luxurious life peppered with lectures on the price and cost. Harold was expected to take direction from his mother and push the family forward.

Harold did just that up until his mom died in 1995. For his 57 years, Harold was a bachelor. No girlfriend, not even his 14-year-old girl next door first sweetheart who was the daughter of Betsy's best friend, was good enough for Harold's mother. That's not to say Harold didn't experience the ladies on more than a regular basis. Harold learned for harmony's sake, it was best to stay a bachelor and enjoy women outside of the view of Betsy.

In the early 1990s, video poker became legal in Louisiana. Legislation fueled by the nationwide growing gaming legalization and a huge budget deficit made for an acceptable change in the Louisiana community. Edwin Edwards was elected governor, and he himself was a boastful gambler and womanizer. Harold saw a great opportunity. The legislation allowed small casinos filled with video poker machines at truck stops on state highways or interstates. With Rosenblum Interests, Inc.'s holdings and available real estate, video poker presented an excellent opportunity to grow the family fortune. It took some serious convincing, but Betsy eventually agreed.

Harold developed casinos all over the state. Considering how regulated video poker was along with the deep politics in Louisiana, Harold found himself in Baton Rouge, the State's capitol, often. It was in 1996 when waiting to meet the Ascension Parish president that Ashley would say, "May I get you something, sir?" Harold was struck by Ashley's long blonde hair as he gazed into her big blue eyes. Harold fumbled for words and finally his standard, "Coffee, black," came out. Tori was born less than a year later.

Harold was as involved as any dad could be in his daughter's life. Tori was into pageants, dance, gymnastics, and cheer over her years growing up in Gonzales. Ashely was from Gonzales, and she and Harold decided to make that home, so Tori would be close to her grandparents. Ashley's parents, Cary and Tina, were younger than Harold. Quite hesitant at first about the age difference, Cary and Tina saw how invoked and loving Harold was to Ashley and Tori. Also, Harold by far was the richest and most successful man in town. Harold became loved.

His time with Tori forged a bond that would make the two best friends by the time Tori went to LSU. Tori stayed back her first-grade year in school, and after, she excelled. She was in the honors program at LSU, working a dual degree with almost a year of AP credits. Harold pushed Tori to work hard, go to summer school, and make her education the first priority.

Tori and her mom also got along well. As an only child and with Ashley a stay at home mom, Tori was the center of her mom's life. Ashley worshiped Harold and always treated him like the working-class girl Harold had found in a café when he was rich and successful. Harold, Ashley, and Tori all discussed frequently that Tori would one day take over Rosenblum Interest.

Much like her father, Tori didn't date much before and in early college. She was driven, spending a majority of her time studying, working out and in school clubs and activities. Tori, on the debate team and a cheerleader in high school, was somewhat intimidating to boys. Most of the girls liked her, yet she didn't really remain close friends with any after she went to LSU and became part of the Fab Five. The Fab Five were her LSU family, and Brit was its leader.

Gonzales was so close to LSU that Tori went home many weekends, and her parents came to visit often, especially football weekends. Partly from being a cheerleader and mostly from her parents, Tori grew up a huge sports fan. She loved football, baseball, and basketball the most. Of those, basketball was her favorite.

For most of her life, Tori went to New Orleans, which was about an hour away from Gonzales for Saints and Pelicans games. There were also trips to Houston to see the Astros play, and for she and her mom to shop at the Galleria.

Tori had an amazing wardrobe, and her tastes were conservative. The most fun for Tori outside of school was LSU football. Harold and Ashley were part of a group that tailgated before the games from Friday night until Sunday morning. Tori grew up at these parties and around family friends. She had so many "uncles," she couldn't count.

LSU was the kind of school where football was a religion, and the tailgate attracts many more people than go to the game. These home game parties were essentially family reunions. Harold had numerous groups of friends and business associates all over. Everyone seemed to know Harold, and Tori admired him greatly. From what Tori could tell, her parents' relationship was perfect. Like her mother, Tori had a very submissive personality.

While at LSU, however, Tori started to feel like Harold used his money and relationship as her best friend to manipulate her future. Tori didn't know anyone whose parents were such a big part of their life or who was as spoiled financially. Part of her began to resent, as teenagers often do, Harold's constant questions and direction. There was a growing part of Tori wanting to be independent. This part was attracted to Brit, who seemed to know everything and worked hard to pursue what she wanted. Their freshman year, Tori brought Brit home and to the tailgates often. Harold and Ashley liked Brit just fine, but could see the powerful influence Brit had over Tori and warned Tori against becoming too close.

4

VooDoo Fest is held every year in New Orleans on a weekend near Halloween. In 2017, the festival was October 27-29. The Fab Five showed up in New Orleans on Friday, October 26, around noon, prepared with fake IDs they had ordered off the internet from Dubai and more than enough cash for college sophomores to have a good time

Checking into two adjoining rooms at the Ritz Carlton would be delayed until 3:00, so Brit asked if they could store their bags until later. The five took off to the French Quarter for lunch at Galatoire's. A new cyber friend had offered to buy the group lunch as a pre festival kick off without even meeting any of them. This one was Tori's catch. Since the night Brit enlisted her troupe, the Fab Five had been seeking with a vengeance.

Brit laid out preliminary rules that night for the girls, which for the most part had been followed. The primary objective was to generate money. To do this, the girls picked generous middle-aged men who wanted more than just sex. The girls would use their "good girl" status to meet and get to know the men for a while before agreeing to sex and, during that time, allow the men to establish an emotional connection. No girl was to ever fall for any of the liars, as the relationship was impossible to work long term.

"Just have fun, stretch it out, and get as much money as quickly as you can," Brit would remind the girls.

Although they didn't pool their money, over the brief several weeks, each had been on several dates and, collectively, they amassed enough money to go on a dream trip. New Orleans was not far, and Electronic Dance Music (or EDM as it's called) was a passion for all of the girls. VooDoo Fest is one of the top places to rave with a dedicated EDM stage and tens of thousands of disciples. Attendees, costumed mostly, and ragers get lost in the loud, pulsating computer generated music while jumping and dancing fueled by uppers and adrenaline.

None of the Fab Five were heavy drug users. All of them had tried pot and no harder drugs except Adderall and MDMA (or Molly). Both Adderall and Molly produced a euphoric high for two to four hours with peaks and valleys. These drugs emphasized the feelings from heavy beats and bright colorful lights. The experience was pure stimulation in every respect.

Only Brit, Colette, and Cassidy had been physically intimate with a man from SA by this time. Tori and Valarie were not only hesitant, but they could find guys to give them money just to meet and take them out. Sometimes, these men would pay for them to go out with their friends without even meeting. While the money might not have been thousands, it was hundreds at a time.

Tori stood up at lunch and asked a waiter to take the Fab Five's picture. Tori forwarded the photo to Randy with a nice text, "Thank you so much. We're having a blast." She told the group, "Randy and I have been messaging for a couple of days. I told him I didn't have time to meet given I needed to get my work done before our trip. All I did was suggest we didn't know where to go for a nice meal in the French Quarter, and he offered to buy us this lunch on his account. He's so…"

"Be careful, Tori" Brit instructed.

"Oh, don't worry, girls, I may never even meet him. I have almost $2,000 for this weekend, so let's do it," Tori responded. The Fab Five often talked about their SA experiences most nights, and it was a common bonding experience. Today at lunch was no different as Tori read a text from Randy, "Order the souffle potatoes and Grand Goute."

The Five did just that while they drank endless champagne. The first bottle was at the table when they arrived and Charlie, the waiter, said, "Mr. M. told him to keep it coming."

Just as Randy had said to Tori, "When the lunch is over, thank Charlie, and you're free to go; I've paid."

After turning heads in Galatoire's and on Bourbon Street, the well-dressed cute 19- and 20-year-olds made their way to the Ritz for check in and transformation. Today's outfit was schoolgirls. The Fab Five purchased three matching outfits (schoolgirls, devils, and angels) for the three day festival. The planning for the Five was as much fun as the festival experience, perhaps more. Getting dressed together in long while socks, pigtails, and plaid skirts, which intentionally showed just a sliver of butt and the whole V was especially fun for the five. These pictures would make great bait to catch the SA fish, Brit thought as Tori questioned why the all-white shirts had an apple sewn onto each breast.

"VooDoooooo," they all screamed as the elevator door opened for them to board. Downstairs, coats were put on quickly to cover the costumes while they waited for the Uber. Inside the Uber, Brit made arrangements with the driver to hold their coats in the luggage area in back and pick them up at 11 PM. The Fab Five exited the car at the entrance to City Park and walked toward the door. Bouncing, giggling, and smiling, these girls knew how to get attention.

VooDoo had a stage dedicated to EDM, and that's where the Five headed. Between acts, they made their way up to the front after stopping to use the restroom and get water. At the portable potties, Cassidy ran into a friend from high school who had Molly. Colette haggled with the other girls on the appropriate amount of the bag containing the white powdery substance to take. Now the trip was complete with enough stimulants for the long weekend.

Before the next act started, the girls put the powder substance into separate water bottles for each of them. Valarie was in charge of this task and, apparently, messed up the amounts because during the show Tori was way too high.

"My heart is about to jump out of my body, and I can't stop my anxiety," she told Brit.

Brit motioned to Valarie and said, "Take care of this, please."

Valarie took Tori out of the crowd, and the two walked to the back where they sat on the ground.

Right as they sat, the bass dropped from the act on stage, and the crowd screamed. Tori jumped as if someone was robbing her. Valarie rubbed Tori's arm and spoke as calmly as she could over the music to soothe Tori.

"You're with your friends. We can do anything together. You're going to be alright," Valarie said. Over Valarie's voice was the computer-generated thumps and repeated lyrics, which seemed to Tori like they would not go away. "Suck that dick mother fucker, suck that dick," was all Tori could really hear.

Many people take drugs to deal with anxiety and, in fact, amphetamines had been given to women in the 50s, 60s, and 70s to help with anxiety. In Tori, the drug did not calm her at all. It heightened all of her awareness and sensitivity. She looked at she and Valarie, thinking how many boys out there were contemplating having sex with them, particularly with "suck that dick mother fucker suck that dick" being repeated. Then it hit her, the message was for Tori and the thousands of girls like her there. She and the Five had chosen to play into the objectification of young women and the aggressive sexual nature of youthful society. Tori felt completely naked and afraid sitting down in the field. She felt like everyone was watching her. Tori could feel the negative sexual energy all around her. It was terrifying.

Meanwhile Cassidy, Colette, and Brit were jumping up and down, waving their arms in the air shouting the mantra as if they had dicks they wanted sucked. Cassidy looked over at Brit to smile and could see in her eyes anger and fear when the lyrics were bellowed. Slowly, Cassidy stopped saying the words and, rather than being lost in the moment, which was one of the purposes of rave, Cassidy could feel a problem.

"Where's Tori?" she blurted. There was no response. Cassidy's movement and participation slowed until finally the show was over.

Brit checked her phone.

"I'm taking Tori back to the hotel. Y'all have fun, and we'll see you tonight," Valarie wrote.

Brit responded, "See ya then."

On the way back in the Uber, Tori stared out of the back seat passenger side window. She insisted Valarie could go back, and Valarie insisted she was staying. Tori wondered about the men on SA. Were they essentially saying "suck my dick mother fucker"? Tori felt for sure boys her age sent this message not only indirectly, but they said it directly all the time. Porn was everywhere with people her age, and the demands boys made hardly knowing girls was amazing. "Come to my room, you're going to give it to me, and if you don't your friend will." Tori had never, ever, given in to such behavior. She had heard too many stories from friends about girls who went to boys' dorms freshman year and, after drunken sex, passed out, only to be placed naked in the hall outside the boy's door with the door locked. This was a badge of honor for the boys.

Sure, that was the attitude of boys her age, but what about the SA men? The ones Tori had met so far, after sifting through those who just wanted sex or were attempting to scam her, seemed nice and genuine. Was that all a lie or a front to get what they really wanted; a misogynistic message defeating women for sex? Tori asked Valarie what she thought. Valarie responded, "I haven't thought about it at all. I think boys and men are, just like Brit says, all liars sometimes and animals motivated just for sex."

"If the SA men are liars who just want sex, then how is what we're doing not prostitution?" Tori asked.

Valarie responded, "Do you ever offer sex for money?"

Tori responded, "Of course not."

To which, Valarie replied, "Then it's not prostitution."

Tori seemed satisfied with this response, but she continued to stare out of the window, feeling cheap and used. Tori felt dirty from the inside, like one gets when they think of something completely unsettling.

Back at the hotel, Tori started to come down off the Molly. She showered and then put on her furry, long pant pajamas with a button up top to the neck line. Tori crawled into bed. Valarie went into the other room where she was sleeping, saying, "I'm going to change, I'll be right back." Tori didn't respond and had her back to the door, so Valarie could not see her face. When Valarie came back, she said, "Okay, what do you want to watch?"

Tori didn't respond as she played like she was sleeping. Valarie laid next to her in bed with her lap top out and began SA searching.

Tori's mind raced with the conundrum of her age, friends, and chosen activities versus society as a whole. Tori wanted to toss and turn, but she did not dare. She was not interested in any more conversation tonight. Tori would lay there with Valarie by her side, who fished SA for hours before Tori heard the door open.

It was about 1:00 AM when the door opened. Tori had quieted her mind almost enough to sleep. Brit was drunk and had taken more Molly. She was ready for the Five to hit Bourbon Street.

Tori played like she woke up and said, "Brit, I'm not feeling very well. Would y'all please go without me, and I'll be ready to party again tomorrow."

Brit was insistent.

"You missed such good shows today, and these super cute boys we teased after the last show. They thought we were going to go home with them, or at least out. We talked to them for almost an hour before we got an Uber home. They were so upset."

All of the girls giggled except Tori, who was not impressed and just wanted to be left alone. Eventually, all the girls left and went into the other room. They ordered room service, including Veuve Clicquot Champagne, the type they had first experienced and enjoyed earlier in the day at Galatoire's.

Now alone and able to hear the girls next door, Tori took out her phone and explored SA. She had 43 new messages since she looked at the site less than 24 hours earlier. Tori did enjoy the search. Having so much adoration, albeit electronically, made her feel special. Tonight, she particularly welcomed the feeling while maintaining her picky, selective nature on the site. Tonight, there were no men online to converse with, but it took her three hours to respond to the 40-plus messages, including reading the profiles. Tori also searched for men recently joining or online, so she could message a few she hadn't seen before.

Tori felt better and better the more she searched. It was so fun to fantasize about the pictures while reading men's backgrounds. Tori daydreamed visions of what the men were like and how they would get along. These were, of course, only the profiles from men who had messaged politely. Tori had established a practice of first reading a message before reading the profile. There was no use in reading a profile from a man who used profanity, was looking for PPM, or who made sexual references or asked sexual questions. These were not prospects for her. If a man passed the message test, Tori would review the profile and dream a little. She had no particular boundaries on the profile evaluations except men who were very overweight. She would send a polite and somewhat inquiring message back to all who passed the test. With the significantly overweight or over 70 ones, Tori would indicate she was only interested in platonic friendship, which was a polite way of saying Tori would text or meet them for money just to talk.

Tori was surprised at least two in 10 men she suggested friendship only with would respond. Of the ones she suggested being interested in more than friendship, all responded to Tori. When Tori found a guy whose picture or profile she liked (not all the profiles had pictures; as a matter of fact, less than half did) using SA's feature of showing the men who recently joined, Tori would hit the button to favorite the man. Favoriting was a somewhat discreet way to tell a man Tori was interested without sending the first message. Tori did this, too, for her last task on SA, which was to search the pool of all men by a certain criteria and rank the men by the ones who had recently been online. SA allowed Tori to select age, geographic range, race, weight, height, income level, net worth, and more. Tori's only criteria were income over $100,000 and within 100 miles because that would include New Orleans and Lafayette, as she programmed her location as Baron Rouge.

It was almost 5:00 when Tori fell asleep. Tori had forgotten all about her anxiety earlier and was content. The girls next door had slept instead of going out, and had left Tori to rest. Around 10:00 AM, Colette started to stir and this woke up Tori who got up and showered. Tori was excited to rave today and for the Devil outfit she was wearing.

"Let's go, my little Devils," Tori said as she opened the door between rooms. Most everyone was up, although Brit and Valarie we're still laying down. "I'm so sorry I freaked out yesterday," Tori said as she entered the room bouncing with enthusiasm and completely dressed in her Devil outfit, including red tail and horns.

"No worries, my Devil" Brit exclaimed as the Five all started talking at the same time. When would they leave, who would help who with makeup and hair, where would they eat, how much Molly should Tori take, the guys from the night before, the EDM acts from yesterday and today, and more were the topics.

By noon, the Fab Five were costumed and on their way to Liuzza's restaurant, which was near the festival location. Harold had recommended this neighborhood treasure to Tori, and the Five ate PO-Boys, fries, and onion rings. With their fake IDs, the little Devils were able to get schooner mugs full of beer. Although Tori was not drinking age and was very protected by her parents, Harold believed Tori and her friends would drink anyway, so he preached responsibility and tried to direct Tori towards beer and wine. The girls enjoyed lunch on Harold, who told Tori to charge it on the credit card he gave her only for approved charges.

Tori didn't need much money. She had a nice new 370Z her dad had bought her along with all her bills paid and a spending allowance. Tori also had all the clothes she could ever want from her many shopping trips with Mom. SA was a way for Tori to get extra money, she thought, for things like the Ritz, fancy champagne, and music festivals.

"Today," Tori said, "we are going to raaaaaaaaaave," as the Fab Five walked into the gate at VooDoo. Heads turning as the Devils made their way to the front, they took their Molly and started to jump. Even during the day, the pulsating music and laser lights were intoxicating. Heightened by the right dose of Molly, Tori exclaimed, "I love you!" to all the girls over and over again. Individually, collectively, or to two or more at a time, Tori must have hugged her buddies 100 times during the day, professing love. As the sun dropped, the crowd got tight and pushy.

More Molly and vodka. Today, Cassidy had snuck vodka in a flask that looked like a wallet. From the purse, the flask would come, and out of it, a concoction Cassidy called "Devil's juice." It was a mixture of vodka, Molly, and flavor drops to mask the taste. This was a perfect drink for the Five to pass around and keep the roll moving.

During the final act, Tori and Brit went to the potties and ran into a group of much older men. Brad stopped Brit and Tori, asking, "Hey Devils, are y'all looking for some souls to take?"

Brit quipped, "Are y'all sinners enough for us?"

To which Brad responded, "Let us take you backstage and show you."

"Backstage?" Tori blurted out before realizing it sounded totally uncool how elated she was for the chance.

Brit wasted no time looking at Tori for the smile and, receiving the same, she said, "Only if we can bring our three friends; were a package deal."

Brad said, "Sure. We're with the promoter."

Those words meant something, although all they meant to Tori and Brit at this moment was, *let's go get the girls.*

"We'll be right back," Brit said, and they were, in fact, back in less than five minutes. Little Devils, as they were, Brit and Tori skimped to the crowd and pushed their way up. No one seemed to mind being rubbed on by the sexy Devils, even if the motion towards the front was aggressive.

"Time to go, girls," Brit said and continued, "No time to explain. We're going backstage."

Brad and his two friends escorted the girls to the side of the stage, where the barricades had a slight opening and a 6'4", 300-pound man stood. Brad walked up to the bear and said, "They're with me."

The large man said nothing as he nodded down, and everyone passed.

As Brad walked the girls up to the stage stairs, Brit said, "These are my girls," and pointing to each one as an identification as they all walked, Brit said, "Tori, Cassidy, Valarie, and Colette."

Brad motioned, too.

"I'm Brad, and these are Charles and Colin."

The girls all said hi in a peculiarly weird, high-pitched voice, and all at the same time. It was one of those turning point moments where everyone could feel the energy of the world at work, knowing something significant was getting ready to happen.

To the side of the stage outside of most of the crowd's eye shot were bleachers and some chairs. The front row of the chairs were for the most part empty, and Brad motioned for the girls to take a seat by pointing to the chairs and saying, "Y'all help yourself."

The artist on stage looked over with his hands still on his computer and headphones on. He smiled from under his baseball cap put on low and crooked. It was apparent Brad was known by the artist, and the artist loved the Fab Five, as they could tell from his facial expressions. The girls could see the front of the crowd as well as the artist perfectly. The special monitors for the back stage listeners had an impeccable sound. The girls couldn't help moving up and down nonstop to the beat.

After 20 minutes, Brad walked up to the girls and said, "The set is almost over. Y'all want to have some serious fun with the crowd?"

Without thinking, the girls yelled, "Yes!" and, immediately, Brian motioned with one hand to the front of the stage and with the other hand moved the girls out.

"Go dance and rave until the end" Brad said.

Before they could think, the Five were out on stage jumping and dancing, totally caught up in the moment. When the music stopped, the screens on the side of the stage showed the Devils laughing, hugging, and screaming.

5

Saturday morning at 8:00 AM came very early for Tori. Naked in the bathroom on the floor, which was soaked in water and towels, Tori couldn't remember how she got here. In fact, Tori couldn't remember coming home at all. While trying to remember, Tori threw up, which made her feel slightly better physically. There were no dry towels and no clothes of hers in the bathroom. Tori walked out naked to see Brit passed out on top of one bed with her red stockings ripped to shreds as if by Edward Scissorhands or worse. She thought of Freddy. Brit's leotard was also rippled, and there was dirt and grass stains on her legs and arms. Brit's beautiful hair was a tangled mess.

Tori looked near her bed for her clothes. Tori's stockings, tail, and horns were nowhere to be found. Her leotard was on the floor. It had been cut in two. Top half and bottom half. Tori wondered how she looked coming into the hotel and more importantly how they all got back. The hotel all of a sudden didn't feel luxurious or like home. Feeling naked from the inside out, Tori quickly put on some clothes before going into the other room.

Cassidy, Colette, and Valarie were all passed out on top of their covers. There were no horns or tails to be found. Valarie and Cassidy had only their leotards on with knife slits in their stockings. The leotards were cut, and she could see signs of some scratches on them from whatever knife was used. There wasn't any fresh blood, only dried blood on the scrapes, which weren't deep but were terrifying.

Colette was different. She had a trench coat on, and there was no sign of her Devil outfit whatsoever. The coat was tied in the front so no one could see inside, yet Tori knew she was naked. Slightly hysterical, Tori could remember noting of what looked like to be a mass molestation, at best, or a mass rape, at worse. She went back to her room quietly, not wanting to invite any of the horror to her friends. There she looked around for clues. There was no indication anything violent happened in the rooms. As a matter of fact, the rooms looked amazingly clean with the beds made and nothing out of place except the inhabitants and Tori's bathroom.

It was strange that Tori could not remember anything past being on stage and dancing. It was likewise strange that Brit was on Tori's bed. Tori searched Brit's bed where Tori had found what was left of her outfit on the floor. On the bed side table was Tori's phone and a note. Written on Ritz Carlton stationary was, "Dear Tori, I sincerely hope y'all are okay. Please call me immediately when you wake up. I would have stayed, but I didn't want to scare anyone or make you think I had anything to do with what happened. Love, Randy."

What happened? What happened? What happened? Tori looked at her phone. She would never have called Randy. They hadn't even seen each other once. Tori picked up her phone and looked cautiously. It was out of juice.

"Shit," Tori exclaimed boisterously. No one stirred. Tori found the plug and waited after hooking it up. Tori didn't know if she wanted the apple to appear on the screen sooner or later and then it did. Tori checked her calls. None from last night in or out. A few missed from Randy between midnight and 1:37 am was the last one. Tori checked her texts. At 11:58, she texted Randy, "I think we need help. I'm in the bathroom and having trouble."

Randy had responded almost immediately, "What's wrong? Where are you?"

Tori, at 11:59, sent Randy a pin, which is an iPhone way to show someone your location.

Randy responded at 12:20: "I'm on my way to your pin location now."

Tori checked and Randy had called her at midnight and three more times before 12:20. There were three more missed calls after 12:20 at 12:48, 12:53, and one at 1:37.

Tori knew Randy lived in Baton Rouge, and it would have taken over an hour to arrive in New Orleans. But arrive where? Tori wanted to call Randy despite her embarrassment yet not before she discussed the matter with the other girls.

Tori hesitantly said, "Brit, Brit please wake up." Brit didn't move. Tori then shook Brit's arm and, again, said "Brit, please wake up."

Brit finally responded, "Let me sleep, Tori."

"So you know what happened last night, Brit?" Tori replied.

"Uh, we went to VooDoo, and we were up on stage," Brit said without opening her eyes or lifting her head.

"How did your stockings get cut and my leotard cut in half?" Tori asked.

"What?" Brit exclaimed as she rolled out of bed.

"Look at yourself" Tori said inspecting more of Brit's front. It was apparent Brit had been cut and scratched, as well as had grass stains on her.

Brit turned and looked into the large mirror on the wall near the vanity.

"Oh my God!" Brit exclaimed. The two sat on the bed trying to see what Brit remembered. She recalled leaving the stage and being given bottles of water, one each, by Brad and his friends as well as meeting the artist and his manager. Brit could not remember names and barely recalled talking backstage with the guys. Brit could not remember getting back to the hotel at all. Tori explained all she knew from the note, texts, and missed calls with Randy.

Brit, not remembering Randy at all, asked, "Well, where was the pin?"

Tori picked up her phone and looked at the address. It was a street close to City Park where the festival was. It seemed to be a relatively large street, but residential, when Tori pulled it up on google maps. Neither Brit nor Tori had any recollection of the house whatsoever.

"Let's call Randy," Brit suggested.

"No" Tori responded. "I want to know what we all know first."

Brit agreed, and the two went to wake up Colette, Cassidy, and Valarie. The five didn't feel so fabulous this morning and, after several minutes of talking, Tori said, "I think we were raped."

All the girls in unison hung their heads in silent agreement, acknowledging in a way only a woman knows when they've recently been penetrated.

"Everyone?" Brit said angrily to the replies of slow solemn nods.

After talking, Colette remembered all of the girls and guys getting into an artist's bus. Valarie recalled they were supposed to be going to a party. No one could remember anything after that until Randy at the hotel. Valarie recalled Randy in the valet drive of the hotel asking them for their room number or key. She also recalled being carried into the room but didn't remember by who and how.

"Randy," Tori said softly when he picked up.

"Are y'all up? I'll be right there," Randy said and hung up.

A few minutes later, there was a knock on the door. Tori opened the door never having seen Randy in person before, at least that she remembered. Tori was originally attracted to Randy from his photos exchanged on SA and later through text messages. In person, she surprisingly felt a pull. Perhaps it was the fact Randy apparently dropped everything and saved her and her friends, Tori thought. It didn't matter; Randy was amazing and all of a sudden Tori felt ashamed and embarrassed. After all, consider the girls' condition and who knows how Randy found them.

"I'm so glad everyone is awake and alive," Randy said.

"Alive?" Brit responded.

"Yes, I'm just so happy to see y'all up and okay," Randy said, adding after a short break and in a low, solemn tone, "I was very worried about y'all." Randy continued, "After bringing you to your rooms I…" Randy stopped mid-sentence. He didn't know what the girls did or didn't want to know, and he knew the girls were traumatized. They would be forever.

"Would you please tell us what happened?" Cassidy asked Randy.

"What do y'all remember?" Randy wanted to know.

Brit took over the conversation as the other girls shuffled their feet. No one made eye contact with Randy. Brit, noticeably trying to be strong, said "We remember going backstage at VooDoo fest with three guys we had just met and getting in an artist's bus. After that, all we recall is waking up, except Valarie recalls you getting us here and maybe to our room."

"Would you like to know everything I know?" Randy asked.

"Yes, from the beginning" Brit responded.

Before Randy could start talking, Tori blurted out, "Thank you, thank you, thank you," while grabbing Randy for a huge hug. At no time did Tori's eyes meet Randy's eyes. Cassidy and Valerie chimed in, too. All of the girls were very thankful. Most of the girls seemed like they didn't want to know yet.

Brit, the obvious leader to Randy, said, "Please just tell us."

Randy explained how he received a text from Tori, who indicated she was in trouble and scared. He then received a text with a pin of Tori's location.

"I tried to call and got no response," Randy said. He continued, "When I couldn't get Tori back on the phone, I got out of bed, got dressed, and headed for New Orleans. In the car, I tried to call a few times with no answer. I was more and more terrified—"

Randy was interrupted by Brit, "What happened? Tell us what happened for God's sake."

"I walked into the address where the pin was and found all of y'all there in two different rooms," Randy said.

During what seemed like a forever pause, Brit exclaimed, "What was happening?" Brit's tone was terrified. None of the other girls could remember seeing Brit so shaken. No one was really surprised, as they all were starting to think they didn't want to know what happened.

Randy continued, "Y'all were at a house which looked kind of like a business in that it was oddly shaped with all flat sides and at the top. I have the address for y'all. There was loud music playing when I approached the door. No one could hear me knocking or ringing the doorbell, so I tried to open the door. It was locked. I went around the side of the house and could see some of you all with some guys. It was dark, and I started beating on the window so hard it might break and, then, one of the guys saw me. I continued to knock harder and harder. The guy who saw me pointed me out to a few other guys, who all ran into a back room. I could see three of y'all on the sofa or floor and picked up a board that was on the ground. I smashed the window."

All of the Fab Five were now sitting on the edge of the two beds anxiously awaiting more of the story. It was apparent that their fears were a reality; this was a mass rape.

Randy continued, "As I was breaking the glass, several men ran through the living room and out of the front door. When I ran to the front of the house, the door was open, and the guys were halfway down the street clothes in hand and at least one without shoes that I could see. I ran into the house to find three of y'all in the front room." As Randy continued, he pointed to Brit, Colette and Cassidy, "Tori, you and—" pointing to Valarie "—you were in the only bedroom."

Randy didn't really know the girls' names yet. He was tired having been up all night and waiting for the girls to call. Randy hated not calling the girls by name, but thought it would be worse to get their names wrong. He paused here attempting to use discretion as the girls might not want to know about the manner in which he found them.

Randy, after the pause to think, added, "I didn't call the police because I couldn't wake you and didn't know what you would want. We can call them now." It was obvious reading between the lines Randy knew it was rape. The girls wondered what to do.

After a brief silence, Randy asked, "Would y'all like some priviacy to talk? It doesn't appear anyone needs the hospital, but I will take you there particularly if you…"

Tori hugged Randy again and thanked him profusely. She squeezed harder than most any hug she'd ever given.

"I'll be downstairs. Call me when you're ready," Randy said as he opened the door to leave. Several of the girls said, almost whispering, "Thanks." Brit, uncharacteristically silently, stared out of the window onto Canal Street.

"Don't we want to know more?" Cassidy asked.

"Will it change anything?" Brit responded.

"What do you mean?" Valarie asked.

Brit turned from her window starring position and, while waving her right hand across the room in one fell swoop, said, "We were all drugged and raped. We know that. Are we going to dwell on the past by making a big deal of this or are we simply going to learn from our lesson and move on?"

Tori asked, "What if they do this to someone else?"

Brit, now calmer and quite calculating, said, "My girls. We were taking drugs and underage drinking. We were dressed up as Devils. We got on stage and danced in front of tens of thousands of people. If we push a rape case, it will become public, and everyone will know what happened to us—including our parents and friends. Perhaps worse, it will be in the news and on social media forever. We will never escape the humiliation and embarrassment."

"They should go to jail," Cassidy exclaimed louder than she intended.

"I agree," Brit said. Everyone else chimed in with agreement. "But Brad and the other criminals will just say it was consensual, and we are heavy-partying, loose women. We don't have any way to prove them wrong other than Randy. And how will we explain Randy? A much older man we met on SA."

All of the girls realized at this point there was no way they could challenge the rape and drugging conduct. They were victims with hollow rights.

"These attackers knew what they were doing and that we wouldn't say anything. They are lying manipulators like all men; users of women," Brit said without adding the words, but including the obvious insinuation that all men used women and would as much as they could get away with. These words were not all Brit had to say. Brit continued, "We are going to be big girls. Let's get up, pull ourselves together, do up our makeup, hair and clothes; and go to VooDoo having the best day we ever had. We will use this experience to make us stronger as friends and teach us how to deal with men. Just as they deal with us."

6

Randy didn't know what to think as he drove back to Baton Rouge. Tori called his cell phone and said, "Thank you for saving us. We've decided to put all of this in the past and move on. Please don't tell a soul. Goodbye."

She hung up before Randy could say anything. Admittedly, Randy was stunned and didn't get a word out as quick as he would have liked, but he figured later he would get more of an explanation or time to talk. Or, was it over with Tori? Randy knew she had been raped, and he didn't care. In fact, it made Tori more attractive to him in some unexplainable way. Randy texted Tori on his way home, "I'm ready to talk when you are and want to pursue us."

Randy, unlike many of the men on SA, was not married. He was divorced. An ugly affair caused by Randy's drinking and cheating. Randy's ex had secured most of the time, custody wise, to their two children, Seth and Bridget. Randy, a land use expert and former city councilman who lost his seat in the wake of the nasty divorce, was a political consultant who now made good money and could, he thought, enjoy life fully. This quest for life and broken heart along with his need for ego soothing are what brought him to SA. Randy liked the youthful fire and look of young girls. And Randy wanted to meet young girls who he knew were after older men. Randy didn't want to hang out in bars being the old man lurking or even ask around through friends.

SA provided a good platform for Randy to keep somewhat private and find girls who should know he was not going to remarry. From Randy's perspective, the whole idea of an arrangement was to negotiate the parameters up front, so there were no surprises. He and Tori were doing just that when this long weekend began. Buying lunch for Tori and her friends was a way to show Tori how generous he could be while at the same time how much he could really care for her wellbeing. Randy grew up in New Orleans and wanted Tori to experience the legendary Galatoire's. Randy's childhood was spent in the Garden District, son of a successful lawyer and law professor, who moved to Baton Rouge when Randy was a sophomore in high school at the age of 15. Randy was 42 now.

Almost two hours after Randy got home, the Fab Five walked into VooDoo Fest. A little less screaming and bouncing as the prior two days, but still with a spring in their steps and a bit less focus on them from bystanders than the last two days. No Molly or drinking so far today for the Five. Brit said, "To the EDM stage. If we see Brad and his friends, we act like we don't know them at all, and give them no time of day whatsoever. Agreed?"

All the girls, feeling the adrenaline of showtime and not focusing on the fact Brit rarely asked for acceptance of her instructions, said at the same time, "Agreed."

Pushing their way up to the front was easier today, as there were fewer people in the crowd. The EDM staging area was a large rectangle with the stage in front. On either side of the stage were screens that showed images, mostly psychedelic or bright colors intermittently alternating with video of the artist and the crowd. On the stage, there was a long table behind which the artist(s) stood. That table was up on an elevated riser and covered in a draped cloth. The cloth was black.

The Five were ready to forget yesterday and rage. As the Five approached the front, the artist table became easier to see. On the front of the black cloth was some design. Getting closer, the girls could see it was their Devil costume tails shaped in a circle with the horns covering the top of the circle.

Brit looked at the girls and angrily said, "Let's go."

No one said a word all the way back to the hotel, which was amazing in and of itself. Not a second usually passed when the Five were together without one of them saying something, and usually several were talking at once. As the elevator opened, Brit said, "Pack your stuff girls, let's get an early jump going home."

In the car on the way home, Cassidy and Valarie slept while Colette drove. Brit and Tori were on their phones and quiet. Both were on SA. Brit and Tori didn't share with each other much information about prospective men to meet. This was the same for the rest of the group. A sort of unwritten rule. However, after a bad experience, few or huge warning signs, the experienced girl would enlighten the others with a text message in the group text called "Brit's girls."

Despite the events of the last 24 hours, SA soothed Brit and Tori. *What an amazing way to pass time*, Tori thought as they pulled up to the house. A drive that should have felt like it had taken forever just seemed to be a minute. SA has such a satisfying effect.

Tori still had not opened Randy's text when she crawled into bed. Tori did look at Randy's profile on SA. An experienced SA user now, Tori had turned off other members ability to see when she looked at their profile. This allowed Tori to look at anyone's profile any number of times without the member knowing. She didn't want Randy to know she was thinking about him and looking.

Randy sent another text at 11:00 PM, saying, "I see you were online today. Please give us a shot. You won't regret it. Let's meet. I'm here for you."

While Tori had turned off the ability on SA for users to see her looking on their profile, she could not turn off users being able to see when she was last online. A user could do a group search and see who had been on recently via the members recently online function. Randy sent the same message to Tori on SA.

Tori had so many mixed emotions from the weekend. She was humiliated, embarrassed, afraid, angry, yet still interested in men not only as a source for money, but also for her to feel good about herself. The attention of men definitely did that to her, and SA was a landslide of attention. Randy had seen her get raped or at least close and, at a minimum, he knew about the rape. He did care and saved her, however.

Tori responded, "I'm not sure I'm ready."

Randy texted, "How about we just have lunch or coffee one day?"

Tori relented, "Okay, coffee."

The two scheduled coffee for late Monday afternoon.

It was colder than usual, inside and out, on this late October Monday afternoon. Tori wore gloves and a blinding Pink furry hat with black tights and a large pink coat. She was adorable by all counts, and Randy told her so as soon as she sat down. Randy got her coffee, and the two talked for hours. The weekend never came up. Tori asked Randy questions about his career, marriage and love life. Randy explained to Tori his various experiences with girls from SA. He openly told her about his deep attraction to young women and desire to mentor and share life with them. Tori was drawn to Randy and found herself with him at his house after coffee under the covers snuggling.

Tori and Randy would not consummate their arrangement that night. In fact, no details had been discussed. Tori fell asleep in Randy's arms. She felt safe and secure. That fundamental need that women seek from men mostly without knowing it or wanting to admit it. Randy had it there and was waiting for Tori. And, Tori instinctively felt it, perhaps unconsciously. When she awoke the next morning, Randy was sitting there looking at her lightly stroking the top of her head.

"So how do you feel this morning?" Randy said while kissing Tori's forehead.

"Safe," came out of Tori's mouth before she thought. And then she wondered whether she felt safe at her apartment. There was no particular reason Tori was afraid of the apartment. It was perhaps the stigma of the situation and the reminder of it all at home with the Five together. What had the Five done with their brash conduct, Tori wondered.

Randy and Tori consummated their undefined arrangement and fell back asleep. Tori never skipped school, but she did today. Randy worked briefly on his phone in the afternoon while Tori napped. For the most part, Randy, too, spent the day in bed sharing intimacy and resting. Early Wednesday morning, Tori got up at 5:15 AM.

As she was leaving, Randy said, "Thank you, angel. Have a great day. I'll miss you."

The two had not made another date, yet both understood completely it would be Wednesday night as early as they both could be available.

Randy texted Tori right after he heard the door shut.

"Will $500 per week be acceptable?" he asked. Randy added in a second text immediately, "I didn't want to bring financial support up while you were here, but don't want you leaving thinking I'm not going to do it either; or think you just committed and don't know what my commitment is."

Tori was pleased with the amount and Randy's thoughtfulness as to her feelings. There was something about the text which shook in the reality of the world and erased some of the peace, rest and comfort of yesterday. Tori percolated on the idea of Randy all day. She looked at his web page, read articles about him as a politician, and studied his pictures from SA. Mostly, she daydreamed about being in his arms once again.

Randy and Tori spent months together, learning each other and mostly staying inside. With Tori's family connections and Randy's political background, it made no sense for the two to wander out, and they liked that just fine. Tori and Randy never spoke much or in any detail about the VooDoo Feat weekend, simply referring to it as "when we met." Tori spent her time in class, seeing her family, and at Randy's house. Tori would go home to the Five's apartment daily for clothes and to say hello. She also attended at least one night a week of the Fab Five getting together and drinking.

Her heart was with Randy, and all of the girls knew it. One Friday night before school ended in May, Brit, at a Five drinking night, was quite into the White Claw. A deceiving little bugger, White Claw tasted so good to Brit that this night she had too many too fast. Black Cherry was her favorite, and Brit had been through five in an hour and half. It was the end of their second year, and Brit had significant steam to release.

The Five sat around in the kitchen/living room. Brit, out of nowhere, said, "Tori, you better watch yourself with Randy. You've fallen for him, and it can't and won't work. You could never be public about your relationship and, more to the point, you know he's using you and will break your heart with lies and deceit. We are all using men through SA to fund our adventures and you, not even needing the money and absent of late on our expeditions, are being used. Wake up!"

Tori had missed the most recent trip to Hangout Fest in Gulf Shores, Alabama. She didn't know if this was jealousy or concern coming from Brit. Perhaps a bit of both, or simply Brit not wanting another man to oppress another woman. Everyone else in the room took it upon themselves to agree with Brit, more from a place of wanting to be with Tori and not from being concerned for the heart. The Bonnaroo was coming up, and Tori had not yet committed. The plan was for them all to take a large van and camp together. VIP tickets had already been purchased for the four. Tori hadn't said whether she'd come. Everyone suspected she wouldn't.

"I feel like we have lost touch," Colette said.

Valerie chimed in.

"We're all in this together, having the time of our life in college, and you're missing big parts of it that you'll regret."

Cassidy, the last to talk, finished the peer pressuring off with a velvet touch when she said, "We love you and realize you are pushing yourself hard in school to graduate in three years. We all admire that and may be a little jealous of your AP credits and amazing intellect, but this is summer now, and you don't have to miss anything school-related for the Bonnaroo trip."

Named after New Orleans artist Dr. John's seminal album from the 70s by four college friends who created the biggest camping music festival in the US, the Bonnaroo had long lost its Jam roots and headed more towards the mainstream for college students and that meant, EDM extreme. Twerking butts, bass drops, tons of uppers, half naked women and shirtless boys; mostly middle-class whites singing misogynistic rap style lyrics and jumping up and down smiling. Tori still had the image of the tails and horns in her head and deep down in her subconscious more. Randy had helped her heal these mistakes and was always there for her, she thought. Under the pressure and knowing it wasn't what she wanted to do, Tori said "I'm in."

Randy wasn't excited to hear about the trip whatsoever.

"Remember, please," Randy said.

Tori insisted it was what she wanted to do even though it wasn't. She didn't want to give Randy an opening to talk her out of the trip. In some ways, Tori knew Cassidy was right. She would graduate next year and go off to graduate school or to work. This was, in reality, her senior year, and it seemed lifetime friendships hung in the balance.

On the night before she left, Randy finished cooking his barbecue shrimp for Tori, and as they sat down in his kitchen to eat, he said, "I love you and want you to be safe. That's it. Go and have fun. I'm just a phone call or text away if you need me."

Although the last part was meant to be comforting, it hit a nerve.

Tori was worried. Not only from the last trip, but Bonnaroo was on a farm out in the middle of nowhere. It was hard to get to and out of. It didn't have the comforts of the Ritz or anywhere else. Mostly, the people scared her. Thursday morning came at the 3:00 AM alarm, and Tori was up already. Being held by Randy in their sleep cuddle position, she lightly kissed his head and got up.

Randy whispered, "Don't go." And after a brief second added, "Please don't go."

Tori wondered as the van drove away from their apartment if leaving with the Five was the right thing to do. She knew it wasn't right not to have responded to Randy at all and silently walked out. She had to shower and make the 4:00 AM departure. Bonnaroo was an eight- to nine-hour drive, and the Five wanted camp pitched and completely set before the first shows Thursday evening. *Was that an excuse for not talking a bit?* Tori thought.

Regardless, the Fab Five were off, and Tori disappeared into the joy of friendship that road trips can produce.

7

When Tori returned to Randy's, he was suspicious. There had been little communication via text, and no calls while Tori was gone. Randy saw more posts to Tori's Instagram than he received in texts. The age gap between them seemed huge to him, and Tori did little to rekindle where they were when she wanted to spend the entire night she returned sleeping. The Five returned Monday night at 8:00 PM. Tori walked in, gave Randy a huge French kiss, and fell into his bed fully clothed on top of the covers. Tuesday morning at 10:00 AM, she was still sleeping. Thoughts ran through his head. Randy was not the kind to text jealousy or insist on attention. However, he felt neglected and, worse, somewhat abandoned. Randy needed significant attention from his romantic interests. Tori was well aware of this need. That's why Randy was suspicious.

Randy worked from his home office Tuesday and happened to be on the phone when he heard Tori moving around in the bathroom.

"Well, how was it?" Randy asked.

Tori, looking at Randy in the bathroom door, said, "May I have a little privacy please?"

The please was not in a nice suggestive tone but in one of aggravation. Randy shut the door and sat outside continuing in a loud voice, "I'd like to hear about your trip and, openly, I must say I'm feeling very distant."

Tori said, "Please wait until I'm finished." This time please in a halfway decent tone.

When Tori came out of the bathroom, she did not tell Randy about the boy and two girls she had kissed in some of the hotter, thrashing EDM moments, or about all the insisting she had received from Brit about Tori living her life and protecting herself from being hurt.

"We had fun," Tori said.

"Just, we had fun?" Randy questioned with a slightly insinuating tone.

"Yes, Randy, I'm free to live my life, and what's going to come of us anyway? You expect this to eventually be something that will last?" Tori was parroting things she heard the girls say and, more than a little scared, she had already fallen for Randy past the point of heartbreak. *What was she doing, and should she just get out now?* Tori thought.

Rather than tell him anything, Tori distanced herself. Tori was young and not quite sure how to process her emotions or relate to how she felt. Randy was also becoming her first true love. Should she stop it here? Randy didn't know what to make of Tori. He assumed she was hiding something. Randy decided to let it go for now.

The kisses were innocent. Randy would not likely understand. More than the kisses with the boy, the kisses with Brit and Valarie were on her mind. Randy was likely her first true love. That could be stopped now perhaps. Tori was bi-curious, she was just starting to realize. Had they been alone, Brit, Valarie, and Tori would have likely continued their heavy kissing and grinding without clothes. In the end, none of this would be shared with Randy. Tori was distant because she didn't know how to process and relate to herself much less Randy. The situation was impossible to reconcile with Randy, too. Randy was left to believe Tori had something major to hide and would never tell.

Randy left Tori in his bed to go for dinner at his ex-wife's house. Much of Randy seeing his children was dinner at his ex-wife's house. There were infrequent weekend and vacation visits to and with Randy, but Celeste made sure the kids were at home weeknights, especially during school season. Randy's mind was on Tori, and Celeste knew there was another girl. She always knew it when the two were married if Randy would fall for one of his girlfriends. Randy was hard to talk to and seemed to not be paying attention. He would ask the kids a question, and when the kids were answering, he would check out, being nonresponsive to the answer or asking another question, obviously not having heard the kids' original answer.

As Randy left, Celeste kissed him and asked, “Would you come by tomorrow when the kids are at camp perhaps around 2:00?”

“Sure,” Randy responded. Randy and Celeste were friends now, having been divorced two years before. Celeste didn’t date, and Randy did, although nothing too public and never anything the kids knew about. The divorce had been messy with public affairs, sometimes coworkers, and many young girls, too. Often, Celeste regretted her vengeful conduct to expose Randy. All in the interest of the kids, she rationalized.

Still in love with Randy and torn between never being attracted to anyone else and her friends and family insisting she move on, Celeste still had heavy physical needs and would sometimes turn to Randy. The two had a seldom spoken, “only when Celeste wanted rule”; Randy would have sex with Celeste whenever she asked without discussion or expectation after.

Randy walked in the side door Wednesday at 2:00 unsuspecting. Celeste summoned him periodically for face to face discussions about the kids. It had been since Christmas; well once Christmas night and once the week after New Year’s, since Celeste had asked to be intimate. Randy hadn’t mentioned these to Tori, partly because their relationship was new at the time and partly because he knew she wouldn’t understand. Randy had rationalized to himself that he had been faithful to Tori. The two had never talked about not seeing other people, but given the tenor of the relationship, it could certainly be understood. This time, when Celeste asked, Randy’s mind wanted to say no, but his heart and body couldn’t.

After they had sex on the living room sofa, Celeste said, “Who is she?”

“What do you mean?” Randy said, not being able to help acting clueless and innocent even though he knew exactly what she meant. Randy still could not get away being evasive with Celeste. She knew him so well.

Celeste said, “Really!”

“Okay, okay…” Randy continued, “Her name is Tori, and you wouldn’t know her.”

Celeste said, “Whoever she is, she’s got you pretty deep I can tell. You’re going to tell her about this?”

After laying silent on the sofa for a while together, Randy got up to go. He would return the next day at Celeste’s request. As far as Tori knew, Randy was out for work meetings. Tori was still recovering from what was four days with little sleep, lots of drugs, and heavy dancing nonstop. She had rebonded with the girls and was content making plans for more festivals in the fall. Her dad had a summer internship for her in July, and the first part of August working at a law firm in Baton Rouge. Tori had another week or so to rest before the internship. She would do that mostly in Randy's bed.

Meanwhile, Celeste asked Randy to come home. Randy had been to the house almost every day while the kids were at camp. After thinking it over for a few days, Randy said, "Under what conditions?"

Celeste responded, "None." Randy looked at Celeste with disbelief, and she added, "We're better off with you here; all of us."

Randy looked at her and pleaded, "I want to be here so badly, but it will take me a week or so to unwind what I've got going on. If I'm to do this, please tell me your serious about 'no conditions.'"

Celeste knew exactly what Randy meant—no prohibition on other women so long as he kept it discreet and no prohibition on his drinking and smoking pot.

Celeste said, "Just get home and let me know when you're coming, so I can prepare the kids."

She wanted Randy sober and monogamous; however, she had learned she could not change him and saw the lengths he would go to to have his drugs and women. It was true; the kids flourished when he was home, and she needed him. Celeste could sense she was losing Randy in some way with Tori.

Randy wondered whether his decision would have been any different had Tori not been distancing him post-Bonnaroo trip. Or, would it be justified for sure if he knew what she was hiding? There was really no way to know, as he didn't seem to be able to talk to Tori. Every time he brought up feeling distant, Tori simply said she was tired; nothing was wrong, and she loved him. In the end, Randy concluded it would likely not matter at all what Tori said or did. He wanted Celeste and the kids at any cost.

Tori and Randy had a beach trip to Dolphin Island planned, leaving the evening he last saw Celeste, on June 22 for a week. Randy borrowed the condo from a client. As the two packed for the trip, Randy considered how he would break it off. Tori was going to drive them in her sports car, so Randy drank and smoked. By the time the two left at 6:00 PM, Randy was shit-faced. He jammed music in the car the entire ride while singing and being generally lovable, Tori thought. When the two arrived, Randy could not make the passcode to the parking lot gate work and generally had a hard time getting them into the property after calling the manager and his owner friend. Eventually the two were in the condo, which had a beautiful view of the beach and water. Tori began to drink from the case of fine wines Randy brought and, before too long, they were drunk.

Tori said, "Randy, things seem different lately."

Randy replied, "They are. You didn't call me or text at all while you were gone and have been asleep or at your parents almost the whole time since you returned."

"Do you really love me, Randy?" Tori asked.

To which Randy without hesitation replied, "Yes."

Tori felt like she owed it to Randy to be honest with him, and she looked at this trip in the moment as an opportunity to drive their relationship to the next plateau.

"My friends want me to be distant from you because they say you'll lie to me and hurt me. When I'm with them, it's hard for me to believe in you totally unlike when I'm with you. I'm thinking I might not want to be so close to them, and we can be close like we were before." Tori stopped, holding both of Randy's hands, looked at the ground and said, "I kissed a boy and two of my friends." Randy didn't say anything, and Tori then looked in his eyes and continued "it was nothing, just drunken party kissing and nothing else."

Randy knew right then and there he had an out. It would be cowardly and fake, but he could use this conduct by Tori to break it off and go back home. He was drunk and scared to lose Tori, who he thought he had a chance of keeping while he was with Celeste, so he was honest instead.

Randy confessed, "Tori, I have something to tell you too." Tori looked up crying and still holding Randy's hands while Randy continued, "I'm sleeping with my ex-wife. It's been going on since several months after the divorce was final. She doesn't want to see other people and asked me to sleep with her when she needed it. It's been happening long before you and I met, and it only happens when she wants to, which is sporadically."

"When was the last time?" Tori asked.

Randy sheepishly admitted, "This week."

"When you told me you were out working?" Tori said, beginning to get noticeably angry. She picked up her drink and walked to the kitchen. Just as she put the glass down on the island, Tori turned around and said angrily, "How can I believe anything you tell me?"

Tori opened the door and was gone in a hurry. Randy got up to go after her, and by the time he was out of the door on the deck, he could see Tori almost all the way to the beach entrance running down the walk. It was night, and after she got to the beach, Tori disappeared into the darkness.

Back in the house, Randy sat at the island scribbling on a pad left there for notes.

"How can I believe anything you tell me?" Randy wrote and then stared at it for some time. He knew he had not told Tori everything, and her level of trust for him was diminished, if not completely gone. Randy decided he would tell Tori everything. He wanted Tori after he moved back home.

Over an hour passed, and Randy became worried. He went out to the beach to find Tori. But where did she go—west or east? Randy went right to the west and walked for an hour almost until he reached the end of the island where it turned into a bay area. Tori was not to be found. He walked back half the time and ran the other half. Exhausted and wanting another drink, Randy went back to the apartment, and Tori was there on the sofa waiting for him as he entered.

"I've got something to say," Randy said panting.

Tori insisted, "No, me first."

Randy cowardly let Tori go.

"I can forgive you if you stop sleeping with her and agree to be honest," Tori blurted out. On her walk, she had reflected on Randy saving her and making her feel secure. She didn't want to lose it or him. He was worth fighting for, and she could build a life with him despite the age difference. Her parents were a great example.

"Tori, there's more" Randy said, realizing he had been paid his cowardly dues.

"Who else?" Tori questioned.

Randy just came out with it, "Celeste wants me now with no restrictions, so I can go home and still see you. I'll keep the house, and we can be together there daily."

Tori packed her things and without a word she was gone. Randy's contact was blocked, as was her heart.

8

By mid-August, the Five were back in their glory at the apartment. This was Tori's last year. She was going to make the best of it. Having clerked at a law firm, Tori decided she was ready for law school. In Tori's observation, there was a certain credibility and prestige being a lawyer garnered. Tori knew with her father's connections and her intellect, she could advance nicely. Tori would use all of her assets to her ability, she decided.

Brit was the first to ask Tori how things were with Randy. All Tori would say was, "It's over, and you were right. Lesson learned."

From then on, 2018-2019 was to be a year using men for money and playing with her friends. Tori's conclusion was no one would love and appreciate her like her friends. After all, they may be a little shy in telling her (other than Brit), but they were practical and realistic, too, holding this same belief.

In the fall, Tori took the Law School Admissions Test and received a 166/180. This was in the ninety-third percentile and, with Tori's GPA of 3.79, she could go to any Louisiana law school. There was no thought of going to school out of state. Tori planned a life with her father in business with his contacts and those she would make at Tulane. Prestigious Tulane University located in New Orleans was her choice, and she would have no problem getting in with her scores.

Also in the fall, the Five went to Hullaween, a music festival in Florida at a camping park where EDM was rampant. Unlike VooDoo, EDM was on more than one stage there and, after the old people petered off from String

Cheese sets around 11:00 PM, the place turned into a play school for the bravest of EDM characters. The Five, fresh off of Bonnaroo and some with individual summer EDM experiences, considered themselves masters. This time, they stayed in a cabin one of their friends owned. Many artists and neighbors were there and around for after parties, where everyone raged until 5:00 or 6:00 AM each morning. The girls were far away from their VooDoo experience and had learned not to let any boys near them. No drinks from anyone was their rule, and no drugs from anyone they didn't know or when they didn't know someone who had tried them

On Saturday night for Hullaweeen, the Five dressed in black tights with large eyes on the thighs (front and back). It was a great message, the Five thought, to all the men who constantly stared at their young, fit bodies: "We see you looking at us," they screamed. For the most part, the Five were done with boys their age or even close. The girls often discussed boys were so immature and big liars, treating girls like the Five with no respect. Brit's girls now all believed, particularly Tori, who was becoming more a preacher than a student: older men, no matter how nice, and they were across the board nice at first, would eventually lie and cheat. There was no reason the Five shouldn't lie and cheat their way into money and a good time. Lying for money was becoming the Five's game and taking no prisoners an attitude.

The Five were having fun with the deception at this point. Sitting on the porch of the borrowed cabin, Brit suggested, "Let's start advertising on SA as a group. We can do 'all for one and one for all.' We will tell men we've all never done something like an arrangement before, and we're the 'best of friends.' We will insinuate we're all bi and will be together with him as harem. We will ask for $200 apiece for meet and greets."

Full of vodka, Molly and Adderall, the Five loved this new plan.

On the way home Monday, Brit made a new SA page for the Fabulous Five. Under that name appeared the phrase "All for you." The profile included pictures of all five girls taken from their Instagram posts. The profile included the following description: "intelligent, young beauties looking for just one Daddy to share us all." It continued with language that made it obvious the Five were romantically involved and would add a partner for support and, of course, "more." None of the Five had ever been with each other except drunk kissing and only one, Cassidy, was truly bi.

Brit gave her girls the login and passcode to the profile. They were off. November of 2018 was full of meetings and $200 apiece. At least two a week up until exam time when the Five slowed down meeting, but not looking on the SA page. The thought of older men to get five girls together who were innocent and had never been in an arrangement was as alluring as Brit anticipated. Their inbox overflowed. An unwritten rule of the group was after the Five met him in one form or fashion anyone could take him for more money individually. The group had a pact: all money, no sex.

On December 12, 2018, a message came in from a man in New Orleans who was 41, married with kids, and a professional. Tori saw the message first and responded, "How are you? We love New Orleans."

The unnamed man was up early on the thirteenth, and at 5:12 AM, he responded, "I'm well. I'm very intrigued by having an arrangement with five girls. I'd like to learn more."

Tori, always an early riser who now checked SA as a matter of habit before she did anything, responded at 6:04 AM, "What's your phone number, please? I'll get you in a group text, so we can all get to know each other."

A response came almost immediately.

"My name is Gregg. I'm very thrilled to meet y'all. My number is 504 723 1330."

A text came soon to Gregg, and the conversation sparked. First, Gregg asked for pictures of the girls and their names. All of the girls were quick to reply and, before Gregg knew it, they were set to have lunch in New Orleans the Monday after exams. Early on in the conversation, Brit named the group text "Gregg's Girls." Gregg loved the sound of that, and Brit knew he would. The girls had learned how to spot a good mark. Gregg was polite, successful, generous, willing to take things slow, and most importantly, he bought their story hook line and sinker (meaning he was gullible).

The texts flowed for the first day until the Five tired of Gregg because other men were closer and more available. It was the weekend after exams, and the girls wanted to party as well as make some cash in the meantime. Gregg sent a few texts which were not responded to and felt very let down after a rocket start. Gregg had been fantasizing about being with all five in bed at once; actually, one in the bed and four around the bed.

On Sunday, Gregg sent a text that said, "Are we still on for lunch tomorrow?"

All of the Five responded with excuses. Not one apologized for failure to communicate or for making a date they were cancelling. All of the respect and manners the girls had grown up with were gone and, in fact, the Five got pleasure out of treating men with no respect.

On New Year's Eve, Gregg received a text from Brit at 9:53 on the Gregg's Girls group text which read, "We miss you. Happy New Year."

Given their lack of interest and failure to make the arranged date combined with over a decade of searching on SA dealing with girls who were unreliable, Gregg should have known not to respond. Part of him did know, but the thought of an arrangement with the Five, and all that entailed propelled him to the keys. He texted, "Happy New Year. It's great to hear from y'all. Doing something fun?"

Within two minutes, all of the Five texted back. The attention was grand when it came. All of the Five were in different towns for this part of their break. The texting attention thoughtfully continued into New Year's Day, when Gregg felt comfortable enough to send his girls a song.

Gregg was a Costco Regional Manager. At 41, Gregg was over Louisiana, Arkansas, and Mississippi. He hired and supervised the store managers. Having grown up in the Pacific Northwest moving first from Seattle to Portland, Gregg was a career Costco employee. Gregg started first in the warehouse at 16 and worked his way up to store manager by 29. He was a rising star at Costco who, despite no college education, was promoted at 35 to Regional Manager. Gregg moved with his family's New Orleans and set up life in the suburb Metairie.

An amateur lyricist and lover of music, Gregg wrote songs. New Year's Day, Gregg woke up next to his wife Seltha and wrote a song he titled "New Year's Day." This piece discussed the hope, promise, and opportunity the New Year brings for people and was inspired by the promise of an arrangement with his girls. He sent the song to the Five, who adored the lyrics, according to the return hearts and words of appreciation. Gregg wondered if any of the girls got the not so subtle portions that were intended for them encouraging a real and significant relationship. What the Five saw, of course, was a delusional older man they referred to as a SIMP. To the Five, a SIMP was a man who foolishly overvalued a woman and could be taken advantage of for it.

After texting back and forth for days about Gregg's songwriting and having Gregg send more songs, Gregg offered to buy a welcome home dinner for the Five on their return to school. The Five went to Ruth's Chris in Baton Rouge and had a wonderful meal Gregg arranged with no check delivered. There was champagne waiting at the table, just like Randy did at Galatoire's in the fall of 2017. No one thought about Randy except Tori, who grimmaced and wiped her mind clean. There had been so many admirers the last few months, and none of them meant a thing.

Several days after dinner, the Five found themselves at the Palace Café on Canal Street in New Orleans. Gregg arrived early, and the girls were 40 minutes late. The Five had texted on the way asking Gregg to Venmo the $1,000, so Gregg figured they were coming. He had been stood up many times before by SA dates, so he responded suggesting he would give the Five the $1,000 on arrival. While waiting, Gregg had the time to doubt whether meeting in such a public place was a good idea. While he lived in the suburbs and his wife would certainly not be at the Palace Café, he could see other people who might gossip and, worse yet, they could see him, and he would not know. It wasn't unusual for Gregg to have lunch downtown with conventioneers and the restaurant was in the middle of tourist and convention central. No matter how much Gregg tried to rationalize away the risk, he still felt nervous.

When the Five walked in, Gregg's nerves didn't dissipate. Wow, they were so gorgeous, he thought. A midlevel sex addict, Gregg's mind wandered immediately to which one he'd like first and then the next.

"I'm glad you guys could make it," Gregg said, showing he was obviously not from the South. Brit introduced everyone and sat on Gregg's left side. Gregg handed Brit an envelope containing $1,000. Tori sat on Gregg's right. The conversation seemed strained at first with small talk here and there.

Once Brit asked Gregg, "Tell us about your experience with arrangements," Gregg talked for quite a while. An extensive record going back to 2011 on SA and through strippers before.

"Over the last seven years, I have had some significant arrangements, which were very emotionally rewarding," Gregg concluded and just added, "in one of my arrangements, we had a relationship with a couple who were girls, so there were four of us, but this would be six. How do you envision it would work?"

Brit answered, "We are all very close, and one or any number of us may be available when you want. We can come as single or a group depending on what you and we want at the time."

Gregg asked "Would it always be $200 a piece a time, or should the gift vary?" Gift was a term used in the SA environment, so as not to make the exchange seem as transactional as price or cost. Gregg's experience led him to want some sort of fixed monthly or weekly amount. Despite the question regarding a set allowance, the girls avoided giving a number. The lunch lasted about an hour and 15 minutes. When it broke up, Gregg was not any clearer on what allowance may look like for the group and was left wondering why the Five would spend so much time and effort for nothing substantive when he obviously had wanted to continue.

After the girls left and in the car on his way back to the office, Gregg texted, "Thank you for the time today. Please let me know how you want to proceed."

In the Gregg's Girls group text, Valarie responded, "We're going shopping. Would you like to help us out?"

Brit texted, "Thanks for lunch. We are going to write you a song on the way home."

Gregg, now in the parking lot at his office responded, "A song would be perfect. As we get to know each other better, shopping for sure."

Later in the day, there was no song. Gregg had been checking his texts very frequently. He also went on SA. The Fab Five were online. Gregg did not understand what was happening because the Five had told him at lunch they were new to arrangements, and they all just wanted one guy. Gregg had asked them to get back to him on an allowance structure. Rather than do that, they were back on SA.

He texted Gregg's Girls, "I see y'all are on SA. I'm serious about our arrangement and ready to start if we can agree on an allowance weekly or monthly. I don't want to do PPM because it's too transactional and objectifies you and me."

After an hour, there was no response from Gregg's Girls.

They were gorgeous, smart and so unreliable, Gregg mused. His fantasy of a harem overwhelmed any realistic thought.

Finally, Tori texted him separately, "I'm interested in an arrangement with you."

"What about the others?" Gregg responded.

Tori answered, "They're okay with it. We just go in groups, and we say we were all together for safety reasons. If you want one or more than one of them to come with me sometimes, we can work that out. But for now, I'm wanting to establish an arrangement with you."

Gregg and Tori texted all afternoon and evening. She told him she had only one prior arrangement, and that was with a doctor from out of town who traveled to Baton Rouge frequently for work. This doctor took her on many trips all over, and he loved her deeply, she said. It ended because he wanted to get married and, while she adored older men and "it was in her genes" she said to like older men, she didn't love this doctor. This affair lasted for two years, Tori told Gregg, and Tori also added, "I found him organically; we met in an airport. I've never been with someone from SA before." There was not a shred of truth in this web, and Tori didn't mind one bit.

Tori and Gregg made a date for the next day to have lunch again. Mr. Ed's Seafood was an out of the way place in the French Quarter. Off the beaten path and very low risk of being seen. It was odd for Gregg to take off two days in a row during lunch given it was a heavy traffic flow time at Costco. While he didn't work the stores per se, he liked to walk them daily and also meet with his managers in the mornings. Afternoons were usually the time Gregg liked to meet in his apartment with girls. This day, Tori would meet him for lunch and come to his apartment to get a feel for the location. They did talk significantly about prior arrangements and expectations including money.

Tori told Gregg she was going to law school, having aced the LSAT, in just a few months. Tori told Gregg at the end of the summer, she'd move to New Orleans and start Tulane Law. Before that, the two discussed Tori coming to New Orleans at least three times a week and an allowance of $500 weekly plus monthly parking. Gregg told Tori he'd look into parking for her. The two also talked about LSU Tiger football and how Gregg was becoming a big transplanted fan. Just about everyone in South Louisiana was a fan. Denying all of her family upbringing and heritage in this statement, Tori said, "I don't really like sports. I am a homebody." Somehow Tori was instinctually learning the right lies to say to a man after reading him to hook him hard.

When they left, Gregg promised to look up parking options near the apartment, and Tori said she'd think about everything. Gregg did too. Before long, Gregg texted Tori, "I want to pay for your parking and gas today. What's your Venmo, and I'll send you $100."

Tori responded, "Thank you very much for the offer, but I want you to know how important the relationship aspect of this is to me. And, I'm not all about the money."

"Wow! I'm ready to start now," Gregg responded. It was not until the next morning when Gregg woke up at his usual 4:30 AM that he saw Tori had not responded that night to his text. Gregg texted again, "I just want to let you know I'm well worth your decision and will care for you financially and emotionally."

At 8:23 AM, Tori responded, "Yes, I will do it. When shall I come next?"

Gregg, thinking it so opportune his wife had her weekly Bible class and dinner on Thursday nights, said, "Please come tonight for 5:00 PM."

Tori agreed, and Gregg was ecstatic. He turned to looking for parking right away not being able to think of anything else other than Tori. He found a lot for $200 and texted Tori about it with a link. She replied, "Could you Venmo me the money please?"

Gregg replied, "Of course. What's your Venmo?"

After Tori sent her Venmo, Gregg sent the parking and first weekly allowance totaling $700.

At 5:30, Gregg texted Tori, "How are you coming? Did I tell you I'm excited!"

Tori replied. "I had to get someone to watch my dog and am stopping for gas."

Gregg responded, "What's your ETA?" at 5:38.

Tori didn't respond until 6:25 and then said, "The traffic is so bad, I'm hardly moving on the I10 coming into New Orleans."

Gregg, unsure about why there would be traffic inbound at this time, said, "No worries, dear, I'm waiting for you."

At 7:30, Gregg, having looked on his phone for traffic or accidents, texted again, "Are you okay?"

Tori responded, "I got a flat tire and had to fix it. I'll be there soon. Sorry."

Gregg responded, "So sorry."

By 8:45 he had not heard from Tori and was needing to go home soon. He Facetimed Tori, but being suspicious, he programmed the phone, so Unknown Caller appeared. This was a trick he had learned from a stock boy recently. *Kids knew everything about technology*, Gregg thought when he called.

Gregg's suspicions were confirmed when Tori picked up. Tori answered in what she thought would be a cute way with her back to the basketball court, so the caller could see she was at the Pelicans game.

"Heyyyyy," she said until the sight of Gregg caught her eye and she disconnected immediately

When the final buzzer sounded, Tori could feel her body vibrate inside and out.

9

The first year of law school was as intimidating for Tori as everyone made it out to be. Weinmann Hall is a large brick building on Freret Street in New Orleans, right in the heart of the Tulane University campus. About 40 percent of the incoming class in the fall of 2019 were from Louisiana. Future politicians, judges, and managing partners of major law firms sat in the school's auditorium. The Law School Dean addressed the couple hundred incoming students, including Tori, on a hot August morning for orientation. All of the full-time faculty was in attendance.

Tori was intimidated by the new place and faces. She was also thrilled to be at Tulane, and proud of her accomplishment to get in with no help from Daddy. Tori was also a year younger than almost everyone there having finished school in three years, and she was surprised that the class had what appeared to be 10 percent or more members who were substantially older than the 22-25 age range of most of the students. After the orientation's main presentation, Tori walked around the school to find her class rooms. Tori's first class was Torts, which was on Monday, Wednesday, and Friday from 9-9:50.

Tori's section of Torts was taught by Arthur Tomlinson. That night, Tori googled Professor Tomlinson and found out that he was 41 years old. *The same age as Gregg,* Tori thought. Having graduated from Yale Law School and Georgetown Undergrad (History and Philosophy), Arthur Tomlinson taught 1L Torts and upper-class ethics classes. Professor Tomlinson practiced law as many law school professors did on the side by consulting with other lawyers and doing some research and brief writing. Professor Tomlinson's web page contained information about his family, wife Christine of 15 years and two children, a boy and a girl. A native New Orleanian, Professor Tomlinson went to Jesuit High School. He was significantly involved in the Catholic Church and various charities, including numerous Catholic affiliated boards.

What the web didn't tell Tori was the teaching style of Professor Tomlinson. Law school primarily involved teaching under the Socratic method. Simply defined, this style was to ask open ended questions provoking thought and discussion on the topic at hand. Just like every other incoming 1L, as they're referred, Tori was nervous to get called on her first, second, and for that matter, any day. The night before her first class, Tori commiserated about her nerves with Taylor, her roommate. Taylor was a friend of a friend from LSU who Tori had approached about being roommates in March of last semester upon finding out they'd both be attending Tulane in the Fall.

Taylor was from Shreveport, Louisiana. More Texas in personality than Louisiana, Tori thought, Taylor was very serious about law school. Her father and grandfather were lawyers in Shreveport, and Taylor wanted to graduate as they both had from Tulane and return to their practice. Taylor had a business degree from LSU. While the two were not really friends before this first week moving in other than through social media, they both could relate to each other being from established families and wanting to go to work for family at some point after school. While Tori wasn't exactly sure if she would practice law at a firm or go directly to work for her dad, she knew she would be working with her dad eventually and, even if at a firm, the firm would work for her dad. Having employment already was a fact that separated Tori and Taylor from their classmates and allowed them to bond. There are also great pressures that come with familial expectations which both shared.

"Good morning, class. Welcome to Torts and, more importantly, welcome to law school. Your life will never be the same after today. Congratulations, it's quite an honor and privilege to be an attorney. You are on your way there, ladies and gentleman," Professor Tomlinson said. Tori was so excited to hear those words. Becoming an attorney was Tori's dream.

She sat in a large classroom with what looked like to be 75 people. Taylor sat next to her, and they were in the third row a bit off to the left of center. The two felt overdressed somewhat. Tori always dressed higher than the norm for an occasion, especially to make a big first impression. She had on a white mini skirt with a pink blouse. While Tori was one of those young girls who didn't have to wear any makeup to look stunning, she had it on today, and her hair up in braids. More "cute sorority girl" than professional, she stood out and was a head turner. Taylor also wore a skirt and blouse. The two certainly turned all heads when they walked in early, even if there were only 20 students or so already waiting 15 minutes early. Tori could feel the nerves not only from her but from the class collective.

Professor Tomlinson asked the class, "Who can tell me what a tort is?"

Several hands went up. Professor Tomlinson pointed at a young man in the second row not far from Tori and Taylor. The young man said, "Negligence."

Professor Tomlinson said, "Yes, negligence is a type of tort but any others?"

Another hand was called on.

"Wrongful acts which cause damages."

"Yes," Professor Tomlinson said.

"An act, whether intentional or accidental, from which injury occurs to another. Torts include all negligence cases as well as intentional wrongs which result in harm," Professor Tomlinson said as he wrote the definition on the black board. "And who can define negligence for me?" Professor Tomlinson asked.

Tori wondered how people might know these definitions; she didn't. There hadn't been any homework or required reading assigned. Tori had researched the teacher but not the subject before class. A mistake she wouldn't make again.

"Negligence is when someone doesn't do something they should or does something they shouldn't," a voice volunteered from the back.

"Please, sir, wait to be called on for proper order in my class," Professor Tomlinson said. "This is a good time to pass out the room seating chart and have you fill in your name in large print and legibly at the spot you are sitting in. This will be your place in class. I will call on you from this chart and take a roll, too. You are only allowed three unexcused absences from the class, or you will be subject to a whole letter grade drop. For your fourth and each other absence, a grade drop for you. Given that there is only one exam for your grade here at the end of the semester, and we cover significant ground each class, I suggest you don't miss class ever," Professor Tomlinson said.

Tori could feel her nerves rumbling. So far, Professor Tomlimson seemed nice and professional. He wasn't dictatorial or rude like she feared from a 1L professor. He was not like the professor in the *Paper Chase*, an old movie her dad suggested she watch. But the thought of one exam. She could come to class daily, no problem. She could study and research, no problem. She could participate in class likely with some nervousness. But one exam scared her. What if she had a bad day? What if she froze up?

While Tori was getting lost in daydreaming horrific exam possibilities, Professor Tomlinson said, "Back to negligence. Yes, negligence is where a person has a duty to perform a task and her conduct does not live up to the standard in such duty. Who can think of an example?" Professor Tomlinson said.

A volunteer from the back suggested running a red light, which was a perfect discussion starter. The class began a group-type discussion on what Professor Tomlinson described as duty risk analysis. The duty at issue had to encompass the foreseeable risk that harm such as that which resulted would come to the injured.

Professor Tomlinson then asked, "Must the conduct be intentional?"

The class started its first real pro and con debate. Several hands went up and opinions back and forth came on holding people accountable for things they didn't intend but which were consequences from their actions. Professor Tomlinson described that regardless of intent or mental state, duty was a question of law.

"In a certain circumstance, does the law require a standard of conduct" Professor Tomlinson explained. The class then discussed examples of failing to act, which were not intentional such as failing to stop a car soon enough or swearing into another lane when not checking for cars first and pushing someone off the road.

Driving Torts were good examples because almost everyone drove, and accidents are so prevalent, particularly among young people. The discussion slightly veered off when a pretty young woman named Sissy suggested accident litigation was too prevalent, given the aggressive attorney advertising which had become part of the current culture.

"You need to take my ethics class in the spring, and if you're really interested, my class on philosophy and ethics in the Law when you're a 2 or 3L. So, what about intentional acts?" Professor Tomlinson asked. "Who can think of areas of the law where injury occurs from an intentional act?" Professor Tomlinson asked.

Taylor raised her hand, and when called upon by her first and last name since the seating chart was complete and back in the Professor's hands, she said, "How about stealing from someone?"

"Yes," Professor Tomlimson said, adding, "when you take from someone or even attempt to take from someone without them knowing or by deceitful conduct, the law holds you responsible."

"Who knows what this is called?" Professor Tomlinson asked. After a brief silence with no hands being flung in the air, Professor Tomilinson asked "Taylor, Ms. Taylor Reeves, what's this called in the law?"

"Fraud or theft," Taylor responded

"Yes, in the criminal law, we refer to deceitful taking as theft, robbery, and sometimes fraud. In the civil law, it's referred to as fraud or conversion which brings up an interesting point. Intentional conduct can be both a crime and an actionable tort. The state or federal governments prosecute crimes, and individuals who are harmed may bring civil suits for damages." Professor Tomlinson then gave the class the example of Bernie Madoff, a highly publicized case involving an investment advisor who lied to get people to invest with him and took their money for his own purposes. Madoff was found guilty of criminal fraud and at the same time sued civilly by his victims for taking money from them using lies.

Professor Tomlinson abruptly said, "Time is up. For next, class read the materials noted on the class syllabus I have here for you. Pick one up on the way out. Please also read the definitions of tort, negligence, and fraud. And finally, each year, I have a 1L research assistant. I'm taking applications. If you're interested, see the posting referenced on the syllabus."

Leaving class, all Tori could think about was how cute Professor Tomlimson was. She adored his way of talking and moving. He dressed business casual in a preppy style, khaki pants and a tailored button-down oxford, blue and white striped. He had brown hair, which was about one quarter grey. Arthur, as she was already calling him in her mind, was tall at well over 6 feet and a large build but not overweight. Arthur wore cute circular glasses with frames clear colored with brown spots. Arthur projected confidence in a kind, humble way. Tori wanted the research position for sure.

When Tori settled in the library after coffee and her second class, Contracts, she took out her phone and first thing checked SA. The library offered individual areas for students to study. Tori set up shop in one area where she planned to always be before, after, and between classes, weekdays like a job. This was a suggestion from the lawyer she worked for over the summer. The goal was to focus and make the best of her time.

Tori continued to work her system of checking and responding to messages and new member profiles on SA. Since in New Orleans full time, the number of potential candidates had grown exponentially. This meant there were more men willing to give up money for just dates with a little encouragement by Tori's stories. Tori had become an expert at reading the men from their messages and knowing which one to pick for dates. Since her parents paid for essentially everything, Tori spent her money on luxury spa days and some clothes and accessories that her parents might balk at paying for, although they didn't say no much. This meant Tori saved a nice little stash of cash.

SA always gave Tori confidence. All the compliments and adoration she received was welcome and, now, part of her every day routine. Tori was addicted to the feeling, although she didn't quite realize it. She would wonder occasionally if she could go without SA. Periodically, she would tell herself she was not going to look at it except every three hours. Once she started to do it only twice daily; once in the morning and once at night. That plan didn't last more than one day.

After working SA upon arrival in the library, Tori took out the syllabus for Torts. At the bottom under the heading Research Associate it read "1L student needed for 10-15 hours a week of research. No pay for the position; however, it looks good on your resume and is wonderful experience in writing on ethics. Apply in person with your resume Friday, August 23 between 3:00-5:00 PM."

Tori needed to update her resume and went to work on it immediately. She would include the interning she had done periodically at her father's companies here and there as well as the summer law firm job. Although she had done little more than filing and running errands, she had got to sit in on a deposition and strategy sessions for discovery planning. These duties could be colored up nicely for her resume, Tori thought. Of course, Tori highlighted graduating in three years summa cum laude as well as her LSAT score. Tori was confident this job was hers. She wanted to get close to Arthur, although she didn't really spend any time thinking about why. Tori just knew she wanted a relationship with him.

Tori next turned to her homework for Torts. She read the page allotment. It was a case about negligent conduct. She was a little surprised at what constituted negligence and what didn't in certain circumstances, such as the epileptic who had a seizure, which could not be anticipated, and wrecked into someone else. Tori looked up and studied the definitions relating to negligence suggested by Arthur.

Next, Toni turned to fraud. She read the Oxford definition "deception intended to result in financial gain." *Wait,* Tori thought, *there had to be more to it than that.* Digging further, Tori found the following in US Legal, "Fraud is generally defined in the law as an intentional misrepresentation of material existing fact made by one person to another with knowledge of its falsity and for the purpose of inducing the other person to act, and upon which the other person relies with resulting injury or damage."

Falsity to induce another to act rang in Tori's brain like a gong. This was her. Tori reflected and realized that she was engaging in fraudulent conduct all day long on SA and when meeting men. In fact, she even engaged in this conduct with her parents, the law firm over the summer, and others. It had become a way of conduct, as a habit if you will. Tori refused to believe she could be a fraudster. And her friends, the Fab Five, were all fraudsters, too. *No way,* Tori thought.

Tori started thinking of all the shading of the truth done every day in life by everyone. All of it was harmless really. Recipients in everyday life knew they were being lied to right. This was just part of being an adult. The more Tori read and pondered she kept coming back to the fact that her mistruths, no matter how small or well-intended, were all "intended to gain some advantage." *This just can't be the law,* Tori thought.

Tori set out on an extensive reading mission about fraud. What she uncovered was somewhat terrifying for her. It was a federal crime to make untrue statements via text, direct messaging, or any social media, including SA. Wire fraud, it's called and many people were prosecuted for such conduct by the federal government. Google searches uncovered all sorts of instances where acting for financial gain liars had been indicted of wire fraud for making false statements. Lying in person to gain advantage was likewise fraud.

Tori sat unusually idle. She stared off towards the library ceiling, not believing what she had become. The air felt heavy like it was bearing down on her. Tori thought of herself as a law-abiding, good girl. Yes, that's who she was. Tori began to rationalize. She was not in business; she was taking money from men who wanted to give it to her, and most importantly, the men should know better. These all sounded like reasonable exceptions to the rules on fraud.

Tori went back to her computer started to look. She could find nothing allowing any exception to a lie made to gain money. It didn't seem to matter if the lie was to someone ignorant and, further, it didn't matter why the lie was made as long as it had something to do with getting an advantage, like money. It didn't matter if the recipient wanted to believe the lie in a particular situation. Tori kept coming up with one thing: there was absolutely nothing about the recipient knowing better.

"I'm a criminal," Tori said out loud in a soft voice with a hint of disbelief.

10

Friday morning, Tori was up early for a run down St. Charles Avenue to Audubon Park, around the park, and back home. Tori and Taylor lived on St. Charles Avenue, almost downtown, in an apartment building with a doorman and secure parking. There was a concern Tori's parents shared about her safety, and Taylor was happy to have the security. Taylor's parents valued the influence they thought Tori and her family would have on Taylor.

Eighty degrees before sunrise was how this morning presented itself; just right for Tori, who wanted to sweat. Tori pushed herself hard as the upbeat playlist pounded in her ears. Even Drake could not move Tori's attention from her newly analytical mind's conclusion of self judgement. The human born technique of self-denial from unseemly truths was no longer working. The minute Arthur introduced her to the law, Tori started to apply herself in a most studious way to research.

Things need to change, Tori thought to herself. As she entered the park, the sun was rising, and Tori was making a list of things to do. On the top of the list was no more lying on SA. Second was get that research job and get close to Arthur. Something drew Tori to him, and it had started to occur to Tori it was Arthur's dedication to the study and application of morals and ethics. For self-discipline, Tori committed to herself this morning to two-a-day working outs and a rigorous eating regimen. Tori didn't need to watch her weight for physical body's sake. Standing 5'7" and weighing 125, Tori had a lovely figure with double D breasts and a firm, plum butt. Nothing too big, but healthy for a young white girl. She was paid much attention running every morning and would now be in the evenings too for her second run of the day. The tight booty shorts Tori had on this morning didn't hurt the attention eye.

Tori pondered what to wear after she got out of the shower. Her outfit needed to be attractive, somewhat professional and not too flashy. Thinking of the type of women's dress that might attract Arthur, she picked out a white skirt which landed right above the knees, very long for her usual taste, and a yellow blouse. Under the blouse, she wore another layer that protected her bra from being seen through the light fabric. Blue flats and small, not her large, pearl earrings. No rings or necklaces today for Tori. Simple yet refined for her age, Tori thought.

Tori's hand went up at the first questions Arthur asked. She knew an impression not just visually but substantively would need to be made in class to get the job. Thursday night, she had reread the materials two more times to make sure she could evaluate the cases and answer any questions that came up. It worked. Not only did Tori review the case of Fisher v. Hernandez which Professor Tomlinson asked about first, she also was able to chime in later about a group discussion comparing two other cases. Tori was careful not to volunteer too much. She didn't want to seem completely over anxious. Tori was pleased with her performance.

Later in the day, she presented herself at Professor Tomlinson's office at 2:55. Not wanting to be too early, yet needing to show she was thoughtful and attentive, Tori knocked on the door and entered when she heard Arthur say, "Please come in. You're the first here," Arthur said, continuing, "I like you're on time."

Tori responded, "I'm enjoying your class and very interested in legal ethics. Here is my resume as requested."

Professor Tomlinson looked at the resume to read her name and said, "Victoria, it's nice to meet you. Very nice comments in class today. It takes courage to be one of the first volunteers, and your eager participation helps calm the raging nerves of most of the 1Ls in the room."

"Thank you, Professor," Tori responded, adding, "please call me Tori."

"Please call me Art outside of the classroom. In class, I prefer Professor Tomlinson," Art said. "What makes you interested in ethics?" Art added quickly.

Tori stuttered at first and breathed in deeply to collect her thoughts. She responded, "It's so important to me to be the best representative of my future clients and myself that I can be. My dad is a successful businessman and comes from a line of family business. I want to be able to help him and maintain the highest reputation for his interests."

Art was impressed. Not only by her response, but by her confident demeanor and well intentions. He thought Tori seemed perfect. Tori's looks and dress couldn't help but grab his attention, too, although he had grown accustomed to not allowing his animalistic intentions to show, moving to quash the feelings soon. Art studied the behavior of men and ethics regarding the treatment of women in the workplace. He also was a believer in the sin of even the thought about women physically when married. Art was able to move his mind quickly when it deviated from all of the skills he developed through reading on the subject.

Tori didn't push her womanhood to get the job, Art noticed. As an attractive, relatively younger professor, Art had his fair share of female students act suggestively toward him in the past. Tulane Law School certainly had its male professors with a reputation for enjoying female students. The movie *The Pelican Brief* made significant mention of the style. Art was far from those professors and knew how to immediately shut down the approaches. He also bent over backwards to keep his distance and stay always businesslike and professional.

"You understand the job does not pay," Art asked Tori.

"Yes," Tori responded and asked, "What will I be doing?" The affirmative statement as if she had the job was not lost on Art. He appreciated Tori's vigor and confidence.

"You'll be looking at ethics issues I'm writing a paper about for the Catholic Church. I'm on a counsel that assists the Archdiocese of New Orleans and have been asked to comment on the ethics involved in the Church and other not for profits getting property tax breaks." Tori looked eager and didn't ask any questions. Art added, "Sometimes I get other issues or cases from outside to work on and, then, if I'm paid, I will make sure you get a reasonable hourly rate."

It wasn't lost on Tori that Art was speaking like she had the job. There was some more discussion on Tori's background. No one else had come to the office at 3:25 when Art said, "The job is yours. I'd like to meet with you weekly at this time, and you may work from anywhere. When we meet, please have your hours detailed on what you did and how long it took as well as send to me in advance of the meeting a memo on your progress from my weekly assignments. I really don't want you to work more than 15 hours a week, which I think is the maximum so as not to interfere with your grades."

Tori responded, "Thank you so much."

When Tori was about to turn to leave, not knowing what else to say, Art handed her a flash drive and said, "Here are my current thoughts in the form of a memo on the issue at hand along with some authorities. Familiarize yourself with these and my desired form of writing a memo. I've included a couple of memos from my last year's assistant on the drive."

Tori smiled and nodded her head, she grabbed the drive and walked out while thanking Art again for the opportunity.

After a dinner that night with Taylor and a few new friends from school, Tori sat down at her desk in her apartment. The apartment was nice and spacious for the two girls. Both Tori and Taylor had bedrooms which could fit a queen size bed, a dresser, and a desk. Tori took the master, which had a bathroom in the room, and Taylor had a full bath accessible by her room and also the hallway from the living area. There was a large living dining combo, which had a sectional sofa, easy chair, entertainment center with TV, and dining room set. Tori and Taylor's moms had picked out furniture with them and, then, coordinated the move in and set up the weekend before school. The apartment was appointed comfortably in the way Tori had always known.

Tori looked on SA. She had also looked on Wednesday after class and Thursday several times. On those occasions, Tori had been careful not to send any messages which contained a lie. She stuck to "Hi, how are you doing?" and general background questions and answers. Tori looked at her profile Wednesday and edited it as it contained suggestions about who she was and what she wanted that were not accurate. What did she want? This question stuck in Tori's mind tonight as she stared at her inbox full of messages. She had made a promise to herself about SA and to run twice a day. Here she was on SA and not having a run. Tori clicked off SA and got dressed to run.

St. Charles Avenue in New Orleans was a main street joining the downtown area with the Uptown area. It runs through several sections of town and ends up at Tulane University near Audubon Park. The street has a neutral ground or median as it is referred to in other cities. The neutral ground has tracks for street cars, which are a historic form of public transportation. Along both sides of the street on the sidewalk sides are large oak trees that form an arc over much of the street. These trees are more prominent in the residential section which starts about at Tori's apartment and runs towards the park. A well laid out historic avenue where many people usually ran, but not any this Friday night at 9:30.

It was a short run. Just to the park and back. Tori didn't want to run in the park this late at night. The park was theoretically closed after dark, although there were no gates and wide-open areas to enter. The running track in the park was a large oval, about two miles around lagoons and a golf course. Tori's run this night was a little over five miles total.

Tori bagged the music tonight and contemplated the week. Mostly, Tori thought about Art. She loved the name first off. He was so welcoming and didn't ogle her in the usual fashion. Art treated her with respect and complimented her in a professional way. She knew he was going to have a big influence on her. Not knowing how, Tori did anticipate why. She was dead on accurate when she described to Art her desire to present in a truthful and ethical way. Tori wanted impressions of her to be fair and, she decided, she, too, wanted to be fair and just. This, and changing her ways, which haunted her, were the legacy of a relationship with Art.

Once home again, Tori loaded the flash drive into her laptop, and she began to read Art's draft memo about the tax issue. Tori didn't understand why it made much of a difference if nonprofits didn't pay property tax. They didn't really have money because they operated for education or other purposes, right? These groups didn't make a profit, she thought. Not taxing them helped keep down tuition and service costs she assumed; it kept the Church's standing.

Tori didn't read long before she nodded off. Tori slept well and woke up to another early, hot run through the park.

Saturday morning early was playtime for Art. While he saw his children every night for dinner and helped read to them before bed since they were infants, Saturday mornings usually meant a trip downtown to cafe Du Monde for beignets and/or a trip to Audubon Park to play. Art had a boy, nine, and a girl, seven. Arthur and Estelle were the light of Art's life along with his wife Christine. Christine and Art met in tenth grade, and neither had ever dated anyone else. They were married right after graduating from Loyola University which is a Catholic school. Like Art, Christine grew up Catholic attending Sacred Heart of Jesus School from nursery through graduation.

Both Art and Christine's parents lived locally and were in their 60s. Spending time with family was Art and Christine's pastime. This weekend was no different. Christine, a stay at home mom, made sure the chores and errands were done before the weekend, so all they had to do as a family was play unless she had something for Art to do around the house she couldn't get to. Christine was very accommodating as a wife, not only doing the cleaning, laundry, and cooking herself, but making sure the kids were always where they needed to be and prepared. Art left the house early most days, off to the gym and then work before the kids woke up. Like clockwork, Art would be home between 5:00 and 6:00 daily. Christine even took care of cutting the small backyard and front patch of grass they had as well as any other usual "honey do" type chores around the house, so Art could focus on his work and family.

Christine admired Art so much. He was always the smartest person she ever knew. Valedictorian at Jesuit and Summa Cum Laude from Loyola in Religion. They both knew Art was not going to be a priest; however, had the Catholic Church allowed priests to marry, Art might just have chosen that path. He still might if the rules were changed. Recently, there had been changes to allow priests to be married if converting from other faiths and coming to the Catholic Church married. Art didn't question the fairness in this rule as he respected and followed his Pope, who knew best. The Church was in need of good priests, these days that's for sure.

Art served any way he could. Upon returning from Harvard Law together where Christine worked as a school teacher to help support them, Art went to work for the Archdiocese of New Orleans as an attorney. His boss was an older man who enjoyed some outside practice from a family firm. Art's boss started the inside legal department at the Archdiocese. The Church had significant real estate holdings and ministry operations outside of the main Church such as senior care and apartment complexes. The Church also owned business interests. The Church needed wise counsel not only for the day to day transactions but also to act as outside negotiators and strategists for their holdings.

Art worked for three years in this position before a position at Tulane opened to take over the study of legal ethics as part of an endowed Chair. Art was by far the youngest person to ever be hired for an endowed Chair. If ever anyone was qualified and prepared, it was him. Art was allowed by Tulane to continue to work for the Archdiocese as outside counsel when needed. Art did this for free, donating time to endless committees and projects. Art's first love was the Church.

Art grew up as an altar boy at the Holy Name of Jesus Church on Loyola's campus across the street from Audubon Park. This was where his family would be tomorrow morning for service. Today, it was French donuts at 8:00 AM when the outside of Café Du Monde opened. Fried bread with powdered sugar dunked by the kids, as was tradition, in Art's café au lait.

Art loved these Saturday morning trips, which occurred every few weeks. The kids liked to get a table all the way toward the Canal Street side of the outside, so they could watch the balloon man blow up all sorts of creations. Art was pleased to accommodate since the trumpet player who worked the sidewalk just outside Café Du Monde played beautifully. Art's favorite was "Amazing Grace," where the musician alternated between trumpet and singing. A chilling rendition every time he heard it.

No matter where he was, "Amazing Grace" struck at the heart of Art's soul. "A wretch like me…" Art thought of himself as a sinner constantly on the path of asking for God's forgiveness. The beauty of the intimate gift of Christ was still memorizing to Art like a child hearing it for the first time.

Art struggled with sin like most. He had drank too much several times and said things he shouldn't. Art thought way too much about his success and image, he would contemplate, not placing enough thought in the less fortunate. Many books had been read by Art about the great temptation of man: woman. This was the topic of a men's retreat Art had been on recently and was something Art struggled with, as most men do daily.

A recent read had suggested men look away, and Art did. Not one to masturbate frequently, Art had committed to only sexual activity with his wife and no self-pleasure years ago. He had never been with a woman other than Christine, and he succeeded without self-pleasure for the last year and a half. There were many impure thoughts about his mother-in-law, too, although nothing out of the ordinary.

Today, no illicit thought clouded Art's mind, and after breakfast, he and the family went for balloons. Arthur got a blue boat and Estelle a pink poodle. The kids ran up the Moon Walk toward the river as Art and Christine followed hand in had, just like they were school kids. The Tomlinsons beamed with delight as their kids experienced the joy of the city they loved. From the top of the walk, one could view the Mississippi River and even wander out to the levee which ran on its edge, keeping the city from flooding. On the other side was the best view in town, Art told his kids always. St. Louis Cathedral was built by the French originally in 1719. It and it's successor were destroyed. The third Church to bear the name and sit in the location was built by the Spanish in 1789. Having been added on to and restored many times, the elegant structure watched over Jackson Square and the entirety of New Orleans. The Catholic Church not only dominated New Orleans' history; it dominated Art's life.

After the walk this hot August morning, Art decided to take the kids and Christine on a carriage ride through the French Quarter. Not one to spend money wastefully and living on the $245,000 Tulane paid him with two kids in private school, Art could splurge now and again for the kids' education. Not that the carriage driver's history lessons were close to accurate. They were amusing, and Art narrated himself for more than half of the ride. This was only the third time Art had taken the kids for a carriage ride through the French Quarter, and he was all three times noted by the driver to be a local with very useful information. Not one to outdo anyone, Art always agreed with the driver and supplemented. Christine adored Art's style. He was her hero.

The Tomlinsons found themselves at home a little before 11:30 AM with the parents wanting to nap and the kids talking nonstop. A movie was in order. *Aladdin*, the non-animated one, was ordered up and everyone sat on the sofa cuddled up watching. Art dozed off here and there. The kids wanted to squeeze his nose as he snored, but Christine would not let them even though she had taught them the trick.

"Not today," she whispered to the kids. "Daddy worked hard this week as school just started."

Tori was anything but relaxed around noon this Saturday. After her run, shower, and coffee, she hit the flash drive. While first wondering again into the memo to file partly finished by Art, she started to think about money and its uses. How did the Church use their property and get its money? Why did it need to be exempt from tax? Was this the government favoring religion?

Pondering these questions, Tori went to the kitchen for water. She stopped to talk to Taylor, who was hanging out on the sofa covered up by a furry purple blanket and watching Netflix on their 65-inch TV.

"How was your night, Tay?" Tori asked.

Tori called Taylor "Tay" as an endearing nickname. Taylor liked it and would sometimes tease Tori affectionately in response, as she did this morning, by saying "Victoria." Taylor continued, "Thanks for asking. It was divine." Literally no one called Tori Victoria, not even her parents. Taylor enjoyed poking a little at Tori's usual seriousness this way especially when Tori was trying to be casual.

"I had a great night drinking with the gang at Cooter Browns," Taylor said. Continuing, she added, "I'm feeling it though."

Tori responded, "Going to do any homework today? I'm working a bit on the research project for Art."

"We're calling him Art now?" Taylor responded.

"Yes, that's what he prefers when not in class," Tori said and continued to tell Taylor about the job and research project. After a while the conversation turned to Art.

"So, what do you think of him?" Taylor asked.

"He's very nice and super smart," Tori responded.

"That's not what I meant, and you know it" Taylor giggled.

"Oh, well…" Stammering for a second and, after some hesitation, Tori just came out with it "he's hot!" Taylor agreed. This started a lengthy conversation about older men and their attraction to them. Tori was interested to hear Taylor's attraction to middle age men, too, and they talked about Art and others.

After a while Tori asked, "Have you ever heard of SA?"

"SA?" Taylor asked.

"Yes, Seeking Arrangements, it's a web site for girls to find older men to be sugar daddies," Tori responded.

"Oh yes I have heard of it," Taylor said and, just before Tori could say another word, Taylor continued, "Modern prostitution."

Gasping for breath internally, yet showing no signs of emotion externally, Tori sat quietly for a minute.

"So, are you going to study today?" Tori asked after about 15 seconds.

"Why do you ask, Tori?" Taylor said.

"I've heard of girls having meaningful relationships through SA with older men, and since you like them, too, I thought maybe you…"

Tori was then interrupted by Taylor.

"Oh, no, that's payment for sex."

Tori nodded her head and said, "Cool."

She then excused herself to go study and work. Back at the desk, Tori googled prostitution. "Engaging in sexual activity for payment" was the definition Tori found from the New Oxford American Dictionary. The title sounded so formal. Certainly, she hadn't had sex for money, Tori thought.

Tori though more—she had had sex. She had gotten money. But they weren't one for another. The money was a gift. Would she have gotten the money without the sex? Tori asked herself. Soon she realized this was a dumb question. Tori then thought, well, lately and for the most part, she had gotten money without sex. She had offered sex or at least suggested she would in exchange for money.

More google research indicated this, too, was a crime. She went into SA and reviewed her most recent messages. There appeared a discussion about the number of times per week men would want to meet and the amount of allowance. Being as objective as she could, Tori had to realize she'd been committing fraud in offering prostitution.

Taylor was right!

11

Tori began to read Art's memo, which recited the history of tax exempt status in the nonprofit world for property taxes. The Catholic Church, like many nonprofit organizations, was exempted from income tax under the United States tax law by having filed and obtained tax exempt status. This allowed the Church, or any other recognized nonprofit for that matter, to accept donations and not pay any sort of income tax on the donations less operating expenses of the nonprofit. Also, interesting to Tori, the nonprofit can operate a business, such as an apartment complex, which would typically be a for-profit venture and not pay any income tax so long as it was operated to generate revenue to be used for the overall mission of the nonprofit. There were three levels of operations for the Catholic Church categorized by Art in the memo: (1) Church specific operations; (2) related ministry operations (such as nursing homes, hospice, and elderly housing); and (3) non-directly related operations (for example in New Orleans the Archdiocese owned a TV station).

Over the last several decades, a debate had arisen about the propriety of exempting non directly related operations from tax. Certain nonprofits, such as churches and universities have gigantic holdings. For example, Tulane's endowment was over $1 billion, not including its real estate holdings according to Art's memo. The Catholic Church was rumored to be the wealthiest organization in the world, although no one knew for sure considering the secrecy around its finances. The apparent and actual wealth of some nonprofits had governments at every level looking to pay for their increasing budgets with taxes on nonprofit assets or revenue. This debate was at the center of Art's research.

Most particularly, states and their local jurisdictions like cities or counties collected property tax. Only in Louisiana were sub geographical jurisdictional areas not called counties. They are called Parishes as a holdover from French influence.

For businesses, the value of real and personal property was by state law to be assessed each year by a local assessor who levied a tax pursuant to the legislatively determined tax rate. This tax on your land, buildings, inventory, equipment, etc., is a cost of doing business, Art's memo laid out. Historically, nonprofits were exempt, however, from the State and local real estate taxes on their assets. The last couple of decades had seen a move toward taxing the assets of a nonprofit's non directly related operations.

Art's memo contained citations to various articles, papers, laws, and legal authorities. For now, Tori wasn't drilling down past the words in Art's memo to look at any of the source material. The crux of the matter seemed to be that in order to assess if an operation or asset related thereto was directly related there had been developed a series of questions or a test. The answers to these questions needed to be certified in affidavit form by the nonprofit. Art had been asked to comment to the Archdiocese of New Orleans generally on the rules and certification process as well as detail guidelines to the Victor General for completing and signing the form. Where there were any questions by the Victor General, Art was to be consulted.

Art's memo defined drafting these guidelines for the Archdiocese as the ultimate task. Also, Art indicated he wanted to provide a thorough history of property taxation and the case for and against taxation of nonprofit's assets in all classes. Art expected the Archdiocese would likely face, in the future, a move by the State and local taxing authorities to have more of their asset classes taxed. Helping make the case to law makers for the Victor General was part of Art's assumed responsibilities.

Tori understood the issue now, but she was uncertain as to what Art wanted her to do. She turned to reviewing the memos included on the flash drive from prior assistants of Art. Art had given her these memos as examples of how Tori should report to him. There were two memos. Both followed the same form. In the beginning, there was a statement about what had been asked to be done, such as, "You requested I research the relationship of the city of New Orleans to the state of Louisiana for who had the ultimate authority to pass property tax legislation and, specifically, what the city could do if the state didn't have a specific law for a specific situation," the first memo read. After the question presented, there was a discussion outlining the results found with citation to almost every sentence. Tori didn't know how to use the legal citation form and began feeling overwhelmed. Then, finally, the memo contained a conclusion section of a few sentences summarizing the result of the author's efforts and indicating other tasks to be done.

The form seemed simple enough. Tori was no legal researcher, she thought. And what about all the citations? This really intimidated Tori who, on Saturday night by now, couldn't wait to see Art and ask him these questions. She knew that wasn't the only reason she wanted to see Art.

Tori put away the flash drive and set off for her evening run. Tori was not Catholic, and she really didn't know anything about the Catholic Church. Having been to New Orleans many times and now living there, she had noticed large churches all over downtown and the uptown area where she lived and went to school. Catholic schools were big in New Orleans, and Tori knew Art had been to one, Jesuit, from reviewing his bio on Tulane's webpage. In her hometown of Gonzales, the Catholic Church was well known in the community.

Directly across St. Charles Avenue from Audubon Park were Loyola University, then, Holy Name of Jesus Church and, then, Tulane University. Tori thought about the association geographically of those institutions and all the real estate they covered in an area, which was filled with grand houses and no vacant land other than the park. *All of that property must be so valuable*, Tori thought. She wondered what the connection was among the institutions and how much property they really had. Tori also wondered what it was all used for within Art's three categories, and the value. *Must be astronomical*, Tori thought.

Holy Name was a beautiful Neo-Gothic built Church from the early 1900s, Tori learned when she googled it on her return home. It had services several times a week including one Saturday afternoon and a few on Sunday at 8:00, 10:30, and 6:30. Tori decided to go tomorrow at 10:30. While her family was conservative and religious, they were non-denominational Christian. Tori did not like the heavy evangelical style and had all but abandoned religion in college. That was four years ago, and she hadn't really been to

Church other than Christmas, Easter, and occasionally on weekend visits to her partners, although Tori had become quite seasoned at not going to Church on her visits. Tori was curious and wanted to check out what she was working on. It would impress Art, too, she thought.

Tori was not alone as a single, college age student at Holy Name. There were many late teens and early twenties sitting by themselves mostly in the back. Tori had a few Catholic friends growing up, so she knew that she was not welcome at communion but certainly for the service. The building was gorgeous, particularly the altar and the stained glass. Tori also admired the high ceilings. Not paying attention to the service so much as checking out the parishioners and the architecture, Tori thought about the cost of the building and the land. She had no real way to know, but instinctively knew the cost was significant. While spanning the crowd during communion, Tori saw a beautiful blond girl skipping back down the aisle. She had a yellow dress with white lace and a pretty red ribbon in her hair. Tori looked up, and behind her was Art along with a woman and a boy. *Art's family*, she thought. Feeling a hint of being a stalker, Tori turned her head and looked back. Art hadn't seen her, and as the service continued after communion, Tori snuck out during the closing prayer.

After Torts Monday, Tori stopped to talk to Art.

"I have so many questions after reading the material and am ready to start working," Tori said. Understanding this meant Tori spent her weekend working on the research, Art was impressed and wanted to make some time.

"Are you free today at 3:00?" Art asked.

"Yes," Tori responded eagerly.

As he was walking out of the class room and motioning for her to start walking, too, Art said, "Please come by my office after my 2:00 ethics seminar, and we will discuss your questions and the next steps."

Art explained as they sat in his office talking that the Catholic Church was divided into jurisdictions all over the world. Each jurisdiction was a Diocese and within each Diocese were parish churches and other ministries as well as non-directly related operations. The Diocese was run by a Bishop and, in this case, the Archdiocese of New Orleans was run by an Archbishop. The Archbishop had a first assistant, Art explained, titled the Vicar General, whose responsibility is to run the business and administration of the Archdiocese. There wasn't much difference between a Diocese and an Archdiocese just the size of the area and title of the spiritual leader.

As they talked, Tori learned that Art was on several committees where non-priests can assist the Vicar General and the Archbishop in running the Church. These committees were advisory. A particular committee on sustainability of the Archdiocese had been formed in 2006 after Hurricane Katrina hit New Orleans and devastated much of the city. Art was appointed to the committee at its inception and while he was employed as in-house counsel for the Archdiocese. Art had faithfully served since his appointment.

Art described the particular effect Katrina had on the Catholic Church to Tori. While the Church finances were solid pre-Katrina, the membership had fallen since and the Church had trouble recruiting priests. The pedophile scandals certainly didn't help matters.

The Archdiocese was run as a separate financial unit from the rest of the Catholic Church and was required to pay certain money to the larger Church. Art wouldn't elaborate and indicated he was bound by confidentiality agreements on many financial and related issues. In general, Art indicated that the Archdiocese had significant property which was under insured and, in some cases, not insured. This combined with the fact that over half of the parishioners didn't return to Church right away and, to some extent at all, put the Church in a strained financial position. Administering this financial nightmare was the job of the Vicar General who Art knew well. Art worked with the Vicar General the entire time he was at the Church in its employ and since while at Tulane. Art had become an independent outside counselor to the Vicar General and the various committees needing his services. Art was a trustee and reliable servant of the Church.

"Has the Church recovered?" Tori asked.

Art timidly looked at the floor and then up.

"We continue to struggle with sustainability and the work we are doing relative to taxing is very important to this cause." Art couldn't say how much property the Archdiocese had or even how much in the non-directly related category. He did indicate to Tori's detailed questioning that post Katrina, the Church suffered by owning many properties in every category without the funds to restore or the need to restore (in the case of lack of use). This had created animosity with parishioners over loved church buildings and priests as well as in the neighborhood communities where damaged properties sat without any sign of rebuilding when Katrina had occurred in 2005.

Art was impressed with Tori's enthusiasm as well as her ability to grasp the concepts. They discussed the test for non-directly related to ministry, the ambiguities and, importantly, the certification the Vicar General had to give. It was critical to Art that the Vicar General answer truthfully all questions so as to not expose the Church to scrutiny. The Church had enough scrutiny recently and, also, it was imperative the Church follow the law like it or not.

"No matter what the reward or cost, the law is our societal foundation which must be honored and respected for civilization to function equitably," Art said in a mentoring fashion, adding, "if you don't like the law, your option is to work to change the law."

Tori got it, and she adored the high respect Art had for principled society. This is exactly what she wanted to assist and shape her future; not only the law, but her moral compass, too.

Art added that what they would be working on this year would be ideas on changing the law, expanding definitions in the law, and potentially fighting new laws on more taxation of Church property.

"This is important work for the success of a great institution; one that's necessary for the city," Art added. Art elaborated that the outcome of the tax situation would impact development of Church property and putting it back into commerce. Also, the Archdiocese's future could hang in the balance. Tori didn't need any pep talk, and she wasn't sure if Art thought she did.

Tori did want to know about citation form and rule though. It was 5:20 when Art said he had to leave so as not to be late for family dinner. Tori thought about Art's family she had seen in Church and, for a second, wondered if Art knew she was there. It couldn't be. He would have mentioned it. Armed with her further information and an assignment, to review citation form and provide examples from the memos she had, Tori left for home and her evening run.

12

Johnathan Detweiler was appointed Vicar General for the Archdiocese of New Orleans in the wake of Hurricane Katrina. Whether the former Vicar General was asked to retire by the Archbishop due to mishandling the insurance for Church property, or whether he had just become complacent in his job and new blood needed for the rebuild, was of no moment to Father Detweiler. Father Detweiler was not one to question authority or gossip. In fact, he had no such aspirations for the post of Vicar General. The Archbishop plucked Father Detweiler from seminary and expedited his completion.

Johnathan Detweiler was a practicing Certified Public Accountant who was a faithful New Orleans Catholic. Schooled at St. Francis Xavier, Christian Brothers, Jesuit, Loyola and, then, a Masters in Accounting and Business from the Wharton School. He had returned to New Orleans following school to practice at a local, medium size firm, which assisted the Catholic Church. Specializing in forensic auditing and consulting, Mr. Detweiler developed a significant reputation as an expert. A bachelor and called to the cloth at 52, Mr. Detweiler had spent years adversarially picking apart clients' and opponents' positions and books in Court. Well-seasoned at posturing and strategy, Mr. Detweiler was highly respected in the New Orleans legal community and among judges for being aggressive yet credible.

The long hours and love for his work passed the years quickly, and Mr. Detweiler found himself with only two other dedications outside of work. Those were his mother and the Catholic Church. Mr. Detweiler served on committees, as did Art, and got to know Art in connection with their sustainability work. Both had gone to Jesuit and Loyola, although Art a decade later. Both had an affinity for service to the Lord. On the Sustainability Committee, right from the start, Mr. Detweiler showed an aggressiveness and drive towards rebuilding the Church. His bottom-line approach was not always valued by the more systemic members of the committee, Art being among them. Although Mr. Detweiler was among the minority who viewed the only possible path to sustainability, survival really, was a business-like approach, the Archbishop agreed.

Mr. Detweiler had been in seminary for only two years having left the accounting practice at the urging of his mother for the cloth. The Detweilers had money, and Mr. Detweiler made his share, saving quite a bit living his entire adult life after school in the family home. Mrs. Detweiler was widowed when Johnathan was only 11 and, then, her life focus had become the Church and Jonathan. She was nicely taken care of with a house and a few million dollars. She lived relatively frugally. She attended Church every day and encouraged Johnathan always towards service.

Johnathan was quite submissive toward his mother, although in the rest of his life he dominated. Old for his class, at seminary, he was first in everything. The Archbishop was familiar with Johnathan before Katrina and, right after, decided with his background, to put Johnathan on the Sustainability Committee. Johnathan's work for the Committee while in seminary was a vision the Archbishop didn't particularly like but accepted. The bitter pill needed affirmation, and the only way for it to be done would be to make Johnathan a priest and Vicar General.

The Archbishop received significant scorn and warning from behind the velvet curtain which is the Catholic Church. The appointment was discretionary, and Father Detweiler was immensely qualified substantively, although he knew little about the Church finances specifically.

"This has been his job at the highest level for years; evaluating poorly performing businesses and shaping their future," the Archbishop would say to the committee members and some of his close advisors behind closed doors. No one officially questioned the Archbishop.

Art respected the Archbishop's choice and worked well with the Vicar General. The two were close outside of committee work attending retreats and Bible studies together frequently. And, the Vicar General's plan was working. Although a long way from solvency on a cash flow basis and heavy in debt to rebuild, there was a light at the end of the tunnel. Taxing of non-directly related assets could cost the Archdiocese millions of dollars and was a large impediment to the survival of the institution. Expansion of the law would for sure cripple the Church, requiring wholesale liquidation of many assets to survive. One thing the Sustainability Committee fought hard on against the Vicar General was the sale of Church properties. Current mandate was restructuring needed to be done without liquidation unless urgent in a situation. The Committee specifically didn't want Church or mission property being used for non-religious purposes after any sale. This would cut at the heart of the neighborhood fabric where sometimes up to 10 generations of families had been raised in these institutions.

"Saving face," as the Vicar General called it, was no way to approach survival, but he was outvoted on this point even by the Archbishop, who constantly told the Vicar General he had faith God would provide a way without wholesale liquidation and damage to tradition and neighborhoods. The Church was already suffering from lack of attendance pre-Katrina and post Katrina was a nightmare.

"Keep them closed if you have to, but don't sell," was the call for Parishes that could not afford to rebuild or did not have the congregation to support the property. By all accounts, the Vicar General had done an amazing job sifting, organizing, and plotting through the muck which was the Archdiocese finances post Katrina.

Art would not share with Tori any information about the Sustainability Committee or its inner workings, much less the Vicar General, other than their existence and mandates. The politics and financial strategy of the Archdiocese was far from Tori's consideration. All she was focused on was how to meander legally within the evolving tax law and suggest changes. To this end, Tori dedicated her time. She also prepared for class, ran, and occasionally checked SA. She found herself by October not having been on any dates or taking money from any men. Tori checked every few days now as she was so busy and committed not to lie or prostitute herself. Tori needed, however, the adoration of men. Cyber adoration, and all the attention Art showed her over the last two months, motivated her.

Tori and Art started meeting on Monday, Wednesday, and Friday afternoons. Tori had been to dinner at Art's house and even shopping with Christine. Tori had begun to use Christine as a source for girl referrals like nails and clothes in town, and Christine and Art used Tori as a babysitter four times so far.

Tori admired the relationship Art had with his family. He was safe, too. There was no chance he would approach her, which was perfect because she knew she couldn't resist him if he did. Tori's affection for the kids, friendship for Christine and respect for Art's family aside, Tori was in love with Art and knew it. She was content to love him from afar and as his mentee.

On October 23 at their 3:00 meeting, Art started by saying, "We have an issue the Vicar General needs us to look at."

"Okay," Tori said, excited to hear about the new task. Constant research and writing in the same subject, no matter how important and desirous to help Art with, needed some spicing up. Tori was used to these meetings taking until Art had to go for dinner and, sometimes, she'd be asked to come. Christine prohibited law talk at the table.

"The Vicar has several properties that are not multi-use," Art said, elaborating, "the question is how will they be taxed and what can he honestly say in the affidavit required to be submitted."

"I think we should pick one to analyze first and, then, when we have a firm grasp on the parameters, we can tackle the others," Art suggested. Tori nodded agreement, of course, like you would imagine a soldier did hearing a general.

Art described a building which was part of a Parish complex. The Parish was shut down effectively, and as the start of rebuilding, the Parish was renting out one building as a preschool, which operated for profit. Art said this was a good example of how the Archdiocese could and was rebuilding slowly their neighborhood presence with tenants that were consistent with the Church's mission but not funded by Church monies. There were several questions here, considering only a small part of the whole complex was rented. Also, the purpose of the tenant was consistent with the theme and mission of the Church.

Tori quickly pointed out the literal reading on the tax form was how much of the property was used and occupied by the nonprofit for mission related issues. She observed, "If the Church is not using any of the property at this time, isn't all of the use technically not by the Church?"

Art responded, “Even if so, and I’m not conceding the point, the use is consistent with the mission.” The two debated the matter and pulled out the statutes and forms applicable. Art then decided, “Let’s get the Vicar General on the phone”.

“Art, this is simple as far as I see it. The Church is using the property by renting it out to support the rebuilding which is within its mission,” the Vicar General said.

“But Vicar, that’s not the Church using the property; the real estate,” Art said.

“Of course it is,” responded the Vicar. “We are using it by renting it to pay for the rebuilding of the property as a whole, and the school, although not operated by us, is within our mission.”

This explanation seemed circular to Art but somewhat convincing. Equitably, it seemed completely fair not to tax this property and, in fact, because the property was not separated into sections, the whole property’s value would be taxed if 50 percent of the use was not qualifying.

“That tax would exceed the rent. How are we to do anything?” the Vicar General said. “Find me a way to do it, Art. We have so many situations like this and need the money. I can’t tell you what this means to the survival of the Church. Thanks.”

And the Vicar hung up.

His tone was pleasant yet somewhat strained and rushed. Tori could tell he was under a lot of stress. The two discussed the issues to research, and Art asked Tori to search all jurisdictions nationwide to see if there was any guidance here.

Then he said, “I know this weekend is VooDoo Fest. I’m sure you’re going. Do you know anyone who could baby sit for Christine and me Friday night?”

Tori thought about the Devils. She looked down and started to cry just barely. Tori felt so comfortable with Art. She was completely caught off guard here. Quickly gaining her composure, she looked up and said, “I’ll be there. What time?”

13

After a week and a couple of days looking, both Tori and Art could find nothing to support the Archdiocese's position that partial rental qualified as use by the nonprofit for its mission or that the vacant portion was still being used for the mission even though it was dormant. It seemed completely unfair that an entirely vacant property should be viewed by the law considering its last use and intended future use; however, the statue and small authority out there all indicated that even the slightest use of the property would be considered all of the use of the property. In these situations, the law applied was clearly inequitable, Art thought. Tori agreed.

Art and Tori recommended to the Vicar General that the Archdiocese take the matter to the New Orleans City Council and ask for an ordinance to be passed. Art offered to draft the language which would solve the problem. Art was disappointed when the Vicar General told him and Tori over the phone not to bother and asked Art to come to the Archdiocese's offices the next day for a meeting.

"Just you please," the Vicar General said right before goodbye.

Meeting with the Vicar General on a Saturday was unusual and, in person, less unusual but infrequent.

"Glad you're here, Art" the Vicar said as Art entered the conference room. Continuing, the Vicar said, "I'd like you to meet Thomas Sanders and Judith Templeton. They are counsel for the Archdiocese in a matter we have not discussed. Please sit down."

After getting Art coffee with cream, half and half, Art's favorite, and sugar, the Vicar asked Thomas to proceed.

Thomas introduced himself to Art as a senior partner at a prestigious downtown law firm. Top floor ivory tower type, Art guessed. Judith was his partner, and they had years of experience working with the Vicar General when he was serving as a forensic expert. Thomas reviewed briefly a few case types and successes he and the Vicar shared.

Art wondered why he was there. It was starting to feel like he was there to hear Thomas talk about himself and the Vicar. Just about the time Art was missing his Saturday morning play time with Arthur and Estelle and wondering why on November 2, All Souls Day, the Vicar General didn't have the dead to mourn, Thomas got to the point.

"A woman has passed away and left an amazing sum to the Archdiocese," Thomas said.

Art looked to the Vicar wondering again why he was there, but he was pleased at the news.

The Vicar looked Art dead in the eye following this hollow silence and said, "Enough to right the ship."

"That's wonderful news," Art bellowed. Continuing, immediately Art said, "Wow! Thank God for providing. This is amazing. We should tell the Sustainability Committee at once."

"Well, I haven't brought it to the whole committee yet Art because there is a possible snag," the Vicar said. The Vicar explained that Barbara Mason passed away almost a year ago. She was a close friend of the Vicar's mom, Mrs. Detweiler. Mrs. Detweiler and she were friends from college, Mary Baldwin. The two had been separated geographically for years until Mrs. Mason's husband died, leaving her in his will over a $100 million estate.

Mrs. Mason was a second wife and, candidly, was surprised her husband cut out the children from his first marriage and grandchildren. Apparently, the Vicar explained, he had provided businesses and support for years to his lineage who were ungrateful and spoiled. Mrs. Mason moved to New Orleans from Savannah to get away from the family mess her husband left. Mrs. Detweiler, her lifelong dear friend, was the reason she settled in New Orleans.

In fact, it was Mrs. Detweiler, the Vicar explained, who convinced Mrs. Mason to donate her estate to the Archdiocese. Mrs. Mason died in late 2018.

"We have got a snag, Art," the Vicar said timidly which was an unusual tone and style for the Vicar. Art assumed this change in demeanor of the Vicar had to do with the amount of money involved. "You see Mrs. Mason has a son from a prior marriage who challenged the will as being executed under duress or when Mrs. Mason was incompetent," the Vicar explained. The Vicar elaborated, "I don't have to tell you how important this is to us."

Art was so excited for the news. While not a seasoned litigator, he suspected most will contests settled, given each side had everything to lose potentially. And here, when the donee was a nonprofit like the Archdiocese, it would weigh the equities in its favor. Art spoke up and confirmed both of these facts with Thomas. So why was he there, Art thought?

"What do you need from me?" Art said.

"Art," the Vicar authoritatively said, "we want you to be an ethics expert in the case."

"Why do you need an ethics expert?" Art asked very curiously.

Thomas joined in.

"The question of undue influence involves alleged pressure brought to bear by Mrs. Detweiler on Mrs. Mason." Thomas paused briefly and then followed with, "We can prove Mrs. Mason was competent, the question of pressure by a close, lifetime friend to donate to the Archdiocese where she had not lived previously may be more difficult. It's not an area where there is much authority, and our judge is not Catholic. We would never want to try this case to a jury in New Orleans because Mrs. Mason's son may have more sympathy given the Catholic Church's reputation recently."

Everyone knew what Thomas was referring to. It didn't need to be elaborated on whatsoever. Art, still wondering what use he could be as an ethics expert, looked at the Vicar, who said, "Art, your reputation is beyond reproach and your ethics impeccable. You know me and my family. You know there was no undue influence here."

Now, Art felt somewhat pressured, yet he wanted to help. Art understood when Thomas explained that Mrs. Mason's son had a serious lifetime cocaine problem having been in and out of rehab. He had not even seen his mom since the funeral of her husband, and that wasn't a pretty sight. There were witnesses to his intoxication and her embarrassment at the wake. And further, Art understood when the Vicar explained that almost half of the estate would go to taxes if the son inherited all of the estate.

"I'll do whatever I can to help the Archdiocese," Art volunteered.

Thomas scheduled to meet Art at school Monday at 3:00. The Vicar General thanked Art as he walked Art to the door.

While the two were alone, Art asked the Vicar, "What are your thoughts about the tax issue."

The Vicar replied, "I appreciate your work, Art. We're going to take the risk and say the property is used by the Archdiocese for its mission."

Art asked, "But what about an ordinance clarification or clear statement?"

The Vicar assuringly said, "We don't have political favor at the City Council, and anyway, any attempt to clear or change the law will alert the city to what we're doing."

On the way home, all Art could think about was the Vicar was not only failing to follow his advice, which was bad enough, but the Vicar General just admitted he knew he was not following the law and didn't want to get caught. *Is that what the Vicar General said?* Art thought. *Am I exaggerating this too much?* Art wondered.

Art wrestled with the final back and forth all Saturday night. He could not believe what the Vicar said: "…any attempt to clear or change the law will alert the City to what we're doing." Was it clear what the Vicar meant? Art decided it was clear to him in the moment with the tone and knowing everything which had been advised by he and Tori. The Vicar knew the Archdiocese was breaking the law.

What would Art do about this information? Should he tell the Archbishop? Art knew when a lawyer represented a client who was an entity and the lawyer knew something inappropriate was happening, the lawyer should raise the issue with a higher authority in the entity.

Going to the Archbishop would detract from the Vicar's confidence in Art and may result in Art being minimized or dismissed from his position in the Church leadership where he could do good on so many levels. In the end, Art knew the right thing was to take the matter to the Archbishop, no matter what the fall out.

Sunday morning came painfully, as Art couldn't sleep. He texted Tori at 7:00 AM, which was the earliest he could get away with, he thought.

"Call me," Art texted.

The phone rang at 7:04, and Tori said, "What's up?"

Art asked Tori to come into the office for 2:00 after he went to Church and lunch, which was tradition on Sundays in the Tomlinson home. Tori agreed, and Art searched the ethics rules for an answer on his phone. The answer was what he thought.

A second set of eyes was always good on any issue, Art knew. He wanted Tori to be those eyes. Not because she was an ethics expert, but because she already knew much of the situation, and Art could not violate the confidence of the attorney/client privilege. Since Tori worked for him, she was bound by the privilege and could receive client communication and not have to disclose the same. He wanted assurance that he was right to bring this to the Archbishop.

Tori listened to the entire situation intently. She then said, "I get that you want to maintain the peace and continue in the work of the Church. Also, the result is fair and equitable regardless of the law. However, knowing you the way I've come to know you, you believe the law must be followed. Not only the tax law, but the ethical rules that require you to go to the Archbishop as the higher authority."

Tori was giving Art the advice he had told her was his foundation the first day they met. Art was so thankful for the advice. Tori believed she was just telling Art what he already knew. Art still had doubts about what to do.

14

Thomas and Judith were waiting for Art when he arrived at his office a little before 3:00 Monday afternoon. Tori was there, too, waiting for Art having been mulling over the issue at hand; going to the Archbishop. Art walking in said, "I hope I'm not late. My seminar discussion was really heated today. I see y'all have met." Thomas looked curiously at Art, who added, "Thomas and Judith, this is Tori my research assistant. Tori, Thomas and Judith are here to consult with us about a matter for the Archdiocese."

Thomas accepted without question Tori would be helping. Tori wondered if this related to the tax legislation and, perhaps, the Vicar General had changed his mind.

Thomas spoke, "We've brought you a drive containing all the relevant information pertaining to the matter of Mrs. Mason's will."

Tori knew then and there this was not their tax issue. She took the drive and just listened.

"On the drive you will find the will, succession proceedings initiated by other lawyers in my office, the challenge to Mrs. Mason's will, some written discovery and scheduling related documents," Thomas stated. He continued, "As a will contest, this matter is entitled to priority over other pending matters, and it is currently scheduled for trial in June. We have depositions to prepare for and take from January through March, including a written expert opinion from you and your deposition.

"And I almost forgot," Thomas added, "we have a folder of materials related to Mrs. Mason's son, Ray Namer. The file details his persistent drug use and poor relationship with his mom. We believe this is enough to demonstrate why Mrs. Mason would not leave him any of her prior husband's estate."

The four talked for over an hour. Tori and Art learned that Mr. Mason had made his money in shipping on the East Coast. A rough, hardworking man, he married Mrs. Mason later in life after he started to make his fortune and was divorced from his first wife. Mr. Mason had three children from his first marriage and several grandchildren. He was 92 when he died, working all the way up until his death.

Thomas explained that Mr. Mason had tried to bring his children and even his grandchildren into his businesses over the years. All of them were spoiled in the way a man with hard-earned, newfound success sometimes does. He and his first wife separated over the fact Mr. Mason wanted to take a harder line with the children and his granddaughter, who was being groomed to take over the reins. She was a feisty brat with a personal assistant working for her when just a junior executive at the age of 23.

Mr. Mason had enough, divorced his ex-wife and married Mrs. Mason, who was his kids' age; he 77, and she 54. Mr. Mason cut off his family at that point and lived another 15 years with Mrs. Mason, which he would say were the happiest days of his life. Mrs. Mason, who was a demure Southern woman from Birmingham, Alabama, cared deeply for Mr. Mason and, while she knew she stood to inherit some money at his death, had no idea Mr. Mason left it all to her.

Judith joined in here. Neither Art nor Tori had heard her speak other than pleasantries until now.

"Mrs. Mason and Mrs. Detweiler were roommates at Mary Baldwin, and they had maintained a close friendship, writing over the years," Judith noted. She added, "Mrs.Detweiler convinced Mrs. Mason to move to New Orleans, where she could get out of the family shadow in Savannah. Here they could live out their later years as widows. Both lived as very close friends, devoting most of their time to the Church and various clubs until Mrs. Mason died."

"How long was Mrs. Mason in New Orleans?" Tori asked.

"She moved four years after Mr. Mason's death. It took forever to liquidate the companies and settle the estate. She moved to New Orleans in 2009, and she died in December of 2018," Judith said.

Art asked point blank, "What again do you want me to do?"

Thomas responded, "We need an opinion from you as an ethics expert providing that using one's friendship to persuade someone to leave their property to a nonprofit is not undue influence as undue influence would be something only applicable when you benefit yourself."

It sounded reasonable. He would have to research the issue of benefit.

Thinking there may be an opinion in other facts combined with what Thomas suggested, Art stated, "I'll need to know all the facts."

"Of course," Thomas replied. He added, "that's why we're here. We assumed you would want to interview the witnesses, sit through the depositions, and attend the trial." Thomas looked at his watch and then said, "We've taken over an hour of your time. How about you read the materials we've put together, call anytime with questions, and send me dates when you would like to interview Mrs. Mason's doctor, Mrs. Detweiler, the attorney, and the other witness to the will."

"This sounds like a plan," Art responded as they all stood close to at once and headed for the door.

Once the door shut, Tori said, "I love this case Art. It's so exciting to work on something so important. Thank you for including me. I have to ask, how much money?"

Art, feeling very comfortable by now with Tori and a bit estranged from the Vicar General, let his guard down a bit and said, "Over $100 million." Tori sat in awe with her mouth literally wide open. After a brief pause, Art said, "It's enough to get the Archdiocese out of its huge hole and make it close to, if not, sustainable again."

Tori didn't know any details before now about the depth of the Archdiocese's financial issues and understood slightly, as much as an early-twenties student could, the matter was dire.

"Congratulations," Tori blurted out. She added, "I know how hard you have been working on sustainability as your main passion. This is it."

After an awkward pause where Art and Tori both felt instinctively like this was too good to be true, Art said, "Thanks be to God."

Neither spoke of their feelings.

Art explained to Tori Mrs. Detweiler's relationship to the Vicar General and decided he should call the Vicar.

"Vicar," Art started, "I've just completed my meeting with Thomas and Judith. I'm excited to work on the matter. It seems like God is working for us here no doubt."

The Vicar General responded, "Thanks, Art. No doubt. You're a great friend."

Art followed with, "One thing; since this case is going to be the fuel we need to solve our financial problems, perhaps we should be less aggressive with the tax issue."

The Vicar immediately said, "Things are far from over, Art, and I want to make sure you know the significance of the tax issue. We can't afford any other position."

Art was disappointed and, somewhat in a desperate tone, said, "You know, theoretically, where you disagree with my advice, and I think something inappropriate is occurring. I have to raise the matter with the Archbishop."

"Feel free, Art. No hard feelings. I've already reviewed it with him, and I'm sure he would welcome your call," the Vicar General said.

After a polite goodbye, Art was more perplexed about what was going on and what to do. He didn't even get paid for any of this work, although it didn't matter ethically, he thought. Art's motivation was serving the Church.

Tori said, "I think you should call the Archbishop for sure, but what if he supports the Vicar? What then?"

Art leaned back in his recliner, looked at the ceiling and said, "Then theoretically I have to put in writing I will withdraw and, also, write to the Archbishop's supervisors, which would mean higher up in the Catholic Church. That would undoubtedly harm the Archbishop and, then, the Archbishop would likely work to banish me from Church involvement.

"And," Art added, "depending on the legality, I may be obligated to report the conduct to legal authorities if nothing gets done."

"Wow," Tori responded.

Art looked at Tori getting up from his chair, and he approached her. She stood instinctually, and they suddenly hugged. It was a soothing necessity. A long, firm grasp during which Art said, "Thank you for being here to help me with this. You understand me, and it's a great relief to have you."

Both then left feeling warmly bathed in a moment of significant discomfort. All Tori could think about on the way home was the hug. Meanwhile, Art was wrapped up in his mind about how to approach the Archbishop and what the Vicar had said already.

At home, Art was absent mentally, as he had been over the weekend. Christine didn't question Art's having to work on Saturday, which was unusual. She knew better than to ask him about what he had to urgently deal with at the Archdiocese. Christine had asked Art why he needed to go in on a Sunday when Art said he was leaving.

Art's reply was, "It's confidential and dealing with the Archdiocese." Art had not been mentally present when he returned or Monday morning. Likewise, he came home Monday night and might as well not have been there. Christine tried to politely suggest to Art he interact more with the kids, who in Art's eyes were oblivious as was Christine.

Art recoiled stating, "You can't be involved and wouldn't understand. It's a major ethical dilemma."

Now Christine wanted to know and pushed a tad. Sensing he had said too much and trying to avoid a fight, Art said he needed to do some reading and hurried to bed from the kitchen where the two were cleaning. Christine would have to handle bed time, and Art would be no more talkative when she arrived after putting the kids to sleep. Art stayed up in bed on his computer researching various cases looking for an out with the Archbishop. Art knew he wouldn't find one, and he didn't. Shutting down the computer and turning off his bedside light, Art snuggled up to Christine and said softly to her from behind "I'm sorry. I'll snap out of it. Everything is fine. Love you."

Both knew everything wasn't fine.

The Archbishop's office wasn't particularly grand in size, yet the appointments were fine woods, leather, and silver. A comfortable space Art had only been twice before. Art was intimidated about the position and its closeness to God. He hesitantly said, "Archbishop, I'm here to review with you a position the Vicar General has taken about property taxes on vacant properties we are slowly putting back to use."

The Archbishop was very friendly and to the point.

"Yes, yes, I spoke on that with the Vicar just last week. He explained to me your advice to seek a new ordinance and, you know, we just can't accomplish that now politically."

Art nodded understandingly and said, "I respect that, Archbishop. It's just that I appreciate the Vicar plans to proceed with renting small portions of property, yet claiming the majority of the property is used by the Church when most of the property is not in use and the portion used is not used by the Archdiocese."

The Archbishop said, "Well, isn't it?"

To which Art replied, "No, technically, if it's vacant, but for some use, the use, however minor, is all the use. This subjected the entire property to tax as a matter of law."

The Archbishop responded, "That can't be. It's not equitable and will keep us from rebuilding."

Art understood, he told the Archbishop while agreeing. However, the only opinions legally were for the law to be followed or changed. The Vicar General didn't intend to do either.

"Now Art," said the Archbishop, "we have this matter involving Mrs. Mason ,which the Vicar General is coordinating with his mother. We can't do anything to disturb that at this point. It means too much to the Archdiocese, as you know. I understand your helping with the matter and am so grateful for your service."

"Yes, Archbishop," Art insisted "but these are separate issues and don't need to be dealt with together. The only extent to which these two might be related is we may want to hold off on leasing completely until we get the money from Mrs. Mason's estate."

The Archbishop sighed and, shaking his head, said, "Jonathan told me he disagreed with you and was already proceeding. I can't challenge him under the circumstances."

Art understood the Archbishop meant that so much of the future of the Archdiocese was in the Vicar General and his mother's hands, there could be no real challenge at this point.

"Can it wait, Art?" the Archbishop asked.

"No, and it sounds like the Vicar General has already knowingly exposed the Archdiocese to tax fraud," Art said.

The Archbishop said, "Can't we remedy this with legislation later or pay the taxes if they become assessed."

"That's the problem, Archbishop," Art said. "Doing this now can't be undone as a matter of law and, worse, if you don't agree to stop the Vicar General and make this right, I am technically supposed to go over your head and report the matter."

In a grandfatherly fashion, the Archbishop said, "Now, now, Art, it won't come to that. Let me talk to the Vicar General. You focus on the Mason matter, please, and I assure you, I'll let you know when this is remidied."

Art felt assured somewhat, but doubtful. He was also very disturbed the Archbishop seemed so beholden to the Vicar General. While leaving, the Archbishop assured Art the future of the Archdiocese was secure with Mason and all focus needed to be placed there. Art agreed, given the Archbishop gave his word everything was going to be dealt with on the tax issue. Art thought, *perhaps my suggestion of going higher up was the ultimate end to the issue.*

That Tuesday night at home, Art felt better and was present. Christine and the kids were happy. Art offered to do bedtime and was in bed with Christine to share long overdue intimacy before they fell asleep. Checking his phone to set the alarm, Art saw Tori texted earlier in the evening.

"How did the meeting go?"

Oh my, Art thought, he forgot to tell Tori. He shot off a text, "Great. We'll review it all tomorrow."

Christine asked, "Who is that?"

To which Art responded, "Just Tori. Something I forgot to tell her."

Christine smiled and kissed Art.

"Thank you for tonight," she said.

"Are you crazy?" Tori said after she sat silently while Art ran down the entire meeting with the Archbishop.

"What do you mean?" Art asked.

"You're blind to what's happening here, Art," Tori said. Art was silent knowing maybe there was something to be uneasy about. "You want to believe in the Church and the Archbishop, Art, and I admire that greatly," Tori paused and then continued, "but the Archbishop clearly won't do anything about the tax issue and is putting you off past the Mason resolution."

With all the instinctual awareness he ever had, Art knew Tori was right.

"Oh my Lord, Tori, you're right," Art said. He continued, "And I'm being put off and used at the same time."

Tori added, "The Vicar General clearly has all the power here."

Art was distressed. He looked at Tori and said, "You're so insightful and just know me and the situation so very well. I'm blessed to have you." Both we're thinking about the unspoken hug and the room was silent as they looked down. Finally, Art said, "What am I to do? The Archbishop has told me he will take care of it. That should be the end of the inquiry, except I don't believe him and know he won't upset the financial applecart. I just can't bring him to the higher authority and lose my position in the Church," Art said, continuing, "The Archbishop will just say he was taking care of it, and I didn't let him do it. I'd look like a fool."

Art began to rationalize.

"The tax issue is so unfair anyway," he said, adding, "and I can rely on the Archbishop acknowledging it and saying he will cure the problem."

Tori stared at him, wantonly knowing what it was like to need to convince yourself of something that wasn't true. She stood up without thinking about it, and he stepped toward her.

"I'm right to do nothing now, Tori, right?" Art said.

Tori didn't answer, being lulled by the force of the moment towards him to soothe, he then bent down slightly, and they kissed. Not just a short kiss. A long, passionate French kiss with strong embracing and gentle caressing. The moment was an energy roller coaster starting with passion followed by lust followed by a calming hum and then guilt. When the guilt kicked in Art moved back from the kiss, looked at Tori, who didn't want to stop, and was shocked.

She said, "I know," turned and walked out.

15

The Monday after exams ended, Tori and Art met at Thomas and Judith's office with another lawyer from the firm and Mrs. Detweiler. The Vicar General was there. Mrs. Mason's doctor had been deposed. Mrs. Mason had some slight memory issue and perhaps early dementia, but incompetence wasn't a question anymore. The remaining issue in the case was undue influence. Art and Tori were there to interview Mrs. Detweiler and the attorney, Janet Haines, who had prepared the will.

Janet was Mrs. Detweiler's lawyer. Janet had trained under Mrs. Detweiler's husband's lawyer, both of whom had business dealings with the Vicar when he was in practice. Having had her mentor pass away, Janet inherited most of his clients, including Mrs. Detweiler. Mrs. Detweiler had some real estate and small company stock she needed help with from time to time. Janet was called by Mrs. Detweiler to consult with Mrs. Mason on the will.

Janet and Mrs. Detweiler said all the right things. Yes, Mrs. Detweiler had been in all the meetings with Mrs. Mason and assisted in answering questions, but Mrs. Mason wanted her friend there and was quite adamant herself with Janet about wanting to give the money to the Archdiocese. Janet recalled that Mrs. Mason specifically said in the meeting about preparing the will that Mrs. Detweiler and the Church were her life and, further, that her son completely abandoned her emotionally years ago.

Mrs. Detweiler was a nice elderly lady who volunteered that it was Mrs. Mason's idea to do the will, and she merely called her lawyer and came to the meetings. Mrs. Mason, according to Mrs. Detweiler, was devoted to the Church, and there were 20 or more people who could testify similarly.

The Vicar General sat silent and was mostly on his phone texting. It appeared he was only there at the request of his mother. Everything seemed completely fine with the case, and an expert report should be no problem. Art had questioned everyone about the meeting leading up to the will, the general surroundings, and the habits of Mrs. Mason.

"Now I want to talk about the singing day for the will," Art said. He pulled out a copy and looked at Janet. "Tell me about that day please, Janet," Art asked.

Janet indicated she went to Mrs. Detweiler's house with the will and a durable power of attorney to make medical decisions. Both of these documents were prepared after the initial meeting at Janet's office with Mrs. Mason and Mrs. Detweiler.

"What happened between the meetings?" Art asked.

"I have my billing records here," Janet said. She showed Art and Tori when she had the initial meeting and, then, the two days where she drafted and revised the will. "Here is the letter and draft I sent Mrs. Watson to her house which followed the drafting." Janet said.

Art asked, "Did you mail a copy to Mrs. Detweiler, too?"

Janet said, "No."

"And what do your records show occurred next?" Art asked.

Janet responded, "My bill indicates Mrs. Mason called me on April 5. I recall we discussed everything she intended, that the will was accurate as drafted, and she was ready to execute."

Art stopped and looked up from his notes and asked, "So Mrs. Detweiler was not on this call?"

"She was not," Janet responded.

Art continued, "How did you come to execute the will at Mrs. Detweiler's house?"

Janet explained, "Given her age, I had indicated to Mrs. Mason I would come to her house for execution. It's on my way home. I told her I could bring two witnesses, as is required for this will if need be." Janet added "This is something I've done before with elderly clients who live close by."

"Tell me more about the phone call, please," Art asked.

"Sure," Janet responded, continuing, "Mrs. Mason thanked me for preparing the will. Mrs. Mason indicated she had read the will and was ready to sign. I asked her if she wanted me to come over one afternoon towards the end of the day to sign, and she said she would but could we do it down the street at Mrs. Detweiler's house, where there were witnesses. I agreed." Janet continued, looking at her billing records, "And there was another brief call the next day where we scheduled the stop for the ninth."

The facts were such that Art could not imagine much of an undue influence claim, and he was thrilled. There was independent review and contact with Mrs. Mason along with time between the request and execution.

Art followed up, "And the day of execution, what happened then?"

Janet looked at her records and said, "On the ninth, I met Mrs. Mason at 4:00 PM at Mrs. Detweiler's house. We all three live in the Garden District."

Art followed up, "Please describe the meeting."

Janet looked up and said, "It wasn't much at all. We sat and discussed my kids and their earlier lunch date at a ladies' club. After brief pleasantries, I read the will out loud, asked Mrs. Mason if this was her will and her intentions and, then, we signed after she agreed."

Looking at the will, Art asked, "Who is Deloris Taylor?"

Judith responded, "Yes, yes, Ms. Taylor is Mrs. Detweiler's long term housekeeper as I understood it."

Art turned to Mrs. Detweiler and confirmed all the facts as Janet recalled. He asked Mrs. Detweiler about witnessing the will, and she said, "On the way home from our meeting with Janet, I offered my house because we were told the Will would require two witnesses and, while we both have housekeepers, I'd need to be there unless we went downtown."

Art continued, "Why your house?"

And Mrs. Detweiler replied, "To make it easier on me. Mrs. Mason was very appreciative for my help." Mrs. Detweiler added, "We had lunch that day, too, and many days after lunch we would come to my house to sit, visit, and pray. When Mrs. Mason moved here, we started meeting at my house mostly until she got settled. It just became our place almost all of the time, although I went to Mrs. Mason's house sometimes, too."

Art asked, "Why the Archdiocese?"

Mrs. Detweiler, a very believable and forthright elderly woman, said, "My dear friend didn't have any close family. She was torn up by her son and him throwing his life away. She became close to God after she moved, and I suggested the Archdiocese needed the money."

Art followed up, "What did you know about the Archdiocese's need for money?"

Mrs. Detweiler answered, "Only that Katrina had left it in a dire place with damaged properties, lack of insurance proceeds, and less than half the congregation. It was no secret and discussed constantly." Mrs. Detweiler added, "Mrs. Mason was proud to make this her legacy, and while no one locally ever knew how much money she had but me and her investment advisors, she told many people at Church she had made the Archdiocese her beneficiary. She was proud of this fact and wanted to encourage others."

"And you can provide us with witness names, Mrs. Detweiler?" Art asked.

"Of course."

Art didn't ask about the Vicar General's conversations at home regarding Archdiocesan finances. It wasn't material, and he didn't want to know if Johnathan talked about his work at home. The Vicar General continued to sit without speaking, mostly on his phone working and briefly stepping into the hall for a call so as not to interrupt anyone. It was clear to Art that Mrs. Detweiler knew what she was doing and had a good recall. She would make a terrific witness.

"I'm just about ready to get to work on my report," Art said. "I'd like Tori to follow up with calls to at least five friends from Church who knew about Mrs. Detweiler's wishes and passion for the Archdiocese as well as Mrs. Detweiler's housekeeper. And I need to, then, interview Mrs. Detweiler's housekeeper, the other witness."

Tori was provided names and phone numbers for five of the Church friends of Mrs. Mason, and all agreed to reconvene Friday at 10:00 AM at Mrs. Detweiler's house to talk to Deloris Taylor.

In the car on the way back to Tulane, Art asked Tori, "So how were your exams?"

Things had been strained personally since the kiss. Neither had discussed it. Tori didn't want to bring it up, assuming it would be forgotten. She longed for another, but she didn't dare do anything to initiate. Tori valued her relationship with Art and his commitment to his family. It was an emotional mistake he made in the depths of crisis to feel better. It wouldn't happen again, yet she couldn't undo in her mind.

Art had prayed frequently asking for forgiveness, but he, too, could not get Tori out of his mind. He now wanted her physically and found himself a couple of times thinking about her while he and Christine had sex. Art had been able to not have physical feelings for Tori, stopping the same at initial desire in the past, yet, since the hug, it was growing every time he was with her and couldn't stop the desire. He didn't want to talk about the feeling or the kiss, trying to suppress them and move the relationship back to strictly business. It helped that Thanksgiving and then exams were upon them. Tori spent, as she should and Art encouraged her to do, significant time at home visiting family and also studying for her finals. Art very much wanted Tori to do well.

"Oh, I was so nervous, especially for yours. I think I did well. It's just having one test all semester decide your whole grade. I wish I knew the scores now," Tori said. It would be weeks before grades were out. Fortunately, Tori thought, she got to spend the break working with Art.

On Friday, Tori and Art met at Art's office to prepare for the meeting at 10:00. Tori had spent several days talking to the witnesses and making statements for them to sign in a form Art provided. Everyone had cooperated and responded as anticipated. The case and report were shaping up nicely, Tori thought. She said as much to Art when she walked into his office with two coffees, one for her and one for him. Art reviewed with her the comments he had made to the statements Tori emailed him the day before, so she could make the changes after they discussed some minor points Art thought needed discussion. The statements were to be sent to Judith for review and supplementation by she and Thomas before Judith arranged with the witnesses to sign. Art asked Tori to arrange everything. Tori was excited to have the experience of preparing a case.

Art asked Tori, "Get your stuff and let's talk more on the way about this meeting."

Tori asked, picking up her coffee (which was all of her "stuff"), "What do we know about Deloris Taylor?"

Art replied, "Nothing other than she's Mrs. Detweiler's housekeeper." Art added "Everything's adding up fine, I don't expect any surprises."

Tori volunteered, "I googled her and came up with nothing except an obituary from her father."

Art and Tori discussed the report form as Art drove them to the Garden District. Arriving early, which was always Art's tendency and a habit somewhat lost on the younger generation, he thought, Art looked at Tori and said, "We'll wait until five minutes till and then ring the bell."

There was silence in the car for what seemed like an eternity. No music was on, and neither looked at their phones just ahead. Art fidgeted with his files containing the notes from prior meetings and research, checking it again for who knows how many times.

Tori said, "Do you think about it?"

Art looked down and said, "Little else."

Tori responded "I know it weighs on you—your decision not to question the Archbishop."

This was not what Art thought Tori was referring to at all. He was thinking about the kiss. Relieved that she was referring to something else, Art said, "I've come to the reluctant rationalization of accepting facially the Archbishop's word and not pushing the Vicar General."

Tori realized from Art's tone and veiled response, he was talking about two things.

"Let's go in. I wonder if our friend the Vicar General will be here today," Art said somewhat indignantly. The prior conversation had hit two nerves. Art continued with, "Let's go do the Lord's work."

Deloris Taylor opened the door and let Tori and Art in while at the same time introducing herself. Mrs. Taylor was in her sixties and quite plump. She moved around with a wobble and mostly looked down. Mrs. Taylor didn't speak much and seemed to want to get everything over with immediately, not even wanting to be in the room at first. Art sensed her discomfort and said, "Mrs. Taylor, would you please get us both something to drink, you and me, so we can sit at the table and talk." Art motioned to the kitchen breakfast table.

Mrs. Detweiler walked in with the Vicar General. Thomas was with them. Judith was running late. Thomas asked to wait for Judith, which left everyone sitting around the six-seater breakfast room table with not much to talk about. This made Deloris uncomfortable, and she wanted to get up and work. Work soothed Mrs. Taylor, and it was her calling. She had been a housekeeper for over 40 years and with the Detweilers for 30-plus.

Finally, after much stained talk of the Saints winning the Super Bowl even after losing to San Francisco and likely home field advantage, Judith arrived, and the meeting began.

Art started, asking, "Mrs. Taylor, had you met Mrs. Mason before the will was signed?"

"Yeah," Mrs. Taylor responded. Art knew it would take some prying to get Mrs. Taylor to say more than yes or no. He decided to ask some open-ended questions.

"When did you meet her?" Art asked.

"Years ago," Mrs. Taylor responded.

"Do you recall how long ago?" Art asked.

Mrs. Taylor said, "A while back."

Art wasn't able to loosen up Mrs. Taylor at all. She didn't have anything to hide. It was just not usual at all to be questioned by several lawyers from big firms and Tulane about something her bosses thought was so important. Mrs. Taylor had heard on more than one occasion the Vicar and his mom discussing how significant the Mason gift was to the future of the Catholic Church in New Orleans. She was rightfully out of place and nervous.

"What was your impression of Mrs. Mason?" Art asked.

"Impression?" Mrs. Taylor responded.

Trying again, Art asked, "What did you think about her?"

Mrs. Taylor responded, "Nice lady."

Art followed up more specifically, realizing open ended or opinion questions weren't getting anywhere, with "Did Mrs. Mason ever seem like she didn't know what she was doing or saying?"

"No," Mrs. Taylor said.

"And how about Mrs. Detweiler, did you ever see her tell or make Mrs. Mason do anything?"

"No," Mrs. Taylor said.

Sensing Mrs. Taylor couldn't be ever made to say anything directly bad relating to Mrs. Mason, Art asked, "Are you a religious woman?"

"Yes, I am" Mrs. Taylor said. This provoked some emotion.

"What religion?" Art asked.

"Baptist," Mrs. Taylor said.

"Do you understand the significance of why you are here today?" Art asked.

"Yeah," Mrs. Taylor said.

"And what is that, Mrs. Taylor?" Art asked.

"To tell you about me signing Mrs. Mason's will."

"Did you sign Mrs. Mason's will?" Art asked.

"Yeah," Mrs. Taylor replied.

Art reached into his folder and pulled out a copy of the will. He turned to the last page and pointed to the signature of Mrs. Taylor.

"Is this your signature?" Art asked.

"Yeah," Mrs. Taylor said.

"And underneath where your name is printed, is that your handwriting?" Art asked.

"Yeah I wrote that" Mrs. Taylor said, adding, "The lady asked me to."

"What lady?" Art asked.

"The lady who came with the will," Mrs. Taylor said.

"Was her name Janet?" Art asked.

"Don't recall," Mrs. Taylor said.

"Well what do you recall?" Art asked.

"She told me to sign and write my name, and I did," Mrs. Taylor said.

"Do you see here the name Janet stamped under the Notary Public title and the signature above it, Mrs. Taylor?" Art asked.

"Yeah," Mrs. Taylor said.

"You saw Mrs. Mason sign this page, and Janet, too?" Art asked.

"No, it was signed when I walked in," Mrs. Taylor said.

Art looked at her and said, "Are you sure?"

"Yeah, all the signatures were on there when I came in but mine" Mrs. Taylor said.

Art paused, wondering if anyone understood the significance of this matter. Everyone was looking at him waiting for the next question.

Judith said, "Mrs. Taylor, you were right here in the kitchen next to this table just across the room when these papers were signed, right?"

"No, I was in the laundry room. Mrs. Detweiler called me to come," Mrs. Taylor said.

Then Thomas joined in, asking a series of questions that made Mrs. Taylor crawl into her shell and not say much. Thomas was intimidating and spoke in an accusatory tone, even when talking about the Saints. Finally, to break from the revelation, Art suggested he was very happy to meet Mrs. Taylor and thanked her for her time.

Art asked everyone to step into the dining room.

Thomas immediately said, "Art, this has no bearing on if Mrs. Detweiler exercised any undue influence whatsoever over Mrs. Mason. It seems you have everything you need for your report."

The Vicar General innocently put out his hand gesturing curiously to Art, not understanding what had happened. In fact, the only persons who got it were Judith, Thomas, and Art.

Art didn't know what to do. Technically, Thomas was right. He had everything he needed to write an opinion on undue influence, and it would be completely favorable to the Archdiocese. Not knowing what to say and somewhat pushed by Thomas, Art agreed and motioned to Tori for them to leave. Mrs. Detweiler was very gracious, and she insisted on walking Tori and Art to the door, saying, "What you're doing here is what Mrs. Mason wanted. God bless."

When they got in the car, Tori said, "What's wrong? I can tell something happened, but I don't know what. All the lawyers were nervous and scared. I could smell it. Hell, I could see it in your faces. The Detweilers were as pleased as could be and I'm clueless."

Art looked at Tori and grabbed her arm lightly, saying, "In Louisiana, each witness has to watch everyone sign a will for it to be valid, enforceable, and legal."

"You mean the will is not valid?" Tori said excitedly.

"Yes, it's very simple, and there are no exceptions," Art quickly responded.

"What are we going to do?" Tori asked.

Art, still holding Tori's arm, looked her in the eye and said, "Thomas is asking us to forget what we heard because it has nothing to do with our job or our opinion."

Tori said, "That can't be. Everyone agrees Mrs. Mason knew what she was doing. Clearly there was no pressure or influence from Mrs. Detweiler, I've talked to the witnesses, and the will was signed by a notary and two witnesses. Mrs. Taylor knows it was Mrs. Mason's will. And, Art, the Church will lose all the money to the drug dealing middle aged punk."

Tori couldn't help but think of the Devil incident, imagining hoards of men out there like those. The thought of the damage a man could do with $100 million was frightening.

"None of that matters in the law, Tori," Art said.

Tori pulled her arm from Art's hand and angrily said, "You can't let this happen."

"But I don't know how to stop it," Art said. They were talking about two different things again. Art didn't know how to let the truth come out for the law to be followed, and Tori couldn't fathom the son getting all of the money. After a few seconds of conversation where each talked over each other with the tone getting harsh and angry, they understood the other's perspective.

16

Brian Johnston was short and unassuming. Mostly balding and from rural South Louisiana, he spoke with an accent and, most often, at a slow pace. Brian's pace speaking could be deceiving. It would appear he didn't know where he was going with a topic given the lack of speed and, then, almost by surprise, one would realize Brian knew much more than he let on.

Brian was a lawyer practicing in the New Orleans area with his offices in Slidell, Louisiana, a town just outside of New Orleans. Ray Namer was referred to Brian Johnston by a friend from Birmingham who had been involved in an accident on the Greater New Orleans Causeway Bridge. Ray's friend's wife's car barreled through a rusty road hazard barrier straight into the Lake. She died. Brian Johnston was able to determine that the Bridge's General Manager knew the barrier was an inferior product to another option and, resultantly, the rust and death could have been prevented. The general manager wanted his friend to get the contract. A tragedy.

It was common knowledge at the Watering Hole in Birmingham where Ray sometimes hung out that there was this lawyer in New Orleans who could fight the crooked establishment and win.

Brian was not particularly fond of Ray Namer, yet he couldn't ignore the prize. Yes, will contest cases were difficult. There was a presumption in favor of capacity. And, undue influence cases were equally hard given the heightened standard of proof and presumptions. Who could really say what influence was right or wrong?

In all of his 30-plus years practicing law, Brian had never seen anything like Art's expert report. Not only were Art's credentials impeccable, as the endowed ethics Chair at Tulane law, the report was amazingly thorough, detailing both facts and law. Brian knew he could attack Art on the grounds of bias given Art's affiliation with the Archdiocese, yet he wondered how far that would go with the judge in this case, as Art's reputation was impeccable.

Art's deposition was scheduled for April 13. To prepare, Brian had taken the deposition of all the witnesses the Archdiocese listed as may call for the trial, including Mrs. Mason's church friends. The case was shaping up to be difficult. Brian had taken the case for only one reason. With over $100 million involved and the reality that most will contests settle, no matter what the resolution here, it proved to be a big pay day. Bigger than big, in fact. It would be the most money Brian had ever made with "one lick," as he called it. Brian had a 40 percent contingency interest in the outcome. Even with a bad case, Brian figured the Archdiocese would pay at least 10 million (less than 10 percent) to make it go away. That would be four for him and six for Ray.

It wasn't that Brian needed the money. He lived quite frugally on a farm by himself having been divorced for over 10 years with grown children. He loved the work; lived for it. Brian had a few associates, but in this case, other than some research, Brian did everything himself.

All of the depositions Brian took, Ray attended. Brian wanted Ray to see firsthand what they were up against and, also, wanted a cleaned-up Ray front and center for the Archdiocese to see. This would demonstrate to the Archdiocese that Ray was not going to appear like everything the Archdiocese would say he was, assuming reputation testimony and bad acts were to come into evidence. The Archdiocese had hired private investigators to dig into Ray's past arrests, fights and failed jobs, marriages and businesses. It was an ugly portrait, yet there were evidence objections to keep much of it out potentially and redemption was always possible with addicts. Most everyone loves a good addict recovery story, and Ray knew how to play the role.

Brian had gotten Ray clean right off the bat. Rehab and AA meetings with a sponsor and all. For this kind of money, Ray could stay clean. Ray dreamed of being high all the time, forever, once the dough rolled in. And, the case would be over by June.

Ray presented very well clean and sober. Brian rented Ray an apartment in Slidell, and the two were together every day, including weekends. Brian protected his investment by watching Ray like a hawk. Brian even had Ray thinking, sometimes, he'd recovered with all the positive affirmations daily. Brian cared about one thing only, victory. And victory was 10 million or more.

Not that the Archdiocese knew this. From the beginning, Brian's strategy would be to call witnesses from Savannah, who would say that Mrs. Mason crawled into a shell after her husband's death and was not herself. They would add that Mrs. Mason was not religious whatsoever before the move to New Orleans, and she had no affiliation with the Catholic Church. And Brian could prove no one in Mrs. Mason's old life knew Mrs. Detweiler at all, as she had never been to Savannah to visit. It wasn't hard to find old friends of Mrs. Mason's who would help. They all felt abandoned and scorned after Mr. Mason died as well as somewhat vengeful when the money had left Savannah. This on top of the beloved Mason heirs being left without.

Art dealt with all of this testimony in his report as having been old and outdated information related to Mrs. Mason. It had been years and years since these witnesses had seen or heard from Mrs. Mason who was, clearly, from the medical testimony and many cooperating witnesses, a thoughtful, competent, and faithful Catholic who loved her Church and its community. To prepare for his deposition, Art and Tori both read through every deposition and outlined them. Together, they would meet every other day and compare notes to assemble an outline for anticipated points to be asked and the suggested response. This matter was a life saver for the Archdiocese and Art treated it as such.

Art had not convinced Tori that the invalidity of the will, the truth in the law, should prevail in this matter. Tori was, conflictingly, not so convinced equity should prevail either, allowing the Archdiocese to get the funds for its rebuilding, particularly seeing Ray recovered.

Tori was puzzled. Tori's past haunted her, and she believed a man wouldn't change his dog nature, ever. However, she was still stinging from the tax issue and how the Vicar handled the matter. She wanted to do the right thing, too. even if it wasn't equitable. Art had made quite an impression on her in that regard although she didn't give in totally. She wondered why.

Primarily, it occurred to Tori she may like the intellectual discourse with Art more than she cared about the outcome. Tori loved the way Art pushed her to follow the law and truth, regardless of personal thought. This was the foundation of society, he would say. It's what makes the safety and security of the population possible; "the impartial administration of justice."

Tori didn't know what to call it but could see that Art was projecting when it came to the tax issue. No one had asked the Vicar or the Archbishop over the intervening months if the tax matter was corrected. Art knew it wasn't based on the actions being taken he was familiar with from his Sustainability Committee work and what he could see happening around town. Did Art know for sure? No. But he was more than 70 percent sure.

Plausible deniability was becoming harder and harder for Art to take. He didn't dare challenge the Archdiocese, however. This situation with the Mason inheritance made Art feel better and worse, depending on the day. Better in that with the money the Church was safe and could rebuild strong, yet not bringing to light the will's defect was hiding the truth. No, it wasn't his province to raise the issue with the Archdiocese or even his job as an attorney, for Art wasn't counsel of record. Art was troubled by the truth and took it out, not fighting for it, but with Tori.

Tori and Art started sleeping together after school started in January. At first, it was in his office with the door locked. After a week of being nervous and feeling guilty, the two moved to a hotel halfway between Tulane and downtown that had a restaurant next to it. Tori could get the room, and Art would park in the lot, so it looked like he was coming and going from the restaurant. The restaurant had an entrance where the hall also led to the hotel. It seemed perfect, although the guilt didn't wear off.

The two were now, by April, very entrenched into their affair. Art used it as an outlet for his frustrations with the Archdiocese, he thought. Tori was in love.

After the two finished one afternoon, as they always met from 3:00 to 5:30 when they did the deed, which had become four to five times a week, Tori asked Art, "What about Deloris Taylor's testimony. Have you reviewed it yet?"

Art answered, "Yes I also got the email with the deposition last night. Brian didn't even ask Mrs. Taylor if she witnessed Mrs. Mason sign the will."

Tori said, "Secretly, I guess I had hoped Brian would ask, and the truth would be out. I know the consequences, but it is the law and…"

Tori paused, and Art added, "I know. What can we do? I feel as if we have to convince Thomas he is perpetuating a fraud on the court by having probated the will, or his firm is through Janet. But, we know that will never happen."

Tori responded, "What about the Bar Association?"

Art indicated it would be appropriate to refer a lawyer for perpetuating a fraud on the Court. But, there was the great possibility Mrs. Taylor would be pressured to change her story by her employer and the Vicar General. After all, look at how much the case was worth. Then, Art's reputation would be ruined as having gone against the Archdiocese. There didn't seem to be a way out as the two discussed the matter. Art was, for a second time, handcuffed by fear of preserving his reputation and not wanting to be cast out from the Church.

Leaving, Tori asked, "Still want me to babysit this weekend before your deposition Saturday night?"

Art said, "Yes, please."

Tori added, "It's starting to seem very weird to me, being friends with Christine. I know we said we wouldn't talk about her, but…" Tori never finished.

17

Thomas and Judith's offices were on the top floor of the tallest skyscraper in New Orleans. Marble floors adorned the lobby as Art and Tori got off the elevator. The offices were finely apportioned and detailed in every possible manner. A statement was being made by the location and decor. It wasn't lost on Art this day.

Before Brian and Ray arrived, Thomas met with Art and Tori to prepare Art for his deposition. Art considered himself very well read on the case, having been through all of the depositions, including the ones recently completed, such as Deloris Taylor. Art's deposition was the last before close of discovery and, after the close, a mediation before trial. The mediation was set for Monday, May 11, and the trial for the week of June 1, Thomas told Art. The Archdiocese's strategy was to settle by giving Ray Namer 10 to 15 percent of what was at issue. Thomas and Judith outlined the entire strategy which included Art defending his expert report and, then, an easy mediation.

After reviewing the strategy and anticipated testimony points, Thomas turned to Art and said, "If Brian asks you about Deloris Taylor, what do you intend to say?"

Art was distracted, wondering if a settlement got him off the hook morally, ethically, or legally. There were three different standards Art ran through in his mind. A settlement certainly doesn't absolve Art for allowing the Archdiocese to perpetuate a lie by knowingly probating the will, which was legally defective. The will contained a verification from Janet, too, which said it had been signed in the presence of the two witnesses and the notary. Janet, Judith, and Thomas, at least, knew about this falsity. Did the Vicar General? Did the Archbishop? A settlement really wouldn't make all these issues go away.

"Art," Thomas said, "are you with us?"

"Sorry, Thomas, what's the question?" Art responded.

"If you're asked about Mrs. Taylor witnessing the will being signed, what are you going to say?"

Art angrily stood up and pointing at Thomas said, "I will not lie for the Archdiocese."

The room was silent. Judith and Tori didn't dare to say anything, and Thomas was speechless.

Art added, "You better hope he doesn't ask."

Thomas realized the effect of what he was saying.

Yes, it was true he had to only answer questions asked and not volunteer anything. Yet, Art was a lawyer, and he had taken an oath. Also, he owed an obligation to the court. But most importantly, he owed an obligation to himself and God. Art knew he was coming up short everywhere he turned lately. The walls were closing in, Art felt. Somehow, Art saw strength in taking a stand on not overtly lying.

Finally, Thomas said, "You know what this means..."

Art interrupted him.

"Let's go in the room for the deposition. This meeting is over."

Sitting in the main conference room at Thomas' firm was nerve-wracking. You could see the Mississippi River and the ships maneuvering its crescent turns through the floor to ceiling windows. *You could fit a plane in the room. Not a 747, but a G6*, Art thought. At one end of the table sat the court reporter, who would take down every world Art said. With his back to the wall, Art sat on one side of the table. Next to Art were Thomas and Judith. Tori had to stay in another room, as she was not allowed in the deposition not being a witness, party representative, or counsel. She had made big eyes at Art when they separated. For now, she doodled on her legal-size yellow paper, blue lined with a red pen.

On the other side of the table in the deposition was Brian and, next to Brian, Ray. No one from the Archdiocese was in attendance. Art had not discussed the case again after the day at the Detweilers with the Vicar General other than being told how significant the case was when the Vicar was thanking him for participating and helping. Art wondered what that really meant. Art had not brought up the tax issue again. Art had not talked to the Archbishop on either matter. Art wondered if he was being a good Christian soldier or the Archdiocese's truth quasher. It didn't take long to figure out the answer.

Brian Johnston had a peculiar way of asking questions. He talked around issues instead of being direct. While he asked Art what Art did to prepare the report, and Art indicated he or his staff interviewed witnesses and listed them off from a reference to his report, Brian never asked him exactly what anyone said. All of this was in the report, Brian thought. No questions about his meeting with Deloris Taylor. Art was relieved.

On the other hand, Brian spent most of his time making Art feel and seem like a lifetime disciple of the Catholic Church. The insinuation was Art would do and say anything in its interest. And all of the background and affiliations were true. Brian made much out of Art's work on the Sustainability Committee, the Archdiocese's financial problems post Katrina, and the Mason windfall. The suggestion was apparent. Art felt guilty from it although for different reasons than implied. *I am guilty of it*, Art thought.

When the deposition was over, Brian looked at Thomas and said, "I'll expect an offer from you soon. This didn't help you today."

Thomas didn't reply although he did politely walk Ray and Brian to the elevators outside of the large conference room down the marble path through the lobby.

The team reconvened in the small conference room where Tori waited.

"Well?" Tori said when Art walked in.

Thomas responded, "Art did fabulous. He is our key witness, and we really don't have much to be concerned with. And, there was no real mention of Mrs. Taylor."

Art looked at Thomas and said, "But what about what Brian said leaving?"

"Posturing," Thomas spouted, adding, "Trial lawyers do that to intimidate witnesses and send strong messages for settlement negotiation purposes."

"You're still going to settle, right?" Art said insistently.

"Yes, yes I'm sure we will, Art. Don't worry. These cases always settle. Would you like to come to the mediation? It will look good to the mediator if you're there. And you can bring your assistant."

There was something in the way Thomas said assistant that gnawed at Art. Did Thomas know something? Was this paranoia? Guilt? Art didn't know;

there seemed to be so many things Art was guilty of this could be pushing a button related to anyone. Perhaps it was Art didn't care for Thomas, Judith, and Janet given what they were doing defrauding the court.

Art said, "Yes, please."

In the elevator going down, Tori asked, "So what did Brian say leaving the deposition?"

Art told Tori Brian made a comment like Art's deposition went very well for Ray's case and that the settlement offer should be huge.

Tori asked, "If it settles, no one ever finds out about the will's defect or the fraud of probating it, right?"

"Right," Art said, dejected.

Tori couldn't read Art, and he didn't want to talk. Usually open and polite, Art was exhausted and wanted to forget about the day. Art insisted the two stop at their hotel, as the deposition didn't go as long as planned. Leaving the hotel, neither felt any better.

It was getting close to the end of Tori's second semester as April turned into May. She had received mostly A's with two B-pluses the first semester. Very good grades, and Tori was in the top 15 percent of her class. She wanted to keep up the grades, so she studied relentlessly to make up for some lost time focused on the Mason case. One of the B-pluses she received was in Art's class. They never discussed it.

18

Art had been to a few mediations in his practice before going to work at Tulane. Nothing like this one though. It was held in neutral territory.

The Windsor Court Hotel was the finest luxury hotel New Orleans had to offer. On the second floor down the hall from the bar and restaurant were several conference rooms. This Monday morning, May 11, the Archdiocese team was in one and Ray Namer and Brian Johnston in another.

When Tori and Art arrived, they were shown to the Archdiocese's room by the mediator, Rodger Simon. Rodger was a lawyer from Lafayette, Louisiana, who had a reputation for getting the largest, most complicated cases settled. Rodger made his way to Lafayette from Arkansas to get married and settle where his wife's family lived. Rodger and Courtney met at LSU during college, and Courtney's dad gave Rodger a job in his oil field services company. Part time operations work using his finance degree helped Rodger to develop more people skills than most young lawyers would have. After Courtney's dad sold the company and Courtney left her firm job, Rodger had been given nice bonuses, which allowed him to start his own business. Mediation was a growing field, and Rodger liked the role of peacemaker.

Both Brian and Thomas had heard of Rodger, yet neither had worked with him directly in the past. The judge at a pretrial conference in March suggested Rodger when he pushed both sides to seriously discuss settlement, saying, "Your clients have everything to lose."

And this was true. The Archdiocese came prepared to settle. In fact, once the day got started at 9:30, everyone from both sides were in the large conference room assigned to the Archdiocese at first. Brian made a presentation where he reviewed heavily the Archdiocese's newfound wealth was a surprise from Mrs. Mason's Savannah community, as was her fledgling Catholic faith. He pushed Art's lifetime affiliation with the Archdiocese as well as Ray's recovery. Ray was particularly presentable this day.

Sometimes mediators would back channel with judges and, here, since Rodger was refereed by the judge, Brian wanted to make a big impression with Ray. Brian's presentation reviewed Ray's recovery process and sober life accomplishments. Thomas was not surprised by anything Brian had to say and, for that, he was grateful. With no surprises, Thomas proceeded as planned.

In the room were the Vicar General, Tori, Art, Judith, Janet, and Thomas as well as a paralegal from Thomas' office. The sides sized up in quite the David and Goliath fashion. Thomas began by saying the Archdiocese heeded the judge's comments and appeared in good faith to resolve the case that day. He then reviewed the stated challenge of capacity and demonstrated surgically why under the law there was no chance of success. Likewise, Thomas took the undue influence claim apart using the law, Art's report, and the facts, including so many witnesses from Mrs. Mason's Church groups. Thomas last relied heavily on Art's report and reputation. In the end, Thomas painted a picture of no chance of success for Ray, yet he reiterated the Archdiocese wanted to follow the judge's instructions and be reasonable.

The mediator thanked both sides for their professionalism and asked the Namer team into their smaller room where he would follow. Before the mediation, both sides shared papers which were confidential with the mediator. Rodger had read the voluminous materials and evidence submitted. He looked right at Brian once everyone sat down and said, "Not much of a case here. It seems the best thing you have going for you is this case woke up Ray, and he has wonderfully recovered from his addictions." Knowing all good and well the recovery was showmanship, Rodger wanted a facially positive way to say to Brian and Ray they should be thankful for whatever they got this day.

Brian ignored the comment and said, "We are waiting for an offer from the Archdiocese. I asked Thomas for one after their disciple Arthur Tomlinson prostituted himself. Nothing has come," Brian spoke in a confident, calculating tone, which was on the high end of the aggressive scale. Rodger knew he had work to do.

Customarily the plaintiff gave the first offer. However, given Brian's tone, Rodger played the complicit card and said, "Let me see if I can't go get you that offer. While I'm gone, please think about whether you are willing to walk away from eight figures today. Bird in hand, fellows." Rodger was sending the message to Brian and Ray that he thought they should take $10 million and that Rodger would try to accomplish the same.

Rodger explained to the Archdiocese team, speaking mainly to the Vicar General with his eyes that a $70 to $80 million windfall donation was once in an entity's lifetime. Rodger continued, why would they risk blowing it not knowing what the judge might think? Laying everything on the line to one judge who had immense discretion was reckless, Rodger pushed.

"Everyone has a 20 percent plus chance of losing any case in a state court with a single judge," Roger said. The Vicar General knew this was true with all the years of his forensic expert work. The Vicar was no stranger to mediations and judges who ruled for or against parties without much apparent regard for the facts or law.

"It's just not customary," Thomas protested to Rodger when asked to make the first offer. Eventually relenting after the Vicar General, with a cooler head, said "Thomas, I have no problem going first," Thomas asked Rodger to excuse himself, so everyone on the Archdiocese team could discuss the offer. Art suggested they go right to it. Fairness considering Mrs. Taylor and Janet's slip ups required a large allocation. The Archdiocese would be just fine with half, Art stated firmly.

The Vicar General calmly said, "Half? Art, that's not commensurate with the facts."

The Vicar General understood exactly what Art meant by the Mrs. Taylor comment as Thomas dutifully had reviewed with the Vicar in detail the significance of Mrs. Taylor not having been in the room when the will was executed. Thomas had not focused on it being Janet's responsibility and fault for failing to have Mrs. Taylor present. The Vicar was no fool though and, rather than be direct, had asked Thomas how much their malpractice policy was. Thomas indicated he didn't believe a beneficiary in a will had a cause of action for malpractice. It would only be the client for the will. This polite yet veiled posturing conversation occurred in January, and it had not been revisited since.

None of this could be discussed with the mediator, of course. Even though the mediator was sworn to confidence, a flaw unknown by the other side was not to be disclosed at any time to anyone. The Vicar General did add in his statement to Art, "We'll do what's right and fair by Ray to equalize what's occurred here and honor the equities."

Tori seethed seeing the rationalizing, manipulating power monger at work. This was the man who knowingly violated the tax law. Now he was ignoring the truth in the name of fairness. And, worse possibly, look what he had done by getting a firm, moral sounding man in Art to prostitute himself.

"Who does he think he is, King Soloman?" Tori said to Art when the two were walking to the restroom on a break from the discussion about a first offer. Tori lingered in the bathroom. Art, not wanting anyone to notice him waiting too long, went back to the large meeting room without Tori. He thought about how frustrated he and Tori were.

By the time Tori got back, the Vicar General and Thomas were going back and forth in the $1 to $3 million range. Thomas wanted to start at $1 and the Vicar General at $3 million.

"I've seen people walk out when an offer is too insulting or, worse yet sometimes, demand a party bid against themselves," the Vicar General said. The two decided with some suggestion from Art on $2.5 million.

Judith went to get Rodger, who responded to the offer as, "Y'all have to be more serious than this. I've predicted a likely outcome for y'all in the $20 to $30 million range. It's now 10:40, and you're going to start there." The room was silent for a few seconds. No one looked down or seemed ashamed except Tori and Art. Both had been taking notes, and at this point, they were looking at the Vicar General.

Thomas spoke, "That's our offer." Thomas understood as did the Vicar General that the mediator played both sides hard to find middle ground. Tori didn't understand. She was worried there would be no settlement. Rodger walked out, and Tori, after making some more notes in her legal pad, asked Art, "Do I need to be in here right now. I'm feeling disgusted and need to go to the bathroom again?"

Art responded, "Oh, I'm sure we'll be in here for quite a while waiting. It could be an hour. Feel free to take a break and walk around downstairs if need be. I'll text you when Rodger is back. I can see you're stressed and upset. Cool off. This is out of our hands."

Tori took her folder and note pad along with her laptop, which all fit in a very stylish girly thin case. Art was right. It was noon when Rodger came in with the waiters delivering lunch.

"A working lunch today. Please set up over there," motioning to the waiters, Rodger said. He continued, "Y'all please grab a plate and sit down. I have the response."

Art knew this wasn't good news from the tone and request to get comfortable. He texted Tori, who was back in a few minutes. Rodger had just started to tell everyone that Ray's counter offer was, "If the Archdiocese doesn't offer at least $5 million we're leaving," Rodger said. Rodger explained that he thought this was a positive sign. While Rodger couldn't tell the Archbishop's team what was said in the other room, he assured everyone that the case was settleable eventually within his range if the Archdiocese came up to five million to start.

The Vicar General said, "Yes, we will." Thomas cleared his throat as if to show displeasure with the quick decision or the decision period. The Vicar General looked at Thomas and, with his eyes, was clearly saying "Don't go there."

The Vicar felt surrounded by incompetence. Janet didn't get the simple execution of the will right. Thomas pushed him when Thomas' firm was to blame. The Vicar General said out loud passive aggressively, "How did we get here, Dear Lord."

The statement was made right after Rodger shut the door leaving. In the smaller meeting room, the mood had changed. Before, Rodger had secured the informal commitment from Brian that if Rodger could get the Archdiocese in the $10 to $20 million, range the case was settleable. The plan had been for Brian to respond with $50 million to the $5 million and try to work the number into that range.

"Let's offer $90 million" Brian said.

Rodger looked at Brian and said, "That wasn't the plan." Brian stood up and began to pace. He thought for a while. Rodger and Ray could tell Brian was formulating the exact words he wanted to use.

"Ray has had second thoughts. I'm afraid I acquiesced in your approach, Rodger, without appropriate consultation with my client." Rodger looked at

Brian in disbelief, yet tried not to show it. Rodger remained friendly, as was protocol no matter what.

"So Ray made this decision?" Rodger asked.

"Yes," Brian responded, adding, "and I'm terribly sorry to you and he for the miscommunication. Ray didn't feel comfortable speaking up until you left."

Rodger wondered if he had put the cart before the horse. Rodger usually asked the client, confirming with the client directly, their acquiesce in the strategy. Perhaps he had not followed his usual path, Rodger thought. There were significant dollars and pressure.

"May I speak directly to Ray now with you in the room?" Rodger asked.

"Of course" Brian responded.

"Ray, you understand your chances of winning the case must be less than 20 percent," Rodger said. Ray didn't respond. Rodger added, "if you want to settle today or anytime for that matter, you'll need to come into the $10 to $20 million range eventually. Are you prepared to do that?"

Ray again didn't respond.

Brian then said, "I'd like to talk to my client alone."

After Rodger excused himself from the room, Ray said, "What are we doing?" Brian was silent, and Ray continued "I'd take $10 million today. That's six for me and four for you. Brian?"

Brian looked at Ray and said, "You're going to have to trust me on this. Negotiation is a mind game. We need the other side to believe in our confidence. I assure you, by the time we get to June 1, the number will be substantially higher than 10 million. It will only go up from what the Archdiocese is willing to pay today."

Ray responded, "But we agreed coming into today what we would do and sat and planned the strategy with Rodger. Why did we do that? Why didn't you tell me?"

Brian looked at Ray in almost a fatherly fashion and said quietly "Ray, we've got something big here. Bigger than we ever thought. You just need to trust my experience level."

Ray fought a little harder and then relented. Brian assured Ray no matter what happened today, there'd be more money pretrial.

Once Rodger, armed with no real explanation for the about face by Brian and Ray, received the go ahead to make the $90 million offer, he went to the larger meeting room.

"Ninety million!" the Vicar bellowed. Tori smiled. She liked seeing the Vicar General so upset. To pass the time, Tori had been flirting with Art via text message. She was feeling frisky, and there didn't seem to be a chance of finishing early today, so she thought she'd get the next best thing.

Thomas added, "Why would we stay. How do you get to $10 to $20 million from $90? What kind of approach is this?"

Rodger, of course, couldn't argue with Thomas or even tell the Vicar he was overreacting. Rodger instead said, "I think you should call their bluff. Tell Ray you came up to $5 million and bid against yourself, showing good faith and that Ray must come to 50 million or half of what's at issue to show good faith as to the facts and law. If they don't, you leave and put the pressure on them pretrial. They'll be back soon."

Eventually everyone agreed, and Rodger went to deliver the message.

Rodger was back in five minutes. He said, "They left." Rodger explained he delivered to Brian and Ray the message as a "take it, or leave."

"They said alright, as matter of fact, politely thanked me for my time, and said to tell y'all 'see you in court,' he said.

"What do we do now?" the Vicar exclaimed.

Thomas said, "Prepare for trial. The judge will pressure Ray to settle before trial at the pretrial conference and, if not then, once he hears the evidence. No judge in their right mind is going to rule for Ray."

Knowing this to be most likely the absolute truth, the Vicar said, "You'd better be right, and you know why I'm saying this. You have as much to lose as we do."

Rodger had no idea what the Vicar was talking about. Art was pleased to see the Vicar threatened and backed into a corner, nervous. Tori simply loved it. And she would get Art that afternoon, as there still was time.

19

When Tori left the hotel on May 11, 2020, at 5:48, she knew deep down it was the last time she'd sleep with Art. Things had gotten out of hand, and she needed to be the one to stop. *Tori loved Art dearly and didn't want to break up his home*, she thought. Or, she thought, *was it the fact he was not living up to his spiritual self?* Tori had grown as close, if not closer, to Art in these last several months, in the way only two people can who share a deep secret. She had to end this for Art.

It was difficult, yet not impossible, to explain her being busy to Art. Work for the Archdiocese was done pending trial, and she had exams. Once exams were over, Tori explained she wanted to take a few days at home in Gonzales before she returned for the trial. These days would turn into quite a while. Art never questioned Tori wanting to study or be with her family, and the heavy texting continued without interruption.

Tori did study dutifully. Her grades would be even better than the first semester, she planned. Two a day runs were also on the agenda as a way to work off the stress. She felt well.

Rodger had stayed involved somewhat, trying to move Ray. His only communication was with Brian, and Brian seemed confident in his case. Rodger couldn't understand. Unlike the suspicions, however, Rodger didn't have a back channel to the judge. The Archdiocese became bolder as the trial approached that the judge would consider Ray's $90 million settlement position absurd.

The pretrial conference was set for May 27. Everyone was there early in the waiting room. The judge arrived 45 minutes late. He walked through the waiting room. He shook hands and met the parties and counsel. Art and Tori weren't there.

After 20 minutes, the secretary said, "The judge will see you now."

Judge Katz was the last vestige of a white on the bench in New Orleans. He had been on the beach since 1982. No one ran against him when election time came around. He was a man of all people in New Orleans as a community activist. He had no affiliation with, and also no animosity towards, the Archdiocese.

Judge Katz said, "How come this case isn't settled?"

Thomas used this as his opportunity to attack, saying, "Judge, they've offered $90 million, which is 90 cents on the dollar, and they won't come down."

Literally, this struck at an equitable cord. The judge had read the pretrial memoranda, which summarized the evidence and the law.

"Both sides have everything to lose," the judge said.

"It's a matter of principal," Brian said.

"Principal is for ethics class in school, Mr. Johnston" the judge said, continuing, "Today is for making sure your client gets some money walking out of here because from where I sit, he's not likely at all to get any if this case is tried."

"Judge, please don't predispose yourself. We want our day in court unless, bottom line Judge, right now, the Archdiocese is prepared to split the $100 million plus. Not a penny less," Brian said. Confident and stubborn, Brian wanted his trial.

No one in the judge's chambers understood why Brian and Ray we're taking such a hard line. All suspected it was positioning for a larger settlement, but with the judge now leaning on Brian about the merits of the case, the Archdiocese was not moving. Brian politely introduced some trial presentation issues and evidence matters. There was significant discussion about whether there would be witnesses admitted who could testify about what Mrs. Mason told them—all of the Church friends and, to a certain extent, Mrs. Detweiler and Janet. These statements were hearsay, Brian argued. Thomas argued exceptions to the hearsay rules.

Both sides had briefed the issues thoroughly. Judge Katz, after hearing arguments in chambers, decided to rule from the bench during the trial on a witness by witness basis. Judge Katz reasoned that out of court statements made by Mrs. Mason were inadmissible, even if she were deceased except in very limited situations, which could be specific to each witness.

"It's better to deal with these issues as they come up," Judge Katz indicated.

Thomas protested one last time.

"Judge, this will extend the trial significantly if we have to cover the issue over and over again."

Judge Katz firmly ended the conversation, saying, "I've made my ruling."

Thomas replied, "And this applies, Judge, to Ray Namer's witnesses from Savannah, right?"

Judge Katz was growing frustrated with Thomas, as judges tend to do when being requested to discuss a topic on which they have already clearly ruled, said, "Of course, except those witnesses are more reputation and habit based on observations not words from Mrs. Watson's mouth."

Thomas and Judith were frustrated both because there was no further progress on settlement ($50 million was not progress, as the Archdiocese wouldn't pay) and because now a large part of their case and Art's report foundation might not be admissible.

Leaving the court and walking to the elevator, Thomas asked Brian, "So what's your bottom line in this matter?"

Brian didn't hesitate, as he usually would, to think. Having anticipated these questions at this moment, Brian said, "Half." Thomas threw up his hands saying nothing, to which Brian said, "Most of your witnesses on undue influence are out, and your faithful disciple's wings are clipped."

Thomas was obligated to take this information to the Vicar General, and although he didn't say anything to Brian, Thomas was actually starting to think, as he and Judith walked back to the office, perhaps half or close to it would work.

"Vicar, this is Thomas and Judith, we've just come back from court," the conversation started. "The judge pushed Brian on settlement and preached to us both about how our clients had everything to lose. The judge clearly is looking at the case favorably to us if we get in all of our testimony, but there's the hearsay issue we've talked about." It was true Thomas had brought up the hearsay issue to the Vicar on May 15 when he received the Namer Pretrial Brief. The Archdiocese addressed the issue in its brief filed May 22, and the

Vicar had been told it was a threat, but the Archdiocese would win without the testimony. Today, Thomas's tune was a little different.

"You indicated to me, Thomas, we will win without the testimony about what Mrs. Mason said," the Vicar General insisted.

"That's true, and I think we will, but there is a heightened risk," Thomas said.

"Thomas, my mother and I have worked diligently to save the Archdiocese, and we won't stand by and let your incompetence ruin it. Your firm screwed up execution of the will. You better win the evidence issue and this trial."

Thomas couldn't really say anything in response. He understood the significance of Janet's mistake.

The Vicar General refused to consider a settlement of half, indicating the Archdiocese would double its offer from $5 million to $10. Thomas instructed Judith to research the law from every jurisdiction in the United States for helpful cases on the hearsay exceptions.

He next called Janet into his office, who defensively said in response to Thomas's scolding, "Thomas, I don't recall Mrs. Taylor being called in to witness. What's the big deal? Mrs. Mason was there, and it's obviously her signature." Janet continued, "I saw everyone sign and can testify to that. Also, Brian hasn't alleged a defect or picked up on this issue."

"Yes, you're right it's not an issue for the case, but our client is aware of the mistake. It makes us look incompetent," Thomas said. He asked Judith to meet with Deloris Taylor and Mrs, Detweiler without him Friday to prepare everyone. "Make sure they remember Mrs. Taylor being in the room for the signature," Thomas said.

Janet assured Thomas that, "Mrs. Detweiler can handle Mrs. Taylor."

Thomas waited until the morning to call Brian. Not wanting to seem too anxious, Thomas delayed the call.

"Brian, my client offers $10 million," Thomas said.

Brian quickly said, "Half. You've now bid against yourself twice. You know my case is strong given the evidence issue, we both have everything to win or lose. Half."

Thomas called the Vicar General back and suggested they meet with the Archbishop Friday afternoon. The Vicar frustratingly agreed. He was getting quite nervous. And worse, he had allocated in his mind $80 million dollars to a new plan for rebuilding.

Friday's meeting with Art to prepare for trial had to be moved to Saturday. When Art told Tori, she indicated she would like to stay in Gonzales for the weekend.

Art politely said, "No need to come back, I have this. See you in court Monday."

They both told each other they loved each other, and Art hung up. Tori listened to the click and lingered, not only on the phone but in her heart.

Art had not been made aware of the evidence issue before Saturday morning. Why Thomas had not given it more credence or at least notified Art right after the conference, Art didn't understand. Thomas did. He was scrambling to try to get the Archdiocese to settle.

"You just never know. Many times, a judge doesn't follow the law or the facts. Just does what he wants," Thomas told the Archbishop. "Vicar, what do you think?"

The Vicar General thought for a while. He'd been to battle many times. A wise mentor once told him to treat any matter the same whether it dealt with $5 or $5 million dollars. Yes, the size of this pot was distracting everyone. The Archdiocese had a good case. The presumptions were in its favor. The standard of proof was heightened under the law. All Ray Namer had was his short-lived recovery and decade-plus old habits of Mrs. Mason.

These thoughts swirled through his mind. He let them all out explaining himself to the Archbishop, adding, "I've been involved in many cases that settled during the trial. Once the nerves of trying the case are gone, and we start, Brian will see we're not scared, and he cannot escape the reality of his flawed case." The Vicar continued, "There are two dozen witnesses, and the case will take a week and a half or more. Let's be patient. No more offers until Brian comes down."

The Archbishop agreed.

Thomas' nerves quelled some. The Vicar General was right.

Thomas focused Saturday on working with Art to evaluate how the detailed reasoning in the report changed, although not the conclusion, if certain testimony didn't come it. Most of the day was spent preparing an alternative report. Thomas texted Tori throughout the day, as usual. The two were very close and shared many parts of their personal lives. Even though they hadn't slept together since May 11, Art didn't doubt her love for him or the fact exams kept her busy with the following much needed visit home. Tori reassured him constantly through her texts that he was her most important. Art was comforted by Tori's love. It pacified his other ills.

Sunday, Art texted Tori, "Want to meet at the office before court tomorrow?"

Tori responded, "What time and where is court?"

Art said, "Thomas wants us there at 8:15 on the corner of Poydras and Loyola. Meet in the lobby."

Tori responded, "My parents want me to stay for a Sunday dinner, kind of a tradition here, so I'll just drive and meet you in the morning."

Art replied "I can't wait to see you there. It's been too long. And of course, after…"

Tori responded with a face with hearts emoji.

20

It was raining Monday, June 1. Brian and Ray lugged their own boxes into the court. They walked past Thomas, Judith, Janet, the Vicar General, Mrs. Detweiler, Mrs. Taylor, and Art who were all standing in the lobby off to the side near the small store for food and drinks. Brian and Ray smiled, and Brian politely waved. Not to come over, but as a hello. Thomas, Judith, and the Vicar General smiled. Everyone else looked nervous and serious.

At 8:30, more witnesses for the case started coming into the doors. All of the witnesses for both sides of the case were subpoenaed. The total was 16, including the Savannah contingent who all came in together. Ray met them in the lobby at 8:45 after he came back down from unpacking with Brian. Right before they came in, everyone on the Archdiocese team, including the Church witnesses went upstairs together.

By 9:00 AM, all attorneys were set up and ready to proceed. Ray sat with Brian at the counsel table, and the Vicar General sat back with his mother. The Archdiocese counsel table included Thomas, Judith, and Janet as well as two paralegals who had brought and set up all of the materials. It looked like a mountain. The fight over one woman's estate boiled down to white file boxes filled with papers and a gallery of witnesses seated on sides like at a wedding.

When the judge took the bench there had been no talk of settlement by either side. Tori hadn't arrived yet, and Art texted her, "We're starting. Where are you?"

The judge asked if both sides were ready and, when Thomas and Brian said yes, he then said, "If you're a witness in this case, please stand." He swore all of the witnesses and admonished them not to talk about the case whatsoever to each other or any of the lawyers while the trial was proceeding. The judge then asked all of the witnesses to stay in the hall outside of the testimony being taken, except experts. Art was the only expert, and he moved to the first row of the gallery. The Vicar General came and sat next to Art when he returned from walking his mother out to the hall.

The Vicar General had shared all details of the settlement discussions and the recent evidence motions with Mrs. Detweiler. Mrs. Detweiler agreed with her son's strategy about settlement and, frankly, didn't want to see Ray get anything. Much more emotional than her son on this point, she had no doubts they would prevail.

"I know the truth about what she wanted, and God will make sure the truth comes out in the end," Mrs. Detweiler told her son on their way to court that morning.

The judge said, "Both sides have filed extensive pretrial briefs, and I see there are many witnesses, so let's get right to it. Mr. Johnston. Please call your first witness."

Brian said, "I call Mrs. Deloris Taylor."

Thomas and Judith looked shocked. Why would Mrs. Taylor be the first witness? They looked for Janet to get reassurance everything went well with Mrs. Taylor Friday. Janet was in the hall with the rest of the witnesses. Then Thomas and Judith looked back to the Vicar General, who shrugged and gave Thomas the thumbs up look by moving his eyebrows up and smiling at the same time. Art looked at Brian, who stared back at him like they both knew something. Art didn't know what.

The clerk swore Mrs. Taylor again, and Brian said, without any introductory questions whatsoever, "You didn't see Mrs. Mason sign her will, did you?"

Mrs. Taylor didn't respond. She was shocked and couldn't speak.

"Do you need me to ask the question again, Mrs. Taylor?" Brian said.

Mrs. Taylor didn't respond again.

"Mrs. Taylor, do you understand the question?" Judge Katz said.

Mrs. Taylor responded, "I know she signed it."

Brian raised his voice a little. Not to sound accusatory or aggressive, only to draw attention to the next question. It was unnecessary. By now, everyone in the room, including the judge, was looking at Mrs. Taylor and listening intently. Art subconsciously was praying she told the truth.

"I didn't ask you if you knew Mrs. Mason signed the will. I asked you if you saw it happen."

Mrs. Taylor said, "I know she signed it."

Adding a bit of frustration to his tone, Brian asked, "Do you believe in God?"

"Yes, sir," Mrs. Taylor said affirmatively.

"And did you swear an oath to God just now you would tell the truth?"

"Yes, sir," Mrs. Taylor said timidly.

"Tell me then before God, did you see Mrs. Mason sign her will?"

"Objection," Thomas stood and shouted. "The question has been asked and answered. Mr. Johnston is pressuring the witness for another answer when he doesn't like the one he has received," Thomas said.

"Overruled," the Judge said and looked at Mrs. Taylor. "Now Mrs. Taylor," the judge said in a light, friendly tone, "Yes or no, did you see, with your own eyes, Mrs. Mason sign her will?"

"No, Your Honor," Mrs. Taylor said.

The courtroom was a whirlwind with sighs from everyone except the judge, who looked like he had no idea what the significance was on this testimony. Art was immensely relieved, as if water rushed through his whole body and cleaned him completely. Immediately thereafter, Art felt guilty for not being the one to harvest the truth. Art next wondered where Tori was.

He texted Tori, "Mrs. Taylor said she didn't see Mrs. Mason sign the will."

At the same moment Art was texting, the Vicar General shrunk down into his chair in disbelief. By that time Brian was up at the witness stand reviewing Mrs. Mason's will and Mrs. Taylor's signature. Mrs. Taylor explained to the judge she was not in the room when everybody signed.

"Judge, I move for the probate of the will to be annulled and Ray Namer, the only heir, to be named administrator of Mrs. Mason's assets," Brian said.

The judge asked Thomas, "What's your position?"

Before Thomas could speak, Brian said, "Thomas's firm knew of this defect and perpetuated a fraud on the court today and with the probate. I move for the firm and all its lawyers to be removed immediately."

The judge asked, "Is this true?"

Thomas asked for a recess, and the Judge denied him. Pressed for an answer, Thomas refused to address the question. The judge then ruled, "The will of Mrs. Mason is a nullity, and its probate rescinded. I appoint Mr. Namer as sole and rightful heir, administrator.

"What proof do you have, Mr. Johnston, regarding counsel?" the Judge demanded.

Brian pulled from his old black trial bag a single, yellow blue-lined legal pad page which was folded into thirds. He opened the paper and said, "Judge this paper was given to me anonymously," and reading the page, he said, "Mrs. Taylor didn't see Mrs. Mason sign the will. Janet the lawyer knows this, as does counsel for the Archdiocese. They will deny it."

Art looked down at his phone, which was buzzing with a message from Tori. It read: "Everything I've done is for you. Be the man we know you are. I love you. Don't contact me. Go to Christine and start over."

Art left the court and returned home immediately. Christine was on the porch crying. She ran to meet Art in the driveway and hysterically said, "Tori was here begging for forgiveness and pleading for me to give you another chance."

CPSIA information can be obtained
at www.ICGtesting.com
Printed in the USA
LVHW051457161221
706394LV00002B/163

9 781636 615110

Kindred Spirits

Thomas Jefferson
&
Aeschylus

The Memoirs of UVA graduate, C. Barry Buckley, whose serendipitous acquisition of 7 books from the Retirement Library at Monticello led to an unimagined journey of unexpected revelations about Thomas Jefferson's lifelong connection with the Ancient Greek tragedian Aeschylus.

Maureen Stack Sappéy and C. Barry Buckley

Chester River Press
2015

ISBN: 978-0-578-16640-7

Chester River Press
www.chesterriverpress.com
Chestertown, Maryland

The Journey

Preface

In the 1820s, one or more editions of Aeschylus' tragedies traveled from bookshops in London or Paris to a bookseller in Philadelphia, to Thomas Jefferson's home in Charlottesville, Virginia, to a bindery in Richmond to be rebound into 7 volumes, to Jefferson's Retirement Library at Monticello, to an auction-house in the nation's capital, to a purchaser's private libraries in New York City and Fishkill, New York, to his descendents' homes in Sloatsburg and Greenwich Village, New York, Teaneck, New Jersey, Denver, Colorado, and Chestertown, Maryland, and finally, two years ago, to my home.

For me the journey began in the spring of 2012, when I received a call from my good friend, the accomplished author and historian, Maureen Stack Sappéy. Knowing of my keen interest in Thomas Jefferson, she alerted me to the fact that Gerard (Gerry) Cataldo, a Chestertown bookseller, had been sought out and engaged to sell 7 books that were owned by Jefferson and held by him in his last library at Monticello during the final years of his life.

I caught up with Gerry and was immediately impressed with his passion for all things bound, and by his knowledge and professional approach to his business. His story of how Jefferson attained the written works of Aeschylus and the painstaking steps he took to conflate them into 7 books was fascinating, but more so to me were the endless coincidences that brought about my acquisition of Thomas Jefferson's volumes—books now referred to as the *Seven.*

To make this part of the story short, I could not resist the temptation to purchase the *Seven,* which carried the concurrence of my two sons, Barry and Dekker.

The rest of the story was placed in Maureen's very capable hands since she started this adventure of books. I asked her to write about the journey of the *Seven* from Thomas Jefferson's library to mine, with the understanding that she would accommodate my involvement as the O. I.

~C. Barry Buckley

Thomas Jefferson's Book Room, his library at Monticello. *Watercolor by Bridget Hassan, 2013*

Imagine this . . .

Thomas Jefferson encloses himself in the quiet of his library. His hair is now white, his clothes are patched and worn, and beyond the confines of his sanctuary his house has fallen into disrepair as ill health, debts and family disputes mount, but he will escape through reading to a more perfect world than the one in which he lives.

Settling into his red leather chair he opens one of the Aeschylus tragedies. Perhaps Agamemnon or Thebae or Persae . . . it doesn't matter for he intends to read all of them, to hold each volume in his hands, to turn the pages to the very last . . .

The candle flickers, its wick drowning in wax as he closes the book with a deep sense of contentment, and rising again, he returns the volume to its assigned place on a particular shelf in his library.

Take, then, one of Mr. Jefferson's books into your own hands to turn the pages as he once did, and when you finish reading, return that volume to its new shelf in a quiet corner of the cove.

Step I

The Acquisition

I can't recall a single time my father ever purchased anything that didn't benefit someone else. This is the first time he desired something that would bring him personal fulfillment, and for that reason alone I am very happy he found the books.

Barry K. Buckley

It was nothing more than a lucky coincidence that on the evening of March 2, 2012, Maureen Stack Sappéy overheard complete strangers discussing a "fascinating" lecture given earlier that night by Gerard Cataldo at the Geddes-Piper historical house in Chestertown, Maryland. Because Gerry was a longtime friend, her curiosity was piqued and listening closely (eavesdropping) she learned he was representing 7 books once held by Thomas Jefferson in his Retirement Library at Monticello—significant books, a complete set of the 7 tragedies written by Aeschylus, the Ancient Greek dramatist.

Knowing that her lawyer, C. Barry Buckley, was a true Jeffersonian, she telephoned Gerry and asked if a private viewing was possible. It was, and she then called Barry to tell him of the golden opportunity he had been offered to examine Jefferson's books before their purchase removed them from public view.

Early the next morning Barry phoned Gerry and a few hours later they met at his place of business, the Chestertown Old Book Co., one of those rare shops as inviting as an old-time library when they were still reverential places, hearth-warmed and lined with leather-bound books.

After introductions were made, Gerry placed one of Jefferson's volumes on the counter. It was a medium-sized book with a worn leather cover, a chipped spine and damaged gold tooling; a handsome book in spite of the damage wrought by time. As he gave an overview of the complete set, he used a spatula-like tool to slowly turn the volume's pages—clean pages, none torn or stained, the print clear and readable on the handmade paper.

Noting the book's fragile state, Barry didn't handle it himself, which took great restraint on his part; instead, he listened intently, firmly decided on purchasing the entire collection, though he kept from saying so. Afterwards, as he made his way back up Cross Street, he outlined the necessary steps of an acquisition; the first step would be a careful reading of the prospectus Gerry had provided.

Provenance:

The Tragedies of Aeschylus
From the Retirement Library of Thomas Jefferson
by Gerard Cataldo (2011)

"The Chestertown Old Book Co. is pleased to offer an historically significant set of books from the personal library of Thomas Jefferson, *The Tragedies of Aeschylus*, in seven octavo volumes: Volume I, Prometheus; Volume II, Suplices; Volume III, Thebae; Volume IV, Agememnon; Volume V, Chorephora; Volume VI, Eumenides; Volume VII, Persae. The seven volumes were assembled and interleaved at Jefferson's direction, specially bound by his personal bookbinder Frederick Mayo, and contain Jefferson's unique quire ownership markings. The books are uniformly bound in gilt-tooled calf skin leather, with titles and volume numbers in gilt on spines, marbled pastedowns and free end papers, all edges marbled, and with gilt dentil design at edges of boards.

"Each volume was assembled and bound to Jefferson's specifications, resulting in varied texts, pagination, paper stock, and language: French, English, Greek and Latin. There are various editions interleaved, including: *Aeschyli Tragoediae Quae Supersunt Ac Deperditarum*

Fragmenta, Halae, 1809; Aeschyli Tragoediarum Reliquae, Parisiis, Typis Republicae, Anno III; Theatre D'Aeschyle, Traduit En Francoiis, Avec Notes Philologiques, A Paris, An. III, Du Theil, 1794; Theatre D'Aeschyle, Premiere Partie, Se debite chez J. L. Nyon, rue du Jardinet; Aeschylus, Oxford, R. Potter, Bliss & Baxter, 1812.

"Following the 1815 sale of the bulk of his library to Congress, Jefferson continued to acquire books. The Retirement Library Catalogue, written in Jefferson's hand, constituted his third and final library at Monticello. After Jefferson died in 1826, his library was listed for auction through Nathaniel P. Poor, in Washington D.C., on February 27, 1829. This Aeschylus set is included in the printed Poor Catalogue.

"Jefferson's habit was to mark his books at quires "I" and/or "T" by placing his initial in ink beside the quire signature. Jefferson's marks are present in each volume with the exception of Volume VI where there is no quire "T" and the last quire is "P", and where at quire "I" the page number "4" is printed close to the quire notation. Jefferson's strike-throughs are present on the title pages of Volumes III, IV, V, and VI. At Volume VI he altered "II" to read "VI".

"Also present is a handwritten notation by G. C. Verplanck, the original buyer at auction, on the verso of the front free end paper of Volume I, stating: "Bought at the sale of the Library of Thomas Jefferson, March 30, 1829 . . ." Verplanck, 1786-1870, was U.S. Representative from New York, Chairman of the Committee on Ways and Means, regent and vice chancellor of the State University, member of the State Constitutional Convention, and professor at General Theological Seminary. This set of Jefferson's books has been in the Verplanck/Johnson family since its purchase at auction.

"This Aeschylus set is specifically referred to in a letter Jefferson wrote to Philadelphia book dealer John Laval on March 27, 1820, requesting Laval to procure a copy of Aeschylus in a Latin translation, "because I wish to interleave them in the edition…" and asking for *Potter's Eng. Translation of Aeschylus.*

"Frederick Mayo was Jefferson's bookbinder, and he is discussed in Hannah D. French's chapter "Thomas Jefferson's Last Bookbinder" in *Bookbinding in Early America.* Jefferson instructed Mayo on the interleaving of the various texts for the seven volumes."

The seven volumes as they were purchased.

Untouched Books

Because Barry's standard approach to every new venture is to first draft a measured and calculated plan, his immediate decision to make the acquisition was highly unusual, even extraordinary—in making it, he did sway between logic and emotion similar to Jefferson's artful conflict in his *Head and Heart Letter*, but unlike Jefferson's, Barry's indecision only lasted 47 seconds before emotion (the books' connection to Jefferson) outweighed logic (the books as an investment-grade acquisition).

Though secure in his "heart over head" decision, he'd later admit with an almost sheepish grin: "My sons, Barry and Dekker, watch me like a hawk, or so they think, but I could not resist the temptation to purchase the *Seven*: Thomas Jefferson's volumes."

Soon afterwards, his eldest son, also named Barry, was asked for his initial thoughts about his father's decision regarding the historic books. As if taken aback by the question, he looked off into the distance, and when he turned again there was a subtle change in his expression, a softer, more emotional one.

"I can't recall," he said, "a single time my father ever purchased anything that didn't benefit someone else. This is the first time he desired something that would bring him personal fulfillment, and for that reason, alone, I am very happy he found the books."

The acquisition set in stone; Barry sat down with paper and his thin, blue pen to record the first steps of the *journey*—his word to denote the passage of the *Seven* from Jefferson's bookshelves to his own. As he wrote, an important issue surfaced:

> *After the call came from Maureen and I immediately met with Gerry, he pulled out one book to show me its condition in comparison to the others. At that point my interest was in the books and not in their condition; my chief interest was that Jefferson had owned and touched the books in his library at Monticello and that they had remained there until purchased by G. C. Verplanck at the auction in 1829. Still later, after the dialogue had started with Gerry and I had read through his packet of related information, I spoke with him about the price listed in the presentation material. After again conferring with my sons, Dekker took it upon himself to begin researching Jeffersonian artifacts, even as I returned to Gerry's shop to make an offer. Jan Ross and Judith Cardenas, descendants of Verplanck and the owners of the books, agreed to my offer, and the transaction for the purchase agreement was completed in Gerry Cataldo's bookshop on March 10, 2012.*
>
> *It was at that juncture in the journey that I became mindful of the books' fragile condition. For that reason, subsequent to the signing of the purchase agreement, I asked Gerry to retain custody of all 7 volumes. He agreed, and I left his shop without touching a single book.*
>
> *I had reached an impasse in this journey. A decision needed to be made; an important decision as to whether or not the books should be restored, or left as found in disrepair.*
>
> *~Barry*

The decision seemed simple, but it wasn't.

Barry's purpose behind his acquisition was to hold and read books once held and read by Jefferson, himself. He had no intention of leaving the historic volumes on a shelf, untouched, like objects of fine art, but casual handling of them would advance their disintegration into unreadable pieces of leather and paper. Not being the kid-glove type, he leaned towards restoration to strength the books' bindings—that is, he leaned in that direction except at odd moments when he questioned his right to alter historical artifacts.

Uncertain how best to proceed, he stopped by Gerry Cataldo's shop to gain his expert opinion. There was ample reason for his confidence in Gerry's estimation of historical book restorations. In addition to his work as a rare and fine book dealer and appraiser, Gerry is professionally associated with The Bibliographical Society of America, The Bibliographic Society of the University of Virginia, The Washington Rare Book Group, The Baltimore Bibliophile Society, The Fine Press Book Association, The Washington Antiquarian Booksellers Association, and The Association of Online Appraisers. Following the publication of his first book, *The Passion for Books: A Guide to Book Collecting* in 2010, a second book, *First in Their Hearts: Early Biographers of George Washington*, was released in 2011. He is also a founding partner of and principal editor at Chester River Press, a fine press publishing house of award-winning letterpress limited-edition reprints of classic works, and numerous trade edition memoirs, fiction and poetry by local authors.

Barry opened the discussion with general questions about the physical composition of a traditional book.

In basic terms, a book is a bound manuscript of words written or printed on leaves, which are sheets of paper (each sheet is a leaf; a page is one side of a leaf). To bind the pages into book form, the leaves are glued or sewn together along one side and attached to the spine between two boards, a front and a backboard (usually made of pressed paper or leather). The boards serve as the cover that protects the most elemental part of a book (the author's words), but its spine is its strength, since a strongly bound, thus well-bound book, keeps the pages from loosening and falling out.

In relation to the Aeschylus set, the front boards of both *Volume I* and *Volume III* were detached, while the front boards of the 5 remaining volumes were barely attached to their spines. Yet worse, the spines of all seven books were chipped or missing whole pieces of leather. Fortunately, the pages of the seven volumes were in excellent condition, and too, the text blocks were all intact.

The meeting ended with a strong recommendation for restoration, after which Barry made two requests: first, that Gerry sign a custodial agreement to maintain the insurance for the books under his own name until the restoration process had been completed; and secondly, that he assume the responsibility of contracting a reputable bookbinder with enough experience and skill to restore the volumes to their original strength and beauty. Gerry signed the custodial agreement, already knowing the ideal candidate for the commission: Jill Deiss, a notable bookbinder of long acquaintance.

Even as Barry closed the bookshop's door behind him, he realized another advantage of having the volumes restored—once they could be held without resorting to kid-gloves, he'd have his first real opportunity to validate the *Theory of Cosmic Transfer*, a theory he formulated during his law school years at the University of Virginia.

> *My visits to Monticello in the early days of my UVA experience were for a single purpose: a transfer. I had convinced myself that it was conceivable that in touching something Thomas Jefferson had touched, there would be a "Cosmic Transfer" of his staggering intellect from Jefferson's brain to mine.*
>
> *While the tour guides at Monticello were helpful, most were more concerned about keeping me from touching anything on the property. It didn't matter to me one way or the other, as my mission was to touch each piece of furniture, doorknob, book, or personal effect that Jefferson himself had surely touched. Admittedly, I didn't care much about Newton's higher order of calculus in his Principia Mathematica (Jefferson was one of only five people on the entire continent who truly understood the higher order of calculus), but I had great hope that a Cosmic Transfer would provide a little help when I sat for UVA's single, therefore critical, law school exam.*

Although the transfer wasn't completed as imagined, my admiration for Mr. Jefferson's soaring intellect was cemented from that time on.

~Barry

Step II
Lifeblood

The Jefferson books are truly amazing, but what is even more amazing is my father's drive to find out as much as he can in regards to the journey of the Seven.
Dekker M. Buckley

Although the 7 volumes were not in his possession, and wouldn't be for several months during the restoration period, Barry drew up a plan to trace their passage from Monticello to the quiet cove he called home.

As a starting point, he arranged a meeting between his sons and Dekker's wife, Maricarmen, and the former owners of Jefferson's books. Judith Cardenas declined because of the distance, but Jan Ross was willing, even eager, to speak of their family's ties to the *Seven*. Gerry and Maureen were invited to the meeting, as well; Gerry had a previous engagement and Maureen also sent her regrets—unaware the acquisition had been made, and thoroughly puzzled by Barry's strong insistence that she reconsider his invitation, she relented and agreed to attend Jan's presentation.

Jan arrived at the meeting with an overstuffed file of documents and prints. Sorting through her papers, she explained her family's connection to Jefferson's books through ancestral accounts and anecdotes.

Her first story centered upon a picture-postcard of an oil painting of 9-year-old Daniel Crommelin Verplanck (1771) by the Colonial portraitist, John Singleton Copley. As was customary in that period,

Daniel Crommelin Verplanck by John Singleton Copley. *Metropolitan Museum of Art, NYC.*

Daniel is attired in adult-style clothes, but it's his facial expression that is most striking in that his eyes are as "bright" as those of the squirrel sitting beside him (pet squirrels were popular in that era; most wore silver collars and walked on leashes).

Why is this portrait relevant?

Daniel or *Squirrel Boy,* as he's affectionately known, grew up in pre-Revolutionary War New York where he attended the city's best schools and enjoyed all of the advantages of being the son of a wealthy man. Daniel married, lost his wife young and delegated the care of his three-year-old son, Gulian, to his parents, Judith and Samuel Verplanck. That toddler grew into the accomplished gentleman who bid on Jefferson's volumes at Poor's Auction in 1829, which began the descent of the *Seven* through generations of his family to Barry's.

Moving from the 17- and 1800s to more modern times, Jan told of her accidental discovery of the Aeschylus volumes in a barrister bookcase after her mother's death in 2006. Recalling how "stunned" she felt that historical artifacts had been overlooked for almost 40 years, she mentioned her sister's own astonishment upon learning of Jefferson's books. Together, they packed the volumes into an old cardboard box in the trunk of their father's Toyota Camry to make the rounds of Denver's bookshops—all to no avail, for no one expressed any interest until Jan carried the books to Maryland and placed them in the hands of Gerry Cataldo.

The stories in Jan's chronology were links in the seemingly endless chain of events and people connected to Jefferson's books. That chain was the reason Maureen had been invited to the presentation—at its conclusion Barry proposed that she, in her capacity as a professional researcher and writer, document the "journey of the *Seven* from car-trunk to bookcase" and publish those findings in a small book.

Maureen's immediate response disappointed him. Though pleased Barry had made the acquisition, she felt his concept of "a book about the *Seven*" was too far-reaching, and that the "journey" would fit more neatly into a pamphlet. In place of a book, she offered to write an essay that would detail the acquisition, as a gift to him and his family. He declined her offer, and asked that she take a week to reconsider his proposal to "write a professionally crafted and published book."

An exchange of letters began nine days later.

Dear Barry,

At your request, I undertook a week of research to reconsider your proposal—in my stubborn way I expected to prove my point that your story would fit more cleanly into a pamphlet, but I was wrong. There's more than enough material to write the kind of book you want for one simple reason—Thomas Jefferson built his incredible life upon his books, and that includes, of course, your 7 Aeschylus volumes.

Unlike you, Barry, I know very little of Thomas Jefferson. Only this past week did I become aware that books were the lifeblood of his achievements; that books were the tools he used to mold himself into a bibliophile, scholar, lawyer, educator, economist, revolutionary, philosopher, author, politician, diplomat, artist, architect, linguist, theologian, scientist, mathematician, mentor, inventor, musician, brewer, winemaker, horticulturalist, engineer, equestrian, agronomist, farmer and librarian. All that—and in his spare time he again turned to books to write the Declaration of Independence, to fight the Barbary Pirates, to purchase the Louisiana Territory (nearly a million square miles!) and to conceive and design Monticello and the University of Virginia—all of which is familiar to you, but for me this is all new and all exciting, for I've only now learned that Thomas Jefferson is America's Renaissance man.

So, regarding your proposal, my suggestion is that we step beyond the transfer of the Seven from Jan's family to yours, by focusing, in part, on Jefferson the book-connoisseur, and on Aeschylus, who started this journey thousands of years ago.

Cordially,

Maureen

Dear Maureen,

Not once since the inception of my idea for a book about the Seven did I think it worthwhile to include Aeschylus other than as a cursory mention in the manuscript. And I did not picture your writing yet another biography about Jefferson; instead, I thought the focus would remain entirely on the Journey of Thomas Jefferson's Seven from Jan's car trunk to my bookcase, but I am open to further discussion.

Sincerely,

~Barry

Barry, I'm pleased you're open to discussion. To begin with, I propose that we co-write the book—your narratives and reflections would give life to a work of this kind. In fact, I'd be more than willing to take on the invisible role of a ghostwriter and give you full credit as the author.

Incidentally, I do agree with you—there are thousands of books about Thomas Jefferson; the market doesn't need another biography, but we could provide another example of his intellect by shining a spotlight on Ancient Greece. To only mention Aeschylus as an "ancient writer of tragedies" would be a disservice to Jefferson—the intimate connection between the Virginian and the Athenian should be underlined in your book to fully explain the value Jefferson placed on the Seven.

Maureen

First, as you suggest, Maureen, we should neither overlook the Ancient Greek's achievements as a playwright, nor undercut Jefferson's recognition of Aeschylus as a major player in literature. At the very least, biographical details could be inserted into the book: highlights of his career as a tragedian, and maybe an overview of the Golden Age of Greek Theatre.

Secondly, the idea of being a co-writer appeals to me (your offer to ghostwrite the book has no appeal).

In the near future, please define your role in this writing project.

~Barry

As always, Barry, I'm struck by your kindness—stepping away from my suggestion that I serve as a ghostwriter, it's a simple matter to define my role in your book project.

As a researcher and writer I will underscore the intrinsic value Jefferson placed on books, in general, and on the Aeschylus volumes, in particular. If my work is successful, your 7 books will be looked upon as priceless possessions—not in terms of dollars and cents, but in measure of the significance of ancient words written in Athens centuries before the birth of our nation—significant in that Aeschylus' words influenced Jefferson's lifework.

In gathering evidence to support this notion, I returned to Gerry Cataldo's provenance, which details the lengths Jefferson took to acquire the definitive works of Aeschylus for his final library—his first step was to commission John Laval to locate a Latin translation of the Ancient Greek's tragedies. Laval found at least one edition, and Jefferson went through that book and others, page by page, to reorder them into separate volumes before his master bookbinder, F. A. Mayo, bound the reassembled pages into your 7 books.

Jefferson was short of cash by then, and surely the search for Aeschylus and the rebinding of the pages cost him a pretty penny, so we have to ask ourselves: why were these ancient writings of Greece so important to Jefferson?

A logical answer seems to be lurking just beneath the surface—at least it seems logical to me after having read a biography of Aeschylus and 7 synopses of his extant tragedies, the ones found in your Jefferson books. Here goes . . .

The effort and cost in conflating and rebinding Aeschylus' tragedies was worthwhile in Jefferson's opinion because he shared a common experience with the Ancient Greek—both men had witnessed the emergence of democracy in their respective homelands. At risk of losing his liberty, land and life, Aeschylus filled his dramas with characters that defy the tyrannical gods and kings of Greece—heroic figures, no less hungry for independence than Jefferson and his compatriots, whose defiance of Parliament and King involved equal risks. Surely, in reading Aeschylus' tragedies, Jefferson would have identified with Agamemnon's betrayal; he would have admired Prometheus' rebelliousness, and would have applauded the fifty brides who fled from marriages mandated by an unjust law . . . the beating heart of your acquisition, Barry, is that intimate and marvelous connection between Jefferson and Aeschylus . . . they were kindred spirits, and they are now connected to you, as well, through your 7 books.

Maureen

Maureen, I read your last letter with interest and wish to schedule a meeting to discuss your many points.

In moving away from the limited premise of books carted about in a Toyota to the intrinsic value of books in Thomas

Jefferson's life, specifically the Aeschylus volumes, it would seem we have reached a balance of purpose.

As for your defined role in this project, it fits my conception of how this book should unfold. I'm pleased you are finally on-board.

~Barry

I am on-board, Barry, and fast at work on a roadmap, a detailed outline of the proposed chapters for the entire book—your memoir, in my opinion.

The chapters are being labeled as Steps in keeping with your concept that this is a "journey." Thus far, each Step in my proposed outline leads to unexpected turns in the history of your 7 Jefferson books, but that's the joy that can be found in writing: each venture takes you along unmarked paths to unimagined places.

It's highly improbable I'll uncover anything you're not already aware of regarding Jefferson and his singular life, but for me each unexpected turn in this journey of discovery adds another layer of richness to my pride of country. I'm indebted to you for introducing me to such a great American—one I'm embarrassed to admit I hardly knew.

Barry, I can now say with confidence that your request for a "professionally crafted and published book" seems within reach of being met in 5 months.

Maureen

Postscript

Five months?

No one would have guessed this project would take more than three years to complete, but beyond the typical tasks of researching and writing a book, there were several rounds of interviews with book professionals in Philadelphia, New York City, Boston, Winchester, Charlottesville, Washington, D. C. and Chestertown.

One of the first tasks was a letter to Barry's two sons:

Dear Barry and Dekker,

As you know, your father asked me to write a small book that traces the movement of the *Seven* from Jefferson's hands to his. Apart from my role in this project, this is your father's book. He will be involved in the research, outlining of the sections, and interviews of all involved. He will decide upon the title of the book, and will approve of the graphics and cover art. He asked that all of the interviews with professionals be presented as conversations, and that all pieces of fiction in the text be presented as Flights of Fancy. He will also be injecting his wonderful sense of reflection and humor through his own narratives, which will be spliced between the sections of the book. Finally, he wishes to include narratives written by you, his sons.

Thus far, my research has proven this—if your dad had acquired one of Jefferson's inventions or pieces of artwork at even greater cost, he'd have come away with an object that held little value for Jefferson. His most prized possessions were his books. Your father's memoir will show that the 7 volumes of Aeschylus were highly valued by Jefferson—not in monetary terms, but because of the written content of Aeschylus' tragedies. From all that the research has uncovered to this point, it can be said with confidence that your father has acquired a unique and rare treasure.

I am very honored to write this book with your dad—he has introduced me to a great man, which is a gift in itself for I am coming to know Jefferson—in turn, I have the pleasure of giving your father a written gift of his own reflections, memories, and humor.

Cordially,
Maureen

The eldest son, Barry, left a message that he'd be more than willing to contribute narratives to the project; Dekker sent his reply by email. He wrote:

"Maureen, what a beautiful note. I know that my Dad is truly indebted for all of your work and input on this incredible project. The Jefferson books are truly amazing, but what is even more amazing is my father's drive to find out as much as he can in regards to the journey of the *Seven*. His thirst for knowledge is insatiable and who knows what his next project will be once this book is concluded. I would be honored to add some narrative. I'll have to think long and hard to equal the quality of writing.

"I remember a great conversation I had with my father when I was about to buy my first car. It wasn't about financing or gas mileage or the typical questions you might expect your father to ask; it was all about the make. When I told him I was considering a European model, because it had the best maintenance record of any car on the road, it was as if I had stabbed him. I can still remember like it was yesterday. 'What? You have to buy American. You have to support our country! It doesn't matter if the maintenance record is not as good. It would be unpatriotic if you did anything else.' That's my father, the consummate patriot. If he gets cut, he bleeds red, white, and blue.

"When my father brought up the idea of buying the *Seven*, it didn't surprise me. Here was a chance for him to have something dear to his heart—a piece of history that would connect him forever to a time that he holds as the most important period in our nation's history.

"Will he ever read the volumes? I don't think so, unless he's secretly brushing up on his Greek, French and Latin. I realize that the *Seven* means more than just having a closer connection to Thomas Jefferson and holding something tangible of great worth—worth in the sense of historical value, not monetary value. His real interest has become the uncovering of the history of the books themselves.

"My father is a voracious reader of history. He reads the books that sit on peoples' coffee tables or that collect dust in their libraries. Buying the *Seven* has started a journey to figure out where they have been and how he has been so fortunate to have them come into his possession. Having the *Seven* on his shelf will be awe-inspiring to anyone who has a chance to see them, but I know he will be most proud of this book, his own book, that stands next to them. Best. Dekker."

Step III
Cat Tail Run

At this point in the game it's easy to empathize with Mr. Jefferson . . . he was known for his impatience while his books were being rebound.

~Barry

At the end of March, the Aeschylus volumes were again boxed and placed in the back of a car. From Chestertown, Gerry Cataldo drove approximately 75 miles west of Washington, D. C. to the Cat Tail Run Hand Bookbinding in Winchester, Virginia, a historic town sited in the Shenandoah Valley between the Blue Ridge and Appalachian Mountains.

The Shop. *Courtesy of Cat Tail Run Hand Bookbinding*

The bindery stands near a winding stream called Cat Tail Run. For over 20 years the proprietress, Jill Deiss, and her staff of 10 (including an apprentice and an intern) have undertaken full restorations of antiquarian books by using centuries-tested techniques. Working in tandem, they re-sew loosened pages, repair torn and soiled leaves (pages), and rebind bookcovers and spines to renew their strength and quality.

Throughout his decade-long professional relationship with Jill, Gerry had taken note of her craftsmanship and dedication to the field of bookbinding. In handing over the 7 volumes, he felt confident that the books would be restored to their original state.

In turn, Jill considered the commission a welcomed challenge, for she intended to follow the techniques of Frederick August Mayo, the Colonial binder who originally bound the *Seven* in or around 1820.

After examining and photographing the complete set of books, Jill exchanged emails with Barry.

Hello Mr. Buckley,

As stated in my report, Condition Prior to Treatment, each binding is broken at the joint, or so very nearly so that it's considered broken. The corners, overall, are in good condition with only minor damage to the worst of them. The endbanding . . . sewn cotton or linen thread . . . is complete on all the books. There are no problems with any text sewing, and no tears are seen with any pages. The endpapers are complete across the set . . . the marbled flyleaves and pastedowns are nice.

The restoration of the spine will involve replacing the missing areas with matching leather, and gold tooling to replace the missing tooled elements. If you study this photograph you will see that it shows the entire spine of a book, and you will notice two notches sawn into the spine of the text on the left end. One notch goes all the way across . . . it's a little hard to see but it does . . . while the notch immediately to its right stops as soon as it reaches the Latin-Greek translation.

Look closely at this photograph (bottom right) and you will see that cords of hemp are in the notches that go all the way across the text . . . that's a normal part of the sewing structure, but the notches that go only part of the way have no cord in them, only adhesive: hide glue, the original adhesive. Those saw cuts are in sound condition and are doing their job as part of the sewing structure. The saw cuts were created to provide a location for the elements of the sewing structure to rest.

The one saw cut across the spine that stops prior to the last third of the book . . . a stand-alone Latin-Greek translation . . . that looked to me to be a place where the binder started to

Condition of the books when they arrived at the bindery. *Courtesy of Cat Tail Run Hand Bookbinding.*

Cord structure across spine. *Courtesy of Cat Tail Run Hand Bookbinding.*

locate the notch for the sewing and then decided to move it over a bit since there are no sewing elements in that location. That same partial notch is on all the volumes, which tells me he was notching the first two-thirds of the texts all at once with the pages all in one group. The last third of the book . . . the separate Latin-Greek translation . . . doesn't have the partial notch, so it obviously was not being sawn at the same time as the rest of the text. The partial saw cut is very shallow and not deep enough for use.

Jill Deiss

Good afternoon Jill,

Please, call me Barry.

I appreciate the photographs you've supplied. Now that you've had a chance to examine the volumes, is there any good news to report?

~Barry

Barry, everything in the set is of excellent quality. It was of the period in which the paper contained no tree pulp . . . just all cotton and linen fiber . . . and it was handmade paper. The printing has a good punch . . . you can feel the imprint . . . that sets the letters well into the page, and the leather is a good grade of calfskin. Part of its problem now is that the set sat where some thing in the order of a light mist of rain fell on the spines . . . it's water damage, but only lightly, which is very fortunate. If it had been extreme water damage the spines would have been so ruined nothing could have been salvaged from them, and in this happy case, most of the original spines will be part of the restored bindings. Excellent materials and a bit of luck brought us to this point.

Jill

Out of professional curiosity, Jill, what prompted your interest in a career in bookbinding?

~Barry

I don't remember anymore if there was a particular moment

when something made me decide to do this work. I opened my bindery in 1991. I had a Bachelor's in Costume History and Design with the thought I might study to be a curator or conservator of costume and textiles or some kind of conservation. I was additionally very interested in books—I have an undergraduate minor in Library Science, as well. After graduation I took a class in bookbinding, which led to an apprenticeship after which I pursued the MLS and began institutional training in conservation studies, first at Cornell and then at the Smithsonian. The chemistry degree came about after I started my bookbinding business. I received my training in bookbinding and the preservation of library materials in the studio of W.W. Streeter in Northampton, Massachusetts, and through internships in the Department of Library Conservation of Cornell University and at the Conservation Analytical Laboratory of the Smithsonian Institution.

While attaining my Master of Library Science degree from Syracuse University I specialized in the study of rare books. Still later, I attained my degree in chemistry by participating in a project on chemical research in leather tanning through the USDA's Hides, Lipids, and Wools Division in Wyndmoor, Pennsylvania.

Jill

Thanks for explaining your background, Jill; all of which is impressive. In the materials provided me, I noted that your clients range from private individuals and institutions to government agencies . . . that you treated John Wilkes Booth's diary for Ford's Theater Museum, conserved the bank account records of Abraham Lincoln for Riggs Bank, provided conservation treatment for a set of books owned by George and Martha Washington, conserved one of William Shakespeare's First Folios, and restored the Bibles of Edgar Allan Poe and Robert E. Lee, in addition to the Pulpit Bible of the Washington National Cathedral. Of all your works, which did you find most challenging or most rewarding as a professional?

~Barry

It's not possible, Barry, to pick one project in particular . . . they each have their rewards and challenges. Overall I'd have to

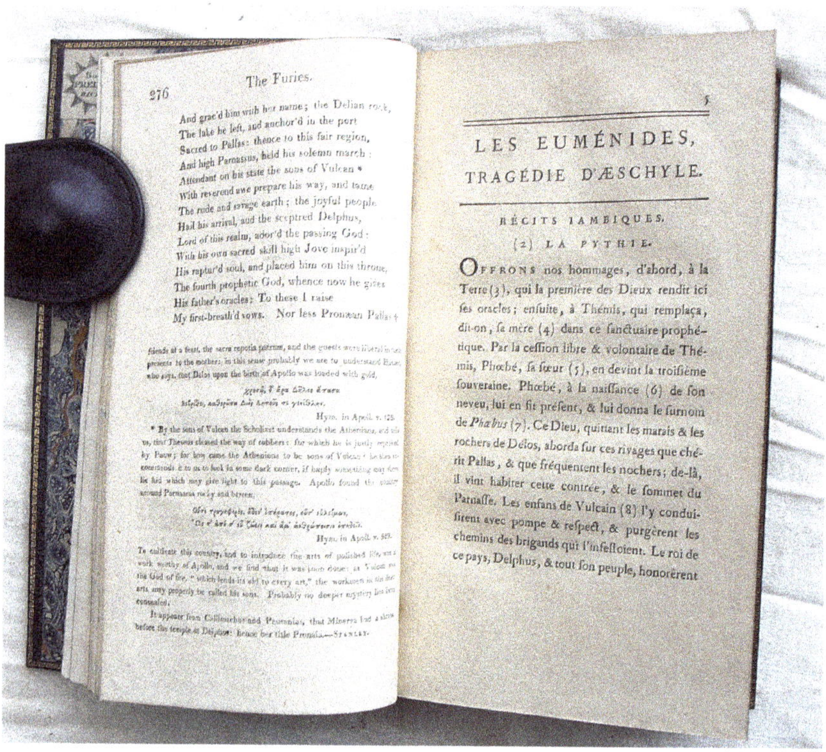

Interior condition of Book 6.

say there is a recurring and satisfying cycle to our interactions with clients and the resulting work. This cycle involves gaining their trust in our abilities coupled with performing our job to a level that meets or exceeds their expectations . . . We look back on those times and allow ourselves to be pleased.

Jill

It would seem that Jefferson worked with a reputable bookbinder, as am I . . . I'm glad you accepted this commission, Jill, and I'm looking forward with eagerness to the completion of your work. At this point in the game, it's easy to empathize with Mr. Jefferson . . . he was known for his impatience while his books were being rebound.

~Barry

Marbled top and bottom of text block.

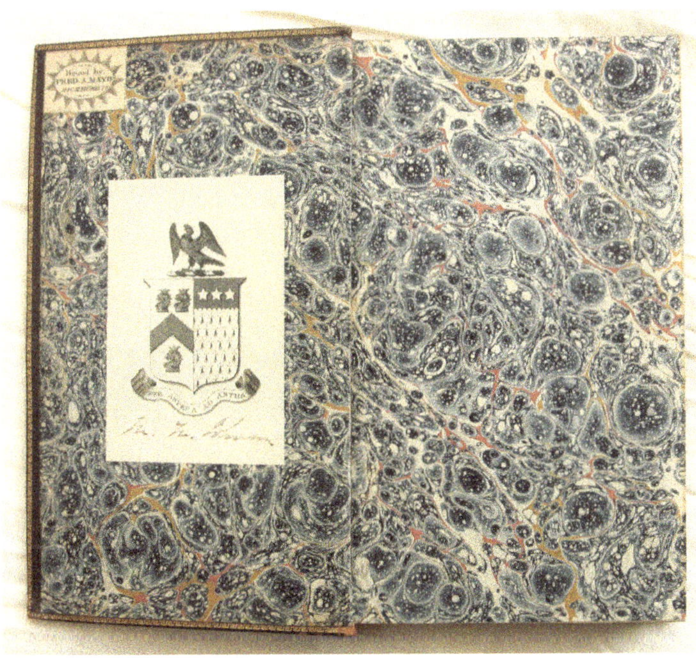

Marbled endpapers with Mayo insignia and bookplate from previous owner.

Step IV

Descendancy of the Seven

Verplanck had the distinct privilege of walking into his library to pull one of the 7 volumes from its shelf . . . As incredible as it may seem, that privilege is now mine.

~Barry

C.G. Verplanck, *Creative Commons.*

On this magnificent journey the Seven came into the possession of a surprisingly gifted man: G. C. Verplanck. He appears in this book to fill my desire to learn about everyone who took part in this journey—everyone who had, at some point, held the volumes in their hands and turned the pages to read the tragedies of Ancient Greece.

Had G. C. Verplanck not purchased the Seven at Poor's Auction and had those same books not passed generationally through his family to Jan and Judith Snyder, they would not have found their way to me. I understood my own reasons for purchasing Jefferson's books, so naturally I was curious about the reasons behind Verplanck's acquisition in 1829.

After his death in NY in May of 1890, a wonderful tribute was paid to him at the NY Historical Society. W. C. Bryant, spoke, stating that in August of 1786, Gulian Verplanck was born on Wall

Verplank's home in New York State. *Courtesy of the Mount Gulian Society.*

Street into a family of old stock colonists from Holland and New York. During the Revolutionary War his grandmother's home had been opened to the British Officer General Howe and others of whom she had many anecdotes to relate to her grandson, Gulian, when he came under her care. In spite of the divided loyalties to which he was exposed, he was his grandmother's constant companion, and was trained by her to love books in foreign languages of which he seemed to have had a natural inherited inclination. It is not much of a stretch for me to assume that Verplanck went to Poor's Auction with the intent to purchase books in the different languages, and did so in tribute to both his grandmother and to Thomas Jefferson, whom he surely revered.

To provide modern relevance to Verplanck's achievements, I asked Maureen to present his résumé in an abbreviated form.

~Barry

Gulian Crommelin Verplanck

Classical studies (foreign languages; literature)
Graduate of Columbia College (Columbia University) 1801
Reader of law and admission to the bar of New York 1807
Member of the New York State Assembly 1819-1823
Professor at General Theological Seminary, New York City 1821-1824
Member of the 19th and 20th Congresses 1825-1829

Elected to the 21st and 22nd Congresses 1829-1833
Chairman, Committee on Ways and Means (22nd Congress)
Whig candidate for Mayor of New York City (lost by a few votes) 1834
Member of the New York State Senate 1837-1841
Governor of New York's City Hospital 1823-1865
Regent of New York State University 1826-1870
Vice Chancellor of New York State University 1858-1870
President of the Board of Commissioners of Immigration 1846-1870
Member of the State Constitutional Convention 1867-1868
Poet (published collections)
Author (published short stories and essays)
Writer of over 70 court opinions (elaborate judgments)
Contributor to the *North American Review.*

Lineal Descent

To trace the lineal descent of the *Seven* through the Verplanck-Johnson-Snyder family, Maureen interviewed one of G. C. Verplanck's descendants, Jan Ross, at her Chestertown home on an uncomfortably warm morning in June. As a follow up to their conversation, emails were later exchanged.

Good morning Jan.
Thank you for your time last week—to confirm my written notes, please map out the movement of the 7 volumes from 1829 to March 10, 2012, when ownership passed from your family to Barry's.
M.

Hi Maureen.
In 1829, Gulian Verplanck bought the books [at Poor's Auction], and two generations later my great grandmother Mary Verplanck Johnson came into possession of them. She added the Johnson family bookplate in 1840 along with her name M. N. Johnson. It is possible she lived at that time in Sloatsburg, New York.
Jan

According to my notes, Jan, the books were then passed down to your grandmother and, after awhile, to your mother. For accuracy's sake, in your own words please retell your story about your discovery of the volumes.

M.

My mother . . . Judith, grew up in Sloatsburg . . . New York, a town . . . named for her mother's family, the Sloats. The books may have been stored there in a barn that was used for storage, or in New York City where my mother worked. The books were most likely kept in a bookcase in her small apartment in Greenwich Village, where she lived and worked after graduating from Barnard College in 1941. The volumes were in such good shape that I believe she kept them with her collection of family books in the city. In 1958, she married in New York, and in 1961, my sister and I were born.

In 1962, my family moved to Teaneck, New Jersey, and the books were kept there in the same bookcase for 10 years. At that time I had no knowledge of them. In January 1972, my family moved to Denver, and the books were moved, unpacked and placed in the same bookcase with other family volumes, mostly leather-bound books from the 1800s. There they sat for 38 years. In 2006, my mother died and in August 2010, I started going through the books in the case.

I picked up the first volume, opened the cover that was loose and asked myself who M. N. Johnson was. I was puzzled, and feeling guilty about not knowing, so I looked up her name in the family tree. I then found a note in that book, the one referring to Jefferson.

Jan

Jan, are your referring to Verplanck's inscription on the inside front cover of Volume I: Prometheus? A few words were difficult to read, but I believe it stated:

"Bought at the sale of the Library of Thomas Jefferson. Washington March 3rd 1829. The volumes were compiled by him-self and bound by his direction. This mode of binding together translations, commentaries, being a favorite with him.

Many of the classics in the Library of Congress are examples of it. G.C.V. "

M.

Yes, Maureen. I then showed Jefferson's book to my father . . . he was then 90 years old . . . I said to him there was no reason why Gulian would have made this up; it must be true. My sister Judith came over and she was stunned, too. We both agreed that Gulian's note had to be authentic . . . We didn't wrap the books up, but we put them gingerly into a cardboard box and packed up about 20 or 30 other books and loaded them into the back of my father's Camry. There was only one antiquarian bookstore in town at the time, The Hermitage Bookshop. We went straight to The Hermitage and sat and waited on their sofa for at least 20 minutes while the owners attended to [customers]—and mostly ignored my sister and me. We told them we had some old and unusual books and specified the Jefferson books.

Jan

When we met, Jan, you mentioned your frustration about the bookshops in Denver—about their overall disinterest in books owned by Jefferson.

M.

Yes, Maureen, but I expected that. The two bookstore owners or managers were skeptical, even standoffish. One checked the titles on the Internet and said that the year was right based on Poor's Auction. He then told us we would have to prove that the books were purchased at Poor's Auction. We explained that the set had been sitting in Mom's bookcase for [almost] 40 years and there was no receipt . . . to procure or locate. Then he suggested that we should do some research to determine the books' value.

Jan

Was that the point at which the volumes ended up at Gerry Cataldo's bookstore?

M.

Yes, almost. I flew home to Maryland and shared my news with my husband. He had been in The Chestertown Old Book Co. a few times and suggested I email Gerry about the discovery of the books. [Gerry] wrote back promptly to tell me he had to see them for himself.

At the very beginning I was very busy and thought this would be an easy project. It seemed obvious to me, but it wasn't. Every time I verified one fact the road would just bend and provide another path of inquiry.

In November 2010, I finally started my research by contacting the Library of Congress' rare book specialist via the Internet . . . I would periodically email Gerry with my findings while he was also doing his own research. He educated me on quires and Jefferson's peculiar habit of adding his initials . . . in the margins.

In January 2011, I returned to Denver to visit my dad and I took photos of the books to share with Gerry. The next step was to pack the books up and bring them back to Chestertown in my carry-on luggage . . . and as soon as Gerry saw the books he found the quires and we started to examine the books for Jefferson's personal marks. By early February Gerry produced a Condition Report to document each volume and the specific markings and respective conditions. The only time the books left my possession was to show them to Gerry . . . I [later] emailed Monticello to . . . contact Endrina Tay, the project manager for Monticello's library project. Her curator, Elizabeth Chew, answered my questions . . . she referred me to a letter Jefferson wrote [to John Laval on March 27, 1820] about his intention to interleave the various editions and translations of Aeschylus.

Jan

When we met at your home, Jan, you mentioned an invitation you had received from the Jefferson Foundation at Monticello.

M.

Yes. My family had never been to Monticello, so we planned a visit and a meeting to share the books . . . but the week before our visit the curators changed their minds . . . and referred me to Vesta Lee, the Book Broker in Charlottesville who has personally appraised most of the Monticello Library and many Jefferson books for the University of Virginia . . . I arranged a meeting . . . my goal was to determine the value and rarity of the interleaved volumes. I showed her the books but she . . . declined to handle them for more than a few minutes.

In August, I received her formal appraisal in which she indicated that Jefferson's practice of interleaving various books was not common . . . the [seven] books were very unique.

Returning to Chestertown, I met with Gerry again. The Library of Congress had told him their ability to collect more volumes was limited by budget cuts. I also learned from Vesta that Monticello was staffed primarily with architectural and fine arts specialists—not book people. Most of their volumes were copies of books that Jefferson would have owned. They were not in a position to acquire the books. Gerry recommended that we reach out to collectors and dealers.

I put the books in a safety deposit box at a local bank here in Chestertown and only removed them for Gerry's lecture at the Kent County Historical Society. The books remained in the bank until purchased by Mr. Buckley in 2012, and delivered to Gerry's bookshop where I met with Barry and his son, Barry, to share my story.

Jan

Having been asked to write conclusive remarks for this section about G. C. Verplanck, I return to that period of his life when the Aeschylus volumes were his to hold and read. He had the distinct privilege, any day or any hour, of walking into his library to pull one of the 7 volumes from its shelf. He could then sink down into a comfortable chair, open that book, and delicately remove an inadvertent drop of grape jelly from a page before reading and enjoying the same pages Jefferson once read.

As incredible as it may seem, that privilege is now mine.

~Barry

Step V
Mark Dimunation, Library of Congress

Mr. Buckley, it is clear you have acquired a golden treasure.
M. Dimunation

The restoration process at the bindery in Winchester had reached a roadblock. Handle tools were needed to replace the tooling (ornamentation) that time and usage had worn from the bindings of the books.

Mark Dimunation.

To replicate the original pattern of tooling, Jill Deiss designed three handle tools that duplicated the ones used by Jefferson's bookbinder, F. A. Mayo, in the 1800s when he bound the *Seven* in "gilt-tooled calf skin leather." Once her designs were completed, she mailed them to a die-maker in England, a firm she has been associated with for over 20 years.

Several months would pass while the brass and wood handle tools were being manufactured, but in the meantime, the research process for the writing of this book continued through interviews with historians, librarians, and specialists in all fields related to historic books.

In July, Barry drove to Washington, D. C. to meet with Mark Dimunation, the Chief of the Rare Book and Special Collections

Division at the Thomas Jefferson Building of the Library of Congress. Mark has had an impressive rise in the field of rare books. After undergraduate studies at St. Olaf College in Minnesota and Christ Church College in Oxford, England, he earned a Masters in American History at the University of California, Berkeley. Engrossed by his work at Berkeley's Bancroft Library, he ended his pursuit of a doctoral degree and accepted a position as a rare book librarian and assistant chief of special collections at Stanford University. Still later, he served as a curator of rare books at Cornell University. In maintaining his affiliation with academic institutions, Mark teaches courses on the history of the book at Catholic University and the University of Virginia where he sits on the faculty of the Rare Book School. And, since March of 1998, with his appointment as Chief of the Rare Book and Special Collections Division at the Library of Congress, he has been responsible for the development and management of America's largest collection of rare books.

Barry's walk from the ornate entrance of the library to Mark's offices in the Rare Book Division was long but pleasant. He later recalled that in passing through the corridors he felt as if he walked through a panorama of our nation's history. Indeed, the wide halls of carved wood, marble and painted plaster are lined with fine art, classic sculpture and stone mosaics, but beyond the first impression you're walking through a museum or stained-glass cathedral, an acute awareness of being in a depository of millions of books and artifacts sinks in—awareness that builds into deep appreciation of Thomas Jefferson's legacy to our nation: *The Library of Congress.*

To unearth the roots of that legacy, it's necessary to return in time to America's first war as a young nation. In 1814, at the height of the War of 1812, British soldiers set fire to Congress' small library. Fortunately, long before fiery torches were flung at the shelved books, Thomas Jefferson had begun work on a *Grand Plan.*

A pure-Jeffersonian plan.

For 44 years (1770-1814) Thomas Jefferson had marked each day (almost every day) by acquiring a book for his library—as posited, he

Library of Congress. *Photo by Maureen Stack Sappéy*

Library of Congress. *Photo by Maureen Stack Sappéy*

viewed books as utilitarian tools to achieve all he desired, but around 1784 he began to earmark his books for Congress' future use. His intent was made known to his heirs: upon his death they were to offer his entire library to Congress, and in turn he felt confident that the government would compensate his family at a fair price. Remarkably, Jefferson stayed the course in building an elite library for the House and Senate, of which he once said, "there is no subject . . . to which a member of Congress may not have occasion to refer." With that sentiment guiding him, he carefully hand-selected books in the categories he regarded as essential to legislators: history, science, law, medicine, philosophy, literature, languages, politics, economics, geography, religion, morals, music, fine art . . .

But in that year of war, 1814, when Jefferson learned of the fire that had decimated the Congressional Library, he amended his *Grand Plan* for two reasons: Congress had immediate need of his books, not later in the unforeseen future of his death, and too, Jefferson had critical need of money. He appealed to a trusted friend to lobby Congress on his behalf, and after several months of heated debate, a vote was taken on January 26, 1815, to purchase Jefferson's collection of 6,487 books.

Unfortunately, a few decades later on Christmas Eve, 1851, two-thirds of those books would be lost to yet another fire caused by a faulty chimney flue in the Capitol building, the site of Congressional Library until 1897.

In that same year, 1897, the first of three buildings that would encompass the Library of Congress opened on Capitol Hill. Its name, *Thomas Jefferson Building*, reflects our nation's gratitude, as does the honorary title given him: *Father of the Library of Congress*. The other two buildings were eventually built and dedicated to Jefferson's fellow Bookmen: James Madison and John Adams.

In that way, Jefferson's legacy became the core of the congressional collection that now reaches over 115 million books. Of greater importance, his *sensibility*—his strongly held notion that Congress requires information on all subjects and in all languages to legislate justly and wisely—remains the library's central tenet for the acquisition of all published works in every language and format. Or, in Mark Dimunation's words: "If it's a record of human endeavor that records thought, that documents an event, that explains motive, then I think that's an important part of the documentation of culture and experience."

The Second Floor of the Jefferson Building

In the 1980s the Thomas Jefferson Building underwent extensive foundation and aesthetic renovations that involved murals, artwork and sweeping marble staircases topped by marble angels. The seond-floor is almost startling to walk through; its ornate beauty rivals any place of old world grandeur. There is a quietness there, a serenity that lowers voices to whispers, as should be assumed in a library over 200 years old.

An exhibit, *Genius of Liberty,* a recreation of Jefferson's Library at

Genius of Liberty exhibit.

Monticello, stands in the southwest pavilion of the second floor. An ongoing exhibit, it opened in April of 2000 to mark the *Bicentennial of the Library of Congress.*

In preparation for the bicentennial, Mark Dimunation was charged with replacing Thomas Jefferson's books—the ones that had been lost in the 1851 chimney-fire in the Capitol. To Mark's credit, more than 4000 copies of the destroyed books have been acquired through monetary gifts, and fewer than 250 white placeholders mark the *lacunae* (empty spaces) on the shelves that line the glass walls; curved walls that remind visitors of the serpentine-shaped walls Jefferson incorporated into his architectural blueprints for the University of Virginia.

The arrangement of the exhibit's books was dictated by Jefferson's preferred method: "sometimes analytical, sometimes chronological, and sometimes a combination of both."

A Conversation with Mark Dimunation

And so Barry continued on through the halls of the Thomas Jefferson Library until he reached the rooms of the Rare Book and Special Collections Division where Maureen waited for the start of the interview with Mark Dimunation.

After introductions were made, Mark invited Barry and Maureen to join him in a reading room paneled in rich cherry-wood and fitted with long tables and leather chairs. As expected, the first topic of discussion was Barry's acquisition of Jefferson's books and the restoration process under Jill Deiss, but as the afternoon lengthened, pleasantly, the conversation shifted with lightening speed from the more serious aspects of historical artifact stewardship to humorous anecdotes about Thomas Jefferson.

At some point Barry mentioned a newspaper article in which Mark had stated: "the best part of working on the [Jefferson library] exhibit was the actual journey through the mind and world of Jefferson." Asked to explain his words, Mark said he had rebuilt Jefferson's library collection by "embrac[ing] a mentality around thought and idea . . . around a study of [Jefferson's] way of collecting and owning books."

Mark was then asked to draw on his deep knowledge of Jefferson's "mind and world" to speculate if Thomas Jefferson's fluency in foreign languages had prompted his conflation of the English, French and Latin translations of Aeschylus' dramas.

"Was he fluent?" Mark countered.

"Certainly he could have been," Barry said. "I have no way of knowing."

With a broad smile on his face, Mark relayed a story about Jefferson's tenure as Minister to France. Supposedly he had attended an elegant dinner party in Paris; afterwards, one of the other guests, a lady, wrote a letter in which she quipped that the level of fluency in French measurably rose after Mr. Jefferson excused himself from the table. Mark pointed out that Jefferson was highly accomplished, but not "perfect, which makes him a more interesting subject."

The topic changed once again when Barry recalled a comment made by Gerry Cataldo that Jefferson directed his grandchildren's education by assigning them certain books—Aeschylus' tragedies were on the Reading Lists.

Knowing of a source that might confirm that fact, Mark left the room and returned minutes later with a thick, aged volume bound in dark leather. Referencing the book's index, he located a letter Jefferson had written on September 21, 1820, to his 19-year-old grandson Francis Wayles Eppes. In that letter, Jefferson urged Francis to undertake in-depth readings of the Ancient Greeks to better prepare himself for the study of law. He wrote:

"I leave at Flood's [Inn] with this letter a packet containing 3 small volumes . . . containing several tragedies of Euripides, some of Sophocles and one of Aeschylus. The 1st. you will find easy, the 2d. tolerably so; the last incomprehensible in his flights among the clouds."

In reading that excerpt aloud, Mark's voice noticeably changed from a more casual tone to undisguised excitement. Pausing, he reread the letter's date and Jefferson's words before pushing his glasses higher onto his forehead. Leaning across the table, he smiled widely and said: "Mr. Buckley, it is clear you have acquired a golden treasure."

The meaning of Mark's words was conspicuous.

First, the letter to Francis Wayles Eppes confirms Jefferson's usage of Aeschylus' works in the education of his grandchildren—a notion that had intrigued Barry from having first heard it said by Gerry Cataldo. Secondly, of equal importance, the date of Jefferson's letter to his grandson is a concrete connection between Jefferson and the *Seven*

Immediate questions surfaced: which of Aeschylus' tragedies had Jefferson left for his grandson, Francis, at Flood's Inn, and why that particular edition or volume? Had Jefferson selected *Eumenides* because of its depiction of a fair trial? Or had he dropped off *Prometheus* in hope that his grandson would be inspired as he ventured into the morally challenging world of law?

Jefferson's selection may never be known, nor if Francis ever commented upon his reading of Aeschylus. It is certain, though, that he returned the edition or volume to his grandfather's library; otherwise, the *Seven* would either be comprised of far fewer pages, or would now be known as the *Six*.

Mark's Gesture

At the end of the meeting, Mark offered Barry his own copy of E. Millicent Sowerby's multi-volume compilation: *Thomas Jefferson's Catalogue of the Library of Thomas Jefferson (1952-1958)*. Her name was unfamiliar, so Mark summarized her work as a researcher, bibliographer, and editor.

Sowerby is credited for making known the books that comprised Jefferson's massive library, the collection sold to Congress in 1815. To complete her work, she had to replace a vast majority of the missing books (the ones lost in the Christmas Eve fire of 1851), which she did by referring to two handwritten book catalogues (Jefferson's first catalogue, and the *Fair Catalogue* he wrote with Joseph Milligan).

At the culmination of her project, Sowerby successfully annotated all of the books that made up the Monticello Library, along with commentaries about his book-dealers and binders. In the 1950s, the Library of Congress published her compilation in five, oversized volumes in commemoration of the *Thomas Jefferson Bicentennial (1743-1943)*.

Endrina Tay, the Associate Foundation Librarian for Technical Services at the Jefferson Library at Thomas Jefferson's Monticello in Charlottesville, Virginia, underlined the importance of Sowerby's work: "Emily Millicent Sowerby's Catalogue has been justly described by Jefferson scholars as *monumental*. The work she accomplished over the span of over 15 years, given the resources she had access to compared to what we have available today, is testament to her skills and thoroughness as a bibliographer. Some of her data has been superseded by more recent information she was not cognizant of; nevertheless, her Catalogue remains the standard reference for the Library of Congress and for Jefferson scholars with regard to the books Jefferson sold to Congress in 1815."

A week after the meeting at the Library of Congress, a box containing Sowerby's compilation in 5 volumes arrived at Barry's office. On July 18, 2012, he wrote:

> *Dear Mark,*
>
> *I find it difficult to find words sufficient to explain my appreciation for the time you spent with Maureen and me at our recent meeting with you to discuss my Jefferson books, which recently came into my possession (which I now refer to as the Jefferson Seven).*
>
> *It was not only the time you spent with us but your genuine enthusiasm and complete command over the subject matter that we found so helpful. I was not only fascinated by your command of the various Jefferson libraries but your ability to communicate to me the significance of my collection (the Seven) which I seem to learn more about every day. I believe that I mentioned that I have commissioned Maureen to write a book about the adventure this project has become and I intend to have her include your wonderful contributions made at our meeting.*
>
> *Mark, on the topic of your generosity, the five-volume catalogue of the library of Thomas Jefferson by Millicent Sowerby arrived safe and sound. The text and map really does impart new meaning and a better understanding of the Seven. Thank you for such a wonderful gift.*
>
> *You commented that you felt that you had the best job in the world. That may be true but my take is that the Library of Congress has the best Chief of Rare Book and Special Collection Division in the world. Again you have my abiding gratitude.*
>
> *Sincerely yours,*
>
> *~Barry Buckley*

E. Millicent Sowerby's volumes now serve as the companion books of the Jefferson *Seven*. The compilation *Thomas Jefferson's Catalogue of the Library of Thomas Jefferson (1952-1958)* includes:

Volume I: Books of History
Volume II: Books of Philosophy
Volume III: Books of Philosophy (concluded)
Volume IV: Books of Fine Arts
Volume V: Books of Fine Arts (concluded).

Chapter XXXVII in *Volume IV* lists the bibliographical citations of Jefferson's tragedies from Sophocles to Boutet de Monvel. References to Jefferson's earlier editions of Aeschylus' dramas are found on pages 529-530.

Conflation

E. Millicent Sowerby's compilation documents Jefferson's unusual practice of conflating books. A conflation involves removing the pages from the spines of at least two books in order to interleave the pages into a revised arrangement that is then rebound as a new book (or books).

Endrina Tay of the Jefferson Library added: "From time to time, TJ would interleave or conflate various translations of the same work for some of his favorite authors on Ancient History (for example, Dio Cassius, Diodorus Siculus, Frontinus, Herodianus, Polybius, and Tacitus), and Ethics (for example Cicero, Marcus Aurelius Antoninus, Epictetus, Seneca, Plutarch, Tacitus and Xenophon), among others, so he could have his favorite translations appear side by side on facing pages. Examples of TJ interleaving different volumes together have been found in Sowerby's impressive Catalogue."

As Endrina suggests, there are many excellent examples of Jefferson's conflations in Sowerby's compilation, but one of her entries is of special interest since it involves the works of Aeschylus. In *Volume IV* (page 530) Sowerby wrote:

"An edition of Aeschylus in 4 volumes was bound for Jefferson in calf, gilt, on June 30, 1807, by John March, cost 4 dollars. Were it not for this binding bill and the entries in the 1849 catalogue, *it would be possible* to assume that Jefferson had conflated the Greek and English texts and bound them in eight volumes."

Asked to clarify the meaning behind Sowerby's words "it would be possible to assume . . . " Edrina wrote: "I think what is printed is what Sowerby meant to say. The sentence construction is odd, but if you read the entire entry from page 529 to 530, it does make sense what she is trying to say. While we are not able to be absolutely sure since Jefferson's copies do not survive, I do believe that this set of Aeschylus (referred to by Sowerby as entry no. 4525) was actually an 8-vol. octavo set."

It should be noted that the 8-volume set in the above example belonged to the Monticello Library, the collection Jefferson sold to Congress; while the Aeschylus volumes referred to as the *Seven* belonged to his third collection, the Retirement Library. Nevertheless, both sets of Aeschylus' tragedies are concrete examples of Jefferson's unique practice of conflating or interleaving an author's original work with translations before rebinding the rearranged pages into a new book of Jefferson's design.

In view of Thomas Jefferson's work as an editor and publisher, we added those skills to his professional résumé found in *Step VII.*

Step VI

The Restoration

The goal of this treatment is to make the books sound for handling, and to make the books look as if they had never needed treatment in the first place.

Jill Deiss

By September 2012, the specialized tools ordered from the die-maker in England had arrived at Cat Tail Run Bookbindery in Winchester, Virginia. Learning that the restoration of the *Seven* was moving forward, Barry emailed the proprietress, Jill Deiss.

Good morning Jill,

Thank you for forwarding the photographs—I'd be interested in learning more about the tools.

~Barry

Hello Barry,

Handle tools consist of a brass positive and negative design attached to a wooden handle. Because some of the tooled areas on the original bindings were missing, it was necessary to re-create several of the brass handle tools to accomplish the restoration work. This photograph shows the three handle tools created off the original Mayo stampings on the Aeschylus covers.

Jill

Jill, what were the specifics that went into your design of the tools?

~Barry

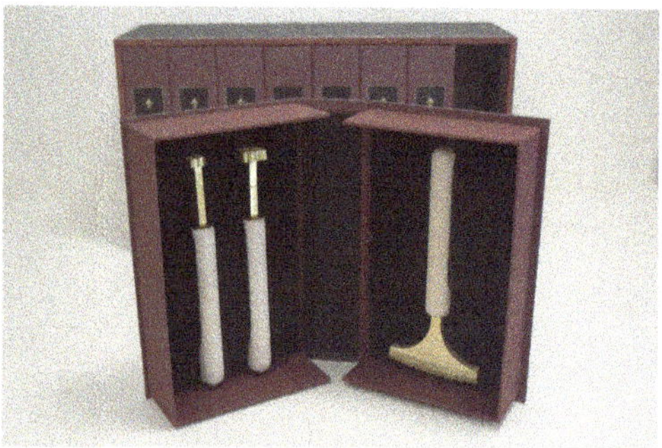

Dies created for the binding ornaments.
Courtesy of Cat Tail Run Hand Bookbinding.

The images at the head [top] and tail [bottom] of most of the spines were missing or badly damaged, Barry, so making an image into a brass tool was necessary to perfectly restore those locations. There was a whole lot of boring graphics work in the process, but thank goodness for Photoshop and Adobe Illustrator. The images from which the dies were made were taken from high-resolution photographs of the original tooling.

This is one of the photographs of the bindings I used to work up the patterns for the die-makers.

Ornament design on original bindings. *Courtesy of Cat Tail Run Hand Bookbinding.*

The images turned out clear, which made a great starting point for me. I made a picture of the large die pattern and sent it to the die-maker to turn into a brass tool.

The version sent him had the millimeter (mm) height and widths so he could size the tool correctly. The die will accompany the finished books, and will not be used on any other project other than the Aeschylus one.

This is a segment of the image around the edges of the cover boards, and at the head and tail of the spine. (Figure 1)

And these are carbon stampings of the designs. (Figure 2)
Jill

Jill, I have two related questions: which die-maker manufactured the handle tools, and are there individual names for the tools?

~Barry

The firm is P&S Engraving near Brighton in the UK. We've worked with their die-makers for twenty years and have always been satisfied.

Barry, I had pet names for each tool such as tree and ball. I'm sure they had numbers or names when first designed . . . one tool was the same kind used in Britain in the 1700s to bind Johnson's abridged dictionary.
Jill

Fig, 1

Fig, 2. Courtesy of Cat Tail Run Hand Bookbinding.

Book in binding press. *Courtesy of Cat Tail Run Hand Bookbinding.*

All very interesting, thank you Jill. Do you have an end-goal for the restoration?

~Barry

The goal of this treatment is to make the books sound for handling, and to make the books look as if they had never needed treatment in the first place. The restoration plan in all cases is to preserve and reuse the original, and provide replacements for any missing elements.

In the photograph above you can see a volume set in a press for the restoration of its spine. The strip of leather that will be used lies over the press.

Jill

With the tools finally in hand, Jill's restoration of the *Seven* would continue on for several months; meanwhile, the focus of this book shifted entirely to Early America and Ancient Athens.

Thomas Jefferson portrait *by Charles Willson Peale. Public Domain.*

Step VII

The Modern Relevancy of Mr. Jefferson

For myself, what I have come to realize about Thomas Jefferson is that he is as relevant today as he was during the period of his enormous contributions to the birth of our nation.
~Barry

I had a thought that it might be instructive, and of genuine interest to some readers of this book, to view an inventory of Thomas Jefferson's many accomplishments.

From there I asked Maureen to outline the scope and breath of Jefferson's achievements in the form of a modern résumé, if only to prove his relevancy today, as it was in past times.

As expected, Jefferson's résumé makes known his vast intellect, but it doesn't show his personal traits, such as his openness to conversations with ordinary people, family, friends, neighbors, and anyone who sought him out for advice on subjects from agriculture to wine. Nor does the résumé disclose how often he'd loan books to anyone desiring further edification of the subjects under discussion—perhaps he loaned one of the Aeschylus volumes to someone who shared his interest in Ancient Greece.

For myself, what I have come to realize about Thomas Jefferson is that he is as relevant today as he was during the period of his enormous contributions to the birth of our nation.
~Barry

THOMAS JEFFERSON

Monticello, Albemarle County, Virginia

Education

Classical studies in Greek, Latin, and Mathematics with Reverends William Douglas and James Maury (1752-1760)
Liberal studies at the College of William & Mary (1760-1762)
Study of Law under George Wythe, College of William & Mary (1762-1767)

Experience

Admitted to the Bar of Virginia (1767)
Lawyer (1767-1774)
Architect: Monticello (1770-1809)
Representative (Albemarle) Virginia House of Burgesses (1768-1775)
Delegate (Virginia) Second Continental Congress (1775-1776)
Representative (Albemarle) Virginia House of Delegates (1776-1779)
Governor of Virginia (1779-1781)
Representative (Albemarle) Virginia House of Delegates (1781)
Representative (Virginia) Confederation Congress (1783-1784)
Officer of the Confederation Congress in Europe (1784)
U.S. Minister Plenipotentiary to France (1784-1789)
Originator of the Patent Act (1793)
Secretary of State under President George Washington (1790-1793)
Vice President under President John Adams (1797-1801)
Third President of the United States of America (1801-1809)
Rockfish Gap Commission on Education and the State of Virginia, Chair (1818)
Founder, Architect and Educator of the University of Virginia (1819-1826)
Rector of the University of Virginia (1816-1825)

Designer of the Free Elective Curriculum for the University of Virginia

Publications/Presentations
Summary View of the Rights of British America (1774)
Declaration of Independence (1776)
Virginia Statute of Religious Freedom (1777)
Notes on the State of Virginia (1785)
First Inaugural Address (1801)
The Philosophy of Jesus of Nazareth (1804)
Second Inaugural Address (1805)
Autobiography (1821)
Editor and publisher of the *Seven: Aeschylus' Tragedies* (1820)
Editor and publisher of *The Life and Morals of Jesus of Nazareth Extracted Textually from the Gospels in Greek, Latin, French and English [Jefferson Bible]* (1824)

Honorary Degrees and Memberships
Honorary Doctorate of Laws, College of William & Mary (1783)
Honorary Doctorate of Laws, Yale College (1786)
Honorary Doctorate of Laws, Harvard University (1787)
American Philosophical Association, President (1797)
British Board of Agriculture, Honorary Member (1797)
U.S. Society of Artists, Honorary Member (1811)
Father of the University of Virginia (cornerstone laid in 1817)
American Academy of Language and Belles Lettres, Honorary Member (1821)
Father of the Library of Congress (1829)
Father of our National Architecture (1950s)
Gold Medal from the American Institute of Architects (1993)

Inventions
Moldboard Plow
Wheel Cipher
Spherical Sundial
Great Clock

Folding Ladder
Portable Copying Press
Lap Desk
Polygraph Copying Device
Mechanical Dumb Waiter (wine)
Automatic Glass Double-Doors
Revolving Bookstand
Alcove Beds
Swivel Chair (improved)
Mechanical Lifting Apparatus (Beds)

Lifeblood

In viewing Thomas Jefferson's extraordinary résumé, an obvious question surfaces: *how could one man accomplish so much in a single lifetime*?

The answer has already been suggested—from his youth to his final days, Jefferson had an intimate, almost obsessive connection with his books—those books were the lifeblood of his momentous achievements.

To support this notion, the next chapter in this book (*Step VIII*) traces Jefferson's life through the books he read, the libraries he built, and the myriad of published writings by him and about him.

Above all else, our objective is to underscore Jefferson's reverence for the written word, and principally, his high regard for the ancient writer Aeschylus.

As our research deepened we became committed to one idea: that in spite of the thousands of years and miles that separated them, Thomas Jefferson and Aeschylus were kindred spirits, united by philosophies, convictions, and truths. The proof lies in *Step VIII*.

Step VIII
Kindred Spirits:
Thomas Jefferson & Aeschylus

... we are then left to speculate if the language and precepts of Aeschylus influenced the hand of Jefferson in the crafting of our nation's foundation documents.

~Barry

Peter Jefferson, William Shakespeare & Jimmy V.

The importance of a father in his son's life is immeasurable.

Two highly regarded men, a dramatist and a college basketball coach, defined the ideal father. William Shakespeare wrote, "It is a wise father that knows his own child," and Jimmy Valvano said, "My father gave me the greatest gift anyone could give another person, he believed in me."

Peter Jefferson fit those definitions. He recognized young Thomas' potential for learning, and predicted greatness in his future. To guide his son along his way, Peter introduced him to books as the essential tools in the construction of a successful life—among those books were the ancient writings of Greece.

In his later years, on January 27, 1800, Jefferson reflected: "I thank on my knees, [my father] ... for having put into my possession this rich source of delight; and I would not exchange it for anything which I could then have acquired, and have not since acquired."

And on August 24, 1819, he added: "I think myself more indebted to my father for this [wealth of ancient writings] than for all the other luxuries his cares and affections have placed within my reach."

Clearly, Peter Jefferson played a vital role in the journey of the *Seven*—in handing his son his first books of Ancient Greece he initiated Thomas Jefferson's lifelong interest in the 7 tragedies of Aeschylus.

Father and Son

In 1740, Peter Jefferson (1707/08-1757) purchased a 1400-acre tract to build a tobacco plantation along the Rivanna River, a 42.1-mile-long tributary of the James River in central Virginia. Three years later, on April 13, 1743, his third child and eldest son, Thomas, was born in the family's frame house: Shadwell.

Thomas' boyhood and youth would be largely spent elsewhere, first at Tuckahoe plantation and later at school, but wherever he resided in those early years his father remained his compass—*aim for the North Star,* Thomas was taught. *Reach for the highest stars through the knowledge gained from books.*

Peter also encouraged his thinly built son to "pursue all matters of physical activity" just as he "exercised his mind" . . . "[since] it is the strong in body who are both strong and free in mind." This was not idle talk on Peter Jefferson's part. His lifework as an explorer, surveyor and mapmaker of "wild lands made dangerous by beasts and Indians" depended upon his almost legendary courage and physical strength.

Thomas admired his father's "noble qualities." He wrote: "Surveyors define new worlds; explorers conquer the unknown; mapmakers bring form to the formless. My father was all three and claimed a central place in my imagination."

In 1748, at the tender age of five, Thomas Jefferson began aiming for the stars. He spent long hours in his father's library; a conventional collection of 40 volumes, typical of the private libraries owned by Virginia's planters.

In addition to books of ancient writings, Peter owned the *Bible, Paradise Lost*, Shakespeare's plays, Alexander Pope's writings, and compilations of the laws of the Commonwealth of Virginia. Thomas read all 40 volumes before his sixth birthday, and though he lacked the maturity to fully comprehend the books' content, his capacity for reading was evolving into a passion for "all things bound."

At the age of nine, Jefferson was placed in Reverend William Douglas' Latin School. An impressionable child, his first walk through the school's library of some two or three hundred books became an illuminating moment for him, an epiphany in which he fully grasped his father's concept that books are the stepping-stones to a successful life. He vowed to build his own library, one that would be the largest in the Commonwealth of Virginia—to his way of thinking Virginia represented the entire world.

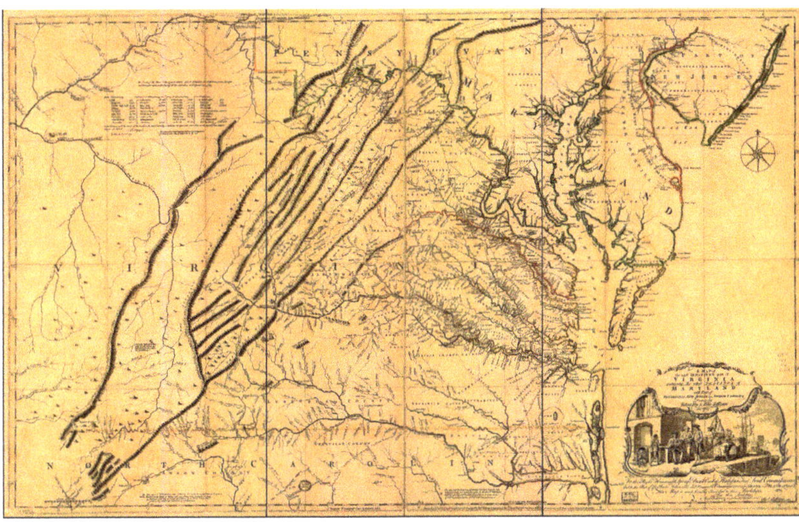

1751 Fry-Peter Jefferson map depicting 'The Great Waggon Road to Philadelphia." *Public domain.*

At once he started purchasing books, as is proven by the notation of a large sum of money under the heading *Books for my Son* in his father's accounts ledger.

In 1757, Peter Jefferson died. At 14 years of age, Thomas mourned, privately, deeply; it was a loss he'd feel throughout life.

As his father's heir, the weight of managing four estates was placed on Thomas' young shoulders. The properties would be held in trust until his 21st year, but from the age of 14 on, he made critical decisions without the benefit of guidance. In his own words, he summed up the challenges of that period of his life:

"When I recollect that at fourteen years of age, the whole care and direction of my self was thrown on my self entirely, without a relation or friend, qualified to advise or guide me, and recollect the various sorts of bad company with which I associated from time to time, I am astonished I did not turn off with some of them, and become as worthless to society as they were."

Shadwell would remain his mother's home until her death in 1776, but the library's collection reverted to 14-year-old Thomas, immediately—it was a gift from a father who had known his son well—a gift of more value to Thomas than anything else that had been placed in trust for him. Those 40 books, in addition to the few he had purchased himself with his schoolboy allowance and the hundreds more he'd acquire during his college years in Williamsburg, would become known as the Shadwell Library.

A foundation built entirely of books was in place to change a boy into a man, America's Renaissance man.

A Taciturn Master, 1760

Peter Jefferson's dying wish was that his eldest son would pursue the Classical education that he, himself, had been denied. Then, as now, Classical studies are defined as schooling in the Humanities, primarily the writings of Ancient Greece and Rome.

To honor his father's final request, Jefferson entered the school of the Reverend James Maury, a gentleman described by Jefferson as a "correct classical scholar . . . without warmth." As for Reverend Maury, he regarded Jefferson as an "unusually apt and studious pupil." Most who observed Jefferson during those two years of his schooling would have agreed with that assessment, for they would have noted the Greek grammar in his hand, at all times.

In spite of Rev. Maury's cold, unapproachable nature, he became a mentor to the fatherless boy by directing his readings, and by initiating Jefferson's lifelong practice of keeping commonplace books.

Commonplace books are filled with blank pages on which inspirational and utilitarian writings are recorded.

In 1706, the Enlightenment philosopher John Locke published a book titled *A New Method of a Common Place Book*, in which he explained that commonplace books "are not journals, which are chronological and introspective" but rather, are records of excerpts from valued writings "deemed important in the shaping of one's character and mind."

Following Locke's directive, Jefferson recorded quotations, measurement charts, prayers, proverbs, letters, poems, political theories and legal writings into his commonplace books—anything and everything he "deemed important in the shaping of [his] character and mind."

As example, in his first *Literary Commonplace Book* he copied a note Reverend Maury had written to his own son, a classmate of Jefferson's. The reverend advised: "Reflect and remark on, and digest what you read; to enter into the spirit and design of your author; to observe every step he takes to accomplish his end; and to dwell on any remarkable beauties of diction, justness or sublimity of sentiment, or *masterly strokes* of true wit which may occur in the course of your reading."

In copying words into his commonplace book, Jefferson etched them into the memory of his mind and heart. The best example is his copy of a poem by Horace, the celebrated poet in the Augustan Age of the Roman Empire. Horace wrote *The Satires* (35-30 B. C.), a two-volume collection of miscellaneous, satirical poems that suggest happiness can be reached through lives of self-sufficiency and moderation. His poem, titled 2.6, stayed in Jefferson's mind throughout his life. An English translation of the Latin verse reads:

O rural home: when shall I behold you!
When shall I be able,
Now with books of the ancients,
Now with sleep and idle hours,
To quaff sweet forgetfulness of life's cares.

Most of his life, Jefferson would long for the leisure to read the "books of the Ancients" but responsibilities to nation and family would continue to deny him those "idle hours." He read, of course, every day and night of his life, but he wanted more than snatched hours; he wanted uninterrupted time with his books to "quaff sweet forgetfulness of life's cares." Those uninterrupted hours lay in his far distant future—his retirement years at Monticello.

Until then, Jefferson continued to copy the "masterly strokes" of the classical writers (Horace, Cicero, Ovid, Virgil, Sophocles, Euripides and Aeschylus) and those of the English poets (Alexander Pope, John Milton and William Shakespeare) into his literary commonplace books. In doing so, he transferred sterling pieces of ancient wisdom into his personal philosophy of life.

The College of William and Mary, 1760-1762

Already tall at sixteen with a thin frame, auburn-red hair, light-colored eyes, and youthful awkwardness, Thomas Jefferson entered the College of William and Mary with unparalleled enthusiasm for

College of William and Mary. *Public domain.*

classes to begin. Though highly disciplined as a student, he did allow himself time for fowling with falcons, riding horses, and hunting—foxes and girls.

Garbed in colored knee breeches and coat, with a chased sword and a fine hat made of beaver fur, he attended receptions, dances, theatres, and evenings at the Raleigh Tavern—it was commonly accepted by Colonial Americans that alcohol "could cure the sick, strengthen the weak, and enliven the aged," and Jefferson stayed "healthy" with bowls of punch, and glasses of beer, rum, brandy, Madeira, and claret.

Apart from his social life and his protracted schedule for study, he prowled through the college's library and the town's bookshops with undisguised pleasure.

Veal and Glasses of Port

All throughout his college experience, Jefferson associated with three gentlemen who were steeped in the philosophy of the Enlightenment. All three—Professor George Wythe, Lieutenant Governor Francis Fauquier, and Dr. William Small—became Jefferson's trusted friends and mentors, but it was Dr. William Small who left the most lasting impression on the young college student.

As Jefferson's principal instructor, Dr. Small is credited with opening his protégé's mind to the study of mathematics. Down the road, Thomas Jefferson would be heralded as one of only five Americans who understood Higher Calculus, a necessary skill in architecture, a field in which he'd distinguish himself. And, many years in the future, Jefferson would again follow the lead of his professor—just as Dr. Small had modernized the teaching methods and curriculum of William and Mary, Jefferson would implement a free-elective curriculum at the public school he'd establish, the University of Virginia.

In his later years, Jefferson wrote: "[It was] my good fortune, and what probably fixed the destinies of my life [to study under] Dr. Small, a man profound in most of the useful branches of science, with a happy talent of communication, correct and gentlemanly manners, and a large and liberal mind [who] most happily for me, became soon attached to me & made me his daily companion when not engaged in the school; from his conversation I got my first views of the expansion of science and of the system of things in which mankind is placed."

Recognizing Jefferson's illimitable intellect, Dr. Small had the good sense to introduce his bookish, reticent student to the elite members of Virginia's society. Over veal and glasses of port, Jefferson, still a teenager, debated philosophical and national issues with scholars and jurists, in particular George Wythe and Francis Fauquier.

Wythe was America's first law professor, a future signer of the *Declaration of Independence*, an abolitionist, Classicist (scholar of Ancient Greek and Latin), lawyer and judge; while Fauquier, the Lieutenant Governor of Virginia from 1758 until his death in 1768 from reoccurring bouts of yellow fever, was a proponent of Enlightenment thought and practice.

Perhaps the dramas of Aeschylus were critiqued in those wine-enriched discussions; perhaps Jefferson suggested to the company of gentlemen that the tales of Ancient Greece's rise to democracy were comparable to the stories of the colonies' rise to freedom.

Perhaps.

Law Apprenticeship, 1762-1767

George Wythe

Before his return to England, Dr. Small arranged Jefferson's apprenticeship in law under Professor George Wythe. Accordingly, at the age of 18, Thomas Jefferson entered into 5 years of intense study in law and the Classics, which included access to the eminent law scholar's private library. Although Jefferson took full advantage of his professor's book collection, he placed more value on their friendship, writing:

"In 1767, [George Wythe] led me into the practice of the law at the bar of the General Court . . . [he]

continued to be my faithful and beloved Mentor in youth, and my most affectionate friend through life.

While residing in Virginia's thriving capital, Jefferson's ravenous appetite for books became known in Williamsburg's market square. Although the records of his purchases from abroad have not survived, his acquisitions from Williamsburg's major bookseller, The Virginia Gazette, are extant. The shop's daybooks show that in two of his years as a law apprentice (1764 and 1765), Jefferson bought 56 volumes (32 titles), an astounding number of books for that time in history. As would be expected, the majority of his acquisitions were law books (9), along with histories of France, Scotland, England and Virginia (5), and Italian grammar books and dictionaries (3) since he was teaching himself that language. He also purchased religious and political tracts and volumes of philosophy, medicine, agriculture and landscape gardening.

In addition, the Gazette's daybooks list Jefferson's purchases of volumes of literature and poetry, from which he copied excerpts into his literary commonplace books. Those excerpts offer another way to track his readings during his law school days. From his notes it's known he read English and Scottish poetry (John Milton to Edward Young, Mark Akenside, William Shenstone and James Thomson) and the works of playwrights (William Shakespeare to the dramatists of the 18th century).

As the years of his schooling unwound, his lodging house became overcrowded—music sheaves, tracts, pamphlets and books of every size filled the shelves, tables and corners of his rooms, but his steps to the market square never faltered.

Voices of the Enlightenment

For endless centuries, Medieval Europe suffered through the darkness of poverty, superstition, famine, disease and violence until a speck of intellectual light appeared during the Renaissance period. Soon after, from the end of the 1600s into the 1700s, the Age of Enlightenment ushered in a brighter era as man began to question his own existence. Rational thought challenged unsubstantiated beliefs, and once illuminated, man advanced slowly, but steadily, towards modern thought.

During his years in Williamsburg, Jefferson delved into the philosophy of the Age of Enlightenment (1685-1815) with primary focus on the writings of Sir Francis Bacon (1561-1626), John Locke (1632 -1704), and Sir Isaac Newton (1642-1727). Jefferson named them the "Greatest [Thinkers] the World had Yet Produced" and credited their works as integral in the formation of the 18th century movement towards rational thought.

By reading and studying their books, Jefferson unknowingly prepared himself for the writing of his most definitive document, the *Declaration of Independence*—a document not yet conceived in his mind, for a republic not yet in existence.

Sir Francis Bacon.

Sir Francis Bacon, a lawyer and Member of Parliament, was a leading figure in natural philosophy and scientific methodology during Europe's transition from medieval to enlightened thought. Jefferson credited Bacon's philosophical, jurist, and scientific writings as the bridge over which Europe stepped from darkness to light.

Bacon's concept of a modern research institute especially intrigued Jefferson, largely because of his abiding interest in science. Jefferson also embedded Bacon's treatises, *The Advancement of Learning* (empiricist natural philosophy) and *Idols,* into his way of thinking. The doctrine of *Idols* argues that the human mind is not a blank slate that receives images of the world, as previously believed; instead, the mind is a "crooked mirror" distorted by "Idols" (empty dogmas of untested concepts). Bacon proposed a new method of analysis to see through "empty dogmas" so that the mind can be freed to function as an acquirer of knowledge.

In like manner, Jefferson admired John Locke, the English physician, social activist (governance and religious tolerance), political

John Locke.

writer and philosopher whose books about republicanism sustained the American revolutionaries. Locke would have a direct influence on Jefferson's philosophy and writings. The finest example is found in the *Declaration of Independence*, in which Jefferson revised Locke's concept of "life, liberty and property" (from *Two Treatises of Government*) to "life, liberty, and the pursuit of happiness." (Jefferson would never have suspected the centuries of debate that would rage over his immortal words: pursuit of happiness.)

And last but not least, Jefferson respected the over-arching intellect of Sir Isaac Newton, the English physicist, mathematician, astronomer, natural philosopher, alchemist and theologian. His book, *Philosophiæ Naturalis Principia Mathematica* (1687), set the groundwork for the laws of physics (such as motion and gravitation) that proved instrumental in the Scientific Revolution, which continued on into the 1800s. Newton's work advanced every branch of mathematics then known—for Jefferson, mathematics was an essential component of his life's work.

Sir Isaac Newton.

It is safe to say that from his college days until his final year on earth, Jefferson considered himself a student of Locke, Bacon and Newton, their books as well known to him as the faces of his children and grandchildren.

Mr. Thomas Jefferson, Esq.

All in all, Jefferson's immersion into the philosophy of the Enlightenment added another layer to his college experience that was largely happy except for one misstep—when his rooms in

Williamsburg couldn't accommodate his expanding collection of books, he shipped many of them to the library at Shadwell—it was a decision he'd bitterly regret.

After passing the bar examination in 1767, he returned to the family homestead on Shadwell Farm. In March of that same year the Imperial Crisis (the conflict over the constitutional relationship between England and the American colonies) began with the passage of the Stamp Act, a revenue tax to offset the costs of the French and Indian War. Parliament imposed the Stamp Tax on all printed documents including contracts, diplomas, newspapers, playing cards, and professional licenses. The highest tax (£10) was placed on attorneys' licenses (coincidentally or not, many of the more outspoken Patriots were lawyers). Throughout the colonies, protests escalated into mass riots, acts of violence and civil disobedience, and in some places, courts closed in defiance of the tax.

In spite of the Imperial Crisis, Jefferson had no intention of hanging out his shingle until he felt prepared to serve his clients to the best of his ability. Turning to books, those written by great legal minds, he meticulously copied hundreds of treatises and reports into commonplace books.

Jefferson focused, specifically, on the writings of Lord Kames and Lord Bolingbroke. Although he had read their works while apprenticing in law, his study of their philosophies deepened as his years as a lawyer lengthened. By examining the lengthy excerpts he copied from their books, and the commentaries he wrote in the margins of his commonplace books, it can be deduced that Jefferson attributed his understanding of *natural rights* (the basic rights governments can't deny) and *theological rationalism* (reason-based faith) to the writings of Lords Kames and Bolingbroke.

Lord Kames (1696-1782) was a prominent Scottish Jurist, legal scholar, and prolific writer—his books *Principles of Equity, Elements of Criticism*, and *Essays on the Principles of Morality and Natural Religion* shaped Jefferson's personal and professional philosophies.

In the same vein, the Deistic arguments of the English philosopher, politician and writer Lord Bolingbroke (1678-1751) impressed

Jefferson—he and many of his compatriots were being drawn to Deism, as they moved into position as America's Founding Fathers.

In our modern times, Deism is often misconstrued as disbelief in God; on the contrary, it is a belief in the existence of God on the evidence of reason and nature, as opposed to Theism, which accepts supernatural revelations of God's existence. Because Thomas Jefferson had a profound interest in faith and religious writings, it is helpful to understand his beliefs as a Deist.

Dr. Samuel Johnson's text, *A Dictionary of the English Language*, (1775) defines Deism as "the opinion of those that only acknowledge one God, without the reception of any revealed religion." The word Deism derives from *Deus*, Latin for God. Practitioners choose personal titles for God, such as Supreme Author, Architect, Providence, Almighty Being, or Supremely Perfect. The Deistic title, Great Governor of the World, appears in the *Articles of Confederation*.

Edward, Lord Herbert of Cherbury.

Edward the first Lord Herbert of Cherbury, England (1583-1648) founded Deism on five points: "God exists; He ought to be worshipped; practicing virtue is the primary way to worship God; sins can be repented of; and there is life after death."

Deism is not so much a religion as a perspective that a Supreme Cause (God) is responsible for all that exists. As advocates of Reason, Deists adhere to the law of physics that nothing comes from nothing, thus all that exists comes from some thing that has no beginning: God. This is similar to the Contingency Theory of God's Existence by the Roman Catholic philosopher, St. Thomas Aquinas; however, unlike Catholicism or most Christian denominations, Deism has neither a formal sect nor a hierarchy with fixed principles and rituals.

Deism can be traced to the Commonwealth of Virginia through a thief. In 1769, Charles Pyne, a bookseller in England, was charged with stealing two volumes titled *Deism Reveal'd* and sentenced to Transportation to America. Four years later he sold those volumes to a planter in Virginia; in all probability Jefferson acquired copies for his personal library for they were books that spurred deep interest in Deism throughout the 13 colonies. It should be noted, though, that Jefferson and his contemporaries who called themselves Deists, stayed faithful to their formal denominations.

Jefferson's Greatest Challenge as a Lawyer

Jefferson was expressly drawn to Lord Bolingbroke's books about republicanism. "Liberty," his Lordship contended in his writings, meant that "one is free not from the law, but by the law."

Lord Bollingroke.

Bolingbroke's definition of republicanism, its cycles in terms of birth, growth, eventual decline and demise, buttressed Jefferson and his close allies, John Adams and James Madison, as they stepped towards independence. But nationhood was more than a stone's throw away, so for the time being Jefferson kept his focus on bettering himself as a lawyer through study and readings. At some point he came across the book, *Study of History*, in which Lord Bolingbroke challenged practitioners of the law to climb up to the "vantage ground" of their profession. Lord Bolingbroke wrote:

"Law—in its nature the noblest and most beneficial to mankind, in its abuse and debasement the most pernicious . . . there have been lawyers that were orators, philosophers, historians. There have been Bacons and Clarendons. There will be none such any more till, in some better age, true ambition or the love of fame prevails over avarice, and till men find leisure and encouragement to prepare themselves for the exercise of this profession by climbing up to the vantage ground—so my Lord Bacon calls it—of science, instead of groveling all their lives below in a mean but gainful application to all the little arts of chicane. Till this happens, the profession of the law will scarce deserve to be ranked among the learned professions."

Bolingbroke's reference to Bacon and Hyde is important Sir Francis Bacon and his fellow jurist, Edward Hyde 1st Earl of Clarendon (1609-1674) labored to abolish the more oppressive practices of England's courts and commissions. Thomas Jefferson would have known of their efforts, and in all probability, he accepted Bolingbroke's challenge to "climb up to the vantage ground."

As a practicing attorney-of-law in the state of Pennsylvania, Barry offered his own thoughts.

> *In my view as a country lawyer, there is a ring of truth in Lord Bolingbroke's words: "Law—in its nature the noblest and most beneficial to mankind, in its abuse and debasement the most pernicious."*
>
> *He had it dead right in challenging us, the practitioners of the law, to honor our profession through proficient, ethical and moral representations of our clients, and by placing their interests above our own.*
>
> *Bolingbroke's statement reminded me of the early years of my practice when I received the first issues of the bar association's directory of lawyers. Each issue carried a face-page that reminded me of my responsibility to up-build my profession to its highest level. Bolingbroke's statement also recalled the early days of my career when new lawyers such as myself were required to fulfill a preceptorship, a mentoring experience under a skilled lawyer, much like an internship in the medical field.*
>
> *The preceptorship I undertook illuminated the distinction between learning the law and understanding the nuances of the practice of law. Would somebody please enlighten me as to why preceptorships have all disappeared?*
>
> *~Barry*

Destiny

Throughout the coming years of his diverse professional life, Jefferson would continue to use books as utilitarian tools in the crafting of himself into a lawyer, farmer, architect, politician, inventor . . . whatever he wished to become. But down the road, he'd voice one small regret that his concentrated readings of Locke, Bacon, Newton, Bolingbroke, and Kames had removed him from intellectual pursuits that were more "congenial to his scholarly temperament." (*The Papers of Thomas Jefferson,* 1769, I: 33-4.)

Perhaps a scholarly life was his larger desire, for he had an aversion to the political life he felt destined to lead for the betterment of the nation. On the other hand, it was a stroke of good luck for America that Thomas Jefferson made such a scrupulous study of philosophical, legal, and political writings, for he would soon draft our nation's most critical founding document.

Montesquieu.

But the writing of that document was years away in 1768 when Jefferson took his first political office as a member of the House of Burgesses (1768-1775). As the saying goes, he didn't rest on his laurels; instead, he pored over books and tracts to improve himself as a public servant. Some of his readings included the treatises of Baron de Montesquieu (1689-1755), the eminent French philosopher of the Enlightenment.

Like Jefferson, Montesquieu had an unquenchable thirst for knowledge, but unlike the rather reserved Virginian, the Frenchman had an acerbic sense of humor as is demonstrated by the "amusement" he found in "thinly veiled despots." Montesquieu's "amusement" led to a political concept in which he contended that nations could preserve themselves from corrupt rulers by adopting a system in which separate bodies exercised legislative, executive, and judicial powers—all answerable to one rule of law. That concept, *Separation of Powers,* influenced the framers of the *U. S. Constitution* (Jefferson participated in the drafting process through correspondence from Paris where he served as Minister to France). Years earlier, prior to his contributions to the drafting of the *U.S. Constitution*, Jefferson served as the war-governor of Virginia, during which time he applied Montesquieu's concept to his fundamental drafting of the state's constitution.

But in turning back to the years of rebellion in the colonies, Jefferson's readings of the books of Montesquieu and other theorists sharpened his political acumen as he stepped closer to that defining moment of his life—the drafting of the *Declaration of Independence.*

READERS OF THE LAW

As a young lawyer and public official of the colonies and, later, as an American statesman, Jefferson opened his private library and his very private mind to the law apprentices he took under his wing. And, as he did in his every venture in life, he set high standards for himself as their master.

Over time he became convinced that "one could [not] become learned by studying mere compiles" of legal facts, but rather one could find excellence in the profession of law through thoughtful readings of primary sources. He deprecated the emphasis placed on *Blackstone's Commentaries* and required his apprentices to use primary works such as *Coke on Littleton.*

Sir Edward Coke.

The *Institutes of the Lawes of England* is the series of legal treatises written by Sir Edward Coke (1628—1644), the great jurist of the Elizabethan and Jacobean eras whose treatises are generally regarded as the foundational documents of common law. In the United States, the *Institutes* have been cited in over 70 landmark cases decided by the Supreme Court.

The *Institutes* are divided into four parts: (I) Commentary on Littleton; (II) an Exposition of Ancient and Other Statutes; (III)

High Treason and Other Criminal Causes; and (IV) the Jurisdiction of Courts. Jefferson abbreviated the first part to *Coke on Littleton.* As a land lawyer, Jefferson would have studied the writings of Sir Thomas Littleton, the British judge and author made famous by his treatise on land law: *On Tenures* (1481).

As a preceptor of the law, Jefferson often provided lists of suggested readings that he considered "highly useful" for both apprentices and novice lawyers. The classic writings of Ancient Greece and Rome were included on those lists.

Several of the *Reading Lists* are extant; the ones given to Robert Skipwith and Bernard Moore in 1771 are documented. Jefferson's accompanying letter to Moore reads in part: "These [books] by no means constitute the whole of what might be usefully read in each of these branches of science. The mass of excellent works going more into detail is great indeed. But those here noted will enable the student to select for himself such others of detail as may suit his particular views and dispositions. They will give him a respectable, a useful and satisfactory degree of knowledge in these branches."

Of interest is Jefferson's letter to his soon to be brother-in-law Robert Skipwith. In counseling Robert as he prepared for the study of law, Jefferson explains how literature, including the tragedies of Ancient Greece, can build moral strength. He wrote: "The entertainments of fiction are useful as well as pleasant . . . when well written . . . everything is useful which contributes to fix in the principles and practices of virtue. When any original act of charity or of gratitude, for instance, is presented either to our sight or imagination, we are deeply impressed with its beauty and feel a strong desire in ourselves of doing charitable and grateful acts also. On the contrary when we see or read of any atrocious deed, we are disgusted with its deformity, and conceive an abhorrence of vice . . . Now every emotion of this kind is an exercise of our virtuous dispositions, and dispositions of the mind, like limbs of the body acquire strength by exercise. But exercise produces habit, and in the instance of which we speak the exercise being of the moral feelings produces a habit of thinking and acting virtuously" (August 3, 1771).

In his later years, Jefferson drew up *Reading Lists* for his nephew,

Peter Carr, and his grandsons, Francis Wayles Eppes and Jeff Randolph. Their lists named books of fiction and drama that would reinforce their studies of foreign languages, and that would also provide digestible moral lessons. Needless to say, Jefferson added the tragic dramas of Aeschylus to the lists.

Chronometrical Notions

In addition to *Reading Lists*, Jefferson asserted that particular books should be read at ascribed times. He formulated a *Reading Schedule* based on his research about the human brain. He theorized "a great inequality is observable in the vigor of the mind at different periods of the day. Its powers at these periods should therefore be attended to in marshalling the business of the day." (*Letter to Bernard Moore*, 1814.)

In applying his theory, Jefferson's *Reading Schedule* paralleled the mind's "vigor" with natural periods of light and darkness, and chronometrical time.

The Vigor of the Brain: Jefferson's Reading Schedule

Before 8:00 A.M.
Books of Physical Studies, Ethics, Religion & Natural Law
8:00 A.M. until 12:00 Noon
Books of Law
Noon to 1:00 P.M.
Books of Political Theory
Afternoon Hours
Books of History (American & Foreign)
Sunset until sleep
Belles-lettres (Literature as Fine Art), Criticisms, Rhetoric & Oratories

Jefferson also devised a plan for those who wished to develop their skills as writers and public speakers. He ascribed:

"[A] portion of time (borrowing some of the afternoon when the days are long and the nights short) is to be applied to acquiring the art of writing & speaking correctly by the following exercises:

"Criticize the style of any books whatever, committing your criticisms to writing. Translate into the different styles, to wit, the elevated, the middling and the familiar. Orators and poets will furnish subjects of the first, historians of the second, and epistolary and Comic writers of the third.

"Undertake, at first, short compositions, as themes, letters etc., paying great attention to the correctness and elegance of your language.

"Read the Orations of Demosthenes & Cicero. Analyze these orations and examine the correctness of the disposition, language, figures, states of the cases, arguments etc." (*Letter to Bernard Moore*, 1814.)

A Herd of Cows

At the age of 21, Jefferson came into his inheritance of more than 5,000 acres in Albemarle County. Faced with the responsibilities of 4 farms (Shadwell, Lego, Tufton, and Monticello) he scrutinized books and pamphlets on every subject from fertilizer to animal husbandry. In time he'd acknowledge the farmer's unpredictable enemies of storms, droughts and floods and the mercurial highs and lows of the marketplace, but he would still refer to himself as the "unskilled manager of my farms."

When not in Williamsburg, he resided at Shadwell with its seven fields (each 40 acres), and the one-and-a half-story frame house he had been born in. Following the terms of his father's will, Jefferson leased the house from his mother (to provide her a residence and income until her death), but he laid claim to the library.

By January 1770, he had accumulated 300-400 volumes, a sizeable collection in that era, even for someone of his financial means. As Douglas L. Wilson, the distinguished author and founding Director of the International Center for Jefferson Studies at Monticello pointed out: "Even for a rich man, which Jefferson was, it represented a tremendous financial investment, being worth as much as a day laborer might expect to earn in ten years, or equal to the cost of a herd of nearly two hundred cows."

At the age of 26, momentous change came into Jefferson's life on the first day of February in 1770, and as one would expect, his books were center-stage. To set that day into history, it was about a month before the *Boston Massacre* in Massachusetts, a riot that the Sons-of-Liberty agitated after which Paul Revere's masterful propaganda provoked widespread protests against England's military presence in the colonies.

But for our purposes we return to the first day of February when fire destroyed the house on Shadwell-farm. Away at the time, Jefferson hastened home, and dismounting at the perimeter of the smoldering ruins, he asked his first question: *Had his books been rescued?* A slave responded, "No master, all burnt, but we save[d] your fiddle."

Devastated, only then did Jefferson inquire about his mother, who had barely escaped the burning house—theirs was a strained relationship. Conversely, his despair about his lost books can be understood—he sincerely believed he could not effectively practice his profession without his law books, and all of them (except a single volume loaned out to a friend) had been reduced to ashes. A few weeks later Jefferson wrote a plaintive letter to his college friend John Page:

"My late loss may have reached you by this time, I mean the loss of my mother's house by fire, and in it, of every paper I had in the world, and almost every book. On a reasonable estimate I calculate the cost of the books burned to have been £200 sterling. Would to god it had been the money; then had it never cost me a sigh! . . . To make the loss more sensible it fell principally on my books of common law, of which I have but one left, at that time lent out."

A smaller house would be rebuilt at Shadwell, but Jefferson had no intention of returning to the family nest, especially one dominated by his mother. A reserved man by nature, he was close-mouthed when it came to his mother, and barely mentioned her in writing other than notations of her marriage to his father, the house fire, and her death from apoplexy along with the funeral costs.

FYI: Jane Randolph Jefferson, February 9, 1721-March 31, 1776.

Born in Shadwell, England, she married Peter on October 3, 1739 and together they had 10 children: Jane (1740-1765) never married; Mary (1741-1811) married John Bolling (served in the Virginia House of Burgesses); Thomas (1743-1826); Elizabeth (1744-1774) mentally ill; Martha (1746-1811) married Dabney Carr (Thomas' good friend and founder of the Committee of Correspondence in VA); Peter Field (1748) died in infancy; Peter (1750) died in infancy; Lucy (1752-1811) married Charles L. Lewis; and twins Randolph (1755-1815) and Anna (1755-1828) who married Hasting Marks. Jane died in Massachusetts in 1776.

Monticello

In 1768, two years before the fire razed Shadwell, Jefferson selected the mountainous, wooded land of Monticello as the future site of his home-farm (resident overseers would manage his other properties, his quarter farms). He had the site cleared for construction, and in 1769 he ordered the laying of the first bricks of a small structure. By the time Shadwell was destroyed in 1770, the brick building (called south Pavilion) was complete enough to serve as his residence while a standing house on the property, Hermitage, was renovated.

Jefferson, being Jefferson, envisioned a grand home for himself and the family he'd have one day. Undaunted by the fact that schools of architecture were non-existent, he turned to his tools of choice: books. He studied the great structures of the world and read the works of Andrea Palladio (1508-1580), the legendary architect who based his designs on the temples of Ancient Rome. Following Palladio's sentiments, Jefferson borrowed Roman concepts, such as columns and pediments, as he sketched his idealized home and its surrounding gardens. Many years down the road, in 1787, he would express his admiration of Roman architecture, writing: "I have been nourished [by] the remains of Roman grandeur . . . Roman taste, genius and magnificence, [that] excite ideas." (*Letter to Madame de Tesse Nismes,*

March 20, 1787.)

In time, Hermitage's name would be changed to Monticello. The first Monticello, a two-story house with 8 rooms, was completed prior to Jefferson's departure for France in 1784. While abroad, he would observe the emerging cultural movement of Neoclassicism, a revival of the Classics (Ancient Rome and Greece) in architecture, music, art and literature. He would purchase books to study the new movement in-depth, and would observe the French architects' interpretations of Neoclassicism from basic skylights to the more complicated features of dome-shaped rooms. Upon his return from France in 1789, he would begin renovations of Monticello, which would only be completed when he stepped down from the presidency in 1809.

By then, the red brick house (11,000 square feet) would include 43 rooms (not counting the pavilions or rooms beneath the terraces), 8 fireplaces, 12 skylights, and a dome room (skyroom) set amidst a network of flower and vegetable gardens, vineyards, stables, and outlying buildings and cabins.

Incredibly all this came about from Jefferson bending over books of architecture, landscape gardening, and engineering for hours on end, as candles melted down into pools of molten wax.

Jefferson's Escape

From its very beginning, life at Monticello was a whirlwind of activity, but as the years passed Jefferson designed the perfect escape: his retreat in the southern corner of his home, a private suite designed around his favored architectural form, the octagonal. The suite was comprised of his Book Room (library), bedroom, greenhouse, and Cabinet, a handsome room with a desk and a barrel-shaped, red leather armchair. The chair, of French design, revolved to allow him ease in turning from book to desk to sketchpad.

The innermost room of his sanctuary was his Book Room, his library. When the house was still known as Hermitage, his books were kept in an upstairs room above the parlor, but once the dome was added, Jefferson moved his entire collection downstairs to his private suite.

Monticello's library would eventually house most of the known books of the ancient and modern world. Granted, he possessed the wealth to purchase the books he needed both professionally and personally, but beyond that, he had the predisposition to acquire debt as he built a library that would be unparalleled in the Commonwealth of Virginia.

He wrote: "Books constitute capital. A library book lasts as long as a house, for hundreds of years. It is not, then, an article of mere consumption but fairly of capital, and often in the case of professional men, setting out in life, it is their only capital." (*Letter to James Madison,* 1821.)

To amass such a major collection, Jefferson purchased a new book almost every day from 1770-1815. As stated earlier, he didn't purchase books to fill shelves like decorative objects; rather, he read the volumes, tracts and pamphlets he acquired to gain the knowledge he needed to do all he wished to do.

Courtship

As he renovated his house, practiced law, held political office, and took an active role in the rebellion and fast approaching war, he found time to court a wealthy widow, Martha Wayles Skelton. There are no surviving portraits of Martha, but she was described as a beautiful, gentle woman "with the greatest fund of good nature . . . which promises to ensure [a husband] the greatest happiness mortals are capable of enjoying." *(Letter from Robert Skipwith to T. Jefferson, 1771.)*

On January 1, 1772, six months after the death of her tiny son, her only child from her brief marriage to Bathurst Skelton (1744-1768), Martha married Thomas Jefferson and in time bore him six children. The happiness of their union was recorded in the family's history. Granddaughter Ellen Wayles Randolph Coolidge wrote: "My . . . grandfather was tenderly attached to her. She commanded his respect by her good sense and domestic virtues, and his admiration and love by her wit, her vivacity, and her agreeable person and manners. She was not only an excellent housekeeper and notable mistress of a family, but a graceful, ladylike and accomplished woman, with considerable powers of conversation, some skill in music, all the habits of good society, and the art of welcoming her husband's friends to perfection. . . She made my grandfather's home comfortable, cheerful, pleasant . . . Her loss was the bitterest grief my grandfather ever knew." And Sarah N. Randolph added: "[My great grandmother was] a singularly beautiful woman, and a person of great intelligence and strength of character; and certainly, if the attractions of a woman can be measured by the love borne her by her husband, hers must have been great indeed, for never was a wife loved with more passionate devotion than she" (no date).

Amidst all the comings and goings of professional responsibilities, social obligations, and daily concerns of children and home, Mr. and Mrs. Jefferson set aside time for music--Martha played the harpsichord and pianoforte, while her husband had mastered the violin. Their favored pastime, though, was reading aloud to each other, especially the works of Laurence Sterne, an Anglo-Irish novelist and Anglican clergyman best remembered for his comic novel published in ten volumes: *The Life and Opinions of Tristram Shandy, Gentleman* (1759). Sterne described his own novel as "a comedy skirting tragedy."

Inheritance of Massive Debts

In 1772, a substantial book acquisition came Jefferson's way from the estate of Reverend James Horrocks, the President of the College of William and Mary. The following year, in 1773, Jefferson inherited two collections: the library of his close friend and brother-in-law, Dabney Carr, and the book holdings of his father-in-law, John Wayles. Unfortunately, Jefferson also inherited Wayles' sizeable debts, which strained his finances from then on.

Still, in spite of his debts and the high cost of books, Jefferson continued to build his library. That was no small feat. Books were hard to come by because of the trade restrictions imposed by England, but Jefferson maintained his association with the Virginia Gazette in Williamsburg. Proud of its reputation as a "major book-dealer," the Gazette kept its shelves filled, and Jefferson stopped in, frequently, and rarely left without making a purchase.

Boston Tea Party

On December 16, 1773, Jefferson's compatriots Samuel Adams, John Hancock, and Paul Revere staged the *Boston Tea Party* to protest the East India Company's monopoly on tea importation—the raid on three tea ships and the dumping of 342 chests of tea into the harbor would resonate throughout the colonies including the Commonwealth of Virginia.

By that cold, winter day in December, Jefferson's library had reached astronomical proportions. In his own hand, he catalogued 1,256 books, not counting the sheaves of music and other volumes left behind in "Williams-burgh."

When Boston's revolt galvanized the colonies in opposition against the Crown and still later when Britain retaliated with soldiers and the punitive removal of colonial rights, Jefferson turned to his books of history and politics with new purpose in mind—to study every subject related to rebellion and nationhood. His readings reached from Britain's parliamentary procedure to the laws of his native colony, and as a result he contributed principally to the revisal of the document, *Laws of the Commonwealth of Virginia.*

By the time Virginia's courts of law closed in 1774, Jefferson had suspended his practice as an attorney—again, books became indispensible tools in his hands as he shifted his professional life from law to politics.

Benjamin Franklin's Lending Company

Most families in the American colonies owned a bible, but only the clergy and wealthy had the means to purchase more than a book or two. Aside from a few private collections such as Thomas Jefferson's, most libraries were found at colleges (holdings were generally composed of publications in foreign languages with a focus on religion and education).

In Philadelphia, Benjamin Franklin and his associates established a philosophical association called Junto, an equivalent of a modern book club. Individually, the members couldn't afford books, themselves, so they conceived a plan--a simple but ingenious plan to combine their monies to open a publicly chartered lending library: The Library Company (1731).

According to the company's articles of agreement, each of the original 50 members invested 40 shillings along with guarantees to invest an additional 10 shillings, annually, to build and maintain the library's holdings. Members could borrow books freely; non-members could make selections on Saturdays from 4-8 P.M. by providing a surety (a thing of recognized value that could be sold if the book wasn't returned). The Library Company's collection had public appeal largely because subjects other than education and religion were included; of equal appeal, most of the books were printed in English. By 1773, the second floor of Carpenters' Hall had to be leased to house the company's expanded collection of 2000 books—some of those books would prove instrumental in the struggle for independence.

On September 5th, 1774, in response to the Intolerable Acts, the First Continental Congress met in Philadelphia. The delegates convened in Carpenters' Hall, mainly because of the "excellent lending library" on the second floor. The librarian had been instructed to "furnish the gentlemen . . . with the use of such Books as they may have occasion for during their sitting, taking a Receipt for them." Presumptively, as the delegates debated the issues of nationhood, they referred to the Library Company's books that documented the world's rebellions, wars and governments.

In the same way, the Library Company offered full use of its collection to the Second Continental Congress when they convened in May 1775. While serving as a delegate from Virginia, Jefferson often climbed the steps in Carpenters' Hall to root through the books that lined the shelves on the second floor. But apart from his congressional duties, he spent hours roaming through the bookshops of Philadelphia. Touted as the cultural and commercial center of the 13 colonies, the city had numerous, well-stocked shops—his accounting ledger records a higher number of book acquisitions in 1776 than in any previous year.

FYI: Ben Franklin's Legacy

In 1787, the Library Company made their collection available to the delegates to the Constitutional Convention, and to Congress when government sat in Philadelphia (1790-1800), thus "unofficially" serving as the first Library of Congress. To this day, the doors of Franklin's Library Company remain open. Distinguished as the nation's oldest cultural institution, it is now an independent research library on Locust Street, Philadelphia, specializing in American history and the cultures of the 17th and 18th centuries; its mission is to preserve and make available its collection of historic books, broadsides, prints, photographs, and art works.

Benjamin Franklin.

In 1789, Ben Franklin laid the cornerstone for a handsome library near the corner of Fifth and Chestnut Streets, but he passed away before the building named in his honor opened on New Year's Day, 1791.

Jefferson's Act of Treason

In the summer of 1776, the colonists' protests for equal rights as subjects of the Crown escalated into demands for liberty. Thomas Jefferson and his fellow Delegates to the Second Continental Congress risked the loss of their liberty, lands, and lives, but they were strengthened by their conviction that America should seek nationhood.

In the middle of June, a five-man committee that included Ben Franklin, John Adams and Thomas Jefferson was charged with drafting a formal statement of separation from England. The chore fell on Jefferson's shoulders, as explained in his own words:

"The Committee of 5 . . . unanimously pressed on myself alone to undertake the draught. I consented; I drew it; but before I reported it to the committee I communicated it separately to Dr. Franklin and

Mr. Adams requesting their corrections . . . and you have seen the original paper now in my hands, with the corrections of Dr. Franklin and Mr. Adams interlined in their own handwriting. Their alterations were two or three only, and merely verbal. I then wrote a fair copy, reported it to the committee, and from them, unaltered to the Congress." (*Letter to James Madison,* 30 August 1813.)

Jefferson's words did him no justice. For two hot, airless weeks in June, he closeted himself in his rooming house in Philadelphia to draft one of the most treasonous documents ever penned in modern history: the *Declaration of Independence.*

He wrote: "The history of the present King of Great Britain is a history of repeated injuries and usurpations, all having in direct object the establishment of an absolute Tyranny over these States."

During those weeks of near isolation Jefferson suffered from migraine headaches that should have left him bed-ridden, but he worked diligently, borrowing ideas and theories and statements from books such as *Holland's Declaration of Independence.* Other reference books came from the Library Company's collection, while some texts were found through correspondence with friends as he wrote his world-changing document.

Working with vital purpose, in a matter of days Thomas Jefferson presented his handwritten draft to his fellow conspirators, as explained below.

A compelling study of Thomas Jefferson elevates him beyond understanding. A case in point: after he wrote his draft of the Declaration of Independence in the long, sweeping flourishes that distinguish his handwriting, he asked Ben Franklin and John Adams for their comments. They made a few suggestions, which Jefferson later inserted into the draft, and on June 28th he returned to Carpenters' Hall where the delegates had reassembled.

Thomas Jefferson took his seat amid the noise of many voices, but he felt all eyes turn towards him. His name was called. In the sudden silence that fell he was asked to read the declaration, but underneath all his intellect was a very shy, unassuming guy, and his shyness made his voice so low he couldn't be heard beyond the first row.

On July 3, debate ensued over the implication of certain words, sentences and phrases in Jefferson's declaration. He listened in silence, mortally offended. He would later write: "The purpose behind the Declaration was not saying some-thing new, but to place before mankind the common sense of the subject, in terms so plain and firm as to command their assent . . . Neither aiming at originality of principles or sentiments, nor yet copied from any particular and previous writing, it was intended to be an expression of the American mind."

I suggested to Maureen that the Declaration of Independence be included in this book, in its entirety, as a result of my abiding conviction that for all practical purposes it has become a lost document, and that too few people are cognizant of its existence, and more importantly, are unknowing of the significance of its content.

~Barry

The Declaration of Independence
IN CONGRESS, July 4, 1776.

The unanimous Declaration of the thirteen united States of America,

When in the Course of human events, it becomes necessary for one people to dissolve the political bands which have connected them with another, and to assume among the powers of the earth, the separate and equal station to which the Laws of Nature and of Nature's God entitle them, a decent respect to the opinions of mankind requires that they should declare the causes which impel them to the separation.

We hold these truths to be self-evident, that all men are created equal, that they are endowed by their Creator with certain unalienable Rights, that among these are Life, Liberty and the pursuit of Happiness.—That to secure these rights, Governments are instituted among Men, deriving their just powers from the consent of the governed, —That whenever any Form of Government becomes destructive of these ends, it is the Right of the People to alter or to abolish it, and to institute new Government, laying its foundation on such principles and organizing its powers in such form, as to them shall seem most likely to effect their Safety and Happiness. Prudence, indeed, will dictate that Governments long established should not be changed for light and transient causes; and accordingly all experience hath shewn, that mankind are more disposed to suffer, while evils are sufferable, than to right themselves by abolishing the forms to which they are accustomed. But when a long train of abuses and usurpations, pursuing invariably the same Object evinces a design to reduce them under absolute Despotism, it is their right, it is their duty, to throw off such Government, and to provide new Guards for their future security.—Such has been the patient sufferance of these Colonies; and such is now the necessity which constrains them to alter their former Systems of Government. The history of the present King of Great Britain is a history of repeated injuries and usurpations, all having in direct object the establishment of an absolute Tyranny over these States. To prove this, let Facts be submitted to a candid world.

He has refused his Assent to Laws, the most wholesome and necessary for the public good.

He has forbidden his Governors to pass Laws of immediate and pressing importance, unless suspended in their operation till his Assent should be obtained; and when so suspended, he has utterly neglected to attend to them.

He has refused to pass other Laws for the accommodation of large districts of people, unless those people would relinquish the right of Representation in the Legislature, a right inestimable to them and formidable to tyrants only.

He has called together legislative bodies at places unusual, uncomfortable, and distant from the depository of their public Records, for the sole purpose of fatiguing them into compliance with his measures.

He has dissolved Representative Houses repeatedly, for opposing with manly firmness his invasions on the rights of the people.

He has refused for a long time, after such dissolutions, to cause others to be elected; whereby the Legislative powers, incapable of Annihilation, have returned to the People at large for their exercise; the State remaining in the mean time exposed to all the dangers of invasion from without, and convulsions within.

He has endeavoured to prevent the population of these States; for that purpose obstructing the Laws for Naturalization of Foreigners; refusing to pass others to encourage their migrations hither, and raising the conditions of new Appropriations of Lands.

He has obstructed the Administration of Justice, by refusing his Assent to Laws for establishing Judiciary powers.

He has made Judges dependent on his Will alone, for the tenure of their offices, and the amount and payment of their salaries.

He has erected a multitude of New Offices, and sent hither swarms of Officers to harrass our people, and eat out their substance.

He has kept among us, in times of peace, Standing Armies without the Consent of our legislatures.

He has affected to render the Military independent of and superior to the Civil power.

He has combined with others to subject us to a jurisdiction foreign to our constitution, and unacknowledged by our laws; giving his Assent to their Acts of pretended Legislation:

For Quartering large bodies of armed troops among us:

For protecting them, by a mock Trial, from punishment for any Murders which they should commit on the Inhabitants of these States:

For cutting off our Trade with all parts of the world:

For imposing Taxes on us without our Consent:

For depriving us in many cases, of the benefits of Trial by Jury:

For transporting us beyond Seas to be tried for pretended offences:

For abolishing the free System of English Laws in a neighbouring Province, establishing therein an Arbitrary government, and enlarging its Boundaries so as to render it at once an example and fit instrument for introducing the same absolute rule into these Colonies:

For taking away our Charters, abolishing our most valuable Laws, and altering fundamentally the Forms of our Governments:

For suspending our own Legislatures, and declaring themselves invested with power to legislate for us in all cases whatsoever.

He has abdicated Government here, by declaring us out of his Protection and waging War against us.

He has plundered our seas, ravaged our Coasts, burnt our towns, and destroyed the lives of our people.

He is at this time transporting large Armies of foreign Mercenaries to compleat the works of death, desolation and tyranny, already begun with circumstances of Cruelty & perfidy scarcely paralleled in the most barbarous ages, and totally unworthy the Head of a civilized nation.

He has constrained our fellow Citizens taken Captive on the high Seas to bear Arms against their Country, to become the executioners of their friends and Brethren, or to fall themselves by their Hands.

He has excited domestic insurrections amongst us, and has endeavoured to bring on the inhabitants of our frontiers, the merciless Indian Savages, whose known rule of warfare, is an undistinguished destruction of all ages, sexes and conditions.

In every stage of these Oppressions We have Petitioned for Redress in the most humble terms: Our repeated Petitions have been answered only by repeated injury. A Prince whose character is thus marked by every act which may define a Tyrant, is unfit to be the ruler of a free people.

Nor have We been wanting in attentions to our Brittish brethren. We have warned them from time to time of attempts by their legislature to extend an unwarrantable jurisdiction over us. We have reminded them of the circumstances of our emigration and settlement here. We have appealed to their native justice and magnanimity, and we have conjured them by the ties of our common kindred to disavow these usurpations, which, would inevitably interrupt our connections and correspondence. They too have been deaf to the voice of justice and of consanguinity. We must, therefore, acquiesce in the necessity, which denounces our Separation, and hold them, as we hold the rest of mankind, Enemies in War, in Peace Friends.

We, therefore, the Representatives of the united States of America, in General Congress, Assembled, appealing to the Supreme Judge of the world for the rectitude of our intentions, do, in the Name, and by Authority of the good People of these Colonies, solemnly publish and declare, That these United Colonies are, and of Right ought to be Free and Independent States; that they are Absolved from all Allegiance to the British Crown, and that all political connection between them and the State of Great Britain, is and ought to be totally dissolved; and that as Free and Independent States, they have full Power to levy War, conclude Peace, contract Alliances, establish Commerce, and to do all other Acts and Things which Independent States may of right do. And for the support of this Declaration, with a firm reliance on the protection of divine Providence, we mutually pledge to each other our Lives, our Fortunes and our sacred Honor.

The 56 signatures on the Declaration appear in the positions indicated:

Column 1
Georgia:
Button Gwinnett
Lyman Hall
George Walton

Column 2
North Carolina:
William Hooper
Joseph Hewes
John Penn

South Carolina:
William Paca
Thomas Stone
Charles Carroll of Carrollton

Column 3
Massachusetts:
John Hancock

Maryland:
Samuel Chase

Virginia:
George Wythe
Richard Henry Lee
Thomas Jefferson
Benjamin Harrison
Thomas Nelson, Jr.
Francis Lightfoot Lee
Carter Braxton
Edward Rutledge

Thomas Heyward, Jr.
Thomas Lynch, Jr.
Arthur Middleton

Column 4
Pennsylvania:
Robert Morris
Benjamin Rush
Benjamin Franklin
John Morton
George Clymer
James Smith
George Taylor
James Wilson
George Ross

Delaware:
Caesar Rodney
George Read
Thomas McKean

Column 5
New York:
William Floyd
Philip Livingston
Francis Lewis
Lewis Morris
New Jersey:
Richard Stockton
John Witherspoon
Francis Hopkinson
John Hart
Abraham Clark

Column 6
New Hampshire:
Josiah Bartlett
William Whipple

Massachusetts:
Samuel Adams
John Adams
Robert Treat Paine
Elbridge Gerry

Rhode Island:
Stephen Hopkins
William Ellery

Connecticut:
Roger Sherman
Samuel Huntington
William Williams
Oliver Wolcott

New Hampshire:
Matthew Thornton

Governor of Virginia, 1779-1781

The very hour the thirteen colonies declared their independence from Britain, Thomas Jefferson addressed a personal concern—the real possibility that the books he had left behind in Williamsburg would be confiscated or destroyed by the British. With immediacy, he sent a letter to Monticello with detailed instructions for the safe retrieval of his Williamsburg collection.

"Monticello Reflection" by Sudhindra. *Public domain.*

In regards to books, the start of the war went in Jefferson's favor. At reasonable cost he purchased the library of the Governor of Virginia who took flight at the first discharge of weapons, and he then acquired the libraries of two scholarly Loyalists who fled in haste to England.

Those books and others became indispensible when he was elected to Virginia's highest office in 1779. As mentioned earlier, Governor Jefferson followed the political theories he had learned from Montesquieu's books to establish the *Separation of Powers* (Executive, Judicial and Legislative) in his fundamental draft of the *Constitution of the Commonwealth of Virginia.*

Jefferson's most pressing gubernatorial responsibilities were his duties as a wartime governor. The long winter of 1778 at Valley Forge had depleted Washington's troops, but Governor Jefferson could not send in fresh reserves, as requested. All able-bodied Virginians were already serving under General Washington's command and the rest of the state's militia had been sent on a clandestine mission to the Great Lakes to take back the lands seized by Britain. In the meanwhile, Jefferson had to deal with the Royal Navy's blockade of the Chesapeake Bay, a ploy that froze Virginia's economy. To further complicate the situation, his attempts to build a defensive force were obstructed by his obstinate Council, a tactic that opened Virginia to invasion by the traitor Benedict Arnold and General Charles Cornwallis.

When a rumor surfaced that the British planned to invade Charlottesville, Jefferson set several evacuation plans into motion: one for his family, and one for the safe removal of his books. In March, General Washington sent French reinforcements under the command of the Marquis de Lafayette to Virginia to bolster the commonwealth's militia. From their first meeting, Lafayette and Jefferson became trusted friends and would remain so the rest of their lives—their friendship was built on a shared love of wine and books.

Marquis de Lafayette.

In spite of the French reinforcements, the British seemed an insurmountable foe at that perilous moment in Virginia's history. Deploring his lack of military training, Jefferson resigned in 1781 in favor of General Thomas Nelson who had filled George Washington's seat in the Second Continental Congress when he assumed command of the Continental Army. Nelson signed the *Declaration of Independence* before health issues forced his resignation from Congress, but he accepted the governorship and was granted almost dictatorial powers to mount a defense against the British General, Lord Charles Cornwallis.

A few days after Jefferson's resignation as governor, British troops marched against Charlottesville. Warned in time, Jefferson sent his family to prearranged shelters and then sat down to a breakfast of poached salmon although soldiers had been sighted in the near distance. His breakfast finished, he wiped his mouth with a napkin before going outside to mount up—a line of Redcoats was charging up the hill towards him and minutes from being captured, he turned his horse's head and rode off.

Thomas Jefferson would have been a prized captive. The British would have felt vindicated in hanging the traitor who had penned the treasonous declaration that thrust another war on England. Rather surprisingly, the soldiers and officers respected Jefferson's property while encamped at Monticello, but Endrina Tay, the Associate Foundation Librarian for Technical Services at Monticello, offered an explanation:

"As far as we know, apart from some of his most valuable papers, TJ did not carry any belongings as he fled on horseback from Monticello when the British arrived on the mountaintop. He wrote later that the British officer, Captain McLeod, had been given strict orders by Colonel Tarleton "to suffer nothing to be injured" and that "McLeod preserved every thing with sacred care during about 18 hours that he remained there" [*Papers of Thomas Jefferson* 13: 363]. The British soldiers did find some of TJ's finest wine, which they consumed."

As 1781 moved from summer to autumn, a large, combined force numbering three French troops to every one American launched an amphibious attack that defeated the haughty Lord Cornwallis. The Battle of Yorktown, also remembered as the Siege of Yorktown, was the final, major battle of the American Revolutionary War. It was a resounding victory that humiliated the British.

FYI: A Patriot

Governor Thomas Nelson (1738-1789) proved himself utterly selfless during the Battle of Yorktown when he offered a money-prize of "5 Guineas" to the first artillerist to strike his family's home in that town—it was believed Cornwallis and British officers were quartered there. (Today, 3 cannon balls remain lodged in the house's exterior walls.) In that year of 1781, Nelson's health issues resurfaced and forced his retirement from public office. He, his wife and 11 children never recovered the 2 million dollars he had loaned to the "cause for freedom."

Betrayal

Jefferson's joy upon hearing of Cornwallis' surrender at Yorktown on October 19, 1781, was curtailed by Patrick Henry's betrayal. A former ally and friend of Jefferson's, Henry spearheaded the official inquiry into Jefferson's alleged failures as a wartime governor. Once the facts became known that Virginia's Council had refused to support Thomas Jefferson's plan to mount a defensive force, he was cleared of any wrongdoing as a wartime governor. Regardless, the scandal impacted his reputation, and he swore he'd never serve, again, as a public official.

After assessing the war damage to his crops, livestock and property, he began rebuilding his farms, but when he had time to spare, he would closet himself in his Cabinet to work on a manuscript, *Notes on the State of Virginia*, as explained below.

> *As a fledgling lawyer, Thomas Jefferson may have been inspired by Lord Bolingbroke's advice to "pry into the secret recesses of the human heart [to] become well acquainted with the whole moral world." It doesn't seem too far-fetched to say that Jefferson pried into the "secret recesses of the human heart" through authors' writings, such as the moralistic dramas of Aeschylus who wrote about "the whole moral world."*
>
> *Still later, when Jefferson put aside his law practice for a career in politics and political writing, he may have adopted Bolingbroke's further advice to "trace the laws of particular states, especially of [his] own, from the first rough sketches to the more perfect draughts; from the first causes . . . through all the effects, good and bad, that they produced."*
>
> *Did Bolingbroke's advice motivate Jefferson, as lawyer and politician, to write his book,* Notes on the State of Virginia? *Possibly. Regardless, sometime in 1781, he finished his manuscript, a significant work structured as a detailed response to questions from Francois Barbe-Marbois, the Secretary of the French Legion to America. Jefferson's book remained unpublished for several years since he had no intention of releasing it to the public; however, after it was translated, poorly, and printed in France without his permission, he revised the draft and published it in 1785 for a select audience of readers.*
>
> *Of keen interest and mild amusement to my co-author is the "drudgery" Jefferson found in the whole process of writing a book. Thomas Jefferson reflected: "A patient pursuit of facts, and cautious combination and comparison of them is . . . drudgery."*

Jefferson never authored a second book, other than the bible he constructed by cutting out scriptural passages and gluing them onto sheets of paper. Obviously, he preferred the pleasures of reading books to the chore of writing them.

~Barry

A Cruel Vow

In March of 1782, Jefferson received a request from George Washington to serve as the new nation's diplomat to France. Determined to avoid public office, Jefferson declined the honor and turned his full attention to his much loved and very fragile wife. Martha suffered from diabetes, which may have brought about her confinement to bed, at times, and several miscarriages.

In their decade of marriage, Martha bore six children, but only two daughters, Martha (Patsy) and Maria (Polly), would live to adulthood. Two daughters, Jane Randolph and Lucy Elizabeth, and an unnamed son died in their infancies; their last daughter, also named Lucy Elizabeth, would die from whooping cough before her third birthday while her father was abroad in France.

After giving birth to Lucy Elizabeth on May 8, 1782, Martha lingered for four months, her husband never far from her side. One night their worn copy of *Tristram Shandy* found its way into their hands. Asking for ink and paper, Martha slowly copied these sentences from the novel:

Time wastes too fast: every letter I trace tells me with what rapidity life follows my pen. The days and hours of it are flying over our heads like clouds of windy day never to return—more. Every thing presses on . . .

She faltered, either too ill or too emotionally distraught to complete the sentence, and so Jefferson took the quill-pen from her hand and finished writing the poignant words:

. . . and every time I kiss thy hand to bid adieu, every absence which follows it, are preludes to that eternal separation which we are shortly to make!

Martha asked her husband to take a vow to never remarry, which he did, but cruel consequences awaited in the future—he might have found love again or companionship, at the very least, that would have softened the hard edges of his sometimes-lonely life. Too, the vow would impact the life of their eldest daughter, Martha. Her marriage would be irreparably damaged by her assumption of the duties as Mistress of Monticello, and later as First Lady of the Executive Mansion during brief visits to Washington during her father's presidency. But at that moment in 1782, when Jefferson vowed he'd never remarry, the future lay unseen by him and his dying wife.

On September 6, 1782, Jefferson opened his accounting book to write: "My dear wife died this day at 11H -45' A.M." The piece of parchment on which they had written the excerpt from *Tristram Shandy* was entwined with a lock of Martha's hair—he kept the parchment close at hand until the day of his own death.

After the funeral, Jefferson fell into a "stupor of the mind" for several months, an endless migraine-like headache. His method of dealing with loss was to internalize his pain—for most of his life he had struggled with expressions of emotion, especially sorrow. He considered himself a modern, enlightened man of Reason, and so he questioned the logic, the practicality of weeping when death was an inevitable biological event in the natural order of the world. And yet, at times, he experienced deep sorrow, and in refusing himself the physical release of sadness through tears, he may have brought on those excruciating headaches that stole away his appetite, sleep, and all desire to carry on simple conversations.

Two months after Martha's death, Thomas Jefferson emerged from his "stupor" as is revealed in his letter to a friend, the Marquis de Chastellux, an officer in the French military. Jefferson wrote: "The state of dreadful suspense in which I had been kept all the summer and the catastrophe which closed it . . . A single event wiped away all my plans and left me a blank which I had not the spirits to fill up . . . [but I'm] emerging from the stupor of mind which had rendered me as dead to the world as [Martha] was whose . . . loss occasioned it."

The Revolutionary War formally ended with the signing of the *Treaty of Paris* on September 3, 1783. At the age of 38, Thomas Jefferson anticipated a sedate life with his beloved daughters and books.

Minister to France, 1784-1789

Jefferson stepped back into political life for one reason: books. Again offered a diplomatic post, he agreed to serve as the Minister to France—a deciding factor was the opportunity he'd be afforded to explore Europe's well-stocked bookstores and book-marts.

He arrived at the harbor in Philadelphia with long lists of the books requested by family and friends. He brought along, as well, his catalogue of the nearly 3,000 volumes and tracts he had collected in only 13 years—included was an addendum of the titles he would search out while abroad.

While waiting for his ship, he met with fellow Bookman, James Madison. Taking Madison into his confidence, Jefferson outlined his *Grand Plan*—to turn his already substantial collection into the finest library in all America. Madison made known his own plan—to convince Congress to establish a national library. To that end, Jefferson would serve as Madison's book-buyer while in Europe. Moreover, before his ship set sail, Jefferson guaranteed that he'd find and mail the books Madison would need to draft the *United States Constitution* at the fast-approaching Constitutional Convention (1787).

Thomas Jefferson captured his appreciation of France in a single letter to his friend Charles Bellini on September 30, 1785. Jefferson wrote: "Behold me at length on the vaunted scene of Europe! . . . You are perhaps, curious to know how this new scene has struck a savage of the mountains of America . . . Were I to proceed to tell you how much I enjoy their architecture, sculpture, painting, music, I should want words. It is in these arts they shine."

Aside from Paris' cultural offerings, Jefferson immersed himself into a study of the city's engineering masterpieces. Of his observations he wrote: "[I] marveled at the hydraulic pumping system that provided the water for the royal gardens and called attention to the quiet magnificence of Parisian bridges."

He also bid on artwork at auctions, learned culinary arts and winemaking, and purchased furniture, ornate candlesticks, clothing, china and, of course, books. Thousands of books.

In his years abroad, 1784 -1789, Thomas Jefferson acquired 2000 volumes, which increased his library's holdings to 5,000. To reach that number took time and effort, and because his diplomatic duties required his full attention, he often asked fellow diplomats to serve as his book-buying agents in the more distant shops of Europe.

He spent an exorbitant sum of money on those purchases, far more than in his earlier periods of book collecting; however, he did moderate his expenditures by seeking out less expensive printings and by bargaining, heatedly, if he felt the price unfairly high. He accurately portrayed himself in a letter to a book-buying agent in London, writing: "Sensible that I labour grievously under the malady of Bibliomanie, I submit to the rule of buying only at reasonable prices, as to a remedy necessary in that disease."

Many years later in 1815, he would reflect back upon his European book-buying jaunts, by writing: "While residing in Paris, I devoted every afternoon I was disengaged, for a summer or two, in examining all the principal bookstores, turning over every book with my own hand, and putting by everything which related to America, and indeed whatever was rare and valuable in every science. Besides this, I had standing orders during the whole time I was in Europe, on its principal book-marts, particularly Amsterdam, Frankfort, Madrid and London, for such works relating to America as could not be found in Paris." (*Letter to Samuel H. Smith*, 21 September, 1814.)

Jefferson's own words verify his attentiveness to books "related to America" as he followed Madison's directive to purchase books for a national library. Regarding his own acquisitions, his correspondence of that period indicates that he had little interest in "embellished" books; his chief interest was the content of an author's work.

MARIA COSWAY

During Jefferson's time in Paris, an unhappily married Englishwoman named Maria Cosway stepped into his life for six weeks. Maria had the reputation of being "coquettish," but she considered herself a devout Catholic and conducted herself, accordingly. Nonetheless, legions of smitten admirers fell at her feet, including, quite literally, Thomas Jefferson. One afternoon in 1786, he showed

Maria Cosway. *Public domain.*

off for her by leaping over a fence. Landing off-balance, he fell on his right arm and broke, or permanently dislocated, his wrist.

Jefferson's passion for Cosway had cooled considerably before her departure for England, but after they parted ways, he wrote her a letter known as *A Dialogue of the Head vs. the Heart.* This artfully written letter presents a debate between Jefferson's Head (the voice of reason) and Heart (the voice of emotion).

Though right-handed, Jefferson had no choice but to write with his left hand because of the injury to his right wrist. He began his lengthy letter by admitting his loneliness, but very quickly he shifted the tone of his letter so that it reads as an entertaining and revealing conversation between "head" and "heart." Speaking first from his "head," he argues against the logic of opening one's door to emotion, for in walk the pains of disappointment, separation and loss. More than once he mentions his crippled wrist, as agonizing proof of the "folly" of love. Speaking, then, from his "heart," Jefferson contends that the pleasures of compassion and love are worth all risks of pain—not love of Maria Cosway, alone, but love of family and friends, compassion for strangers in need, and lastly, devotion to nation.

It is an extraordinary letter in that it transcends a mere love letter to Cosway to become a poignant revelation of Jefferson's approach to living both a judicious and passion-filled life.

The Head vs. The Heart Letter
(Abridged)

My Dear Madam, Having performed the last sad office of handing you into your carriage at the pavillon de St. Denis . . . I turned on my heel & walked, more dead than alive, to the opposite door, where my own was awaiting me. . . I was carried home. Seated by my fireside, solitary & sad, the following dialogue took place between my Head & my Heart:

Head. Well, friend, you seem to be in a pretty trim.

Heart. I am . . . Overwhelmed with grief . . .

Head. These are the eternal consequences of your warmth & precipitation . . . I often told you . . . how imprudent it is to place your affections, without reserve, on objects you must so soon lose, & whose loss when it comes must cost you such severe pangs . . .

All night you tossed us from one side of the bed to the other. No sleep, no rest. The poor crippled wrist too, never left one moment in the same position, now up, now down, now here, now there; was it to be wondered at if its pains returned? [M]y friend, you must mend your manners.

Advance then with caution, the balance in your hand. Put into one scale the pleasures, which any object may offer; but put fairly into the other the pains, which are to follow, & see which preponderates . . . Do not bite at the bait of pleasure till you know there is no hook beneath it.

The art of life is the art of avoiding pain: & he is the best pilot who steers clearest of the rocks & shoals with which he is beset . . .

Hence the inestimable value of intellectual pleasures. Even in our power, always leading us to something new, never cloying, we ride serene & sublime above the concerns of this mortal world, contemplating truth & nature, matter & motion, the laws which bind up their existence, & that eternal being who made & bound them up by those laws.

Let this be our employ. Leave the bustle & tumult of society to those who have not talents to occupy themselves without them . . .

Jefferson then shifted the subject of his letter to his love of family and friends:

Head. Friendship is but another name for an alliance with the follies & the misfortunes of others. Our own share of miseries is sufficient: why enter then as volunteers into those of another?

Heart. But friendship is precious, not only in the shade but in the sunshine of life . . . I will recur for proof to the days we have lately passed [with Maria Cosway]. On these indeed the sun shone brightly . . . From the presence of our charming companion . . . Alone, the scene would have been dull & insipid: the participation of it with her gave it relish . . .

Believe me then my friend, that that is a miserable arithmetic, which could estimate friendship at nothing, or at less than nothing.

Respect for you [Head] has induced me to enter into this discussion, & to hear principles uttered which I detest & abjure. Respect for myself now obliges me to recall you into the proper limits of your office.

When nature assigned us the same habitation, she gave us over it a divided empire. To you she allotted the field of science; to me that of morals. When the circle is to be squared, or the orbit of a comet to be traced; when the arch of greatest strength, or the solid of least resistance is to be investigated, take up the problem; it is yours; nature has given me no cognizance of it.

In like manner, in denying to you the feelings of sympathy, of benevolence, of gratitude, of justice, of love, of friendship, she has excluded you from their controul. To these she has adapted the mechanism of the heart. Morals were too essential to the happiness of man to be risked on the incertain combinations of the head. She laid their foundation therefore in sentiment, not in science. That she gave to all, as necessary to all: this to a few only, as sufficing with a few.

I know indeed that you pretend authority to the sovereign controul of our conduct in all its parts: & a respect for your grave saws & maxims, a desire to do what is right, has sometimes induced me to conform to your counsels.

Again shifting his emphasis, Jefferson wrote about compassion for strangers in need, which clearly reveals his benevolent heart:

Heart. A few facts however which I can readily recall to your memory, will suffice to prove to you (Head) that nature has not organized you for our moral direction. Again, when the poor woman came to ask a charity in Philadelphia, you whispered that she looked like a drunkard, & that half a dollar was enough to give her for the alehouse. Those who want the dispositions to give, easily find reasons why they ought not to give. When I sought her out afterwards, & did what I should have done at first, you know that she employed the money immediately towards placing her child at school.

Without missing a beat, Jefferson expressed, then, his devotion to nation:

Heart. If our country, when pressed with wrongs at the point of the bayonet, had been governed by its heads instead of its hearts, where should we have been now? Hanging on a gallows as high as Hamans. . . . we threw up a few pulsations of our warmest blood; . . . we put our existence to the hazard when the hazard seemed against us, and we saved our country: justifying at the same time the ways of Providence, whose precept is to do always what is right, and leave the issue to him.

And as his Head vs. Heart Letter neared its conclusion, Jefferson chided the "logical" side of himself, writing:

Heart. In short, my friend [Head], as far as my recollection serves me, I do not know that I ever did a good thing on your suggestion, or a dirty one without it. I do forever then disclaim your interference in my province. Fill papers as you please with triangles & squares . . . But leave me to decide when & where friendships are to be contracted . . .

Wealth, title, office, are no recommendations to my friendship . . . We are not immortal ourselves, my friend; how can we expect our enjoyments to be so? We have no rose without its thorn . . .

It is the law of our existence; & we must acquiesce. It is the condition annexed to all our pleasures, not by us who receive, but by him who gives them.

True, this condition is pressing cruelly on me at this moment. I feel more fit for death than life. But when I look back on the pleasures of which it is the consequence, I am conscious they were worth the price I am paying . . . I comfort myself with expectations of their promised return. Hope is sweeter than despair.

Know then, my friend, that I have taken these good people into my bosom; that I have lodged them in the warmest cell I could find: that I love them, & will continue to love them through life: that if fortune should dispose them on one side the globe, & me on the other, my affections shall pervade its whole mass to reach them . . .

And finally, in closing his expressive letter, Jefferson asked that Maria remember him to "Mr. Cosway"—not exactly the words of a man in love. Interestingly, he did not sign his name when he wrote:

I thought this a favorable proposition whereon to rest the issue of the dialogue. So I put an end to it by calling for my night-cap . . . Present me in the most friendly terms to Mr. Cosway, & receive me into your own recollection with a partiality & a warmth, proportioned, not to my own poor merit, but to the sentiments of sincere affection & esteem with which I have the honour to be, my dear Madam, your most obedient humble servant.

Truly this is a singular letter for it reads like an intimate confession, an exposé of self that reveals the heart and mind of a man known, and yet unknown. Those who have read Jefferson's letter often ask if he mailed it to Maria Cosway, and if she replied in kind. Endrina Tay, the Associate Librarian at Monticello's library, provided the answer: "Yes, TJ's letter to Maria Cosway was dated October 12, 1786, enclosed in another letter to Cosway dated October 13, 1786, and forwarded to her via John Trumbull."

On October 30, 1786, Maria Cosway sent a letter in reply to *The Head vs. The Heart Letter*, part of which reads:

"[How I wish I] could answer the Dialogue! But I hon[estly] think my heart is invisable, and Mute, at this moment more than usual . . . Your letter could employ me for some time, an hour to Consider every word, to every sentence I could write a volume . . . . Why do you say so Many kind things? Why present so many opportunities for my feeling undeserving of them, why not leave me a free consolation in admiring a friend, without the temptation [?] to my Vanity? I wish your heart [?] for it is too good. It expands to the Objects he [?] too Much of his own, and blinds the reality of its demerit."

She closed her letter by signing her married name.

Their correspondence continued for several years in spite of their time-consuming responsibilities—his political duties as vice president and president, and hers in the establishment and management of two parochial schools and a convent for Catholic nuns.

The pain in Jefferson's wrist plagued him the rest of his life. At times he was reduced to reading lighter "petit" books, but the worst consequence of his show-off leap over the fence was that his treasured violin had to be put aside.

Wolves Over Sheep

While serving as Minister (1784-1789), Jefferson witnessed the final days of France's feudal economy under absolute rule by king and church. With his ever-observant eye, he wrote a letter from Paris, the center of dissent:

"Societies exist under three forms sufficiently distinguishable. 1. Without government, as among our Indians. 2. Under governments wherein the will of every one has a just influence, as is the case in England in a slight degree, and in our states in a great one. 3. Under governments of force: as is the case in all other monarchies and in most of the other republics. To have an idea of the curse of existence under these last, they must be seen. *It is a government of wolves over sheep.*

"It is a problem, not clear in my mind, that the 1st. condition is not the best. But I believe it to be inconsistent with any great degree of population. The second state has a great deal of good in it. The mass of mankind under that enjoys a precious degree of liberty and happiness. It has its evils too: the principal of which is the turbulence to which it is subject. But weigh this against the oppressions of monarchy, and it becomes nothing. Malo periculosam, libertatem quam quietam servitutem. Even this evil is productive of good. It prevents the degeneracy of government, and nourishes a general attention to the public affairs. ***I hold it that a little rebellion now and then is a good thing, and as necessary in the political world as storms in the physical.*** Unsuccessful rebellions indeed generally establish the incroachments [sic] on the rights of the people, which have produced them. An observation of this truth should render honest republican governors so mild in their punishment of rebellions, as not to discourage them too much. It is a medecine [sic] necessary for the sound health of government." *(Letter to James Madison, January 30, 1787.)*

Jefferson's observations were accurate. While the "wolves" danced minuets and dined off gold plates, the "sheep" were facing ruin and hardship as France raced headfirst towards bankruptcy brought about, in large part, by its role in the French and Indian War (1754 -1763) and its financial and military contributions to the American Revolution (the War of Independence could have been prolonged, or lost without France's assistance).

In 1789, adverse weather spoiled crops, the price of bread doubled, and protestors smeared the streets of Paris with blood. The French Revolution had begun.

FYI: American Exceptionalism

The French aristocrat Alexis de Tocqueville (1805-1859) toured America to purposefully study our government. Highly educated and versed in political theory, he documented his findings in his book, *Democracy in America,* in which he described our nation as "exceptional."

Alexis de Tocqueville.

De Tocqueville had incredible insight. America is qualitatively different from other nations in that we are the fairest-minded, most humanitarian of all the republics that have ever existed in the course of the world's history. The evidence is clear: America has fought more wars to free the oppressed, and has fed, clothed, doctored, rebuilt, and welcomed more people than any other nation, and all we have ever asked in return is a place to bury our war-dead.

Inarguably, Thomas Jefferson defined American Exceptionalism in his political and philosophical writings, and over the centuries, his succinct and brilliant words have buoyed our nation in the deepest, roughest waters.

The French Revolution, 1789-1799

Seemingly overnight, widespread riots throughout France escalated into brutal, indiscriminate acts of cruelty against members of the nobility, church, and government. On July 14, a mob stormed a Parisian fortress, the Bastille, in search of weapons to kill any and all supporters of absolutism, while in the countryside, peasants rose up to protest the feudal tradition of forced allegiance to landlords and king with contractual manorial dues (rents paid by serfs to farm a noble's land).

France's social and political chaos was underpinned by the Enlightenment precept that man's advancement through *Reason* requires freedom of thought and practice; a precept learned through books.

Inspired by America's successful revolution, those outside France's circles of privilege demanded basic freedoms and in the end, the *Declaration of The Rights of Man* (1798) made claim to the freedoms of speech, worship, and assembly; Louis XVI was tried for High Treason and sentenced to the guillotine; arbitrary arrests were abolished; the hierarchy of the Church was restructured; and guilds were eliminated, which opened trades to all citizens.

But in September 1789, the decade-long revolution was just beginning as Jefferson prepared to leave his diplomatic post in France. In that month of September, only weeks after the storming of the Bastille, he personally oversaw the crating of his books for the Atlantic crossing. All his thoughts centered upon his long-awaited retirement to Monticello and the major renovations he would make of his home.

At least that was his train of thought until a letter arrived from President Washington, in which he requested that Thomas Jefferson serve as Secretary of State on the strength of his personal observations of the French Rebellion—insightful observations that would guide American policy during France's cataclysmic shift from a repressive monarchy to a modern republic. Placing nation before self, Jefferson accepted the Cabinet position.

Before his ship set sail, Jefferson amended his book catalogue to include the nearly 2000 books he had acquired in Europe. Most of them were listed under four categories: ancient and modern languages (grammars and dictionaries), and geography and politics (a majority of these works referenced America, many of which were printed in the French language). Throughout the voyage all 86 crates of books stayed secure and dry in the ship's hold—years would pass before any one book would be shelved in Monticello's Library.

Arrogance and Provocative Gowns

Upon his arrival in America, Jefferson observed some disturbing changes in society that had come about during his absence. As example, at a state dinner in New York City, he noticed a shift in the attitude of the privileged class—gentlemen were displaying manners and opinions that bordered on arrogance, and ladies had regressed to wearing "provocative gowns, the kind favored by imperial French women."

He became concerned that America's elite might follow the crooked path towards absolutism.

Secretary of State in the Administration of George Washington 1790-1793

Thomas Jefferson was sworn in as Secretary of State on March 22, 1790. During his three-year tenure, the Department of State would consist of four clerks (correspondents with foreign states) and a messenger. The books Jefferson brought back from Europe became his reference tools for resolving issues such as commerce and territorial treaties with Britain and Spain, and disputes over America's navigational rights on the Mississippi River.

During his stay in office, Jefferson assisted Major Pierre Charles L'Enfant in designing the capital city that would be built in the District of Columbia. Jefferson also took part in the selection of architectural designs for the first government buildings. He accomplished those tasks by referencing books of architecture and history, and by drawing on the observations he had made of neoclassic architecture while in France.

The demanding duties of working with L'Enfant and of serving in Washington's Cabinet kept Jefferson out of bookshops, but he made use of his free time by reading his European collection.

In1793, Jefferson stepped down from public office, fully determined to follow the example of Horace (the Ancient Roman poet) by losing himself in leisurely reading to "quaff sweet forgetfulness of life's cares." But once again, Jefferson's long sought-after retirement at his home, amidst his family and treasured books, was short-lived.

Vice President Jefferson, 1797-1801

Convinced to run for the presidency against one of his closest friends, John Adams, Jefferson soon found himself knee-deep in a scurrilous, mud-slinging campaign that would destroy their friendship for almost 10 years. At battle's end, Jefferson lost the presidential election by 3 votes. To add salt to his wounds, an absurd flaw in the *Constitution* forced Jefferson to serve as Vice President under his new and ardent enemy for 5 long years (1797-1801).

John Adams.

On January 18, 1800, towards the end of that personally difficult period as vice-president, Jefferson mailed a letter to his longtime friend Dr. Joseph Priestley, the theologian, chemist (discoverer of Oxygen), and educator. In his letter, Jefferson wrote of the "sublime luxury" found in ancient books:

"The Greeks & Romans have left us the present models which exist of fine composition, whether we examine them as works of reason, or of style & fancy; and to them we probably owe these characteristics of modern composition. I know of no composition of any other antient [sic] people, which merits the least regard as a model for it's matter or style. To all this I add, that to read the Latin & Greek authors in their original, is a sublime luxury . . . I thank on my knees, [my father] who directed my early education, for having put into my possession this rich source of delight; and I would not exchange it for anything which I could then have acquired, & have not since acquired."

Swampland: Washington, District of Columbia

In the early years of our nation, the capital moved from New York City to Philadelphia and finally, in 1790, to the District of Columbia. The Commissioners of the District offered a 500-dollar prize for an architectural design for the Executive Mansion (White House). Architects, worldwide, entered the competition, including Jefferson who submitted an anonymous entry. The Irish architect James Hoban based his prize-winning design on Leinster House, the palace in Dublin now serving as the seat of the Oireachtas, the National Parliament of Ireland.

On October 13, 1792, George Washington laid the cornerstone of the Executive Mansion, and the site of government officially shifted from the cultural center of Philadelphia to the swampland of the District of Columbia.

With suddenness, Congress lost its access to research materials from Franklin's Library Company and the grey city's numerous bookshops. To amend that problem, President Adams signed an act in 1800 that established an official Library of Congress to be housed in the new Capitol building. The sum of 5000 dollars was appropriated, but the collection would largely be comprised of the books Jefferson had acquired in Europe at Madison's request. In a relatively short time, the library opened its doors to Senators and Representatives—the public had no access to the library.

Meanwhile, the nation prepared for a new administration as the third presidential election came down to a tie between Thomas Jefferson and Aaron Burr.

From the inception of our nation, major conflicts had ensued between two parties: the Democratic-Republicans and the Federalists. Thomas Jefferson assumed the leadership of the Democratic-Republicans, the champions of states' rights, in clear opposition to Alexander Hamilton's Federalists, whose platform called for a strong, centralized government.

The resolution of the tie between Jefferson and Burr rested in the House of Representatives. Although Rep. Hamilton (Pennsylvania) abhorred both candidates, he distrusted Burr and lobbied on behalf of Jefferson. Defeated, Aaron Burr had no choice but to be sworn in as Vice President, another unhappy consequence of the flaw in the *Constitution.*

FYI: Duel in Weehawken

Hamilton and Burr's political arguments intensified during a governor's race (NY, 1804) when Hamilton attempted to thwart Burr's bid as an Independent. Burr lost, and after the publication of Hamilton's "despicable opinion" of the losing candidate, a duel became a question of honor. Burr believed the challenge would increase his political standing, and Hamilton accepted, confident that most duels ended with purposely missed shots, even though his son had been killed in a duel.

On the morning of July 11, 1804, the two men climbed a cliff to the dueling grounds of Weehawken, N.J.; each fired one shot from .56 caliber dueling pistols—Hamilton deliberately fired askew, but Burr aimed with deadly accuracy. Hamilton died in New York City the next day and Burr was charged with murder. Upon ending his term of Vice President he fled south, but in 1807 he was arrested and tried for leading armed forces against New Orleans. Although acquitted of treason, he was publically condemned as a traitor, which didn't stop him from resuming his law practice in New York.

Thomas Jefferson, Third President of the United States, 1801-1809

The French Revolution had ended by the start of Jefferson's presidency, thus all threats of America's involvement in the crisis in France had been averted. Years of peace were anticipated until the pashas of North Africa reared their greedy heads to demand the continuation of America's payment of tribute—a form of extortion to safeguard ships and seamen from captivity by the Barbary Pirates. The Islamic states of North Africa (Morocco, Algiers, Tunis and Tripoli) sponsored the piracy to extort a million dollars a year from the American "infidels."

Several years earlier in 1785, Thomas Jefferson and John Adams had attempted to negotiate an agreement with Tripoli's envoy, but were told: "It [is] written in the Koran, that . . . it [is] the duty of [mussulmen] to plunder and enslave [all infidels]." Jefferson became convinced that the paying of tribute only increased the attacks and ransoms; President Washington, and still later President John Adams, would come to agree with Jefferson, but they felt the extortion had to be paid until the navy could be built up for a successful war against the pirates.

As president, Thomas Jefferson drew the line in sand.

His first weapon was a book. Having made a careful reading of the *Koran*, he had a deep understanding of Islamic philosophy and the religious motives behind "[mussulmen who] sprang to the deck of an enemy's ship, [holding] a dagger in each hand and a third in his mouth." Armed by that knowledge, Jefferson ended the upfront extortion fee of $225,000 paid by each new presidential administration, and stopped the annual payments of $25,000 to each of an ever-increasing number of pashas.

In 1801, Tripoli responded by cutting down the flagstaff in front of its U. S. Consulate, the Barbary style of declaring war. In reply, Jefferson acknowledged: "[I am] unauthorized by the *Constitution*, without the sanction of Congress, to go beyond the line of defense . . ." But in a show of confidence, in his first message to Congress he stated: "To this state of general peace with which we have been blessed, one only exception exists. Tripoli, the least considerable of the Barbary States . . . I sent a small squadron of frigates into the Mediterranean."

Congress never declared war, formally, but Jefferson was authorized "to instruct the commanders of armed American vessels to seize all vessels and goods of the Pasha of Tripoli." Prior to Congress' authorization, Jefferson had already stepped over the *Constitution* to act, in his opinion, for the good of the nation.

When all was said and done, there would be two Barbary Wars: the first against Tripoli (1801–1805), and the second against Algiers (1815–1816). Both conflicts put the U. S. Navy and Marine Corps to the test.

A skirmish in 1804 best exemplifies America's military ingenuity and courage in those wars. In October of 1803, the frigate *Philadelphia* had been captured, its crew held hostage. On a night in February 1804, Lt. Stephen Decatur led a detachment of marines aboard a captured Tripolitan ketch. As expected, the pirates manning the *Philadelphia* floated into close range for a better look—close enough for the Lt. and his men to storm the ship, overpower the Tripolitan crew, and set the vessel on fire to prevent its further use by enemy hands.

British Admiral Horatio Nelson, an officer noted for his own courage, called the Marine's action "the most bold and daring act of the age."

Jefferson's war against the pashas of North Africa clearly illustrates how he acted for the good of the nation although "unauthorized by the *Constitution*, without the sanction of Congress, to go beyond the line of defense."

The purchase of the Louisiana Territory offers another excellent example of Jefferson being caught between the proverbial "rock and hard place" as president in the exercise of his prerogative to act for the good of the nation.

Although no provisions were provided in the *U. S. Constitution* for the acquisition of land, Jefferson borrowed gold from England to purchase the Louisiana Territory from Napoleon (1803). Though widely criticized in his time for his "hubristic act" of stepping over the *Constitution*, we, in our more modern time, can't find a shred of hubris in Jefferson's act; instead, we credit his farsightedness in recognizing the rich potential of unexplored lands and waters that nearly doubled America's area.

Slander

In 1802, the second year of Jefferson's presidency, a political journalist named Callender published a defamatory article in a Richmond newspaper with one purpose in mind: to destroy the reputation of Thomas Jefferson.

James Thomson Callender (1758-1803) was a political writer who fled arrest in Scotland in 1793 after public condemnation of his published criticism of government. In America, he wrote bitterly against everything the new nation held sacred—he denounced the *Constitution* as "undemocratic," and accused George Washington of being the "debaucher" of the people. Fired from the *Philadelphia Gazette,* and deeply in debt, he solicited money from an acquaintance, Thomas Jefferson, who then used his influence to secure Callender a position with the Republican newspaper, *The Aurora.* Jefferson fully expected Callender to attack the Federalists in print, but he never condoned yellow journalism and that was Callender's preferred style of writing. As example, determined to defame the Federalist Alexander Hamilton, Callender wrote an article to expose Hamilton's affair with Maria Reynolds, a married woman.

In 1800, Callender was jailed under the Sedition Act for writing an anti-Federalist pamphlet. Upon his release in 1801, he expected President Jefferson to reward him for his anti-Federalist journalism by making him the Postmaster of Richmond, but Jefferson wanted nothing more to do with Callender. Infuriated, he allied himself with a Federalist newspaper in Richmond to launch vicious attacks against President Jefferson, his one-time benefactor. In turn, Jefferson responded, writing: "I am really mortified at the base ingratitude of Callender. It presents human nature in a hideous form."

Callender stepped up his attack in the press. Beginning on September 1, 1802, he published a series of articles alleging that President Jefferson was keeping a "concubine, his slave Sally Hemings," and that he had fathered her children. The following year, Callender's life began to unravel from alcoholism; in July of 1803 he fell into a drunken stupor and drowned in the James River. It may have been a suicide; he left behind a confessional letter that expressed his regret for writing with a slanderous pen, but he didn't mention Alexander Hamilton or Thomas Jefferson, by name.

To this day, James Callender's slanderous articles tarnish Thomas Jefferson's reputation. It is true that in recent years a DNA link has been found between the Jefferson family line and Eston, one of Sally Hemings' sons, but it should be noted that the link points to Jefferson's entire clan, not to him or any one individual. Sheila Seamans Byrnes, a highly published and widely respected genealogist in Syracuse, New York, explained: "In 1989, DNA samples from Field Jefferson, a living descendant of Thomas Jefferson's paternal uncle and a male descendant of Eston Hemings, were analyzed. The evidence showed a perfect match between Y-DNA with less than one in a thousand chance of being a random coincidence. Although the analysis showed a Y-DNA match between the Jefferson and Hemings families, it does not prove Thomas Jefferson was the father of Eston Hemings. The DNA evidence is inclusive. The study only proves a connection between the Jefferson and Hemings families. Another male member of the Jefferson family could have been the father of Eston Hemings."

Since 1998, many historians have focused on Jefferson's youngest brother, Randolph, as the father of Hemings' children. He resided near Monticello and visited often, usually in an inebriated state. A revealing description of him was provided by the slave Isaac Jefferson who stated: "[Randolph Jefferson] used to come out among the black people, play the fiddle and dance half the night and stay the nights in their cabins."

Not only did Monticello's slaves refer to Jefferson's brother as "Uncle Randolph" but until 1976, Eston's descendents claimed to be the offspring of "Mr. Jefferson's uncle." Of greater significance, a few days after Eston's birth, Randolph filed a will naming his 6 "legitimate" sons as his rightful heirs, presumably to avoid paternity claims by Sally Hemings.

Jefferson's lifelong practice was to avoid public responses to personal attacks, but in 1803 at the height of the assault against his reputation, he denounced yellow journalism by stating: "Our newspapers for the most part, present only the caricatures of disaffected minds." Still later, in 1805, a few days after a Federalist newspaper in Washington, D. C. reprinted allegations that he had had an affair with the wife of his friend, John Walker, and that Sally Hemings was his "concubine," Thomas Jefferson wrote a letter to the Secretary of the Navy Robert Smith. In that letter, he admitted that while young and single he had made improper advances to Mrs. Walker, but added: "It is the only one [charge] founded in truth among all their allegations against me [regarding Sally Hemings]." And in 1816, after another newspaper reprinted Callender's slanderous charge, Jefferson wrote a letter to a trusted friend, the physician Dr. George Logan, in which he stated: "As to Federal slanders, I never wished them to be answered . . . Their approbation has taught a lesson, useful to the world that the man who fears no truths, has nothing to fear from lies. I should have fancied myself half guilty had I condescended to put pen to paper in refutation of their falsehoods, or drawn to them respect by any notice of myself."

Thomas Jefferson was a man of his word, and therefore his own words end this controversy.

Lewis and Clark Expeditions, 1804-1806

Throughout his second term, President Jefferson kept America from becoming involved in the Napoleonic Wars, the conflicts fought between France's Napoleon Bonaparte and several European nations (1799-1815). Unfortunately, the embargoes Jefferson placed on American shipping to combat France's and England's interference with the neutrality of American vessels failed, and embittered the public against him. People have short-term memories; critical of Jefferson as president, they overlooked his reduction of the national

Merriwether Lewis and William Clark. *Public Domain.*

budget by a third, and his elimination of several, highly unpopular taxes such as the Whiskey Tax. In an attempt to restore the nation's faith in his leadership, Jefferson backed the Lewis-Clark expeditions, but his more noble aim was to find a water route that would connect the Pacific Ocean with the Mississippi River system.

Having sealed The Louisiana Purchase the previous year in 1803, Jefferson commissioned army volunteers under the command of Captain Meriwether Lewis and Second Lieutenant William Clark to map out "the most direct & practicable water communication across this continent, for the purposes of commerce." In May 1804, the expedition departed from St. Louis on the Mississippi River to make its way westward through the continental divide to the Pacific coast. Their mission involved critical objectives: to explore and map the newly acquired territory; to find a practical route across the Western half of the continent; to establish an American presence in the vast territory; to study the area's geography (plants, animals, waters, and land masses); and to establish relations and trade with the Missouri, Teton Sioux, Mandan and other tribes. In 1806, Lewis and Clark reported their findings to Jefferson, along with sketches, journals, gifts from the Indian nations, and detailed maps (some of which Jefferson displayed in the front hall of Monticello).

Lewis and Clark's explorations of America's newfound lands of natural wealth and beauty were recorded in numerous books, magazines and newspapers that were read by an astonished world.

The Window into Jefferson's Mind and Heart

Earlier, at the start of his presidency, Jefferson had to deal with criticisms from clerics from different churches (primarily Episcopalians and Congregationalists) who sought to establish a particular denomination as the national religion. Jefferson strongly believed that the government's endorsement of a national religion would constitute "tyranny over the mind of man." Warned by Dr. Benjamin Rush to expect verbal attacks by the more outspoken members of clergy, Jefferson replied to him on September 23, 1800, writing: "I have sworn upon the altar of god, eternal hostility against every form of tyranny over the mind of man. But this is all they have to fear from me." Even though Jefferson swore an oath upon the "altar of god" he opened himself to the charge of being irreligious, which in that era was a death knell for one's reputation.

Quite the reverse, although castigated as being nonreligious, Jefferson possessed a rare spiritual dimension, a centering of his thought on the historical and religious figure of Christ. He viewed compassion as the core of true faith, and strove to be Christ-like in his every word and act. His enemies ignored that part of him. Having failed to destroy him politically with the slander he had fathered a slave's children, they vilified him in the press by accusing him of being as "hedonistic" as the French he admired, a people disdained by most Americans. Labeled a "howling atheist," Jefferson wrote: "Every word which goes forth from me, whether verbally or in writing, becomes the subject of so much malignant distortion, and perverted construction . . . "

How does this controversy tie in with this chapter's treatment of the books, libraries and writings in Jefferson's life?

Ironically, the supposedly "godless" president was secretly working on a religious manuscript, the end result of intimate conversations about his beliefs with trusted friends James Madison and Benjamin Rush. They became relentless in urging Jefferson to make his faith known by writing a book about his beliefs, and he finally conceded. But to avoid the "drudgery" he had found in the writing of his first book, *Notes of the State of Virginia,* he chose an editorial approach to his new project; a somewhat unorthodox approach, but one that fit his rather unorthodox beliefs—after all, he once said about himself: "I am a sect by myself, as far as I know."

And so, throughout his presidency, whenever he had time and privacy, he used a razor to extract the words of Christ from four translations of scripture in Greek, Latin, French and English--words Jefferson viewed as Christ's essential teachings. As a Man of Reason and a Deist, Jefferson did not extract the miracles credited to Christ, for in his opinion, they were not in accordance with natural laws. He then glued the sacred words onto folios of blank paper, rearranging Matthew, John, Luke and Mark's Gospels in a single narrative by pasting the Greek and Latin translations in parallel columns on the left, and placing the French and English versions on the right. Next, using iron gall ink, he wrote a table of contents and added commentaries in the margins.

Jefferson titled his work, *The Life and Morals of Jesus of Nazareth Extracted Textually from the Gospels in Greek, Latin, French and English*, but more often than not his book is referred to as *The Jefferson Bible*. This one manuscript is a perfect summary of his faith. He once stated: "Had the doctrines of Jesus been preached always as pure as they came from his lips, the whole civilized world would now have been Christian." *(Letter to Dr. Benjamin Waterhouse, 26 June 1822.)*

No one has successfully trespassed the innermost thoughts of Thomas Jefferson. To understand a man of such practiced reticence, we study the books he acquired, read or wrote, for they are windows into his mind. *The Jefferson Bible* offers far more than that; the Jefferson Bible is a window into his heart because it contains, in his own words, "The most sublime and benevolent code of morals which has ever been offered to man." (*Letter to John Adams, 12 October 1813.)*

It can be said with confidence that he centered his "code of morals" upon the teachings of Jesus Christ.

Respite

As mentioned earlier, Jefferson viewed the cessation of life as a biological process; therefore, to his way of thinking, an emotional reaction to death seemed fundamentally irrational. Steeped in the philosophy of rationalism, he saw death as a step at the end of life's journey "to an ecstatic meeting with the friends we have loved and lost and whom we shall still love and never lose again." (*Letter to John Adams, 12 October 1818.)*

But just as he rarely smiled, he did find joy in life; and just as he never wept, publically and perhaps privately, he did mourn his loss of loved ones.

In 1804, amidst the mounting stresses of his presidency, his daughter, Maria (Polly) died from complications of childbirth. In the depth of his sorrow he wrote to his close friend, John Page (then Governor of Virginia) about Polly, his "vision of beauty," and confided his sense of emptiness in having lost half of all he owned—he meant one of his two daughters. Jefferson wrote:

"When you and I look back over the country which we have passed, what a field of slaughter does it exhibit! Where are all the friends who entered it with us, under all the inspiring energies of health and hope? But we have the traveler's consolation, every step shortens the distance we have to go; the end of the journey is in sight, the bed wherein we are to rest, and to rise in the midst of the friends we have lost. My loss [of my daughter] is great indeed. Others may lose of their abundance, but I, of my want, have lost even the half of all I had. My evening prospects now hang on the slender thread of a single life [my only daughter, Martha]. The hope with which I looked forward to the moment when I was to retire to that domestic comfort from which the last great step is to be taken is fearfully blighted" (June 25, 1804).

Sorrow brought on one of Jefferson's blinding headaches. To alleviate the pain he paced in his office for hours, or rode his horse along isolated roads, but in the end he escaped the pain of loss through quiet hours of reading—books had become Jefferson's one respite in his often-lonely, often-criticized, and often-troubled presidential years.

As would be expected, throughout his stay in office he acquired a massive number of books. The year before Polly's death, he acknowledged his almost obsessive practice of book-buying to a French bookseller, writing: "My collection of books is now so extensive, & myself so far advanced in life that I have little occasion to add to it." But numerous acquisitions lay in his future.

Some books came to him without cost. Authors, the world over, sent him complimentary copies of their works, and private libraries, such as that of his former law professor George Wythe, were bequeathed to him. Wythe, who died in 1806 as the victim of accidental arsenic poisoning (his great nephew had intended to poison his uncle's other heirs), wrote that he willed his library to Jefferson knowing: "[My books were] perhaps not deserving a place in [Jefferson's] Museum, [but still they would be] most valuable to [Thomas, than] any thing which I have to bestow." Jefferson was deeply moved by his professor's generosity, but their mutual friends weren't surprised, for Wythe had often mentioned his admiration of Jefferson as a Bookman.

During his last years in public office President Jefferson acquired smaller books (octavos and duodecimos) primarily because they were lighter in weight. His wrist, injured from his leap over the fence in Paris, never healed properly so at times it was uncomfortable for him to hold books in larger formats (folios and quartos). Too, smaller formats were less expensive and required less space on his already crowded shelves; however, most of the small books would end up at his estate, Poplar Forest, near Lynchburg, Virginia, where he retreated each year for a few weeks of reading (his "petit format library" would hold 605 volumes, largely works of poetry, literature and foreign languages).

While acquiring titles for his private library, President Jefferson addressed the book needs of Congress, as well. By the end of his second term another thousand books and tracts were purchased for the Congressional Library, and he felt confident that the incoming president, James Madison, would add thousands more. Of course, neither gentleman could see into the future, but in a very short span of years, both would decry the "barbarity" of a wartime act—the burning of the very books they had sacrificed time, money, and effort to accumulate.

But in 1809 all seemed right in Jefferson's world. As his second presidential term wound down to its final hours, Jefferson penned a letter to Pierrre-Samuel du Pont de Nemours, in which he wrote of his anxiousness to be finished with politics, and of his long-awaited return to "family . . . books and farms" (March 2, 1809).

Two days later on Inauguration Day, Jefferson politely declined Madison's gracious invitation to ride in the president's carriage, and instead rode his horse down Pennsylvania Avenue, his cherished grandson, Jeff, at his side. For Jefferson it was the moment he had waited for—the wearing of the coat and hat of an ordinary citizen. Later, at the Inaugural Ball, a guest noted to Jefferson: "You look so happy and satisfied . . . and Mr. Madison looks so serious not to say sad, that a spectator might imagine that you were the one coming in and he the one going out of office." The former president's reply was candid: "There's a good reason for my happy and his serious looks. I have got the burthen off my shoulders, while he has now got it on his."

One "burthen" he would carry back to Monticello was astronomical debt. He later wrote that he left political office with a clear conscience "in having added nothing to my private fortunes during my public service and of retiring with hands as clean as they are empty." (*Letter to Compte Diodati,* 1807.)

Today, Thomas Jefferson's presidential acts are regarded as visionary, but throughout both terms in office, Congress and powerful newspapers scarred him with their criticisms, all of which he fully expected. Prior to his election to the presidency, he rightly predicted he'd become "a constant butt for every shaft of calumny which malice & falsehood could form." *(Letter to Benjamin Rush, 23 September 1800.)*

There were successes, of course, and more than a few opulent "entertainments" complete with the finest wines, but his favored retreat from the burdens of his presidency was a comfortable chair amidst his books.

Sanctum Sanctorum

Freed from the responsibilities of state and nation, Jefferson anticipated years of leisure to fulfill the sentiment he had copied as a schoolboy into his commonplace book: to "idle [away his] hours . . . with books of the ancients." Unbeknownst to him, his library would soon be emptied of books, but that day was years away as Jefferson stepped into retirement.

Retirement?

Not in any sense of the word. Monticello was a hive of activity; the rooms, fields, and grounds were in constant use by family, guests, workmen and slaves, and Thomas Jefferson stood at the very center of all the commotion. Day in, day out, he attended to the tasks of his estate: the cultivation of gardens and fields, the inspections on horseback of his farms and private works, the institution of a brewery (excellent beers) and winery (undrinkable wines), the drawing up of architectural and academic designs for a school of higher learning, the writing of extensive even exhaustive correspondence, the pursuit of knowledge through research, the endless "entertainments" of legions of visitors . . . and so on and so on.

To escape the clamor of his estates, Jefferson would seclude himself in his private suite in the south wing. There he found quiet, but the sense of personal fulfillment he had striven for his entire life was found in only one room: the library, his "sanctum sanctorum."

Margaret Bayard Smith (1778-1844), the novelist and chronicler of society in the early years of the nation's capital, first met Jefferson through her husband, Samuel Harrison Smith, the founder of the newspaper, the *National Intelligencer*. In 1809, she wrote about her visit to Monticello, and in that piece she coined the phrase "sanctum sanctorum" to define Jefferson's library. She wrote: "When we descended to the hall, [Mr. Jefferson] asked us to pass into the Library, or as I called it his sanctum sanctorum, where any other feet than his own seldom intrude...

Margaret Bayard Smith. *PD.*

The library consists of books in all languages, and contains about twenty thousand vols. but so disposed that they do not give the idea of a great library."

The British diplomat and politician Sir Augustus Foster added to Smith's description, stating: "On the ground floor were . . . rooms . . . and the library, which contained several thousand volumes classed according to subject and language . . . In Mr. Jefferson's library there was a picture representing battle, painted by one of the Big-bellied tribes of Indians . . . If the library had been thrown open to guests, the President's country house would have been as agreeable a place to stay at as any I know, but it was there he sat and wrote and he did not like of course to be disturbed by visitors who in this part of the world are rather disposed to be indiscreet."

And so in the privacy of his suite Jefferson thought his large thoughts, wrote in blue ink, and read to his heart's content. To outsiders, his retirement years would have appeared tranquil, even idyllic, but trouble simmered beneath the facade of Monticello.

Logic or Illogic

Isaac Jefferson (1775-c.1849), a slave highly valued for his skills as a tinsmith, blacksmith and nail-maker, became Jefferson's trusted companion. Several years into the future, in 1845, Isaac would record an oral history of his years at Monticello. In one segment, he spoke of a typical scene in the library: "Old Master had abundance of books; sometimes would have twenty of 'em down on the floor at once—read fust [sic] one, then tother [sic]."

Isaac recalled the many times he had interrupted Jefferson's readings to ask a question, and how his "Old Master" without a shred of impatience or hesitation, would take down a book, turn to the exact page needed, and answer the question in detail.

Isaac Jefferson. *PD.*

How could Jefferson have had such intimate knowledge of the content of thousands of books? Did he possess a photographic memory? Possibly, but certainly the logic behind the systematic arrangement of his collection allowed him to place his hand on any book he desired, in an instant.

Jefferson based his library system on a concept from one of Sir Francis Bacon's books in which he conceived the human mind as having three major faculties: *Memory, Imagination, and Reason.* Bacon wrote: "The parts of human learning have reference to the three parts of man's understanding, which is the seat of learning: history to his memory, poesie [poetry] to his imagination, and philosophy to his reason" (1605).

According to Bacon's concept of learning, the Trinity (*Memory, Imagination and Reason*) permits man to comprehend Truth; comprehension of Truth expands into Understanding; and Understanding becomes Knowledge (illumination). If Knowledge is then acted upon, man gains a full experience of Truth.

Borrowing Bacon's concept of the Trinity, Jefferson designed a classification system, in which he organized his books by Chapters, or related areas of knowledge. Bacon's *Memory* became Jefferson's Chapter for books of History; *Imagination* became his Chapter for books of Fine Arts; and *Reason* became his Chapter for books of Philosophy.

The methodology behind Jefferson's Chapters provides insight about his unique view of the world. As example, he shelved books about foreign countries and the American states all together under the Chapter of Foreign Laws—that is, all of the states except Virginia, the only non-foreign state in the union, according to Jefferson.

Another example of Jefferson's orthodoxy was his placement of theology books under the Chapter Jurisprudence. Many questioned his logic, but he reasoned that religion was a "sphere of institutionalized moral suasion" and thus theology books fell under the philosophy of law. Indeed, he saw the world through unique eyes.

As a self-trained librarian, Jefferson modified his classification system for the particulars of a book collection. Back in 1779, while serving as Governor of Virginia, he designed a far different classification scheme for William and Mary's library; in 1818 he would modify that scheme to make it more appropriate for the University of Virginia's library.

Reunion

A war ended and another war began in 1812.

The first war, the one between John Adams and Thomas Jefferson, came to an end in 1812 after 9 acrimonious years, thanks to the intervention of their mutual friend Dr. Benjamin Rush. His earlier attempts to reunite them had all failed, but a casual remark changed the situation when someone overheard Adams say, "I always loved Jefferson, and still love him."

Learning of Adams' sentiment, Jefferson sent a letter to Dr. Rush, in which he wrote: "I only needed this knowledge to revive towards [Adams] all of the affections of the most cordial moments of our lives." He then asked Rush to arrange a reconciliation, which he did by persuading Adams to send a conciliatory letter to Jefferson—a letter concerning a book. Adams' note and Jefferson's courteous reply ended the war between them, and from that time on they kept in close contact through correspondence.

FYI: Peacemaker

Dr. Benjamin Rush (1745-1813) had a litany list of titles: Doctor of Medicine; Professor of Medical Theory at the University of Pennsylvania; Father of American Psychiatry; Founder of Dickenson College in Pennsylvania; Author; Delegate to the Continental Congress and Signer of the *Declaration of Independence.* Highly regarded, he was the first American physician to state that mental illness is not a "possession of demons" but rather a "disease of the mind." Yet, in spite of those accomplishments, Dr. Benjamin Rush is best remembered as the peacemaker between two stubborn men—the reunion he mediated brought about a treasure-trove of letters, the kind written by only the closest and wisest of friends.

Dr. Benjamin Rush. *PD.*

The War of 1812, June 18, 1812 – February 17, 1815

The other conflict began in June 1812, when America declared war against Britain, Ireland, and the Crown's colonies in Canada. The underlying causes were the massacres of frontiersmen, women and children in the Old Northwest by Britain's Indian allies, and the impressments of American sailors by the Royal Navy (British warships needed to be freshly manned in the ongoing Napoleonic Wars, 1799-1815).

To the world it appeared that America was engaging in a Second War of Independence with England, and in the first years of the conflict it looked as if England might win—and might then reclaim her lost colonies. On land, poorly led American forces were being trampled in Canada, largely because the New England states opposed the conflict for economic reasons and refused to supply logistic support and troops (those same states would threaten secession from the Union). On water, the situation was equally grim, in part because the Navy's small gunboats proved ineffective in defending ports from Imperial warships. Britain's blockade ruined agricultural exports, which caused economic hardships for farmers including Jefferson, although the blockade did stimulate the production of America's manufactured goods. In an attempt to divert the British from American ports, hundreds of privateers (mostly former pirates such as Jean LaFitte) were hired to attack England's merchant vessels in open waters, but that ploy largely failed.

Overall, the outlook for the United States looked bleak until 1814 when the tide turned. With the defeat of Napoleon, Britain reassigned legions of war-hardened soldiers to the American front, but by that point the U.S. military was better trained and led. On September 11th, America's small navy defeated the world's greatest naval power at the Battle of Plattsburgh, New York, on Lake Champlain. Defeat of the Royal Navy caused an immediate retreat by British forces to Lower Canada (the Commander-in-Chief, Lt. General, Sir George Prevost would be branded a coward since his army had far outnumbered the American forces).

Days later, on September 13, Fort McHenry in Baltimore withstood 25 hours of bombardment. Early the next morning a massive American flag was raised over the fort; deeply stirred, Francis Scott Key wrote the poem that would become our national anthem. Impressed by the Americans' spirit and courage, the Royal Navy withdrew from Baltimore to prepare for battle in New Orleans, while back in England, government officials prepared as well—for peace.

The *Treaty of Ghent* was signed in Belgium in December of 1814, but the document was slow in crossing the Atlantic for ratification by Congress. Unaware of the peace treaty, General Andrew Jackson (along with Indian allies, frontiersmen and Jean LaFitte's pirates) brutally crushed the King's Men in the swamps of New Orleans on January 8, 1815. Jackson claimed victory at the cost of 101 casualties, while the British reported their number of wounded and dead at 2,037, but the sacrifices were pointless in a war that had essentially ended. A month later, on February 17, 1815, Congress ratified the

Treaty of Ghent. The war over, the former boundaries between Canada and the United States were restored, and the impressments by the Royal Navy ceased, but the massacres on the Frontier would continue for long, bloody years.

Victory in war heightened America's sense of national pride. For the first time our country viewed itself as a world power, and the confidence born of national strength ushered in a long period of prosperity and peace until the states divided in civil war.

Chain Reaction

The War of 1812 played a major role in the history of the *Seven*.In a chain-reaction, our nation's "Second War of Independence" led to American soldiers burning government buildings in York, Canada, which led to revenge by British troops in the burning of Washington's government buildings, which led to the fiery destruction of the Congressional Library, which led to Congress' immediate need for replacement books, which led to Jefferson's sale of the Monticello Library, which led to the start of his Retirement Library and his conflation of Aeschylus' editions into the *Seven*, which led to Poor's Auction and G. C. Verplanck's purchase, which led, in time, to Barry's acquisition—all of which we now explore in this book by returning to the second year of the war, 1813, when American troops torched the Governor's home, the house of Parliament and other government buildings in York (Toronto) Canada.

To exact revenge, the following year British General Robert Ross launched a campaign to burn down Washington, D. C. On the 24th day of August in 1814, British Regulars (4000) advanced East from the Chesapeake Bay, mowed down ineffectual defenses at Bladensburg, Maryland, and marched into Washington, the city all but abandoned by then. Proceeding along a road (now Maryland Avenue, NE), they halted at the crossroads of 2nd Street and Constitution Ave, NE. Bullets were fired from the windows of a private residence, and the British responded by setting that house on fire.

The Union Jack flying over the city, the Regulars spread through the deserted streets, setting fire to the Capitol (the Rotunda had not yet been added), the Navy Yard, and the Treasury building. As a final insult, they advanced towards the Executive Mansion. At that moment, President James Madison (the *Father of the Constitution* and the author of the *Bill of Rights*) stood in the ranks of the 6,000 militiamen marching towards battle in Maryland, while back on the roof of the Mansion, his wife Dolley (a feisty woman noted for her beauty and courage) watched for her "dear husband's return" and optimistically ordered the dining room set for his dinner. Again resorting to her spyglass, she spotted enemy soldiers and prepared for escape, as thousands of Washingtonians had already done. At the last minute she refused to leave without Gilbert Stuart's famed portrait of George Washington; the painting was screwed to a wall so the canvas was cut from the frame and rolled up. Carrying Washington's portrait and a framed copy of the *Declaration of Independence*, Dolley fled to a prearranged place to meet her husband (the Stuart and document were not the originals, but she didn't want them defaced). The soldiers entered the Executive Mansion, and after dining at President Madison's table, they torched his home.

As Washington burned, sudden, perhaps providential rains poured down and quenched the fires even as several tornadoes swept through the city. Terrified, the soldiers retreated, but within weeks they would launch a campaign against Baltimore during which an American sharpshooter mortally wounded General Ross.

Prior to the bombardment of Ft. McHenry (Sep. 13&14, 1814) Francis Scott Key, a highly respected 35-year-old lawyer from Baltimore, boarded a British warship and successfully negotiated the release of a physician, Dr. William Beanes. While onboard, Key overheard the plan of attack, so he and his fellow Americans were detained under guard throughout the rainy night of bombardment on Ft. McHenry. When morning broke the cannons were silenced, and Key searched the smoke-filled sky for the fort's flag—if lowered, it would signal surrender, but an immense American flag showed through the smudged skies. Major George Armistead had ordered a flag so large that "the British will have no difficulty in seeing it from a distance." Yielding to the Americans' fortitude, the British withdrew their fleet and set their sights on New Orleans, never suspecting they headed towards another humiliating disaster.

FYI: Star-Spangled Banner

Though under guard by the enemy, lawyer Francis Scott Key (1779-1843) was so emotionally moved by the sight of the American flag over Ft. McHenry that he wrote the first words of a poem on a scrap of paper . . .

O say can you see, by the dawn's early light,
What so proudly we hail'd at the twilight's last gleaming,
Whose broad stripes and bright stars through the perilous fight,
O'er the ramparts we watched were so gallantly streaming?
And the rocket's red glare, the bombs bursting in air,
Gave proof through the night that our flag was still there;
O say does that star-spangled banner yet wave,
O'er the land of the free and the home of the brave?

Once on shore, he finished the poem and gave it to a friend who had been at Ft. McHenry during the firestorm. Published widely, in November Key's poem was set to the tune of "Anacreon in Heaven," the club song of a respected society in London. Years later, in 1931, President H. Hoover named the "Star-Spangled Banner" our national anthem.

Outrage

Thomas Jefferson was an avid reader of newspapers (over 70 American and foreign publications). Often, he'd cut articles out, add comments in the margins, file them away for future reference, or mail them to family members and acquaintances.

When newspapers reported Napoleon's abdication in April 1814, Jefferson accepted the story as the unvarnished truth, but in August he refused to believe the journalists' accounts of the burning of Washington. He reasoned that the King's Men would never commit such an uncivilized act of warfare, but by September he realized he had misjudged the civility of the British military.

From all accounts he became outraged that "modern" soldiers would have trespassed the upper floor of a building held sacred by a nation, and to then commit the grievous sin of burning books. He took the destruction of the Congressional Library personally, since he had handpicked two-thirds of the collection while in Europe, and had added at least 1000 more books during his presidential terms. Even worst, lost in the flames were the years of effort by his good friend, James Madison, and gone, too, was Congress' broad base of knowledge. With deepening dismay, he learned about the further damage to the few, salvaged books during their transfer to temporary quarters at Blodgett's Hotel.

Jefferson reasoned the library had to be rebuilt immediately, but he was fully aware of the obstacles: the ongoing war with England strained the national budget, and restricted trade with Europe from whence replacement books were more available. He came to a decision: to reveal his longtime plan to bestow his library on Congress—a plan that had been 45 years in the making.

For more than four decades, Jefferson had been purposeful in his accumulation of books "which related to America, and indeed whatever was rare and valuable." Although books were his chosen tools to accomplish all that he strove to do in life, he envisioned his collection in the future hands of Congress. His scheme was simple: upon his death, his heirs would offer his library to Congress at a fair price, but the fiery destruction of Congressional Library amended the original plan—Congress had immediate need of books, not later at the unforeseen time of Jefferson's demise.

Because he had intimate knowledge of the books that had made up Congress' library, he could say with certainty that his personal collection was far superior and broader in scope. But he was also acquainted with many of the sitting senators and representatives and fully expected protests from several quarters of Congress. He needed a spokesman, one who could present his proposal before Congress with enough skill to fend off detractors' verbal attacks. He selected Samuel Harrison Smith, who had founded and edited the *National Intelligencer* during Jefferson's presidential years. By that year of 1814, Smith was widely respected in his very powerful position as the President of the Bank of Washington (1809-1819).

On September 21, while Jefferson sat at his desk composing his letter, Smith was being appointed by President Madison to serve as the Commissioner of the Revenue for the Treasury Department, and by the time the letter arrived in Smith's mailbox, his importance in Washington had risen meteorically with his overnight appointment to the Cabinet as Secretary of the Treasury.

Unknowingly, Thomas Jefferson had selected the perfect spokesman for his cause when he wrote:

"Dear Sir, I learn from the newspapers that the Vandalism of our enemy has triumphed at Washington over science as well as the arts, by the destruction of the public library with the noble edifice in which it was deposited. Of this transaction, as of that of Copenhagen, the world will entertain but one sentiment. They will see a nation suddenly withdrawn from a great war, full armed and full handed, taking advantage of another whom they had recently forced into it, unarmed, and unprepared, to indulge themselves in acts of barbarism which do not belong to a civilized age.

"When Van Ghent destroyed their shipping at Chatham, and De Ruyter rode triumphantly up the Thames, he might in like manner, by the acknowledgment of their own historians, have forced all their ships up to London bridge, and there have burnt them, the tower, and city, had these examples been then set. London, when thus menaced, was near a thousand years old, Washington is but in its teens.

"I presume it will be among the early objects of Congress to re-commence their collection. This will be difficult while the war continues, and intercourse with Europe is attended with so much risk.

"You know my collection, its condition and extent. I have been fifty years making it, and have spared no pains, opportunity or expense, to make it what it is. While residing in Paris, I devoted every afternoon I was disengaged, for a summer or two, in examining all the principal book-stores, turning over every book with my own hand, and putting by everything which related to America, and indeed whatever was rare and valuable in every science. Besides this, I had standing orders during the whole time I was in Europe, on its principal book-marts, particularly Amsterdam, Frankfort, Madrid and London, for such works relating to America as could not be found in Paris.

"So that in that department particularly, such a collection was made as probably can never again be effected, because it is hardly probable that the same opportunities, the same time, industry, perseverance and expense, with some knowledge of the bibliography of the subject, would again happen to be in concurrence. During the same period, and after my return to America, I was led to procure, also, whatever related to the duties of those in the high concerns of the nation.

"So that the collection, which I suppose is of between nine and ten thousand volumes, while it includes what is chiefly valuable in science and literature generally, extends more particularly to whatever belongs to the American statesman. In the diplomatic and parliamentary branches, it is particularly full.

"It is long since I have been sensible it ought not to continue private property, and had provided that at my death, Congress should have the refusal of it at their own price. But the loss they have now incurred, makes the present the proper moment for their accommodation, without regard to the small remnant of time and the barren use of my enjoying it.

"I ask of your friendship, therefore, to make for me the tender of it to the library committee of Congress, not knowing myself of whom the committee consists. I enclose you the catalogue, which will enable them to judge of its contents.

"Nearly the whole are well bound, abundance of them elegantly, and of the choicest editions existing. They may be valued by persons named by themselves, and the payment made convenient to the public. It may be, for instance, in such annual installments as the law of Congress has left at their disposal, or in stock of any of their late loans, or of any loan they may institute at this session, so as to spare the present calls of our country, and await its days of peace and prosperity. They may enter, nevertheless, into immediate use of it, as eighteen or twenty wagons would place it in Washington in a single trip of a fortnight.

"I should be willing indeed, to retain a few of the books, to amuse the time I have yet to pass, which might be valued with the rest, but not included in the sum of valuation until they should be restored at my death, which I would carefully provide for, so that the whole library as it stands in the catalogue at this moment should be theirs without any garbling.

"Those I should like to retain would be chiefly classical and mathematical. Some few in other branches, and particularly one of the five encyclopedias in the catalogue. But this, if not acceptable, would not be urged. I must add, that I have not revised the library since I came home to live, so that it is probable some of the books may be missing, except in the chapters of Law and Divinity, which have been revised and stand exactly as in the catalogue. The return of the catalogue will of course be needed, whether the tender be accepted or not.

"I do not know that it contains any branch of science which Congress would wish to exclude from their collection; there is, in fact, no subject to which a member of Congress may not have occasion to refer. But such a wish would not correspond with my views of preventing its dismemberment. My desire is either to place it in their hands entire, or to preserve it so here.

"I am engaged in making an alphabetical index of the author's names, to be annexed to the catalogue, which I will forward to you as soon as completed. Any agreement you shall be so good as to take the trouble of entering into with the committee, I hereby confirm.

"Accept the assurance of my great esteem and respect. Th: Jefferson"

Included in the letter packet was Thomas Jefferson's handwritten catalogue of his library's holdings. The catalogue listed more than 6,000 books—Monticello Library was the largest, private collection in America.

Vilified

Samuel Harrison Smith appeared before Congress with Jefferson's catalogue in hand, but he neither tendered Jefferson's letter to the members, nor mentioned the former president's request to temporarily "retain a few books [Classical and mathematical books and an encyclopedia volume] to amuse the time [he had] yet to pass." Instead, Smith chose to relay Jefferson's proposal with great and sincere enthusiasm. Of those listening, some were admirers of the former president while others were sworn enemies, but overall there was keen interest in the proposal.

A joint congressional committee was formed and the monetary value of the entire book collection was requested. With characteristic prudence, Jefferson asked Joseph Milligan to calculate a fair price. Milligan, a bookseller and publisher in the Georgetown area of Washington, served at that time as Jefferson's bookbinder.

Having the advantage of familiarity with Jefferson's library, Milligan pored over the catalog to make an exact count of the books, and to gauge their value. He numbered the collection at 6,487 volumes and priced each book according to its size, large to small: ten dollars for a folio, six dollars for a quarto, three dollars for an octavo, and one dollar for a duodecimo. The whole collection was valued at 23,950 dollars, a price uncontested by Jefferson. And so, on the tenth day of October, approximately six weeks after the British torched Congress' library, the joint congressional committee put forth a resolution to purchase Jefferson's library.

Debate consumed Congress—all agreed that Jefferson's books were needed for effective legislation, but resentment towards the former president was strong in some seats of Congress. Jefferson's political enemies, the Federalists, argued that the war with Britain and the growing national debt disallowed expenditures for books that "seemed outside of purview of a Congressional Library." In their mistrust of Jefferson, they discounted his ability to supply appropriate titles, and stubbornly overlooked the fact he had selected most of the books that had made up Congress' original library. The *Annals of Congress* reported: "The objections to the purchase were generally its extent, the cost of the purchase, the nature of selection, embracing too many works in foreign languages, some of too philosophical a character, and some otherwise objectionable."

The strongest objection to the purchase of Jefferson's library was its inclusion of books written by François-Marie d'Arouet (1694–1778), the French philosopher and writer known as Voltaire. The apex of the Enlightenment had come in the publication of the *Encyclopédie* (1751–72), a 35-volume compilation of the works of hundreds of leading philosophes (intellectuals) including Voltaire. Wealthy Europeans and Americans, such as Thomas Jefferson, had purchased more than 25,000 copies of the encyclopedia sets (several sets were part of the collection Jefferson was offering to Congress).

The inclusion of the encyclopedias, and other works by Voltaire infuriated Representative Cyrus King of Massachusetts who vilified the Frenchman as a "godless Deist." Actually, Voltaire did believe in a "Supreme Being" but he criticized church and government through his poetry and fictional writings, which brought him condemnation in some areas of the world—apparently in Massachusetts, as well.

Rebuking Thomas Jefferson for his "infidel philosophy," King wrote: "It might be inferred from the character of the man who collected it, and France, where the collection was made, that the library contained irreligious and immoral books, works of French philosophers, who caused and influenced the volcano of the French Revolution which had desolated Europe and extended to this country . . . [Jefferson's books are] good, bad, and indifferent, old, new and worthless, in languages which many can not read, and most ought not to."

Meanwhile, as the debate on the floor of Congress dragged on from the end of 1814 to the beginning of 1815, Jefferson's need for money became his paramount concern. Noting Jefferson's disquiet, President Madison sent him a letter of encouragement, writing: "[It would] prove a gain to [Congress], if they have the wisdom to replace [the burnt books] by such a collection as yours."

But Jefferson felt as though he stood on a high tightrope while he awaited Congress' decision—his noble aim was to place his books in the hands of Congress, but he had a personal stake as well—the sale of his library would stave off bankruptcy and the possible loss of his home.

FACT OR FICTION

By 1814, Thomas Jefferson's mountainous estate was in need of repairs.

Monticello had been a showplace when he stepped down from the presidency in 1809, but as his retirement lengthened, the house and grounds sank into disrepair because his debts, inherited and accrued, ruled out refurbishments. He had assumed his farms would provide ready-cash in his final years, but crops failed because of seasonal droughts and floods that washed away the soil's nutrients, and too often, trade regulations and restrictions hampered the export of agricultural products. By 1814, he felt weighed down by financial burdens caused in part by the economic hardships of the war with Britain, and by family members' reoccurring bouts of alcoholism and mental illnesses.

And yet, overall, Jefferson's "twilight years" were productive, comfortable, and largely happy, as explained below.

> *The Jefferson Foundation writes that "Monticello is the autobiographical masterpiece of Thomas Jefferson, designed and redesigned and built and rebuilt for more than forty years . . . its gardens were a botanic showpiece, a source of food, and an experimental laboratory of ornamental and useful plants from around the world."*
>
> *The Monticello of today is a recreation of Jefferson's vision of an idealized home. There is, of course, a distinction in all things between reality and fantasy, but the bottom line is that historians and architects rebuilt Monticello by what is known about Jefferson's years on his estate. We, his sincere admirers, can accept the simple motive behind the historians' recreation—after all, a remarkable house is the perfect complement of a remarkable man. Admittedly, I "built" Thomas Jefferson in the same way by drawing from the books I've read about his life and time, all of which has influenced my life in a positive way.*
>
> *An accurate picture of Monticello and Thomas Jefferson during his final years is found in the journal of a young man*

named Francis Calley Gray. A graduate of Harvard, he was the unpaid secretary to John Quincy Adams, who then served as the U.S. Minister to Russia.

In January 1815, Gray took a leave of absence, and supplied with a letter of introduction, he made his way to Charlottesville. From there he hired a hack to carry him to Monticello where he recorded his almost month-long stay as Jefferson's houseguest.

I asked Maureen, a published author of historical fiction novels, to reshape the entries of Gray's journal into a flight of fancy, a narrative of facts and fiction. After she finished this assignment, she explained her approach: to replicate Gray's writing style, she used a liberal hand in borrowing some of his actual words and phrases without resorting to quotation marks that can clutter text. And she gave me her assurance that above all the elements of fiction, she stayed true to Gray's comments about Monticello and Thomas Jefferson. According to my co-author, Gray made it abundantly clear in his journal that he viewed Mr. Jefferson as a gentleman whose home may have fallen into disrepair, but who retained the dignity of his indefinable character and spirit.

~Barry

A Flight of Fancy: The Journal of Francis Calley Gray

January 1815

I had no regrets in leaving behind the iced environs of Russia for the unpaved roads of Albemarle County, Virginia, though the journey seemed overlong on such a bitterly cold day. There were long stretches of deep mud that slowed the hooves and wheels of my coach, and patches of ice that had to be rounded to keep from breaking a horse's leg, but each mile brought me closer to Mr. Jefferson's door—the door of an "infidel" as Representative Cyrus King of Massachusetts has labeled Mr. J., but before long I'd determine for myself who is who in Congress' War over Books.

The hills ascended sharply as my coach crossed the North River at the ford near Milton where I hired another hack and driver to take me on to Charlottesville and points beyond—east of that city sits Mr. J's estate on the summit of a high peak in the Southwest Mountains, south of the Ravenna River.

Too quickly, the road became a narrow path. The sides of the hills were shadowed by a forest of oaks; fallen trees lined the road, some decayed by age, some had been uprooted and twisted by past storms. The driver stopped at a bank of frozen waters. It took hours to break the ice of Mechunk Creek, but finally the horses pulled our carriage through the cold waters and up a shallow bank where a mare lay dead, having drowned, no doubt.

Another mile out we became lodged in black mud, but a small militia of native Virginians happened by—a bedraggled bunch without hats or coats despite the frigid weather. They appeared pale and thin, from the fevers and typhus that had swept through their ranks we were told, and we learned, too, that they had been discharged without pay and were returning to their homes after six months of keeping Norfolk out of British control. They freed our wheels and refused payment, but insisting, I gave them tobacco and clothing from my valise, and what money I could spare. They thanked me, profusely, but I little deserved their gratitude—in my place they had suffered the deprivations of war.

Having reached the foot of South Mountain, we climbed up a steep and savage hill through freezing rain until the carriage was forced to a sudden stop. The driver climbed down to kick a branch out of the road, and wiping the rain from his eyes, he pointed into the near distance at lighted windows, presumably those of Mr. J.

I peered through the falling darkness with sudden impatience for the splendors of Monticello's rooms, its hearths, legendary table and fine wines—little did I realize my expectations were mired, somewhat, in fantasy.

The driveway was muddied, as should be expected in such foul weather, but the door lacked a working bell or knocker—the first clue that all was not right on the estate.

Mr. J's son-in-law, Col. Randolph, took my letter of introduction, and before he disappeared through a side door he suggested I examine the hall's decor—a collection of Indian weapons, apparel, pottery and other tokens of native friendship brought back by Lewis and Clark. Behind me a massive clock ticked away the minutes, but in short order the great gentleman himself came out into the hall and greeted me most cordially.

At first sight, I was struck by his unusual height. Lean and tall (over 6'2" I'd guess), he was the figure of a true Virginian, proud and upright, with broad shoulders, white hair and light grey eyes lit with keen intelligence. His face was streaked with the red veins of broken blood vessels—damage caused, I would soon discover, by the winds that skirt his mountain, and by his daily hours in the saddle under summer and winter suns.

Having assumed a gentleman of his standing would be the paragon of fashion, his attire of stiff, thick cloth took me aback—the cut of his clothes was decidedly old-fashioned from his knee breeches and gray-worsted stockings to his blue waistcoat, day coat, and shoes with pointed toes. Scuffed shoes, I noted. He would, in one of our future exchanges, proudly say that he wore the wool of his own merinos, and that his slaves had carved his buttons from horn. Immensely proud, I should add.

Brought into his parlor, I turned a curious eye to the furnishings, which were less than elegant. The cherry and beech floor may have been highly polished, but horsehair poked through the worn seats of the leather chairs, and a small teatable leaned crookedly against the wall. In a near corner, a slave boarded up a broken window—I had arrived bone-cold, and the chilled air of the room chattered my teeth. Embarrassed, I tried to hide my discomfort, but Mr. J. noticed and graciously built up the fire, himself.

We passed an hour in spirited conversation until a slave ushered us into a more cheerful place, the breakfast room where we sat down to dinner. It was all I had expected of Mr. J's table; an excellent repast of veal and glazed carrots, crusted breads and iced cream. The drinking cups of silver were marked G.W. to T.J., the table liquors were beer and cider, and after dinner we enjoyed wine . . . a thoroughly pleasant interlude that ended a rather interesting and, in some aspects, astonishing day.

And so the weeks sped by; a period of time much too brief, for seldom had I enjoyed more agreeable company.

The mornings were divided between coffee and books. In the early hours before breakfast, Mr. J. would mount his horse and ride off to inspect the dam, mills, and canal he had constructed on the Rivanna—private works, all sources of pride for him.

After breakfast, he'd invite me into his library for an hour. One hour, not a minute more, for he adhered to a strict schedule. But in those single hours I learned much about his collection, his "principal treasure" he called it—the very subject of the fire-hot debate in Congress. With almost juvenile delight he would show off the works of favored authors, and loan me one or two for my reading pleasure. But at the end of each of those hours, he'd wave me out of the library to reclaim his privacy for reading.

The afternoon hours passed like minutes. After luncheon, Mr. J. worked on architectural designs, read newspapers and books, wrote endless letters, met with the slaves and daily visitors that crowded his Entrance Hall, or returned to the saddle for further inspections of his works along the river. At times I was invited to join him, but more often than not he rode out, alone, as that was his first preference. I observed him carefully when opportunities arose, and filled the rest of the hours by emerging myself into the busyness of a large estate.

The evenings were a blend of good conversation and fine wine. Dinner was served in the French style with the wines decanted only after the meal had been consumed and the dishes cleared from the table.

There were assorted guests at Mr. J's table, but more often than not his only daughter, Martha Randolph and her daughter, Anne Bankhead were in attendance along with their husbands, Col. Tom Randolph and Charles Bankhead. When not on call at one of the farms he oversaw for his grandfather, Jeff Randolph also dined with us.

Each night as the clock struck the 6th hour, the evening meal ended and the ladies excused themselves from the room until 7:00 when the tea tray arrived. Customarily they would then pass the rest of the evening in our company of men, however high the topic of conversation may have been for the fairer sex.

Of all the members of his family, the warmth between Mr. J. and his grandson was most evident. Jeff's the good-natured sort—tall, strong like a Titan, and patient with the entire household (his mother would try the patience of a saint). At 23, Jeff's only two years my junior, but he emanates the confidence of a much older man—perhaps the by-product of being the sole manager of his grandfather's farms. He is betrothed to Jane Hollins Nicholas, and they plan to make their home in the dome-room—Jane is the pleasant, large-hearted sort, but I take it Jeff's mother doesn't approve of the match.

Each night, about half past ten, all of us retired to our rooms. Always, Mr. J. bade us a good night of rest, adding that he'd read until sleep befell him. I never failed to inquire the name of his book, and he'd tell me its title with warmth, much like a parent telling the name of a cherished child.

One afternoon towards the end of January a letter arrived, which left Mr. J. in an unexplained, unrestrained mood—that letter aroused my curiosity since much of the time he exuded sobriety and cool reason. At supper that night, the reason behind his uncharacteristic exuberance was made known when Mr. J. produced the letter and read it aloud—after almost 6 months of debate, Congress has cast its vote with the happy result that the government will purchase Mr. J.'s book collection. (Evidently, Rep. Cyrus King's abortion of the rebirth of Congress' library has been botched.)

As Mr. J. read the letter aloud, I glanced about the room with furtive eye so as not to offend him. The draperies lifted from the air moving through the cracked panes, the walls were in need of paint-wash, and the china and crystal glasses were clouded and chipped. Money was much needed by him, just as he remarked several times during our celebration that his books were much needed by Congress.

After the dishes were cleared, Mr. J. uncorked a bottle of wine given him by the Frenchman Lafayette. Our glasses filled, we raised them, one by one, to toast our host's good fortune. After each spoke, he nodded his head, slightly, in appreciation, and added a few words of his own—modest words, I noted, without a speck of arrogance.

The hours passed in that way, the evening ending later than usual, but on a very high note in spite of a sudden storm of snow and hail and gusts of wind that howled down the chimneys.

The following morning when Mr. J. returned from inspecting his properties, I overheard him tell his grandson, "The storm carried away the dam." His voice, his composure, conveyed calmness, so I supposed the restructure of his dam was of small consequence. I would soon learn otherwise.

At breakfast I thanked Mr. J. for the privilege of being his guest, and admitted my regret in quitting Monticello for the barren wastelands of Russia. Graciously, he invited me to return in the near future, which lightened my steps, considerably, when I went upstairs to pack my valise.

Around mid-morning, I began my journey down the mountain's side—a long, stop-and-go drive, for the storm had littered the road with branches that the driver and I had to clear in order to pass through. In time we reached Charlottesville and stopped at a tavern where the dominant subject of conversation was the destruction of Mr. J.'s dam. A calamity, the locals called it, that will cost Thomas Jefferson 30,000 dollars to rebuild.

Taken aback, I recalled the evenness of Mr. J's voice, the equanimity of his whole being when he said: *The storm carried away the dam.* Those few words are etched into my mind; those few words epitomize the resolute strength and quiet dignity of a most singular gentleman, Mr. Thomas Jefferson.

A Harvard trained lawyer, Francis Calley Gray chose to forego the practice of law for a career in politics and writing. His books ranged from art and shell collections to legal issues such as his work about penal reform: Prison Discipline In America (1848). Having read Gray's accounts of his visits to Monticello in The Papers of Thomas Jefferson, I recalled his candid remarks about the estate. I also recalled his keen observation that in spite of broken panes, scuffed shoes, and destructive storms, Thomas Jefferson retained a sense of quiet dignity.

~Barry

10 Votes

It's doubtful that Jefferson rebuilt his dam; no expenditures were recorded in his account ledgers, in which he'd list bills as minor as "$2.90 for cheese, purchased from a neighbor." In all probability, he dismissed the whole idea of reconstructing his dam, for his pockets were empty.

Almost empty.

As mentioned in Francis Calley Gray's narrative, at the end of January, the government's letter reached Monticello with confirmation that the entire collection of 6,487 volumes had been purchased at the agreed upon price of $23,950. Approval had been won by the narrowest margin of 10 votes. The *Boston Gazette's* sarcasm summed up the position of the Federalists, Jefferson's critics in Congress: "The grand library of Mr. Jefferson will be purchased with all its finery and philosophical nonsense," but other newspapers wrote more favorable accounts, noting Congress' advantageous gain of an elite library.

Jefferson had expected a narrow vote, but he was elated it had gone in his favor and that he'd soon have the cash to pay off his more pressing loans. He did express his disappointment, however, that his one request to temporarily keep a few books to "amuse the time [he had] yet to pass" had been overlooked. In a matter of months he would be bookless for the first time in his life, and for Jefferson, a man who equated reading with breathing, that prospect was daunting.

During the next few weeks he became consumed with anxiety, his appetite and sleep all but lost. Until Congress returned his book catalogue, he had no way of comparing the listed books to the ones on his shelves. Some, perhaps many, would have to be replaced and that would be prohibitively expensive, but necessary to honor his contract with Congress. To assuage his conscience, he applied to his spokesman, Samuel Harrison Smith, on the 27th of February, writing: "The only modification to be made [to the list] being a deduction from the compensation in proportion to the size and number of the books which on review shall appear to be lost."

Finally, in March, Congress returned Jefferson's catalogue, and he set about the chore of comparing the list of books to those on his shelves. To his immense relief, the number of missing books was far lower than the number he had mistakenly left out of the catalogue—the expense of replacing certain titles could be diverted, honorably, since the amended count came to 6,707, an additional 220 books over the promised number of 6,487 volumes. Jefferson felt it would be dishonorable to either retain the newfound books, or request additional money (it would have meant another $1,172.50).

In April he penned a letter to the Secretary of Treasury Alexander J. Dallas, writing: "I have not thought it right to withdraw these [220 volumes] from the library, so that the whole delivered exceeds on the principles of the estimates, the sum appropriated."

In spite of his dire financial straits, Jefferson's public-spiritedness prompted him to make yet another magnanimous gesture: he offered to await payment and to then accept the money in installments once the nation had returned to "days of peace and prosperity." But Congress declined his offer, and avowed immediate payment in full, once delivery of the books had been made.

Bittersweet Chore

Jefferson began the bittersweet chore of preparing thousands of books for shipment; a task, he told Samuel Harrison Smith, that "can be done only by myself, and admit of no help." But it was an immense chore, and so he did enlist the assistance of his current book-dealer and binder, Joseph Milligan, who agreed to "arrange and number all the books according as they stand in [Jefferson's] catalogue."

Along with Milligan, Jefferson wrote a new catalogue, which took time and much effort on his part. He asked for Congress' patience, writing "[I am] constantly on my legs, and I ask for indulgence therefore to proceed only as my strength will admit."

After the new catalogue (the *Fair Catalogue*) was completed, he and Milligan pasted a label on the spine of each book to identify the "Chapter" that particular book should be classified under, plus its "Rank" within each "Chapter." Each book was then wrapped in brown paper, and weighed to determine which book-press it would be fitted into. Once the presses were filled, boards were nailed across their openings to give them added security.

After calculating that the books could reach Washington, D. C. in a "single trip of a fortnight," he began interviewing and hiring drivers. In the middle of April, when there was less concern about snow, ten wagons were loaded with the crated book-presses. Jefferson felt confident there'd be no roadside delays, for he had carefully mapped out a fail-safe route that passed through Manassas to Washington. Of their own volition, however, the drivers took their wagons through Fredericksburg to reach the capital city. (Jefferson's and the drivers' maps are sketched on the inside covers of the Sowerby compilation published by the Library of Congress.)

Although greatly annoyed by the change in direction, Jefferson was delighted to learn that the sealed book-presses had been delivered intact to Blodgett's Hotel on 7th and E. St. in Washington by the beginning of May (after the British torched the Capitol, Congress temporarily moved their offices to that hotel). The crates were placed on the hotel's third floor, and once the planks were removed it seemed sensible to leave the books inside the presses in the precise order Jefferson had arranged them. With immediacy, both parties of Congress made use of the books in carrying out their legislative duties.

Thaddeus Kosciuszko. *PD.*

Jefferson, as instructed, drew upon a check from the Treasury Department for the agreed upon sum of $23,950. A major portion of the money went to outstanding loans, and with the remaining $10,580 he retired a 6-year-old debt of $4,870 to his good friend, General Thaddeus Kosciuszko.

Of those he owed money to, Jefferson was most anxious to settle his debt with Thaddeus Kosciuszko (1746-1817). Known as the "Hero of Poland and America," Kosciuszko was once described by Jefferson as "pure a son of liberty as I have ever known." Years earlier, in 1776, upon his arrival in Philadelphia from Europe, Kosciuszko read the

Declaration of Independence with tears in his eyes—all of the principles and beliefs he held most sacred had been captured in that single document, and he hoped, one day, to shake the author's hand. In the meanwhile, the Continental Congress recognized Kosciuszko's elite education and skills and commissioned him as a Colonel of Engineers (his fortifications of battle sites, such as that of the Battle of Saratoga, proved instrumental in winning the war).

Months later, during a military movement, an opportunity arose for a meeting between Kosciuszko and Jefferson; by day's end, the two men had forged a strong bond of friendship based on mutual respect of each other's moral principles. In 1783, after General Washington promoted Kosciuszko to Brigadier General, he returned to his homeland to fight in Poland's unsuccessful struggle for independence. He survived 17 battle-wounds, and two years in a Russian prison before settling for a while in Philadelphia at 3rd and Pine, a modest home that remains open to the public. (General Kosciuszko is also featured at the Polish American Cultural Center Museum, 308 Walnut Street, Philadelphia.)

Margaret Bayard Smith, author of *The First Forty Years of Washington Society*, summarized the depth of Thaddeus Kosciuszko's respect for Thomas Jefferson. She wrote that upon leaving America for the final time, "Kasioskio [sic] left his cloak, with his revered friend Jefferson."

Never Idle

After the sale of his books to Congress, Jefferson sent a prophetic letter to Samuel Harrison Smith in which he had written: "an interesting treasure is added to . . . [Washington, D.C., which has] now become the depository of unquestionably the choicest collection of books in the US, and I hope it will not be without some general effect on the literature of our country" (May 8, 1815).

His words are yet another example of Jefferson as a man of forward thinking—although his collection was slated for Congress, he foresaw it as the foundation of a national library. And yet, even Thomas

Jefferson could not have imagined that his books would become the core of the Library of Congress' collection of over 115 million books in 450 languages.

After the shipment of his library to Washington, Jefferson remarked more than once about the impairments of advanced age, but his daily activities showed no evidence of physical or mental weaknesses. He adhered to a rigorous schedule in the fields and on horseback, and as spring edged towards summer he rooted himself to his desk to draw up plans for 4 major projects:

1. The University of Virginia
2. The Retirement Library
3. The Search for a Master Bookbinder
4. The Conflation of the *Seven*: Aeschylus' Tragedies

Needless to say, each project was designed around books.

The First Project: The University of Virginia

Jefferson's first project had been set in motion in the spring of 1814. Appointed as a trustee of a school of higher learning, he drafted the regulations, proposed funding options, and drew up the architectural designs for Albemarle Academy in Charlottesville, but when its doors opened it would be called the University of Virginia.

On October 6, 1817, only five months after Jefferson had presented his architectural sketches, black carriages crowded a cleared field west of Charlottesville. State and national politicians and distinguished guests had gathered to witness the ceremony Jefferson had long anticipated: the laying of the cornerstone of a pavilion of the University of Virginia. Given that honor was President James Monroe, the fifth President of the United States and the final one to have once served as a Founding Father.

Thomas Jefferson's establishment of the University of Virginia was one of his great achievements. To this day, he stands as the only

University of Virginia. *Courtesy of UVA (Dan Addison/UVa. University Communications.)*

American president to have founded an institution of higher learning, and to add yet another layer to that accomplishment, he distinguished himself as the university's architect and educator.

As prefaced earlier in this book, Thomas Jefferson taught himself architecture through books—he had learned his lessons well, as was proven by his masterful design of Monticello, but by this point in life he had superior command of the art and science of architecture.

The evidence lies in the visually pleasing design of the university's *Academical Village*, the terraced green enclosed by residential and academic buildings and bricked, serpentine walls.

The dual purpose behind the curved walls offers another glimpse into the workings of Jefferson's brilliant mind—both his frugal approach to construction, and his refined sense of aesthetics. Mindful of costs, he calculated that curved walls use 25 % fewer bricks than straight walls since a curved wall supports itself with a one-brick thickness, while a straight wall requires a two-brick thickness. And mindful, too, of the beauty of nature, he worked serpentine walls into his landscape design to provide planting areas with greater and lesser exposure to sunlight to vary the kinds of plants and flowers that could be embedded in the gardens.

The Rotunda, the centerpiece of Jefferson's architectural vision, housed the library. Erected at the north end of the Lawn, the building is half the height and width of the Pantheon in Rome, the model for his design. To Jefferson, the Rotunda symbolized the "authority of nature and power of reason." Sadly, he would never see its completion.

As the university's educator, books again became tools in Jefferson's hands when he designed the curriculum and selected the first faculty.

University of Virginia. *Courtesy of UVA (Dan Addison/U.Va.University Communications.)*

In the planning stage of his "very great and very new" non-sectarian institution, he replaced the standards of a church-defined curriculum with a free-elective curriculum, one based on Sir Francis Bacon's enlightened precept of "using Reason and Scientific Experimentation to teach Knowledge and Truth." The public railed against his "radical" approach, but he argued that America needed professionals to survive—professionals other than college-trained educators and ministers. The new nation, he maintained, required future leaders that were well versed in the related fields of medicine, law, politics, science, and math.

Jefferson handpicked the university's first faculty of eight professors. Throughout the hiring process he ignored the public's criticism; in his learned opinion he had found competent instructors of moral and natural philosophies, mathematics, chemistry, law, medicine, and languages (modern and ancient).

In all these ways as founder, architect and educator, Thomas

Jefferson left his imprint on the University of Virginia—still referred to as *Mr. Jefferson's University*, it is a place steeped in his memory for those who once walked its hallowed halls, as explained below by an alumnus of UVA.

> *No one and I mean no one spends four years at UVA without becoming consumed with the life and times of Thomas Jefferson (Mr. Jefferson, to all). For myself, I had the good fortune to be in the University of Virginia Law School class of 1961, and so benefitted from Jefferson's vision of training lawyers through the case method, a philosophy still practiced at the law school.*
>
> *I was admitted to UVA as a legacy student, which if I understand the concept correctly, means that any child of a UVA alumnus could be admitted as a legacy student on the strength of the family connection with the university, as long as the applicant was upright, breathing, and had passed the LSAT examination. The quid pro quo was that the first year class of 500 students would be trimmed in half at the end of the first year based on class standings, as determined by a single but very comprehensive examination—or as the dean of admissions explained to my father: we'll take him, but we may not keep him.*
>
> *The importance of that single examination finally sank in a month before the exam was to be taken at the end of the first year. In a flight of panic my good friend and fellow student Bill Person and I left the campus to study without interruption. We studied night and day with the help of notes and study material obtained from other classmates, and an ample quantity of Benzedrine supplied by a nurse at the UVA medical school. (Note to my children and grandchildren: do not follow this model.)*
>
> *Bill and I survived the cut, much to our amazement.*
>
> *~Barry*

Artificial Embellishments

Before the university was slated to open in 1825, Thomas Jefferson let his opinion be known that degrees were nothing more than "artificial embellishments."

University of Virginia. *Courtesy of UVA (Dan Addison/U.Va.University Communications.)*

Back in 1762, his two years of college ended without the conferment of a degree. If he had continued on at William and Mary, he could have earned a diploma in education or theology; instead, he undertook a "gentleman's education" with emphasis on the Classics without a paper degree. In the same vein, his years of apprenticeship in law ended without a diploma.

An excellent example of Jefferson's criticism of "artificial embellishments" is found in a letter to his son-in-law John Wayles Eppes, in which it was suggested that Jefferson's grandson, Francis, study worthwhile subjects, rather than waste time pursuing a degree. Jefferson wrote: "The honorary distinction of a Diploma, is a good enough thing to excite the ambition of youth to study, but, in modern estimation, no longer worth tacking, by its initials, to one's name" (September 16, 1821).

The university's Board of Visitors didn't agree with Jefferson. In 1824, a year before UVA's doors opened, the board authorized the school to grant future graduates the degree of Master of Arts, and other educational titles followed: medical degrees in 1828, law in 1842, bachelors in 1849, doctorates in 1883, and additional masters in 1899.

UVA does not bestow honorary degrees (possibly in keeping with Jefferson's viewpoint about paper degrees) but ironically he was awarded honorary degrees from several colleges including Harvard and Yale. Below are some final thoughts about "artificial embellishments."

When I graduated from UVA I received a Bachelor of Laws

degree, as had been the practice of the school since the 1800s. Years later, after I had been admitted to the bar in Pennsylvania and was well into the early years of my law practice in West Chester, I received a letter from UVA announcing that the university had recently adopted a new policy of awarding all law school graduates a Juris Doctorate degree in keeping with similar changes at other law schools in the country.

Thomas Jefferson may have been disappointed about UVA's adoption of "artificial embellishments," but he would have been horrified if he knew I could have swapped my Bachelor of Laws for a Juris Doctorate for the paltry sum of $35.

UVA's offer intrigued me, but I declined in the end when the law school could not assure me that the J.D. would make me any smarter.

Instead I took the $35 and bought a vintage chardonnay.

~Barry

The Second Project: The Retirement Library

At some point in June 1815, after the 10 wagons had carted off his entire collection of books to Congress, Jefferson walked into his library of bared shelves. If he spoke aloud, his voice would have sounded unfamiliar, hollow in the emptiness of the room; a pervasive emptiness felt in the very core of his being. But he was a man of *Reason* and so there was a logical solution: *to refill the shelves.* Even as he closed the door behind him, he knew his next project—the building of his third and final book collection: the Retirement Library.

On the 10th day of June, he sat down to write a long overdue reply to a letter he had received from John Adams almost eight months earlier in October of 1814, during the height of Congress' debate over the purchase of his library. Adams had written: "By the Way I envy you that immortal honour: but I cannot enter into competition with you for my books are not half the number of yours."

In his reply to Adams' letter, Jefferson provided the most evident revelation of self when he wrote:

I cannot live without books . . .

Revealing words, perhaps, but for the purposes of this small book the rest of his sentence points out the significance of the *Seven*. Jefferson wrote:

> *I cannot live without books; but fewer will suffice*
> *where amusement, and not use, is the only future object.*

Thomas Jefferson's words suggest that his third library would be his most intimate collection, for it would only hold books he had previously read and desired to read again for "amusement," for the sheerest pleasure of reading. At that juncture in life he had less interest in books as "utilitarian tools," for he had stepped away from public life and had placed the responsibilities of his several estates on the capable shoulders of his grandson, Jeff Randolph. Of the years he had left in life, Jefferson's only wish was to "idle away his hours" with family and "the books of the ancients."

He started refilling his shelves with an assortment of books, but it's doubtful that novels were high on his list of acquisitions. In his earlier years, he and his wife, Martha, had found contentment in reading novels such as *Tristram Shandy*, but by 1818, he had drastically revised his opinion about fictional works in general, and romance novels in particular. In a harshly worded letter to Nathaniel Burwell, a fellow Virginian, Jefferson wrote: "A great obstacle . . . is the inordinate passion prevalent for novels, and the time lost in that reading which should be instructively employed. When this poison infects the mind, it destroys its tone and revolts it against wholesome reading. Reason and fact, plain and unadorned, are rejected. Nothing can engage attention unless dressed in all the figments of fancy, and nothing so bedecked comes amiss. The result is a bloated imagination, sickly judgment, and disgust towards all the real businesses of life...This mass of trash, however, is not without some distinction... Some is useful for forming style and taste. Pope, Dryden, Thompson, Shakespeare, and of the French, Moliere, Racine, the Coneilles, may be read with pleasure and improvement" (March 14, 1818).

One can only wonder what Jefferson would say about today's million-dollar industry of romance novels—probably, and quite correctly, that it is a "mass of trash" without distinction.

By 1826, Jefferson's third library would hold more than 1600 books, but he leaned strongly towards the Classics, the works of the Ancient Romans and Ancient Greeks. His granddaughter, Ellen Wayles Randolph, wrote: "Books were at all times [my grandfather's] chosen companions, and his acquaintance with many languages gave him great power of selection ... I saw him more frequently with a volume of the Classics in his hand than with any other book."

The Classics that found their way into Jefferson's hands, most often, were the writings of Homer, Virgil, Tacitus, Thucydides, Sophocles, Euripides and, of course, Aeschylus.

The Third Project: The Search for a Master Bookbinder

In the rebuilding of his library, some of the books Jefferson acquired needed to be rebound. At that point his bookbinder was Joseph Milligan, the Washingtonian who had assisted him in the compilation and publication of the *1815 Fair Catalogue* of Monticello's Library upon its sale to Congress. Although he had entrusted Milligan with the compilation, Jefferson had become increasingly critical of Milligan's practices as a bookbinder—in particular, his assignment of Jefferson's books to less skilled workmen at Milligan's bindery. So critical, in fact, that Jefferson launched his third project: the search for a Master Bookbinder to replace Joseph Milligan.

Jefferson maintained that most of the binders trained in Colonial America had elementary skills, at best. He once summed up the vast majority of them by saying: "[The books of the average American binder] are faulty in execution as well as materials. They are so spongy that when once a book has been opened, it will never close shut again."

To find a qualified binder, he scrutinized advertisements, which in his opinion were the only factual sections of a newspaper. On a windy, autumn day in 1818, a boxed ad in the Richmond newspaper, *Enquirer*, caught his eye.

> "Frederick A. Mayo, Bookbinder & Stationer, has just received a large quantity of excellent Russia Calf Skins, which are known to be superior for book-binding to any other skins whatever. Binding can be done

> nearly as low of same as in sheep. Specimens of blank and printed work, bound in Russia calf, can be seen at his Bookstore and Bindery . . . Any work executed under his direction, not agreeable to order, will in no manner be requested to be taken. From his acquaintance and experience in that profession, not only in different parts of Europe but also in the U. states, he feels justifiable in stating to those unacquainted with him, that his workmanship will be inferior to none in point of neatness and durability."

Frederick A. Mayo's reference to his acquirement of bookbinding skills in "different parts of Europe" resonated with Jefferson, for he greatly admired the work of European binders. Hopeful he had found Milligan's replacement, Jefferson wrote a letter on November 30, 1818, in which he challenged Mayo to prove himself the more superior craftsman. He wrote:

"Sir—I have just made up two boxes of pamphlets, which I send to Milton to be forwarded to you by the boats of that place so soon as the state of the river will permit. These contain 39 volumes of which 38 are to be half bound, only moderately gilt on the backs, lettered according to the papers stuck in them respectively, corresponding with the list on the next page, and their leaves to be trimmed. One volume (the correspondence of Cortés & Charles V.) I send merely that you may give me on it a specimen of your best binding. I am particular in my bindings, and have hitherto been obliged to send my choice books to Milligan in Georgetown, because I have found no workman in America but him who can give me such as the London and Paris bindings. Besides the good taste with which he works, a book bound by him is as heavy as a piece of metal, which the common bindings of this country are so spongy, that after a book has been once opened, it will never shut close again. Therefore I repeat that I wish you to shew [sic] on this volume the best work you can do (but not Morocco). When the books are ready be so good as to notify me by mail and send your bill and I will inclose [sic] an order for the amount and direct how the boxes are to be returned to me. I shall be glad to receive them with as little delay as the solidity of the work will admit, and I salute you with respect. Th. Jefferson"

Mayo accepted the challenge, and within months he returned the packet of books, all rebound according to Jefferson's instructions. On April 9, 1819, Thomas Jefferson wrote: "[I am] so well satisfied with your bindings that a box of books which I had made up to send to Milligan I have addressed to you and sent it to Milton to be forwarded by Johnson's boat. [They are to be bound] in your best manner, gilt, and letter according to the labels, and above all, solidly pressed." At long last, Jefferson had found himself a Master Bookbinder. By the same token, Mayo found a prestigious patron who respected his craftsmanship and professionalism.

Mayo's journey to that moment in his career had been physically, emotionally, and mentally challenging, but he was a man of persistence. Born and raised in Saxony (then, a state of Germany), Friedrich Gotthilf Mejo anglicized his name to Frederick August Mayo shortly after his arrival in America around 1808. Of his past he would later tell Jefferson: "I worked at binding in different parts of Europe and in England until my impressment into the [Royal] Navy. [I was] compelled to act the part of a Sailor for nearly four years. I then came by change twelve years ago fortunately by chance to the U. States but in most miserable situation I suppose a person could come without means of any kind and then not in health besides having a very severe wound to contend with which I received not far from Loango, on the coast of Africa having been also up the Congo river in pursuit of Spanish and French Vessels. Some time after, I worked for considerable time in different City [sic] of America" (1820).

Mayo didn't name that city (or cities) but went on to write that upon reaching America, he felt he had "returned to Harbor after a severe storm." Apparently Mayo came to adopt his new country wholeheartedly, as is suggested by the anglicizing of his name, and his disinterest in returning to Europe.

In addition to his skills as a binder, Mayo was unsurpassed as a salesman. To ply his trade, he never failed to mark the books he had bound with tickets, which are small labels that identify a binder by name and city. Tickets, if used by binders, were pasted at the upper left-hand corners of the inside front covers of books. Strangely, of the

700 Colonial American binders, less then 10 percent used tickets to advertise their work.

Jefferson's Impatience

The professional relationship between Jefferson and Mayo is shown through their correspondence; in many of the 40 letters they'd trade, Jefferson's persona as a Bookman comes through, as does Mayo's expert treatment of books.

Quite often they expressed their shared frustration about the unpredictability of the "low state of the [James] river [and its tributary, the Rivanna]" that delayed or jeopardized the exchange of books between Monticello and Richmond. They wrote, too, about the prolonged illnesses that wracked Mayo's family, which slowed the completion of his work. Jefferson would sympathize, sincerely, but at times his impatience surfaced for a vital reason—working against time, he was determined that his more important books would be rebound for his own reading pleasure, and for unknown readers, as well.

Unknown readers?

Thomas Jefferson's intention was to bequeath his Retirement Library to the University of Virginia, thus he desired strong, handsome books that could be held and read by generations of students and professors.

The Panic of 1819

The Panic of 1819 marked a severe collapse in credit, primarily in the South and Midwest. The banks' failures were caused in part by the absence of a national currency system controlled by a federal bank, as the nation moved from a system based on subsistence agriculture to one based on commodity marketing, especially cotton, wheat and corn. The collapse affected Jefferson, as it did most everyone, but whenever he had the means, he'd ship packets of books to Mayo's bindery in Richmond.

For obvious reasons bookbinding was considered a luxury, not a necessity of life, so Mayo also suffered serious reversals in his finances.

Learning of his binder's financial crisis, Jefferson sent him a letter on December 28, 1819, in which he wrote: "[It is my distress] to learn that you had suffered in the common calamities of the times." Not knowing if the bindery had been closed, Jefferson asked in that same letter if Mayo would accept a commission to bind 100 books.

A bookbinder of Mayo's era. *Courtesy of Tim James, a commercial bookbinder and Founder of The American Bookbinders Museum, San Francisco, CA. (a working museum where visitors watch books being printed, sewn, decorated and bound while listening to tales of historic apprentices and binders, such as F. A. Mayo).*

Assuring his patron that his bindery's doors had not closed, Mayo gratefully accepted the commission, and delivered the rebound books to Monticello by March 22, 1820. A few weeks later, on April 2, Mayo wrote Jefferson a long letter, in which he confided that he had sold his book and stationery store to pay off his creditors, but that his binding establishment would remain open. He ended his letter on a solid note, stating he had "held his bindery for almost two years without complaints, and that he'd continue his policy of attending to any unsatisfactory work, without charge." It can be assumed that Thomas Jefferson appreciated Mayo's guarantee of acceptable workmanship.

In the annals of publishing history, F. A. Mayo is marked with the distinction of being Thomas Jefferson's last bookbinder. Their professional relationship is discussed at length in Hannah D. French's book,

Bookbinding in Early America: Seven Essays on Masters and Methods, and is rightfully featured in the American Bookbinders Museum in San Francisco, California.

The Fourth Project: The Conflation of the Seven: Aeschylus' Tragedies

In building his most intimate collection, the Retirement Library, Jefferson acquired fewer books by focusing on the ones he wished to read again for the "sheerest of pleasures."

Since his childhood, the works of Aeschylus had provided him immense enjoyment, and so he undertook his fourth project: the acquisition of the Ancient Greek's tragedies in Greek, English, Latin and French—books he'd eventually send to his binder F. A. Mayo to break apart, conflate, and rebind into the brown, leather volumes now referred to as the *Seven*.

John Laval

By 1820, only a Latin translation was needed to complete Jefferson's collection of Aeschylus' works, and so he turned to John Laval, a Philadelphia bookseller of proven proficiency in locating rare and unusual books. On March 27th Jefferson wrote:

"I have now to request you to procure me a copy of Aeschylus with a Latin translation, the Latin on distinct leaves both recto and verso: because I wish to interleave them in the edition of du Theil. An 8vo would be best, but 12mo might do if an 8vo edition cannot be found. I care nothing about binding, or the Greek leaves, as they will be sacrificed."

Laval read Jefferson's letter with complete understanding of what was meant by the bindings being "sacrificed." If a Latin translation could be located, Jefferson's binder would remove the book's pages and "interleave" them between pages similarly removed from the spines of other books (such as Jefferson's du Theil edition of Aeschylus' tragedies). The revised arrangements of pages would then be rebound into one or more new books.

Jefferson conflated books to satisfy his study of languages and words. Basically, he distrusted translations, but by interleaving an author's original text with its translations, he could fully comprehend the nuances of languages.

His lifelong practice of delving into the exact meaning of an author's words is yet another example of the complex workings of his mind. Or, for a more succinct description of his intellect, consider a comment made by John F. Kennedy at a White House dinner for Nobel Prize winners.

President Kennedy said: "This is the most extraordinary collection of talent, of human knowledge, that has ever been gathered together at the White House—with the possible exception of when Thomas Jefferson dined alone" (April 29, 1962).

In March of 1820, John Laval carried out Jefferson's commission to locate a Latin translation of Aeschylus' tragic dramas. There were only 7 extant tragedies, although the Ancient Greek composed more than 90 works including:

Alcmene
Amymone
The Archer-Women
The Argivian Women
The Argo, or The Rowers
Atalanta
Athamas
Attendants of the Bridal-Chamber
Award of the Arms
The Bacchae
The Bassarae
The Bone-Gatherers
The Cabeiroi
Callisto
The Carians or Europa
Cercyon
Children of Hercules
Circe
The Cretan Women
Cycnus
The Edonians
The Egyptians
The Escorts
Glaucus of Pontus
Glaucus of Potniae
Hypsipyle
Iphigenia
Ixion
Laius
The Lemnian Women
The Lion
Lycurgus
Memnon
The Men of Eleusis
The Messengers
The Myrmidons
The Mysians
Nemea
The Net-Draggers
The Nurses of Dionysus
Oedipus

Orethyia
Palamedes
Penelope
Pentheus
Perrhaibides
Philoctetes
Phineus
The Phrygian Women
Polydectes
The Priestesses
Prometheus the FireBearer
Prometheus the Fire-Kindler
Prometheus Unbound
Proteus
Semele, or The Water-Bearers
Sisyphus the Runaway
Sisyphus the Stone-Roller
The Spectators, or Athletes of the Isthmian Games
The Sphinx
The Spirit-Raisers
Telephus
The Thracian Women
Weighing of Souls
Women of Aetna (two ver sions)
Women of Salamis
Xantriae
The Youths
The Danaids
Daughters of Helios
Daughters of Phorcys
Descendants of 7

Down through the centuries, the 7 tragedies that have survived the ages are: *Prometheus; Suplices; Thebae; Agamemnon; Chorephora; Eumenides; and Persae.*

Aeschylus' extraordinary body of work was only possible because of the rise of democracy in Ancient Greece.

Prior to Aeschylus' years as a playwright, tyrants dictated behavior and thought, and similar restrictions were applied to early forms of drama. But as democracy emerged in Greece, mathematicians, astronomers, physicians, philosophers, historians and scientists claimed intellectual freedom and strove towards knowledge in all things physical and mental. In parallel, dramatists claimed creative freedom, and through the voices of their protagonists, universal questions were asked: How should Man act? Why should Man bear chains? Can Man convert the unjust? Should Man obey despotic gods and kings?

All of these questions, and often the answers provided by the dramatists, centered upon Man's innermost flaw: hubris.

Centuries later, William Shakespeare's protagonists—Hamlet, Lear, Henry V, Macbeth and others—would ask those very same questions. So do the characters in our contemporary dramas though regrettably, too often, hubris is now celebrated rather than criticized. It seems the modern world is infatuated with arrogance rather than repulsed, although the ancients' dramatic lessons regarding the dire consequences of hubris are well documented.

I have no soapbox at hand, but I can assure the readers of this book that hubris is not tolerated on the East Hampton.

~Barry

In addition to his immense body of dramatic work, Aeschylus won the highest number of literary prizes ever earned in Ancient Greece. For those reasons, and because of his innovative techniques as a playwright, he is honored as the *Father of Tragedy*, but that title means nothing without the definition of a tragedy.

Tragedy

The word *tragedy* derives from the Greek words: *tragos* (goat) and *ode* (song). As a form of drama, a tragedy instructs a religious tale that invokes an audience's sympathy and brings about *pathos*: instructive suffering. In a sense, the Ancient Greeks viewed a tragedy as "ritual purification."

In a tragedy, the tragic hero (protagonist) has a prevailing weakness: *hubris*, which is Greek for excessive pride, arrogance. As examples: the protagonist *arrogantly* punishes a god (the hubris of *Xerxes*), or *arrogantly* sacrifices his daughter (the hubris of *Agamemnon*) or *arrogantly* seeks blood vengeance (the hubris of *Orestes*). In dramatic form, the excessively proud protagonist defies gods, king, fate, or society as the play unravels to its tragic end.

The Law of Hubris

In effect, tragedies reflected the Ancient Greeks' deep-seated antipathy towards hubris. Their aversion to excessive pride was so consuming that at the start of Athens' democracy, the Law of Hubris was enacted.

Designed to protect the poor from the rich, the law was a reaction to the city-state's bloody history under tyrants with absolute powers. In the new democracy, aristocrats were not disparaged for their wealth and position in society, but required by the Law of Hubris to act modestly and charitably, and to abstain from hubristic acts such as gluttony, drunkenness, lust, violence, and the withholding of someone's property or rights. Above all else, displays of arrogance were considered tragic flaws of hubris. It goes without saying that the poor were expected to live by the same standards, for the public good.

In Ancient Greece, it was rare to be prosecuted for a hubristic act. Conviction required intimate knowledge of an offender's motive and state of mind, and too, the accuser had to pay the high costs of court proceedings without adequate recompense. Regardless, the mere accusation of hubristic behavior could either affect the outcome of a trial for a different crime, or ruin one's reputation.

Hubris was a subject much written about and discussed in Thomas Jefferson's circles—as in the days of Ancient Greece, Early America regarded hubris as a tragic flaw. Jefferson once said: "Pride costs us more than hunger, thirst, and cold."

The Golden Age of Greek Theatre, 600-200 B.C.

As mentioned, Greece's rise from tyranny to democracy (2/3 of the population remained enslaved) created the environment for the birth of drama. By 600 B.C. Greece had been divided into city-states, and almost at once Athens became known as the center of drama. Its population of 150,000 craved entertainments—their myths were filled with fantastical stories about their gods, but the Athenians wanted more than recitations; they wanted performances—and so, in those early days of Athens' creative freedom, the Golden Age of Greek Theatre came into its infancy.

Consider this: drama was conceived in Athens almost 2,000 years before William Shakespeare's birth in 1564. Billy employed most of the forms, terms, and techniques of Ancient Greek theatre in his own productions in the Elizabethan era, and in turn, he bequeathed the Greeks' methods to our own modern theatres of stage and film.

Knowing all this, an obvious question has to be asked: *how did an ancient people create drama—an art form that still dominates our contemporary culture?*

The answer is wine.

The Greeks' reverence of Dionysus, the god of wine, evolved into drama. Religious rites of intoxication and blood sacrifices brought about *ecstasies* (Greek for ecstasy), which involved uninhibited dancing and intense emotion that purportedly altered the worshippers' mental states. Ecstasies were followed by performances of *dithyrambs*, choric hymns that became critical ceremonies in the veneration of Dionysus. The hymns were sung by bands of men costumed as satyrs (half-human, half-goats) who represented the wine-god's servants. Eventually, the simplistic chanting of choric hymns expanded into complex dramatic productions called *tetralogies.*

A tetralogy was comprised of three tragedies with a related theme, and a conclusive satyr (comedic) play. Each play had four parts: Prologue (sets the scene and plot); Parados (an ode the Chorus sings as they enter on stage); Dramatic Scenes (five scenes, each one followed by a Komos, a lament between the Chorus and the Protagonist); and the Exodus (the climax and conclusion).

Dramatic productions required theatres. Open-air amphitheatres were constructed in half circles on hillsides, which provided natural acoustics and tiered seating. Attentive to the concept of "audience satisfaction," architects designed theatres so that viewers could clearly hear and see the staged productions. A fine example is found in the amphitheatre that stands below the Acropolis. Dedicated to the wine-god, Dionysus, this theatre had a seating capacity of 17,000. Another example is the Theatre of Delphi, which sits on a hill above the Temple of Apollo.

By studying Delphi's design and layout, it becomes apparent how the word *amphitheatre* was derived from Greek words. *Theatron* is defined as a "wooden spectator stand erected on a hillside," and *amphi* means "from all sides," which refers to the viewing ease of the audience.

The Dionysian Festival

In 534 B.C., a drama competition was instituted at the Dionysian Festival in Athens. Its primary purpose was to showcase Greek mythology. Over the years, the annual festival attracted Athens' leading poets, but only a few were permitted to enter their work in the competition. The *Archon* (a royal authority) made the selection, and individual members of the *Choregos* (Athens' wealthiest patrons) financed a poet's theatrical production. There was an attractive incentive for sponsorship: the cancellation of taxes for the year of production.

In the early years of the annual festival, plays were performed during daylight hours over a shortened week with all of the action confined to the orchestral area. Actors wore masks painted with exaggerated facial expressions to represent different emotions, and costumes were the ordinary clothes of a citizen, with the one exception that actors wore *cothornos* (leather boots laced up to the knee). These minimal practices continued until Aeschylus introduced elaborate costumes, props and scenery. He also shifted the dramatic action from the orchestra to the stage, where it remains to our present time, except in avant-garde theatres.

The highest honor a Greek playwright could receive was First Prize for a Tetralogy at the Dionysian Festival. Each tetralogy was judged by the rules and principles of aesthetics, with special consideration given to the audiences' approval or disapproval—the enormous, entertainment-starved audiences demanded excellence.

Aeschylus distinguished himself as the winner of 13 First Prizes. He was regarded with such high esteem that upon his death a law was passed that permitted the restaging of his plays, a rare allowance in a culture in which dramas were only performed once.

Greece's Golden Age of Theatre crossed centuries, but the works of only four ancient dramatists have held up over time. Of those four, Aeschylus is considered the most prominent playwright because of his innovative techniques and creative approaches to his art form. In

Aeschylus.

our day and age, his plays are still widely read, studied and performed, but to gain a full appreciation of his skills as a tragedian, he must be known for the man he was.

A Dream in a Wine Vineyard

Aeschylus was born around 525 B.C. in Eleusis, the town west of Athens that served as the center of Greece's worship of Demeter, the goddess of grain. Demeter was crucial in their mythology—she had to remain appeased, for she safeguarded the Greeks' essential of life: bread. Demeter is best remembered by the mythical tale of the abduction of her daughter, Persephone, by Pluto, the god of the underworld; it is the familiar tale of the coming of spring with Persephone's reunion with her mother, and the coming of winter when she returns to the kingdom of her stern, though loving husband.

In being central to Demeter's worship, the town of Eleusis staged extravagant spectacles, processions, mysterious ceremonies, and nocturnal rites of wild abandonment that were connected to beliefs about the human soul and the underworld. With the passage of time, worship of the goddess evolved into a cult of secretive rituals, the Eleusinian Mysteries, which ranged from inebriation to human sacrifice as initiates performed acts that guaranteed an after-life.

Aeschylus, the son of a nobleman, would have taken part in the pageantry as was expected of aristocrats, but in a deeper sense, his entire life was shaped by his belief in the gods and goddesses of his faith. The story is told that as a small boy he had fallen asleep in his father's vineyard when Dionysus, the god of wine, approached him in a dream. *Go*, the boy was told, *serve Athens and the gods as a tragedian*. And so, upon awakening, he pledged himself to obedience of the gods' desire: to serve them, one day, as a dramatist.

The Battle of Salamis, 480 B.C.

Greek mythology would become the dominant theme in Aeschylus' dramatic writings, but his participation in Athens' slow emergence into democracy would also influence his poet's hand.

In his adolescence, Aeschylus witnessed the rebellion that resurrected Athens from a long and bloody period of tyranny. Democracy was established between the years of 510-508 B.C., but it was a fragile state with enemies from within, and from without the borders of the city-state.

In the years 499-496 B. C. Aeschylus began writing dramas, but he put aside his scrolls to serve in the military. Pledging his life to shield the democracy from all enemies, he fought (490-479 B.C.) at the battles of Marathon, Thermopylae, Salamis, and Plataea in Greece's war against Persia. While fighting at Marathon, one of his brothers, Cynaegirus, died heroically as he attempted to keep a Persian ship from departing. Aeschylus mourned his brother, deeply, but celebrated the victory at Marathon and a later conquest at Salamis, both of which elevated Athens to a position of supremacy over Greece's other city-states.

The Battle of Salamis was a major naval conflict between Greece and Persia. More than 1500 vessels filled the straits between Piraeus and Salamis, a small island in the Saronic Gulf near Athens. The Persians' fleet (over 1207 vessels) proved too large for the narrow channel, while the Greeks' fleet of smaller, sleeker ships (371 vessels) was more easily maneuvered to ultimate victory.

Salamis was a critical military engagement for Greece and for Western Civilization, for it kept Greece from being absorbed into the Persian Empire.

By the time of the Battle of Plataea in 479 B. C., the name of Aeschylus had become known in dramatic circles, and so at battle's end, he resigned from further duty to fully heed the god's directive to serve them as a tragedian.

It is widely accepted that Aeschylus' tragedy, *Persae (the Persians)* is based on his front-line experiences at the Battle of Salamis. His tetralogy won top honors at the annual Festival of Dionysus (472 B.C.), a crowning victory that would be the first of thirteen, unprecedented wins. Afterwards, Hieron I the Tyrant of Syracuse, commanded a court performance. One can only imagine Aeschylus' aversion to that command, for his dramas were thinly veiled criticisms of despotism—the wrong word, the wrong inference in his play could have cost Aeschylus his life.

Although he'd emerge the victor at drama competitions for years, in 468 B.C. he met defeat by Sophocles, an emerging young dramatist. Crushed in spirit, Aeschylus retreated to Sicily (then a Greek settlement), but after a brief period of time he returned to Athens in 467 B. C. with a new drama (the *Oedipus Tetralogy*) and regained his title as Athens' premier playwright. Rich accolades came his way from every corner of the known world, but he secluded himself and continued his writings. As mentioned earlier, by career's end, his body of work would include 90 plays, of which 80 are known and 7 are extant.

From Bloodshed to Reflection

To fully appreciate Aeschylus' work as a dramatist, it is helpful to summarize his role in the development of Greek Theatre.

Aeschylus broke tradition by adding a second actor to his plays, and with that one innovation he changed theatrical performances from simple orations to complex stories of conflict and suspense.

By the end of his career he had completely transformed theatres through other inventive moves such as his reduction of the Chorus from 50 to 12, his addition of casts of *thespians* (Greek for actors), his usage of sophisticated costumes, scenery and props, and of utmost importance, his composition of thought-provoking scripts with universal appeal that satisfied all audiences.

One of Aeschylus' dramatic devices that immeasurably advanced theatre was his ploy of replacing acts of bloodshed on the stage with insightful dialogue about the consequences of hubris. This technique allowed him, as a dramatist, to delve more deeply into the hearts and minds of his characters. In effect, he changed flat characters into complex ones, complete with heart-wrenching dilemmas, failures and successes, all of which drew his audiences' sympathy, thus their deep interest in his dramatic tales.

Felonious Charges

Though honored by all Greece, Aeschylus came close to being disgraced by an ignoble death.

While acting a role in one of his own plays, he made a reference to Demeter that outraged the audience. Believing Aeschylus had revealed an inviolable secret (one of the Eleusinian Mysteries, the initiation ceremonies held every year in veneration of Demeter and Persephone) thousands of angry people surged towards him with murderous intent to stone him to death. Aeschylus fled from the stage to the safety of a sacred altar of Dionysus that had been erected in the orchestral area of the amphitheatre. Though surrounded by verbal abuse, he was unmolested by the mob and once it dispersed, he was left, alone, in the emptied theatre.

At the conclusion of the weeklong festival, Aeschylus stood before the *Areospagus* (the High Court of Appeal for criminal and civil cases). As expected, he was charged with the capital offense of revealing one of the Eleusinian Mysteries. He mounted a defense of "ignorance" stating he had never completed his initiation into the cult of Demeter and so had no knowledge of the secrets he was accused of revealing. Acquitted, largely because of his military service and the heroic death of his brother at the Battle of Marathon, Aeschylus continued his work as a dramatist.

The closing years of his life were passed contently until new criticisms surfaced—the public censured him for revealing his "aristocratic tendencies" through his third play, *Eumenides* from his *Orestean Tetralogy*. This was no small criticism in Athens. Aeschylus stood accused of "arrogance" for having written the scene in which his character, Orestes, is exonerated after committing the hubristic crime of matricide. Aeschylus felt the weight of the public's criticism and disheartened, he again retreated to Sicily.

Killer Vulture

Around 456 B.C. Aeschylus settled in Gela, and as the story goes, he was in his garden when a vulture took flight with a tortoise gripped in its claws. From up high the Lammergeier mistook the poet's baldhead for a marble rock, took aim and dropped the tortoise to crack open its shell . . . Aeschylus' skull was split open. Some discount this story as fable, but research into the species Lammergeier suggests that the circumstances surrounding Aeschylus' death are factual.

Engraver unknown.

FYI: Lammergeier vultures (bearded vultures)

Lammergeier vultures were more common in southern Europe 2,000 years ago than in our modern times. They are the only living bird specie that feeds on the bone marrow of deceased animals. Lammergeiers crack bones that are too large to swallow by carrying them in flight to heights of 160–490 feet and dropping them onto rocks to smash the bones into smaller pieces to expose the nutritious marrow—it takes a vulture 7 years to master this skill. In time, the vultures adapted their method to crack open tortoise shells so as to feast on the delicacy of turtle-bones.

Lammergeiers have excellent aim, unfortunately for Aeschylus who survived war, tyrants and angry mobs only to be killed by a hungry bird.

Shortly before his death, Aeschylus had a premonition his time on earth would soon end, and so he prepared by writing his own epitaph. He wrote of his beloved father, Euphorion, of his assumption he'd die in Gela, and of his service as a soldier and the enemy-Persians who rued the Battle of Marathon. Interestingly enough, he made no mention of his work as a dramatist. Aeschylus wrote:

> *Beneath this stone lies Aeschylus,*
> *son of Euphorion, the Athenian,*
> *who perished in the wheat-bearing*
> *land of Gela;*
> *of his noble prowess*
> *the grove of Marathon can speak,*
> *or the long-haired Persian*
> *who knows it well.*

Jefferson's Epitaph

In comparison, just as Aeschylus wanted no references to his great achievements as a tragedian, Thomas Jefferson's epitaph made no mention of his two terms as the third President of the United States. Before his death, he sketched the monument he wanted for his final resting place, and wrote the epitaph to be inscribed into: "coarse stone . . . that no one might be tempted hereafter to destroy if for the value of the materials."

He further instructed, in a document, that the inscription on his stone be etched "on the faces of the Obelisk . . . & not a word more, because by these, as testimonials that I have lived, I wish most to be remembered." This, then, is how Thomas Jefferson wished to be remembered:

Here was buried
Thomas Jefferson
Author of the Declaration of American Independence
of the Statute of Virginia for religious freedom
Father of the University of Virginia

The epitaphs written by Aeschylus and Thomas Jefferson indicate a trait common to them both: the absence of hubris.

At the beginning of this journey there was a struggle between Maureen and myself as to whether or not the plots of the Aeschylus tragedies had a place in this book. I felt the synopses of the tragedies served no purpose, no real connection to Jefferson, himself, but thanks to Maureen's perseverance, I read the plays and agreed that their histories and storylines were familiar to Jefferson and should be included, in some detail.

Still later, as the journey lengthened and the significance of Aeschylus' writings in Jefferson's life was uncovered, weight was added to the value of familiarizing you, our readers, with the characters and stories of Aeschylus' tragic dramas.

In researching the storylines of the plays, we were struck by the depth of Jefferson's lifelong gratitude towards his father for having introduced him to the dramas of Ancient Greece. On August 24, 1819, at the age of 76, he expressed that gratitude in a letter to his good friend John Brazer (1789-1846), a retired professor of Latin at Harvard, who was then serving as the Minister of North Church in Salem, Massachusetts.

Jefferson wrote: "Among the values of classical learning, I estimate the luxury of reading the Greek . . . authors in all the beauties of their originals. And why should not this innocent and elegant luxury take its preeminent stand ahead of all those addressed merely to the senses . . . I think myself more indebted to my father for this than for all the other luxuries his cares and affections have placed within my reach; and more now than when younger, and more susceptible of delights from other sources . . . The classic pages fill up the vacuum of ennui."

Irrefutably, the "classic pages" of Aeschylus' tragedies were important to Jefferson and so they are included here for your own reading pleasure.

~Barry

Aeschylus

The Seven

Volume I
Prometheus

Volume II
Suplices

Volume III
Thebae

Volume IV
Agamemnon

Volume V
Chorephora

Volume VI
Eumenides

Volume VII
Persae

Synopsis Volume I: Prometheus Bound

Prometheus Bound *by Nicolas-Sébastien Adam.*

Dionysia Festival in Athens: the date of this tetralogy is unknown, therefore it is unknown if Aeschylus was awarded First Prize.

Tetralogy: 1st play *Prometheus Bound*; 2nd *Prometheus Unbound*; 3rd *Prometheus the Fire-Bringer; 4th* (satyr) *unknown title.*

Only Extant Play in this Tetralogy: *Prometheus Bound.*

Notes:

A motif of this play is the tragic flaw of hubris: arrogance, excessive pride.

This play tells the myth of the rebel, Prometheus, who has stolen the god's forbidden fire to benefit mankind. As punishment, Zeus orders Prometheus chained to a mountain, where he remains throughout the play, making this a drama of speeches with a minimum of action.

Zeus and Prometheus are both guilty of committing acts of hubris: Zeus for condemning the Titan, Prometheus, without a shred of mercy, and Prometheus for disrespecting the authority of Zeus.

Aeschylus boldly criticizes Zeus' vengefulness in this play, but the partial texts of the other plays in this tetralogy suggest that the playwright resurrected Zeus as a god worthy of honor.

Lost Plays:

The 2nd and 3rd plays survive in sections. In *Prometheus Unbound*, 13 generations after Io's son's birth, her descendant Heracles (Hercules) unchains Prometheus; and in *Prometheus the Fire-Bringer*, Prometheus warns Zeus to resist the sea nymph Thetis, for she'd bear him a son greater than himself. Prometheus' warning reconciles him with Zeus. The title and subject of the satyr play is unknown.

Characters:

KRATOS (symbolizing Power)
BIA (symbolizing Force)
HEPHAESTUS (blacksmith of the gods)
PROMETHEUS (Protagonist)
OCEANIDES, CHORUS (ocean nymphs; Prometheus' cousins)
OCEANUS (Titan)
IO (beautiful maiden transformed into a cow)

Story Line:

Unwillingly, Hephaestus chains Prometheus to a mountain in the Caucasus, a place the Ancient Greeks labeled "the ends of the earth." Kratos chides the blacksmith's reluctance, reminding him that Prometheus deserves perpetual punishment for his sin of hubris: his defiance of the gods' laws by stealing their forbidden fire for mankind. Their companion, Bia, remains silent.

Prometheus' suffering worsens, for each day a fierce eagle swoops down to devour his liver (nightly, the liver regenerates).

The Oceanides arrive to console their cousin Prometheus, who confides he committed other crimes against the gods. His supposed crimes benefitted mankind (he foiled Zeus' plot to destroy all men after the Titan War, and gave humans the gods' Civilizing Arts of medicine, mathematics, astronomy, writing, metallurgy, agriculture and architecture).

Oceanus appears and outlines his plan to convince Zeus to show compassion, but Prometheus stops him, mindful of Zeus' unpredictable wrath. Oceanus is reminded that Zeus depends upon Prometheus' gift of prophecy to avoid begetting a son greater than himself, and so will have no choice but to eventually unbind the chains. Convinced a pardon is forthcoming, Oceanus leaves, after promising he'll do nothing to deepen Zeus' anger.

Lastly, Io comes. Once beautiful, Zeus changed her into an ugly cow to elude his jealous wife, Hera. Prometheus calms Io by predicting her return to human form, the birth of a son, and still later, a descendant who will be named Heracles (Hercules), who will undo Prometheus' chains.

At play's end, Zeus demands the identity of a feared usurper, but Prometheus refuses to reveal the name. Furious, Zeus hurls a thunderbolt that strikes Prometheus, hurtling him into Tartarus, an abyss of fire-hot lightening and organ-devouring beasts.

Synopsis Volume II: Suplices (The Suppliants)

Danaïdes *by John Waterhouse.*

Dionysia Festival in Athens: in 463 B.C., Aeschylus won First Prize for *the Danaus Tetralogy.*

Tetralogy: 1st play *The Suplices (Suppliants)*; 2nd *The Sons of Aegyptus*; 3rd *The Daughters of Danaus*; 4th, (satyr).

Only Extant Play in this Tetralogy: *Suplices.*

Notes:

A motif of this play is the tragic flaw of hubris: arrogance, excessive pride.

This play tells the myth of the disposed king, Danaus, and his 50 daughters (suppliant maidens) who rebel against the Marriage Law that forces them into marriages with their 50 cousins. Father and daughters flee to Argos for refuge, knowing they will be pursued.

The maidens serve as both the Chorus and Protagonist. In disobeying the Marriage Law, they commit hubristic crimes against King Aegyptus, his 50 sons, and society. This is not a traditional tragedy for there is no single hero who suffers a tragic downfall and the conclusion is not tragic—unlike the modern concept of a tragedy, an Ancient Greek tragedy can end with hope. In this play, once the maidens are rescued from forced marriages, they are bidden by their father to offer prayers of thanksgiving to Zeus, the Upholder of Justice—to the Ancient Greeks this ending would suggest hope.

Lost plays:

The other tragedies in this trilogy continue the story of the suppliant maidens in Argos. Those plays are lost, as is the satyr, *Amymone,* which presents Poseidon's comical seduction of one of the 50 daughters.

Characters:

DANAUS (disposed king)
THE DANAIDES, CHORUS
(Danaus' 50 Daughters)
AEGYPTUS (King)
50 PRINCES (Aegyptus' Sons)
HERALD OF AEGYPTUS
PELASGUS (King of Argos)
CITIZENS OF ARGOS

Story Line:

King Aegyptus, flawed by hubris, usurps the throne from his twin brother, Danaus, and then arrogantly commands Danaus' 50 daughters (the Danaides) to obey the Marriage Law that binds them as brides of the king's 50 sons.

Danaus and his daughters flee from the kingdom to Argos to avoid the injustice of forced marriages. Once there, they ask kind but timid King Pelasgus for refuge within Argive walls. Fearing the Danaides will be pursued, the king vacillates but upon reflection, he fairly and democratically seeks his subjects' opinion.

The citizens urge King Pelasgus to open the city as a sanctuary to the fugitives, but before the Danaides can pass through the gates, Aegyptus' fleet (carrying his 50 sons) sails into the harbor. The herald of King Aegyptus suddenly appears at the gate and orders the 50 brides to obey the Marriage Law. Defiant, they cite their right to happiness, and refuse to go with him to meet the grooms. Infuriated, he drags them, bodily, towards the harbor until stopped by King Pelasgus. Emboldened by the injustice of the law, he sends his warriors to drive off the suitors' ships, and ushers the 50 suppliants into the haven of his walled city.

The play ends on a hopeful note with Danaus urging his daughters to offer prayers and libations to the gods. He bids them to avoid hubristic acts, to purport themselves modestly and to show charity to all. Willingly, they promise to carry out their father's wishes.

Synopsis: Volume III: Thebae (Seven Against Thebes)

Oedipus and Antigon*e by Aleksander Kokular.*

Dionysia Festival in Athens: in 467 B.C., Aeschylus won First Prize for the *Thebes Tetralogy.*

Tetralogy: 1st play *Laius*; 2nd *Oedipus;* 3rd *Seven Against Thebes*; 4th (satyr) *The Sphinx.*

Only Extant Play in this Tetralogy: *Seven Against Thebes.*

Notes:

A motif of this play is the tragic flaw of hubris: arrogance, excessive pride.

This play tells the myth of the battle for the city of Thebes during which Oedipus' sons kill each other for the Theban crown. Their sisters inherit the throne.

In this play, Aeschylus institutes the technique of a prologue. He also introduces a literary form called "reflexion of life" through the character Eteocles who muses on the fate of an innocent man, unfairly condemned to share the fate of wicked associates. Eteocles is considered the first "true" character in Greek literature.

The Women of Thebes serve as the play's Chorus. They criticize the gods' interference in human events (government), and credit the polis (city) with the advancement of civilization and democracy—these were common themes in Aeschylus' works.

Lost plays:

The other two plays in the trilogy continue the tale of Oedipus, while the satyr play comically distorts his myth.

Characters:

ETEOCLES (son of Oedipus)
POLYNICES (son of Oedipus)
ADRASTUS (King of Argos)
SPY
HERALD
THEBAN WOMEN, CHORUS
ANTIGONE (daughter of Oedipus)
ISMENE (daughter of Oedipus)

Story Line:

Daring to equate himself with the gods, Oedipus' hubris brings down a plague on his kingdom, Thebes. Upon learning he murdered his father and bedded his mother, he plucks out his own eyes, and in abject humility, he relinquishes his kingdom to his sons, Eteocles and Polynices. They agree to alternate the throne, annually, but at year's end Eteocles commits the hubristic act of withholding his brother's right to assume the throne. Under mortal threat, Polynices escapes to Argos where he and King Adrastus assemble an army under 6 captains: Tydeus, Capaneus, Eteoclus, Hippomedon, Parthenopaeus, Amphiaraus.

Polynices names himself the 7th Captain.

The play opens with their siege of Thebes. To defend the city's 7 gates, Eteocles chooses 6 commanders: Megareus, Melanippus, Polyphontes, Hyperbius, Actor and Lasthenes.

Eteocles names himself the 7th Commander.

Learning from a spy that his brother stands at a city gate, Eteocles meets Polynices in single combat. The bloody battle between the brothers takes place off-stage, the ghastly details made known through a choral ode.

A herald sorrowfully announces that Eteocles and Polynices died by each other's hand. The battle ensues, and the 6 Argive captains are slain.

The princes' bodies are carried on stage. Their sisters and Thebes' women (Chorus) mourn deeply, blaming the witchy goddesses, the Erinyes, for their role in the princes' deaths. Oedipus' daughters, Antigone and Ismene, want to bury their brothers beside their father, but the Herald condemns Polynices as a traitor. Antigone declares she will bury her brother with her own hands—the herald warns her that disobedience is a hubristic act against society, but she defies him, angrily, and boldly buries both brothers.

Synopsis Volume IV: Agamemnon

The Funeral Procession of Agamemnon *by Louis-Jean Desprez.*

Dionysia Festival in Athens: in 458 B.C., Aeschylus won First Prize for the *Oresteia Tetralogy.*

Tetralogy: 1st play *Agamemnon;* 2nd *Choephori (Libation Bearers)*; 3rd *Eumenides*; 4th (satyr) *Proteus.*

Only Extant Trilogy: the three plays of the *Oresteia Tetralogy* make up the only extant trilogy of Ancient Greece.

Notes:

A motif of this play is the tragic flaw of hubris: arrogance, excessive pride.

This play tells the myth of King Agamemnon's return from the Trojan War to his wife, Clytemnestra, who kills him to avenge his sacrifice of their daughter, Iphigenia.

Agamemnon and the other two plays in this trilogy (*Libation Bearers* and *Eumenides*) can each stand on their own merits, but they share a common theme of justice. The trilogy shows evil begetting evil, but by the end of the third play, Aeschylus shows the good that can emerge from sufferings.

Agamemnon is considered Aeschylus' superlative drama, for several reasons: the story line is fueled by the machinations of the gods and the characters are more dimensional than in the playwright's prior works (for example, Clytemnestra is both a ruthless killer and a loving mother). Aeschylus gave his characters complexity through their revelations of the consequences of hubris.

Lost Play:
The comic satyr, *Proteus*, is lost.

Characters:
WATCHMAN
ARGIVE ELDERS, CHORUS
CLYTEMNESTRA (wife of Agamemnon)
HERALD
AGAMEMNON (King of Argos)
CASSANDRA (daughter of Priam; slave of Agamemnon)
AEGISTHUS (son of Thyestes; cousin of Agamemnon)
ATTENDANTS
SOLDIERS

Story Line:
Joy-filled, a watchman announces his sighting of a distant fire that signals the downfall of Troy. After a decade of war, King Agamemnon is returning home in victory.

The Elders recount the king's virtues that led to his great victory, but Queen Clytemnestra loathes her husband for sacrificing their daughter, Iphigenia (at the start of the war the king slaughtered Iphigenia to appease the moon goddess Artemis so she'd fill his warfleet's sails with winds).

In his absence, Clytemnestra has taken her husband's cousin, Aegisthus, as her lover—he also despises Agamemnon (Aegisthus is the lone survivor of his siblings; years earlier, his brothers and sisters were cooked and fed to their father by Agamemnon's cruel father). Hate-filled, both wife and cousin plot the king's murder, their "sin" of hubris in evidence for they place themselves above all laws, the gods' and society's.

Agamemnon arrives with his concubine, Cassandra, the captive priestess of Apollo and daughter of Troy, who is blessed with prophetic gifts, yet cursed in that her prophecies are ignored.

In a pretense of love, Clytemnestra urges her husband to walk the red carpet into his palace, which is an act of hubris, for only gods are permitted that honor.

Once inside his walls, Agamemnon removes his clothes and weapons and enters his bath. Seizing his moment of vulnerability, Clytemnestra "sacrifices" him, sadistically, with an axe.

Cassandra, who foresaw the murder of the king and her own death by an axe, laments the logic of entering the accursed House of Atreus, but she can't deny fate. Though filled with terror, she enters the house, and is butchered by Clytemnestra with the same axe.

Clytemnestra boasts that the murders are justified, but the Elders reproach her for her arrogance. Aegisthus haughtily threatens the Elders, and in turn they forewarn the usurpers that Agamemnon's son, Orestes, will soon return to take "blood revenge."

Synopsis Volume V: Chorephora (Libation Bearers)

Orestes, Elektra and Hermes
by Cheophoroi painter.

Dionysia Festival in Athens: in 458 B.C., Aeschylus won First Prize for the *Oresteia Tetralogy.*

Tetralogy: 1st play *Agamemnon*; 2nd *Choephori (Libation Bearers)*; 3rd *Eumenides*; 4th (satyr) *Proteus.*

Only Extant Trilogy: the three plays of the *Oresteia Tetralogy* make up the only extant trilogy of Ancient Greece.

Notes:

A motif of this play is the tragic flaw of hubris: arrogance, excessive pride.

This play tells the myth of the on-going tragedy of the never-ending blood crimes of the House of Atreus. Agamemnon's son and daughter, Orestes and Electra, reunite and plot revenge for their father's death.

Orestes, the Protagonist, is urged by Apollo to carry out the ancient practice of "justice by blood" by killing his mother, but he ponders the more modern approach of judgment by trial.

Libation Bearers and the other two plays in this trilogy (*Agamemnon* and *Eumenides*) can each stand on their own merits, but they share a common theme of justice. The trilogy shows evil begetting evil, but by the end of the third play, Aeschylus shows the good that can emerge from sufferings.

In this play Aeschylus highlights the beginning of Greece's moral struggle from an autocracy ruled by ritual to a democracy ruled by reason. By the play's end, the struggle is not yet over as Orestes flees for his life, pursued by the Erinyes.

Lost Play:

The comic satyr, *Proteus*, is lost.

Characters:

ORESTES (son of Agamemnon)
SLAVE WOMEN, CHORUS
ELECTRA (daughter of Agamemnon)
CLYTEMNESTRA (Queen)
AEGISTHUS (cousin of Agamemnon)
PYLADES (Orestes' friend)
ERINYES (3 goddesses of punishment)
ATTENDANT

Story Line:

For several years, Clytemnestra shares the throne of Argos with Aegisthus, their rule corrupted by their excessive pride, hubris.

Clytemnestra is haunted by a reoccurring nightmare in which she gives birth to a snake that kills her by drawing milk, then blood from her breast. Terrified that the snake in the dream will become real, she orders her unhappy daughter, Electra, and the slave women (the Libation Bearers) to pour wine (libations) on the grave of the murdered king, Agamemnon. Clytemnestra's hope is that the gods will be appeased by the libations and will grant her their protection from the snake in her dream.

At her father's grave, Electra is happily reunited with her brother Orestes—many years earlier at his birth, Electra had smuggled him, her infant brother, to a safe haven to keep him from being murdered by their mother who foresaw that her newborn son would grow into a man of strength and hatred; a man who would murder her. Orestes is, in fact, the snake in his mother's nightmare.

Orestes convinces Electra to help him avenge their father's death. They devise a plot. Soon after, Orestes and his companion, Pylades, arrive at the palace disguised as travelers bearing word for Clytemnestra that her much feared son, Orestes, is dead. Immensely relieved, she calls for a feast of jubilation.

Involved in the plot, the Slave Women summon Aegisthus to the throne to take part in the Queen's celebration. Upon entering the room, Aegisthus is slaughtered by Orestes.

His hands bloodied, Orestes seizes his mother. Recognizing her son, she begs for mercy. The knife poised, he falters to ponder the more democratic approach of trying his mother before a judge and jury until Pylades reminds him that Apollo ordered "blood revenge."

Clytemnestra is brutally murdered by her son, and even as he boasts of having taken "blood revenge," the three witchy goddesses, Erinyes, appear before his eyes.

The goddesses are only visible to Orestes. They pound him with their fists, tear at his face with their long, sharp nails, and curse him for his hubristic act against society's laws—in Greek society, matricide is a more grievous crime than that of a woman (Clytemnestra) killing her husband (Agamemnon). Tormented, Orestes flees Argos, pursued by the screaming Erinyes who will physically abuse and curse him for all eternity.

Synopsis Volume VI: Eumenides

The Remorse of Orestes *by William Adolphe Bouguereau.*

Dionysia Festival in Athens: in 458 B.C., Aeschylus won First Prize for the *Oresteia Tetralogy.*

Tetralogy: 1st play, *Agamemnon*; 2nd *Choephori (Libation Bearers)*; 3rd *Eumenides*; 4th (satyr) *Proteus.*

Only Extant Trilogy: the three plays of the *Oresteia Tetralogy* make up the only extant trilogy of Ancient Greece.

Notes:

A motif of this play is the tragic flaw of hubris: arrogance, excessive pride.

This play tells the myth of the Erinyes' pursuit of Orestes for the crime of matricide. Taking flight from their abuse, he goes to Athens where Athena and a jury of 12 Athenians determine if his crime justifies eternal torment by the dreadful Erinyes.

Eumenides and the other two plays in this trilogy (*Agamemnon* and *Libation Bearers*) can each stand on their own merits, but they share a common theme of justice. The trilogy shows evil begetting evil, but by the end of the third play, Aeschylus shows the good that can emerge from sufferings.

Although a tragedy, the play *Eumenides* and thus the entire trilogy ends with hope since Orestes is acquitted of wrongdoing. It should be noted that the tragedies of Ancient Greece could end on a hopeful note, unlike most modern tragic dramas.

Even though this trilogy won the highest award at the Dionysia Festival, Aeschylus was later accused of committing the hubristic act of revealing "aristocratic tendencies" as a playwright by allowing the exoneration of his character, Orestes, for the hubristic crime of matricide. Dejected by the public's criticism, Aeschylus exiled himself from Athens.

Lost Play:
The comic satyr, *Proteus*, is lost.

Characters:
THE PYTHIAN PRIESTESS
APOLLO (god of music & light)
ORESTES (son of Agamemnon)
GHOST OF CLYTEMNESTRA
THE 3 ERINYES, CHORUS
ATHENA (goddess of civilization & law)
ATTENDANTS OF ATHENA
JURY (12 Athenian citizens)

Story Line:

Knowing he has committed the sin of hubris, Orestes flees, tortured and bullied by the Erinyes, three shrewish Underworld goddesses. Hoping to find a moment's respite from their beatings and curses, he seeks refuge in Apollo's temple in Adelphi. Moved by pity, Apollo casts a sleeping spell over the Erinyes so that Orestes can escape his ordeal. But even as he reaches Athens, Clytemnestra's Ghost rouses the drugged Erinyes and they track down Orestes through Athens' forests and streets by the scent of his mother's blood in his every footprint.

Found by the Erinyes, Orestes shields his head from their fists, and begs Athena for help (Apollo and Athena embody justice and wisdom). Compassionate, Athena summons a jury of 12 Athenians, and seats herself as Judge and Instructor of Fair Trials. Apollo defends Orestes; the 3 Erinyes speak for the murdered Clytemnestra, citing Orestes' hubristic act of matricide.

The trial ends with six votes for condemnation, and six votes for acquittal. Athena casts the deciding vote in favor of Orestes, and the Erinyes accept the decision.

Vindicated, and grateful to Athena and the citizens, Orestes departs for Argos, resolved to rule his subjects with great wisdom and justice, having known suffering, himself.

The Erinyes renew their anger about Orestes, but Athena calms them by changing their names to *Eumenides*, the Greek word for "Kindly Ones." Assured of great honor if they act, henceforth, with kindness, they accept their new role as benefactors and all Greece honors them for their newfound grace and goodness.

Athena also declares that from thence on, hung juries must end in acquittals, as that is more just, more democratic.

Synopsis Volume VII: Persae (The Persians)

Xerxes Lashing the Hellespont.
Artist unknown.

Dionysia Festival in Athens: in 472 B.C., Aeschylus won First Prize for *the Persian Tetralogy.*

Tetralogy: 1st play *Phineus;* 2nd *Persae* (*The Persians*); 3rd *Glaucus of Potniae*; 4th (satyr) *Prometheus, the Fire Kindler.*

Only Extant Play in this tetralogy: *Persae* (*The Persians*).

Notes:

A motif of this play is the tragic flaw of hubris: arrogance, excessive pride.

This play tells the myth of the god Hellespont who punished the Persian king, Xerxes the Great, for the sin of hubris.

The Greek historian Herodotus wrote an account of the actual ruler of Persia, King Xerxes (519-465 B. C.) at the Battle of Salamis. Xerxes ordered his vessels lined up, side-by-side, and cabled together like a pontoon bridge for his army to advance over into battle. Herodotus reported that Xerxes' first attempt to bridge the strait of water, the

Hellespont, ended in failure when a storm stirred up by Hellspont (the god of the strait of water), destroyed the bridge's cables of papyrus and flax. Furious, Xerxes ordered Hellespont lashed 300 times, before he threw fetters into the water to shackle the god's ankles. Xerxes' second bridge over the strait held, but his hubristic act against the god, Hellspont, brought about King Xerxes' defeat by the Greeks in battle.

This play is based on Aeschylus' actual wartime experience in the Battle of Salamis.

There are two conflicting interpretations of Aeschylus' tragedy *Persae:* as either a sympathetic treatment of the defeated Persians, or as a celebratory tale of Greece's victory in war; regardless which interpretation is chosen, this tragedy is a dramatic glorification of Athens as a warrior city-state.

Lost Plays:

Phineus tells the myth of Jason & the Argonauts' rescue of King Phineus from the Harpies' torture, and the other play, *Glaucus*, tells the myth of the Corinthian king who angers Aphrodite and is devoured by his own horses. The satyr play, *Prometheus the Fire-kindler*, tells the Prometheus myth with a comedic twist.

Characters:

ATOSSA (widow of King Darius and mother of King Xerxes)
XERXES (King of Persia)
MESSENGER
GHOST OF KING DARIUS
PERSIAN ELDERS, CHORUS

Story Line:

In Susa, a city in the Persian Empire, the Elders (the Council of State) await news of King Xerxes' war against the Greeks. The king's mother, Atossa, reveals to the Elders the bloody battle-scenes that haunt her dreams. She tells them of Xerxes' defeat even before a messenger arrives with gory details about the Battle of Salamis. The messenger names all of the generals who were killed; Atossa is greatly relieved her son, the king of Persia, is not named among the dead.

King Xerxes' arrival is expected within hours.

At her family's tomb, Atossa bids the Elders to summon her dead husband's spirit to learn the reasons behind Athens' victory.

Appearing, the Ghost of King Darius the Great tells Atossa that their son committed a crime against a god, a hubristic act, which brought about his defeat. Having observed the battle in his vaporous form as an apparition, the Ghost tells of Xerxes' arrogance in lashing his ships together into a bridge for his army's advance over Hellespont, the god of the narrow strait between the Aegean Sea and the Sea of Marmara (the Dardanelles).

Atossa listens carefully as the Ghost speaks of the retaliation by the god, Hellspont, who hurled tempestuous waves to destroy the bridge. Infuriated, Xerxes swore retaliation of his own. Using his whip, he flogged the god with 300 lashes before throwing fetters into the strait to bind Hellespont's ankles.

The Ghost tells Atossa that he watched their son stride boldly into a field to cut yet more flax, so as to cable a second bridge of ships over the fettered god (the strait of water). That bridge held, his army marched into battle, but was mightily overwhelmed by the Greeks.

The queen condemns her son's hubristic act against the god, Hellespont, for she is certain that Xerxes' arrogance sealed Persia's defeat before the battle was underway.

Prior to vanishing, the Ghost predicts another defeat at Plataea (the actual Battle of Plataea occurred in 479 B.C.).

King Xerxes arrives home in ragged, bloodied robes. Lamenting to the Elders about his terrible loss to the Greeks, they reply through lengthy, lyrical songs in which they bitterly picture Athens' boastful celebration of Persia's defeat.

Kindred Spirits

In Jefferson's own words, the 7 tragedies of Ancient Greece gave him a lifetime of *story satisfaction*—that fact forms our premise that Thomas Jefferson and Aeschylus were kindred spirits.

To support this premise we turned to studies in the art of fiction-writing that maintain that readers derive *story satisfaction* by identifying with an author, or with one of the author's characters (usually the hero; rarely the villain).

To identify with an author, the reader must recognize shared common experiences, attributes, philosophies or goals—all of which the author reveals through the words and actions of his story. The author in this case is Aeschylus, of course, and the reader is Jefferson; to name them as kindred spirits we must show that commonalities existed between them.

Literary scholars describe Aeschylus as:

"The only man of his age . . . [with] sublimity of conception and grandeur of [ideas]. As to the esteem in which he was held by his contemporaries . . . there is sufficient evidence that he was . . . proud, stern and impatient; his sentiments . . . pure, noble and warlike; his genius inventive, magnificent and towering; his style lofty, bold and impetuous, full of . . . ponderous expressions, while in the . . . arrangement of his [life-work] there was . . . ancient simplicity . . . splendor [in] his talents . . . originality of ideas [with] the force, variety and beauty of . . . language . . . [with] dignity of sentiment."

Other than the reference to Aeschylus being "warlike," the above description fits Jefferson, perfectly. Other parallels in their lives include:

- their high regard for their fathers
- their adolescent decisions to pursue lives filled with books and writings
- their witnessing of the emergence of democracy in their native lands
- their courage to address the principles of freedom in their writings
- their participation in wars to defend the right of independence
- their recognition that their new nations were fragile and in grave danger of imminent collapse.

But the final and most significant commonality between the Virginian and the Athenian is the identical theme found in their writings: *the shift from tyranny to freedom.*

Consider this:

Aeschylus took an active role in Greece's transition from despotic rule to democracy—as a playwright he revealed that movement through his dramas. For example, in writing *Eumenides* he depicted the three goddesses, Erinyes, as foul representatives of Greece's ancient, primitive laws, while he presented Apollo and Athena as representatives of a new order of government based on Reason and democratic principles.

In the same vein:

Jefferson took an active role in the colonies' transition from despotic rule to democracy—as a writer he revealed that movement through his political documents. For example, in writing the *Declaration of Independence*, he depicted King and Parliament as foul representatives of England's ancient, primitive laws, while he presented the unified states as representatives of a new order of government based on Reason and democratic principles.

As for the other aspect of the studies in the art of fiction-writing, a reader can derive *story satisfaction* through identification with one of the author's characters. Did Prometheus or King Xerxes, or possibly Danaus, Agamemnon, Orestes or even Antigone strike common chords in Jefferson's mind and heart?

As the saying goes, the jury is still out regarding our premise that Thomas Jefferson and Aeschylus were kindred spirits, but as Barry suggests below, the whole idea merits further thought . . .

> *Keeping all of the perceived parallels between Aeschylus and Thomas Jefferson in mind, I asked Maureen to step into Jefferson's shoes as he ponders the relevance of Aeschylus' dramas to actual events in his own life as an American Patriot, lawyer and writer. I asked that she keep in mind the timeline of Thomas Jefferson's life, as she considered his ever-changing, or perhaps never-changing reactions to, and reflections upon, the moral lessons of these myths of Ancient Greece.*
>
> *To do so, of course, constitutes a flight of fancy, for she can only imagine, only conjecture Thomas Jefferson's thoughts as he read the 7 plays. Above that, we are left to speculate if the language and precepts of Aeschylus influenced the hand of Jefferson in the crafting of our nation's foundation documents. And we are then left to ponder the notion that they were kindred spirits.*
>
> *~Barry*

Volume I: Prometheus
Flight of Fancy: The Connection to Jefferson

This tragedy tells of Prometheus' heroic defiance of a tyrant (Zeus) for the betterment of humankind. In committing selfless acts of rebellion he accepts the risks of discovery and punishment. Consequently, though a Titan of great strength, he is chained to a mountain at the ends of the earth, his liberty lost, seemingly, for eternity.

As self-sacrificing as the Titan, Jefferson sought constitutional justice for the citizens of the 13 colonies, and in so doing, he defied a powerful tyrant, King George III. And, similar to the character Prometheus, Jefferson understood the consequences of rebellion but, willingly, he accepted the risks of losing his land, liberty and life for the greater good of state and nation.

Volume II: Suplices (The Suppliants)
Flight of Fancy: The Connection to Jefferson

This play highlights the autonomous undercurrents running through Athens prior to the establishment of a democratic government in 461 B.C. Aeschylus illustrates the emergence of independent thought in Greece through the flight of the 50 daughters and their father from the unjust Marriage Law, and through King Pelasgus' democratic consultation with his subjects as to whether or not he should offer Argos as a sanctuary.

In Ancient Greece, daughters were considered property to be doled out in arranged marriages; in Colonial America, wealthy families such as Thomas Jefferson's formed political and business alliances through marriages, but in general, matrimonial unions weren't forced upon the unwilling. In his drama, Aeschylus challenged Greece's Marriage Law—as a proponent of the Theory of Natural Rights, Jefferson would have applauded the runaway-brides' defiance of the law in their pursuit of happiness, one of man's natural rights.

Too, Jefferson would have recognized King Pelagus' egalitarian consultation with his subjects as being consistent with Greece's rising democracy. To Jefferson's way of thinking, the people of Argos were being bestowed the great privileges that we, as a nation, have been given through our founding documents.

This play must have especially pleased Jefferson, for although it is labeled a tragedy, *Suplices* is a story of hope.

Volume III: Thebae (Seven Against Thebes) Flight of Fancy: The Connection to Jefferson

In the writing of this play, Aeschylus censured the interference of the elite gods in human affairs—Polynices' attack on the 7 gates of Thebes against his once beloved brother, Eteocles, fulfills a prophecy—as sons of the accursed Oedipus and at the instigation of the goddesses Erinyes, the brothers battle each other for the kingdom, and tragically, they die at each other's hand.

Just as this play criticizes the interference of the elite gods in the brothers' affairs, Jefferson censured the interference of the elite gods of England (King and Parliament) in the colonists' affairs through unwarranted restrictions and taxation. And, just as the gods drove the Greek brothers to fratricide, the "gods" of England turned brother against brother in the throes of the Revolutionary War.

No matter which form the elites took (King & Parliament or President & Congress), Jefferson mistrusted large governments. As a Democratic-Republican, he envisioned a nation of farmers, thus independent, self-reliant laborers under a limited government—were he here with us today, would he call for a "little rebellion" to end the elitism gripping our nation? Perhaps. And perhaps Thomas Jefferson had the gods of this Greek tragedy in mind when he wrote: "The issue today is the same as it has been throughout all history, whether men shall be allowed to govern [themselves] or be ruled by a small elite."

Volume IV: Agamemnon Flight of Fancy: The Connection to Jefferson

This tragedy draws a thin line between murder and justified murder as ethical questions arise: is Agamemnon *justified or unjustified* in the sacrifice of his daughter, Iphigenia, for the greater good of his people, and is his wife, Clytemnestra, *justified or unjustified* in killing her husband to avenge their daughter's death? Both characters present themselves as having acted honorably, but how would Jefferson have judged them?

As a father who deeply cherished his children, he probably viewed Agamemnon's sacrifice of Iphigenia as murder, plain and simple, but Clytemnestra would have been a more complicated character for him to unravel. Would Jefferson have cast her in the role of the vindictive wife wanting release from marriage for purely selfish reasons, or did he view her as the grieving mother rightly seeking justice for her slain daughter?

As a man of the Enlightenment, Jefferson may have leaned towards the latter, if he recalled Francis Bacon's definition of revenge as "wild justice," which aptly describes Clytemnestra's unrestrained wielding of the ax—apart from the "wild" brutality of the punishment she doles out, she is seeking "justice" for the more heinous crime of Agamemnon's slaughter of their innocent and loving daughter.

Beyond this play, did that thin, almost invisible line between murder and justified murder challenge Jefferson's thinking in real-life situations?

Volume V: Chorephora (Libation Bearers)
Flight of Fancy: The Connection to Jefferson

Clytemnestra fails as a mother, and her son, Orestes, declares his familial separation from her, and yet in a moment of weakness, he falters with the knife. Reminded again of her failures and crimes, his anger is renewed and he slays his mother, brutally, according to the ancient laws of primitive justice—all the while knowing he will suffer dire consequences.

Jefferson would have felt a kinship with Orestes. In the 1770s, the "mother country" failed her "children" (the 13 colonies) and so after much deliberation, he wrote the *Declaration of Independence*, which "killed" the relationship with the mother-country, England—all the while knowing there'd be dire consequences for himself, as a "traitor," and for those who stood with him in the pursuit of liberty.

This play ends tragically, but hope lies ahead for Orestes, as it would for Jefferson and his fellow Americans—its happy ending was only hinted at when Jefferson first read this play as a child and young man, but fully appreciated when he re-read the play after the War of Independence.

Volume VI: Eumenides
Flight of Fancy: The Connection to Jefferson

In this drama, Aeschylus shows Greece's transition from primitive to civilized forms of justice. The play continues the tragic tale of Agamemnon and Clytemnestra with their son Orestes' act of "justice by blood" (his murder of his mother that carries on the curse of the House of Atreus) to "justice by trial" (his trial, sanctioned by the enlightened gods Apollo and Athena). Orestes' acquittal ends the family's curse, and he vows he will rule as a rational, fair-minded king, all of which corresponds with the advancement of Greek civilization.

As a land lawyer, Jefferson primarily dealt with caveats (property issues) and thus he was far removed from jury trials; however, the depiction of Athens' fair trial complete with lawyers, jury and judge would surely have intrigued him as both a practitioner of the law and a private citizen.

Volume VII: Persae (The Persians)
Flight of Fancy: The Connection to Jefferson

In short, this tragedy can either be read as a congratulatory piece about the might of the Greek military, or as a condemnation of hubris as the cause of King Xerxes' defeat in Persia's war with Greece.

Aeschylus' treatment of hubris would have caught Jefferson's eye.

Thomas Jefferson viewed arrogance as a tragic character flaw in fictional works, and as a despicable human flaw in real-life. Reading deeply as he was wont to do, he would have mulled over the accusation that King Xerxes revealed hubris in his arrogant defiance of the god, Hellespont, by building a bridge over the strait for his army to cross over into battle. And above the accusatory words of the Ghost and the Persian Elders, Jefferson would have noted the barbed words of the sharp-tongued queen-mother.

But did Jefferson agree with the accusers, or did he empathize with Xerxes as a leader caught between the proverbial "rock and hard place" in the making of national decisions? Empathy in that Jefferson, himself, while serving as our third president, arrogantly stepped over the "gods" of Congress and the citizenry by his enactment of boycotts that outraged the public, by his purchase of the Louisiana Territory with loans he had no constitutional right to make, and by his furtive and illegal arrangement of the Lewis and Clark expeditions.

Thus, if Jefferson viewed Xerxes as a decisive leader who acted in the best interests of his kingdom, he would not have condemned the Persian king as a man of hubris. In kind, Jefferson, would never have labeled himself as a man of hubris, but rather as a resolute leader who seized unilateral opportunities to best serve the United States of America—perception after the fact proves the forward-thinking of Jefferson's Executive Acts, in particular the territory acquisitions and explorations that measurably increased our nation's standing as a world power.

As a final point, in reading this tragedy, Jefferson may have empathized with Xerxes in one other way: both had strong-willed mothers who were best ignored.

Were Thomas Jefferson and Aeschylus kindred spirits?

As my co-author said, the jury is still out, but the idea that Aeschylus influenced Thomas Jefferson's crafting of our nation's foundation documents has merit largely because of the value he placed on ancient writings.

The evidence lies in Jefferson's own words in the August 24, 1819, letter sent to his friend, Harvard Latin Professor and Minister, John Brazer. In that letter, Jefferson explained the benefits derived from readings of the literary works of the Ancient Greeks, by writing: "To whom [are Greek writings] useful . . . to the moralist they are valuable, because they furnish ethical writings highly and justly esteemed . . . The statesman will find in these languages history, politics, mathematics, ethics, eloquence, love of country."

As a parting remark about the value of the Ancient Greek's writings, I can only add that for those of you who have been influenced to read the Declaration of Independence, I now suggest that you tackle the 7 tragedies of Aeschylus. But as a cautionary note, if you do read Aeschylus' dramas, keep in mind that he lost his life when a vulture snatched a live turtle and dropped it on his head.

~Barry

The Seven

In returning to John Laval's search for a Latin translation of Aeschylus' tragedies, it is unknown if he found one or more books. If he located several editions in different languages, it's probable that he acquired those books for his patron, as well. At any rate, he shipped a book-packet from Philadelphia to Monticello without mishap.

Assumedly, after reviewing the contents of the package, Jefferson felt that his Aeschylus collection was complete. By then he owned:

Aeschyli Tragoediae Quae Supersunt Ac Deperditarum Fragmenta, Halae, 1809;

Aeschyli Tragoediarum Reliquae, Parisiis, Typis Republicae, Anno III;

Theatre D'Aeschyle, Traduit En Francoiis, Avec Notes Philologiques, A Paris, An. III, Du Theil, 1794;

Theatre D'Aeschyle, Premiere Partie, Se debite chez J. L. Nyon, rue du Jardinet; and

Aeschylus, Oxford, R. Potter, Bliss & Baxter, 1812.

On April 10, 1820, Jefferson` wrapped all of the editions in sturdy paper, placed them in a mail-packet, and enclosed a letter in which he commissioned F. A. Mayo to interleave and rebind the pages into 7 volumes, one for each of Aeschylus' 7 tragedies. The packet was carried to Milton and taken from there, by river, to Richmond.

Mayo accepted the commission, and over a series of months, he removed the pages from the books' spines to reorder them as prescribed by Jefferson. Once the original text (Greek) and translations (English, Latin and French) were properly arranged, he attached the pages to new spines between front and back boards, and rebound all 7 volumes in soft, brown calf-leather. Lastly, he stamped a delicate dentil design over the marbled flyleaves before embellishing the leather covers and spines with gold tooling.

In that way, the *Seven* came into existence.

Broken Threads

Jefferson's April 10, 1820 letter to Mayo, in which he gave instructions for interleaving the Aeschylus editions into the *Seven* is lost (details are provided under **Authors' Notes** at the end of this book). Along with the lost letter, there are three broken threads in the fabric of this book; three unknown dates: the day Mayo completed his work on the Aeschylus volumes; the day he shipped them to Monticello; and the day the book packet arrived at Jefferson's door. To recreate the events of those three days, facts had to be combined with conjecture...

A Flight of Fancy

On an unknown day in 1820 or 1821, Fred Mayo cleared enough space on his worktable for the 7 Aeschylus volumes, a jar of glue and 7 sunburst tickets. They were larger tickets than the ones he normally pasted into Jefferson's books, but these were extraordinary books that warranted singular tickets.

He opened *Volume I* so that its front cover lay flat. Uncorking the jar, he applied a thin layer of glue to the back of the first ticket before pressing it onto the upper left corner of the cover. Using a sea-sponge, he dabbed away any excess glue, before moving the book to the side, its cover left open for the adhesive to dry. Working in his methodical way, in due course all 7 were labeled as books bound by his hand.

After his noonday meal of bread and cheese, Mayo wrapped the books, individually, in thick, brown paper and added them to a mailing packet along with the letter he had written the night before.

The skies blackening above him, he carried the heavy package through the alleys and streets that circled down to the wharf; there was strength in the rising winds, enough to push him along the pier as he made his way towards a manned merchant boat. Its lines were being cast off so he quickened his step, but Captain Peyton acknowledged him with a wave of his cap and waited at the side of the boat.

Accepting the package from Mayo, the captain gave his usual assurance that Mr. Jefferson's books would be provided safe and dry

Mayo's sunburst ticket on the inside front cover of Volume I. The ticket bears his name, and the location of his bindery. Each ticket measures about 1" by 1 ¼." The gilt dentil design can be seen on the upper and left sides of the board (the hard cover of the book).

passage—rain fell, and without another word he hurried towards his cabin, the packet shielded by his cap.

From boat to cart, delivery was made to Monticello without incident, and we imagined this . . .

Thomas Jefferson placed the mail-packet on his desk. The cords cut, the seal undone, he removed a letter and several packages wrapped in brown paper. Savoring his moment of anticipation, he first opened the letter and read Mayo's comments with interest, but a reply would only be written after a full inspection of his handiwork.

With deliberate slowness Jefferson unwrapped each of the volumes, placing them side-by-side in their proper order, I through VII. Sitting back in his chair, he appraised the books, confident their similarity in size and color would distinguish them as volumes of the same set.

He picked up *Volume IV* to gauge its weight; though smallish, it felt solid, heavy, which meant thousands of words, and hours of reading pleasure. In hand, the book had the feel of fine leather, the softness of calf; its brown color reminded him of wood, a blend of dark walnut with a lighter cherry. The rich color of the leather gave its gold-tooling an aged look, much like antique gold.

To test the quality of the binding, he opened the book, closed it, and opened it again, all with the ease of a perfectly bound book. He then turned his attention to the inside front cover. Purplish-green marbled paper had been chosen for the flyleaves . . . its edges glimmered under the lamp's light . . . he bent closer . . . a delicate line of gilt dentil surrounded the board. He ran a light finger over the design of repeating blocks of gold, more than satisfied with his binder's artistic skills. Simplicity is the hallmark of elegance, he thought to himself.

But the ticket in the upper corner surprised him. Typically, Mayo added small, unremarkable tickets, never one as large and as ornate as this sunburst. Why, why indeed? A small smile touched his mouth as the reason occurred to him—it was Mayo's way of recognizing the significant position these books would hold in his patron's library. "Intuitive," Jefferson said in a low voice, meant only for himself.

He came to the final aspect of his inspection—a measurement of Mayo's accuracy in the interleaving of the original text with the different translations. As way of checking, he first read the Preface in English, before turning quite a few pages. Pausing, he read Clytemnestra's false words of welcome to Agamemnon in Ancient Greek . . . turning more pages he found its translation in French . . . pages later, Clytemnestra's lies appeared in English . . . still later, at the end of the book, her treacherous words rose up harsh and bitter in the ancient language of Latin. His smile reappeared. All of his instructions had been followed to the tee—he would make note of that in his letter of reply to Mayo.

He placed *Agamemnon* back in its allotted space between Vol.

III and Vol. V to begin a task he had adopted out of his disdain for bookplates; a task that would take several hours to complete, but meaningful in that it connected him, visibly, to his books.

He selected a quill, tested its sharpness, and opened a jar of indigo ink. Starting with *Volume I*, he opened to a signature quire to ink one of his two initials: a "T" for Thomas or an "I" (Latin for "J") for Jefferson. Blotting the ink, he turned to the next quire to ink another initial, and so on and so on, to the next volume and the next, meticulously making his ownership markings.

Reaching the 6th volume, he paused to consider the 4th page; the 4 had been printed very close to the quire notation. He inked an "I" next to the 4, and turning to the last quire he inked a "P." A change of habit; a slip of the hand? No matter, the "P" would stand as written.

Lastly, he checked the title pages of all 7 books, making strikethroughs in volumes III, IV, V and VI. Noticing a small error on the title page of the 6th volume, he altered the II to read VI.

His tasks completed, he carried the 7 volumes into his library, and lined them up on a shelf that had been kept in reserve for Aeschylus' work. He stepped back to regard the books' spines, the gilt letters of the tragedian's name, and the titles of his dramas: *Volume I, Prometheus; Volume II, Suplices; Volume III, Thebae; Volume IV, Agememnon; Volume V, Chorephora; Volume VI, Eumenides; Volume VII, Persae.* Supremely pleased, he decided to read them in order—he'd begin after supper.

Back at his desk he wrote a long note of appreciation to Mayo and included a check to pay him in full. Once addressed and sealed, it was added to the pile of letters that would be posted in the morning. He stretched, widely, and rising from the red chair he went into his room to change his coat for the evening meal.

Dinner seemed interminably long, but at last the food, wine, and talk ended and he could lock his door behind him. Trading his coat for a robe, he lit candles, and sank down into the red chair, a pot of spiced tea at his side. Around him the house had finally quieted in sleep, and confident he could read without interruption, he opened *Volume I* and turned to the first page . . . *drawn back through the centuries to the highest mountain of the Caucasus, Jefferson stands with the chained hero, Prometheus, as he tells of his defiance of tyrants. His words are ageless, invaluable, for they are the words of heroism, the timeless words of courage . . .*

The Seven: Teaching Tools

The Aeschylus books were his to hold and read, and Jefferson did exactly that, but he reserved another purpose for the *Seven*, as explained below.

> *Like a typical grandfather Thomas Jefferson lavished his grandchildren with gifts, all of which has been covered in his different biographies; however, at our first meeting, Gerry Cataldo positioned Jefferson as a grandfather who took his role seriously and the proof lay in the Seven.*
>
> *Supposedly, Jefferson's practice of using books to teach his grandchildren foreign languages included the Aeschylus volumes. That whole idea was intriguing enough, but during the research process for the writing of this book, it was discovered that Jefferson reserved an additional, more essential purpose for the Seven—he used the Ancient Greek's stories of heroes and villains to teach his grandchildren moral principals.*
>
> *Jefferson's approach to teaching morals was based on simple logic. When his grandchildren were small, he guided their studies through advice, and directed their education through Reading Lists that included books in foreign languages, history, science, philosophy, politics, and poetry (Scottish and English). He also suggested readings of magazines and newspapers, and often clipped out articles for them, adding comments in the margins.*
>
> *Later, as his grandchildren matured, Jefferson knew they would hear, but not listen, to lectures about morals, so instead he encouraged them to read certain, inspirational books before their 16th birthdays. Consider, for example, his recommendation to them to read Shakespeare's King Lear—surely in Jefferson's mind, Lear's daughters illustrated the positives and negatives of filial respect, for he wrote:*

"The field of imagination is thus laid open to our use and lessons may be formed to illustrate and carry home to the heart every moral rule of life. Thus a lively and lasting sense of filial duty is more effectually impressed on the mind of a [grandchild] by reading King Lear, than by all the dry volumes of ethics, and divinity that ever were written . . . " (1771).

Still later, as his grandchildren took their first steps into the world, Jefferson supplied them with Reading Lists that included more complex moralistic writings—he placed in their hands the definitive works of Aeschylus: seven books, seven memorable lessons.

~Barry

Jefferson's Beloved Grandchildren: Anne, Jeff, and Francis

A great deal has been written about the happiness Jefferson found in the company of his grandchildren. He once said, "It is only with them, that a grave man can play the fool."

Although he doted on all of them, three of his grandchildren provided him the greater part of that happiness. Those three were Anne Randolph Bankhead (or Ann, 1791-1826), and her brother, Thomas Jefferson Randolph (Jeff, 1792-1875), and Francis Wayles Eppes (1801-1881).

Books became a bridge between grandfather and grandchildren.

Anne was a gentle soul who shared her grandfather's passion for gardening and reading. At the age of 17, she married Charles Lewis Bankhead; the couple resided at Carlton, a farm at the edge of Monticello (4 of their children would reach adulthood).

Her brother Jeff displayed the courage and immense strength of Peter Jefferson, his Great-Grandfather. While still a young man, Jeff became the farm manager and close confidante of his revered grandfather. They spoke often of the ethical lessons found in books; lessons Jeff learned well, for by all accounts he was a "Titan, of much honor."

As for Francis, to his grandfather's great pride, he became a scholar in his own right, venturing into a life of study and public duty. In his future years, in close imitation of his grandfather, Francis would persevere in changing a small school into a university: Florida State University.

Francis offers documented evidence of Jefferson's usage of Aeschylus' writings to ease a grandchild's acquirement of knowledge and moral principles.

Back in 1804, Francis' mother, Maria, died from complications after the birth of her daughter, also named Maria (1804-1806). On April 17, 1804, Thomas Jefferson wrote: "This morning between 8 & 9. aclock my dear daughter Maria Eppes died." In public, he appeared stoic as he carried out his presidential duties, but behind the scenes he devoted himself to his daughter's toddler, Francis.

From that time on, Jefferson remained a strong presence in his grandson's life. Years later, on September 19, 1820, Jefferson wrote a letter to Francis, by then a young man of 19, to recommend that he read Aeschylus and other ancient writers as a method by which he could prepare himself for the study of law. He wrote:

"I leave at Flood's [Inn] . . . 3 Volumes . . . containing several tragedies of Euripides, some of Sophocles and one of Aeschylus. The 1st. you will find easy, the 2nd. Tolerably so; the last incomprehensible in his flights among the clouds."

In our more casual use of language, it is sometimes helpful to take a closer look at a word's actual meaning. Jefferson's choice of the word "incomprehensible," which is defined as "impossible or very difficult to understand," did not imply that Aeschylus was a poor craftsman of words. Rather, Jefferson was emphasizing the complexity of Aeschylus' writings.

The placement of Aeschylus' moralistic dramas in Francis' hands was no idle gesture on Jefferson's part. There was purpose in everything he did, especially when it came to the betterment of his grandchildren's lives.

Heresy

Jefferson's editorial work on the *Seven* has been rightfully commended, but his work on another book brought him public censure.

On the 13th day of October 1824, Jefferson placed the unbound pages of a manuscript into a mailing packet and added a letter, in which he wrote: "[This manuscript] is to be bound with as much dispatch as good pressure will admit. Do it in red morocco with gilt leaves, and two or three leaves of good writing paper at the beginning and end; blank [papers] which will permit writing on. Send it through the mail as soon as [its] ready."

After the packet arrived at the Richmond bindery, Mayo sorted through the pages with growing consternation. If he accepted the commission, he'd risk his career and reputation, for Jefferson's manuscript was nothing short of heresy.

But Mayo was teetering on the edge of ruin—since the Panic of 1819, bookbinding orders had dried up, even while the doctor's bills for his ailing family had piled up. In 1822, to offset the high cost of medicine, he had opened part of his home as the "Garden" where Virginia's gentlemen could be "afforded amusements." In 1823 and into 1824, his financial situation only worsened, and so in spite of any misgivings he may have had, Mayo accepted the commission to bind Jefferson's supposedly heretical manuscript.

As the days of autumn unfolded, F. A. Mayo bound the manuscript in red Moroccan leather—a color Jefferson had never requested before, a color Mayo had assumed his patron disliked. The cover in place, the flyleaves dried, he added the book's long title: *The Life and Morals of Jesus of Nazareth Extracted Textually from the Gospels in Greek, Latin, French and English.* Or as many have come to refer to this book: *The Jefferson Bible.*

Some would denounce the red bible as the work of an "atheist," because as the editor of his scriptural work, Jefferson chose to exclude the miracles performed by Christ. But Jefferson's critics overlooked the words he had once stated emphatically: "I am a Christian, in the only sense in which [Christ] wanted anyone to be: sincerely attached to his doctrines, in preference to all others; ascribing to himself every human excellence; and believing he never claimed any other."

Those who were familiar with Jefferson's nighttime rituals noted that he read his red bible each night before extinguishing his candle—a practice he had begun during his presidential years before the manuscript's pages were bound in red Moroccan leather.

Gratification

The professional relationship between Jefferson and Mayo was successful—just as Jefferson recognized the skills of his bookbinder, Mayo recognized his patron as a Bookman of refined taste.

During their years of patronage, Mayo came to understand Jefferson's contempt for books that were left untouched and unread like "lavish ornaments." Jefferson read his books, and so he expected them to be well-bound to provide "ease" in handling and reading. On the other hand, Mayo knew Jefferson wasn't averse to artful bindings. He expected his binder to provide "handsomely bound [books] with restrained elegance . . . elegant but not opulent . . . with neat bindings, gilt and lettered in the modern stile [sic] with gold and blind tooling and at times, elaborately edged pages."

Keeping all that in mind, Mayo used handmade paper and calfskin leather of one variety or another, but above all else, he made certain the bindings had the "durability" and "ease" Jefferson desired in the opening and closing of his books.

In his last letter to Jefferson, Mayo requested additional commissions, asking for: " . . . a few sizable volumes with liberty to bind them in the best style I may be able to fancy . . . probably they may be of some credit to me, either in your library or in the University of Charlesville [sic]."

Mayo's request is worth mentioning for it confirms Jefferson's altruistic plan to bequeath his third collection, the Retirement Library, to the University of Virginia.

As an aside, for a number of years after Jefferson's death, Mayo continued to use his patron's words of praise in newspaper advertisements, but by 1836, he had to admit that mechanized binding machines were replacing hand bookbinding. Although highly accomplished in his field, he acknowledged the period of his patronage under Jefferson as the peak of his professional career—surely Frederick August Mayo would be gratified knowing he is featured in books and historical sites as "Thomas Jefferson's last bookbinder."

The Tragedy of Monticello

The final years of Thomas Jefferson's life
Setting: his mountain estate near Charlottesville, Virginia

Like one of Aeschylus' dramas, a tragedy was unfolding at Monticello; a tragic tale of physical abuse, attempted murder, and death complicated by insanity, illness, alcoholism and debts. But high above the turmoil, the figure of Jefferson rose up as the protagonist of the story—beaten down physically and emotionally at times but heroic in every sense of the word, he stood at the head of a cast that included:

Jefferson's strong-willed daughter, Martha, and her villainous husband, Tom Randolph;

Jefferson's sweet granddaughter, Anne, and the other villain in this tragedy, her husband, Charles Bankhead;

and Jefferson's honorable grandson, Jeff Randolph, and his virtuous wife, Jane.

The Protagonist: Thomas Jefferson

Jefferson's twilight years meant morning rides throughout his properties, estate projects that occupied his afternoon hours, conversations over glasses of wine, and uninterrupted hours in his library—finally allowed the luxury of following Horace's example, Jefferson would settle into his red leather chair with a book "to quaff sweet forgetfulness of life's cares." The two people he loved the most, his daughter Martha and her son Jeff Randolph, shouldered the burdens of home and estate to provide him those peaceful hours of reading.

The Supporting Characters: Martha and Tom Randolph

Martha (1772-1836) was the eldest of Jefferson's children. Educated in Philadelphia and Paris, she married her third cousin, Thomas (Tom)

Mann Randolph (1768-1828) and bore him 12 children. Because of the vow Jefferson had made to his dying wife to never remarry, his daughter assumed the responsibilities and tasks as mistress of Monticello and accepted the duties of First Lady during two visits to Washington. Her devotion to her father destroyed her relationship with her husband. Or, on the other side of the coin, her relationship with her father was a saving grace in her life, for she had married a monster.

On paper, Tom Randolph had an impressive résumé. He came from one of Virginia's First Families, attended William and Mary College and the University of Edinburgh in Scotland, and worked as a planter. Later, he served as an artillerist in the War of 1812, as a member of Virginia's House of Delegates, as a Representative to Congress, and finally as Virginia's 21st Governor. In his personal life he was a tyrant—an abusive, alcoholic, mentally ill man who was obsessively jealous of his father-in-law. As for his dozen children, he never provided them with educations comparable to his own.

After Jefferson's retirement, Martha and her youngest children spent a majority of their time at Monticello, primarily to escape abuse. No matter where she resided, though, Martha carried the financial strains of both her father and husband. She was, in all regards, loyal to family, even to her loathsome husband—after her father's death, she separated from Tom, but eventually returned to him prior to his own death.

Anne and Charles Bankhead

To make matters worst, the husband of Martha and Tom's eldest daughter, Anne Cary (1791–1826) was equally abusive. To her misfortune, she married Charles Lewis Bankhead, another gentleman who looked better on paper than in person. Although he proved "alcoholic, abusive, and improvident" Anne refused to leave him in spite of the beatings she endured, but she wasn't the only one to have been physically attacked by Charles during his bouts of intoxication. One night, dangerously drunk, he brutally knifed his brother-in-law, Jeff, the grandson Jefferson called the "greatest of God-sends which heaven has granted to me." Upon hearing of the attack, Jefferson climbed back into the saddle (after having spent the entire day on horseback), to tear off to Jeff's side in Charlottesville—he was not expected to survive the night. Miraculously he did, though he was left with a damaged arm that never healed properly.

Anne and Charles would have four children before she died of complications in 1826, after the birth of their fifth child. Anne's death only preceded her cherished grandfather's by months.

Jane and Jeff Randolph

Thomas Jefferson (Jeff) Randolph (1792-1875) was Tom and Martha's eldest son and Jefferson's eldest grandson. He was the true depiction of the hero of a literary work from his rugged good looks to his sterling character. All who made his acquaintance described him as the model son and grandson: a tall (6'4"), handsome, industrious, inexhaustible young man with an aptitude for farm management and finances, who accepted the responsibilities of his grandfather's estates without complaint. Thomas Jefferson had directed Jeff's education and was in favor of his marriage to Jane Hollins Nicholas, a rather plain, but supportive wife and mother. Theirs was a happy marriage that produced twelve healthy children.

The Tragedy Unfolds

With the passage of time, the drama unfolding at Monticello took on tragic lines. Thomas Jefferson suffered from boils of almost biblical proportions on his "callipygian" . . . Martha kept creditors at bay . . . Tom Randolph's erratic behavior moved him closer to commitment in a lunatic asylum . . . Anne's premature death would leave her small children without protection from their father's drunkenness . . . Charles took to the bottle and to secluded hideouts to avoid arrest for the attempted murder of his brother-in-law . . . Jeff, the selfless "Titan" of the tragedy along with the patient support of his wife, Jane, worked the estates with his bare hands and oversaw the financial concerns of his father, father-in-law and grandfather . . .

And throughout those troubled years of dramatic crisis, Thomas Jefferson sought refuge in his books as seen through these excerpts from his correspondence.

"My greatest of all amusements, reading."
(Letter to Abigail Adams, August 22, 1813.)

"My Dear and ancient friend . . . This [correspondence] keeps me at the drudgery of the writing-table all the prime hours of the day, leaving for the gratification of my appetite for reading, only what I can steal from the hours of sleep. Could I reduce this epistolary corvée within the limits of my friends and affairs, and give the time redeemed from it to reading and reflection, to history, ethics, mathematics, my life would be as happy as the infirmities of age would admit."

(Letter to Charles Thomson, one of the more influential Founding Fathers who translated American ideals into his design of the Great Seal, January 9, 1816.)

"My repugnance to the writing-table becomes daily and hourly more deadly and insurmountable. In place of this has come on a canine appetite for reading. And I indulge it, because I see in it a relief against the taedium senectutis; a lamp to lighten my path through the dreary wilderness of time before me, whose bourne I see not. Losing daily all interest in the things around us, something else is necessary to fill the void. With me it is reading, which occupies the mind without the labor of producing ideas from my own stock."

(Letter to John Adams, May 17, 1818.)

And in one of his final, indirect references to the ancient writings of Aeschylus, Jefferson wrote: "I feel a much greater interest in knowing what has passed two or three thousand years ago, than in what is now passing. I read nothing, therefore, but of the heroes of Troy, of the wars of Lacedaemon and Athens . . . I slumber without fear, and review in my dreams the visions of antiquity."

(Letter to Nathaniel Macon, a staunch Jefferson supporter and the first Southerner to be elected Speaker of the House, January 12, 1819.)

The Climax of the Tragedy The Fourth of July, 1826

On the 4th of July in 1826, while the nation prepared to celebrate the fiftieth anniversary of the signing of the *Declaration of Independence*, Thomas Jefferson "ceased to breathe" at ten minutes before noon at his farm, Monticello, Virginia.

Five hours later his much-loved and respected compatriot, John Adams, died at his own farm in Quincy, Massachusetts. His final words were, "Thomas Jefferson survives." Some historians reason that John Adams simply misspoke, since it would have been impossible for him to have had known of Jefferson's death only hours before his own, but Adams hadn't misspoken—he understood that Thomas Jefferson *will* survive in our nation's memory as long as we remember that on July 4th, 1776, he rose from his chair in Carpenters' Hall and stood before his fellow delegates to read, in a barely perceptible voice, these immortal words . . .

IN CONGRESS, JULY 4, 1776

The unanimous Declaration of the thirteen united States of America

When in the Course of human events it becomes necessary for one people to dissolve the political bands which have connected them with another and to assume among the powers of the earth, the separate and equal station to which the Laws of Nature and of Nature's God entitle them, a decent respect to the opinions of mankind requires that they should declare the causes which impel them to the separation.

We hold these truths to be self-evident, that all men are created equal, that they are endowed by their Creator with certain unalienable Rights, that among these are Life, Liberty and the pursuit of Happiness. — That to secure these rights, Governments are instituted among Men, deriving their just powers from the consent of the governed, — That whenever any Form of Government becomes destructive of these ends, it is the Right of the People to alter or to abolish it, and to institute new Government, laying its foundation on such principles and organizing its powers in such form, as to them shall seem most likely to effect their Safety and Happiness . . .

The Final Act

The *Tragedy at Monticello* had not yet ended.

A graveside funeral, to which the public had been invited, was set for July 6th. Rain fell, and a gross misunderstanding delayed a procession of the 1500 mourners who had gathered in Charlottesville. Reverend Hatch and a smaller group did arrive at the gravesite on time, but Tom Randolph insisted that the service be delayed until the procession could march up the mountain's side. His son, Jeff, disagreed; they argued and the scene became ugly.

Finally, ignoring his father and the reverend, Jeff stood at his grandfather's grave and with deep emotion roughing his voice, he read aloud the burial service from the *Book of Common Prayer*—it was the most heart-wrenching moment of that difficult day for those who had truly loved Thomas Jefferson—and it was only fitting that the man who had cherished books was bid farewell through the words of a Holy Book.

Afterwards Martha escaped from her husband to Boston with her two youngest children while Jeff stayed on, having made the vow to honor his grandfather's memory by paying off his every debt. He did. But it involved years of hard work and personal sacrifices, and in the end Jeff sold Monticello, the slaves, artwork, horses, inventions, furniture, and of course, his grandfather's treasured books.

Preordained Failure

Throughout *Step VIII of* this small book we attempted to shine light into the corners of Thomas Jefferson's life, but with preordained failure—he guarded his privacy and perfected the art of reticence, and as a result, no one but Jefferson can know Jefferson.

Biographers all admit their frustration in failing to fully define the person of Thomas Jefferson—that is, all except one historian who explains how he came to know Mr. Jefferson when others could not.

During my law school years, UVA's proximity to Monticello accommodated my many visits to the home of Mr. Jefferson, each of which produced fresh insight as to the man's brilliance and endless accomplishments and contributions to our country's independence.

Each visit prompted the reading of another book about the man, one of which was the six-volume tome of Dumas Malone that probed the scope of Jefferson's intellect. At the end of his book Malone concluded that despite his exhaustive research, which included over 66,000 pages of Jefferson's correspondence, he "never really felt that he had gotten to know the guy." It is my understanding that Malone's admission influenced Joseph Ellis to write his widely acclaimed biography of Thomas Jefferson, The American Sphinx.

In regards to my advantage in knowing Mr. Jefferson . . . unlike Malone, Ellis, Jon Meacham, Alan Pell Crawford and others who never had the opportunity to dine at Monticello, Thomas Jefferson and I shared a glass of wine and discussed the relevant issues of the 17- and 1800s; time, however, did not permit me to probe his thoughts as to the current state of our country.

~ Barry

Step IX

Poor's Auction, Washington, D. C., 1829

Books are indeed with me a necessary of life.

Thomas Jefferson

Although it had been Thomas Jefferson's intention to bequeath the holdings of his Retirement Library to the University of Virginia, his heir, Jeff Randolph, felt honor-bound to pay off his grandfather's remaining debts. Everything of value had to be sold, and Jefferson would have been the first to say that his library was his most valuable possession.

In time, arrangements were made to sell the entire book collection through the public auction house of Nathaniel P. Poor. Heavily advertised, the *Auction of President Jefferson's Library* was held in Washington, D. C. from February 27th to March 11th, 1829. The sales brochure, titled as *Poor's Catalogue,* listed "931 items in some 1,540 volumes," which was almost an identical copy of Jefferson's Retirement Library Catalogue.

The enormity of Jeff Randolph's undertaking in the closing of his grandfather's debts is underscored by an apology printed on the title page of the auction catalogue:

"Poor apologizes . . . for pricing his catalogue at twelve and a half cents, unusual charge that it is, but taking into consideration the circumstances which make it necessary . . . to realize as much . . . as is practicable."

Plainly, every penny was needed, or as Endrina Tay of the Jefferson Library confirmed, the sole purpose of the "sale of Jefferson's library [was] an attempt to help clear Jefferson's sizeable debts at his death."

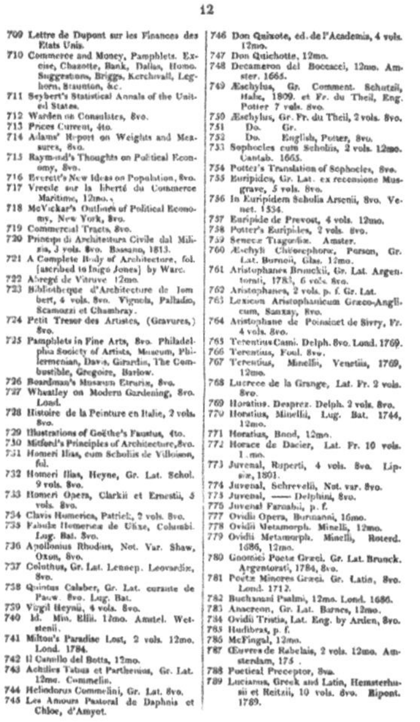

12

709 Lettre de Dupont sur les Finances des Etats Unis.
710 Commerce and Money, Pamphlets. Excise, Chazotte, Bank, Dallas, Homo. Suggestions, Briggs, Kerchivall, Leghorn, Staunton, &c.
711 Seybert's Statistical Annals of the United States.
712 Warden on Consulates, 8vo.
713 Prices Current, 4to.
714 Adams' Report on Weights and Measures, 8vo.
715 Raymond's Thoughts on Political Economy, 8vo.
716 Everett's New Ideas on Population, 8vo.
717 Vreede sur la liberté du Commerce Maritime, 12mo.
718 McVickar's Outlines of Political Economy, New York, 8vo.
719 Commercial Tracts, 8vo.
720 Principi di Architettura Civile dal Milizia, 3 vols. 8vo. Bassano, 1813.
721 A Complete Body of Architecture, fol. [ascribed to Inigo Jones] by Ware.
722 Abregé de Vitruve 12mo.
723 Bibliotheque d'Architecture de Jombert, 4 vols. 8vo. Vignola, Palladio, Scamozzi et Chambray.
724 Petit Tresor des Artistes, (Gravures,) 8vo.
725 Pamphlets in Fine Arts, 8vo. Philadelphia Society of Artists, Museum, Philermenian, Davis, Girardin, The Combustible, Gregoire, Barlow.
726 Boardman's Museum Etruria, 8vo.
727 Wheatley on Modern Gardening, 8vo. Lond.
728 Histoire de la Peinture en Italie, 2 vols. 8vo.
729 Illustrations of Goëthe's Faustus, 4to.
730 Mitford's Principles of Architecture, 8vo.
731 Homeri Ilias, cum Scholiis de Villoison, fol.
732 Homeri Ilias, Heyne, Gr. Lat. Schol. 9 vols. 8vo.
733 Homeri Opera, Clarkii et Ernestii, 5 vols. 8vo.
734 Clavis Homerica, Patrick, 2 vols. 8vo.
735 Fabulæ Homericæ de Ulixe, Columbi. Lug. Bat. 8vo.
736 Apollonius Rhodius, Not. Var. Shaw, Oxon, 8vo.
737 Coluthus, Gr. Lat. Lennep. Leovardiæ, 8vo.
738 Quintus Calaber, Gr. Lat. curante de Pauw. 8vo. Lug. Bat.
739 Virgil Heynii, 4 vols. 8vo.
740 Id. Min. Elili. 12mo. Amstel. Wetstenii.
741 Milton's Paradise Lost, 2 vols. 12mo. Lond. 1784.
742 Il Camillo del Botta, 12mo.
743 Achilles Tatius et Parthenius, Gr. Lat. 12mo. Commelin.
744 Heliodorus Commelini, Gr. Lat. 8vo.
745 Les Amours Pastoral de Daphnis et Chloe, d'Amyot.
746 Don Quixote, ed. de l'Academia, 4 vols. 12mo.
747 Don Quichotte, 12mo.
748 Decameron del Boccacci, 12mo. Amster. 1665.
749 Æschylus, Gr. Comment. Schutzii, Halæ, 1809. et Fr. du Theil, Eng. Potter 7 vols. 8vo.
750 Æschylus, Gr. Fr. du Theil, 2 vols. 8vo.
751 Do. Gr.
752 Do. English, Potter, 8vo.
753 Sophocles cum Scholiis, 2 vols. 12mo. Cantab. 1665.
754 Potter's Translation of Sophocles, 8vo.
755 Euripides, Gr. Lat. ex recensione Musgrave, 5 vols. 8vo.
756 In Euripidem Scholia Arsenii, 8vo. Venet. 1534.
757 Euripide de Prevost, 4 vols. 12mo.
758 Potter's Euripides, 2 vols. 8vo.
759 Senecæ Tragœdiæ. Amster.
760 Æschyli Chöephoræ, Porson, Gr. Lat. Burnoii, Glas. 12mo.
761 Aristophanes Brunckii, Gr. Lat. Argentorati, 1783, 6 vols. 8vo.
762 Aristophanes, 2 vols. p. f. Gr. Lat.
763 Lexicon Aristophanicum Græco-Anglicum, Sanxay, 8vo.
764 Aristophane de Poinsinet de Sivry, Fr. 4 vols. 8vo.
765 Terentius Cami. Delph. 8vo. Lond. 1769.
766 Terentius, Foul. 8vo.
767 Terentius, Minellii, Venetiis, 1769, 12mo.
768 Lucrece de la Grange, Lat. Fr. 2 vols. 8vo.
769 Horatius. Desprez. Delph. 2 vols. 8vo.
770 Horatius, Minellii, Lug. Bat. 1744, 12mo.
771 Horatius, Bond, 12mo.
772 Horace de Dacier, Lat. Fr. 10 vols. 1 mo.
773 Juvenal, Ruperti, 4 vols. 8vo. Lipsiæ, 1801.
774 Juvenal, Schrevelii, Not. var. 8vo.
775 Juvenal, —— Delphini, 8vo.
776 Juvenal Farnabii, p. f.
777 Ovidii Opera, Burmanni, 16mo.
778 Ovidii Metamorph. Minellii, 12mo.
779 Ovidii Metamorph. Minellii, Roterd. 1686, 12mo.
780 Gnomici Poetæ Græci. Gr. Lat. Brunck. Argentorati, 1784, 8vo.
781 Poetæ Minores Græci. Gr. Latin, 8vo. Lond. 1712.
782 Buchanani Psalmi, 12mo. Lond. 1686.
783 Anacreon, Gr. Lat. Barnes, 12mo.
784 Ovidii Tristia, Lat. Eng. by Arden, 8vo.
785 Hudibras, p. f.
786 McFingal, 12mo.
787 Œuvres de Rabelais, 2 vols. 12mo. Amsterdam, 175 .
788 Poetical Preceptor, 8vo.
789 Lucianus, Greek and Latin, Hemsterhusii et Reitzii, 10 vols. 8vo. Bipont. 1789.

Poor's Auction Catalaloge. The Seven appear as item 749. *PD.*

The auction was well-attended, but two gentlemen should be mentioned by name: Richard Rush, who had known Jefferson well, and Gulian Crommelin Verplanck who never had the privilege of meeting the venerable statesman from the Commonwealth of Virginia.

Richard Rush (1780-1859) had served as Attorney General (1814-1817) under Jefferson's fellow Bookman, James Madison, and at the time of the auction he was Secretary of the Treasury (1825-1829) under John Quincy Adams.

Rush's father, Benjamin, was the prominent physician who had signed the *Declaration of Independence,* but who is best remembered for reuniting John Adams and Thomas Jefferson after their almost decade-long quarrel. Like father, like son, Richard became a confidante of Thomas Jefferson. On June 22, 1819, almost seven years before his death, Jefferson wrote the now famous letter to Richard, in which he expressed his personal philosophy in nine words:

Books are indeed with me a necessary of life.

Considering the depth of Richard's respect for Jefferson, it is an easy matter to understand his presence at the auction—in all probability, he was a Bookman, himself, and welcomed the opportunity to acquire titles from Jefferson's elite collection.

As for Mr. G. C. Verplanck, his attendance at Poor's Auction merits further investigation, for he was a major player in the journey of the *Seven . . .*

Step X
Gulian Crommelin Verplanck, Humanitarian

Verplanck distinguished himself as a reputable lawyer and politician in New York, but it was his monumental work as a humanitarian that earned him a place in history with Thomas Jefferson and the other great Americans who sought to better our nation for all.

~Barry

An objective in the writing of this manuscript was to highlight anyone who took part in the journey of the *Seven*, thus the New Yorker, Gulian Crommelin Verplanck, warrants a closer look. As may be recalled, after Verplanck's introduction in *Step I* (provenance), he was again mentioned in *Step IV* (his abbreviated résumé and a descendant's remarks), before his brief appearance in *Step IX*.

C.G. Verplanck. *Public domain.*

This chapter, *Step X,* uncovers G. C. Verplanck as a gentleman unhampered by arrogance; a reputable gentleman who distinguished himself as an essayist, humorist and poet while forging legal and political careers and promoting human welfare and social reforms—all noteworthy accomplishments, but he was an exceptional man in that he was a true patriot who placed nation before self.

Two Questions

As the research broadened, two questions surfaced:
Why did Gulian Verplanck attend Poor's Auction and;
Why did he select the 7 Aeschylus volumes from the 1,540 books offered for sale?

The answer to the first question seemed clear-cut. The second question required a better understanding of Verplanck's mind and heart. We turned, therefore, to the best source we could find: the biographical essay, *A Discourse on the Life, Character, and Writings of Gulian Crommelin Verplanck*, written by William Cullen Bryant, the celebrated poet and editor of the *New York Evening Post.* It is an overlong essay, but supremely perfect for our purposes, for it suggests answers to both questions about Verplanck.

Verplanck and Bryant first met in New York City to discuss one of Verplanck's submissions as a writer. From there they forged a professional and personal bond based on mutual respect for each others' literary works within the tenets of Romanticism, a rising cultural movement centered upon emotional and natural themes that countered the Age of Enlightenment's precepts of rational thought, order and logic. (William Wordsworth, John Keats, Walt Whitman and Edgar Allen Poe typify the style of Romanticism.)

After Verplanck's death in March of 1870, Bryant wrote and published the biographical essay, *A Discourse on the Life, Character, and Writings of Gulian Crommelin Verplanck*, to memorialize his associate's sterling qualities.

The essay begins at the starting point of Verplanck's life with his mother's premature death. His father, who would soon remarry, placed his three-year-old son, Gulian, in the care of his paternal grandparents, Samuel and Judith Verplanck.

Strong-willed individuals, they honed their grandson's mental and moral qualities, thus their backgrounds are worth exploring. About them, Bryant wrote: "Samuel was betrothed at the age of 7 to his cousin Judith Crommelin, the daughter of a wealthy banker in Amsterdam. As a young woman, Judith was particularly accomplished, and versed not only in several modern languages, but in Greek and Latin, speaking fluently the Latin . . . Her conversation is said to have been uncommonly brilliant and her society much sought."

At the proper age for marriage, Samuel and Judith were wed in Holland before returning to America to set up dual residences in a "yellow mansion on Wall Street" and a country homestead in the Fishkill-Beacon area of New York.

Today, the Verplancks' colonial homestead is known as Mount Gulian Historic Site, an active center for programs, events and research that attracts tourists, students and scholars. The site's governing authority is the Mount Gulian Society; Elaine Hayes, the Executive Director since 1992, graciously supplied information and prints of G. C. Verplanck and his two homes. She stated: "I have had the good fortune to be immersed in the site's unique history, surrounded by Verplanck family treasures that include decorative and fine art pieces, family letters and documents, and antiquarian books, some from Gulian Crommelin Verplanck's extensive library."

Centuries ago, Samuel Verplanck's homestead served a vital purpose throughout the Revolutionary Period. During those years of rebellion and war Samuel spent a majority of his time at Mount Gulian "quietly occupied" by his books when, in fact, he put himself and his house at the disposal of the rebels and officers of the Continental Army. The Mount Gulian Society issued this statement: "Samuel . . . became involved with anti-British groups and joined the Committee of Safety of One-Hundred in Manhattan. This patriot group was poised to take over the city in the event of rebellion, which occurred on April 19, 1775 at Lexington & Concord . . . during the War for Independence, Verplanck turned over Mount Gulian to the Continental Army because of its strategic location on the Hudson near the Fishkill Barracks and across from Washington's Headquarters at Newburgh. In late 1782 through the summer of 1783, Mount Gulian was the site of the Continental Army headquarters of patriot General Fredrich Von Steuben. After the American victory at Yorktown, upon learning of the Treaty of Paris, General Von Steuben and other chief American officers created at Mount Gulian on May 13, 1783, the Society of the Cincinnati, America's first veterans' fraternal organization."

Samuel's wife, Judith, spurned her husband's convictions as is revealed by Bryant's essay that details her activities during the rebellion and war. After declaring herself a High Tory and staunch supporter of the King, she chose to reside apart from her husband in the "yellow mansion" in New York City—its doors were kept "open to the British officers, General Howe, and others."

Evidently, Verplanck's maternal grandfather, William Samuel Johnson, the educator (President of Columbia University), lawyer and politician, was an outspoken proponent of liberty. Bryant wrote: "Johnson was the agent of Connecticut in England, and in the revolution he took a zealous part in the cause of the revolted colonies; he was a Delegate to Congress from his State when Congress sat in New York, and he aided in framing the Constitution of the United States." In a later period, Johnson would direct his grandson's formal education in a positive way.

Accordingly, throughout his youth and into his young adult years, Gulian Verplanck was reared on conflicting schools of thought: from his two grandfathers he learned about "inalienable rights . . . revolution and patriotism," and from his Tory grandmother, he learned "of the obligation of loyalty and obedience to the Crown and . . . of the virtues and accomplishments of Cornwallis." In the end he allied himself with his grandfathers' patriotism, but his fluency in modern and ancient languages was deeply entrenched in him by his multi-lingual grandmother. Above all else, Samuel, Judith and William encouraged their grandson's scholarly pursuits—under their combined tutelage he began his life-long interest in acquiring books and writing.

In 1811, Gulian Verplanck married Eliza Fenno, the daughter of John Ward Fenno, the proprietor of Philadelphia's *Gazette of the United States*. She bore two sons, but died very young while they were in Paris in 1817. Devastated, he never remarried.

As Verplanck stepped into his professional life and pursued

philanthropic causes, he blended his over-riding passion for writing into his work as a lawyer, academic, and politician. As examples, in 1825 the writer-lawyer published his *Essay on the Doctrine of Contracts*, in which he maintained that the "transaction between the buyer and seller of a commodity should be [entirely absent] of concealment . . . and that the maxim, *caveat emptor* . . . is . . . immoral." And in 1831, while serving in Congress, he drew on his extensive experience as an author and poet to procure a law to better secure literary property.

Humanitarian

In the 1800s and into the 1900s, thousands upon thousands of starving, largely uneducated people fled Europe's famines and political chaos to start new lives in the "Promised Land." Unfortunately, upon reaching New York, most fell into the grip of criminals bent on luring men, women and children into hellish lives of indentured labor, crime, military enlistments, addictions, and sexual abuse. A man of compassion and a zealous patriot, Verplanck worked tirelessly to provide the emigrants with the basics needed to become law-abiding and productive, thus loyal, citizens.

Crediting Verplanck's humanitarian efforts, Bryant wrote: "[Because of his work,] all soon saw the domes and spires of that great cluster of buildings, forming a vast caravanserai in which the poorer class of emigrants are temporarily lodged, before they can be sent into the interior or find employment here. Here are barracks for the men, a spacious building for the women and children, a nursery for children of a tender age, Catholic and Protestant chapels, a dispensary, workshops, a lunatic asylum, fever wards, surgical wards, storehouses, residences of the physicians and other persons employed in the care of the place, and out-houses and offices of various kinds. Here, too, rise the stately turrets of the spacious new hospital styled the *Verplanck Emigrant Hospital*, in honor of the great philanthropist, for such his constant and noiseless labors in this department of charity entitle him to be called."

In simple words, Verplanck's altruistic work as a humanitarian earns him a place among the great figures of our nation's early history.

The Answer to the First Question

As suggested earlier, Bryant's essay offers the possible reasons behind Verplanck's attendance at Poor's Auction.

Similar to Jefferson, Verplanck was taught the value of books by the most influential people in his early life. For Jefferson, it was his father; for Verplanck, it was the combined force of his three grandparents. And like Jefferson, Verplanck had a voracious appetite for books—Jefferson's libraries may have been grander in volume and scope, but Verplanck's libraries in his two homes were noted as being "large and well-stored."

Clearly, both gentlemen, the Virginian and the New Yorker, were Bookmen of the highest order; therefore, it is reasonable to say that Verplanck was drawn, like a moth to a flame, to the book auction of the nation's most celebrated collector, Thomas Jefferson.

The Answer to the Second Question

To answer the more compelling question as to why Verplanck purchased the Aeschylus volumes, we need only to return again to his early years as documented in Bryant's biographical essay.

Although Verplanck sided, politically, with his grandfathers, he spent a great deal of time with his Tory grandmother and acquired her fluency in French, Greek and Latin. His interest in those languages was not recreational; Bryant's essay speaks of Verplanck as a lawyer and politician who preferred legal treatises and books written in Ancient Greek, Latin, and Old French.

We have to concede that Verplanck would have known of Jefferson's penchant for books written in, or translated into, foreign languages—during the widely publicized congressional debates (1814-1815) over the purchase of Jefferson's library, his enemies openly criticized the large number of books printed in "useless" languages, while his supporters admired those same books. Knowing all that, Verplanck would have walked into the auction fully expecting to find hundreds of books that would satisfy his own partiality for works published in languages other than English.

But why did he choose the Aeschylus tragedies? Bryant's essay reports that Verplanck's library was "large and well-stored . . . with different editions of the Greek and Latin classics, some of them rare and enriched with sumptuous illustrations."

Obviously Verplanck had a liking for ancient writings, but more than that, he was noted as having lived a moral and virtuous life. Had he, like Jefferson before him, shaped his ethical philosophy through his books? Had Verplanck gleaned the moral lessons taught by Aeschylus' heroes and villains—perhaps so, for like Jefferson, Verplanck urged his children and grandchildren to read ancient writings, and so we can only assume he placed each volume of the *Seven* into their small hands.

The New Yorker and the Virginian

W. C. Bryant wrote that Verplanck "loved our free institutions; he had a serene and steady confidence in their duration and his published writings are for the most part eloquent pleas for freedom, political equality and toleration . . ."

Could those same words have been written about Thomas Jefferson?

Bryant continued: "Verplanck rarely, and never, save when the occasion required it, spoke of what he had done for others. I never heard, I think no man ever heard, anything like a boast proceed from his lips, nor did he practice any, even the most innocent expedients, to attract attention to his public services."

Again Bryant's description of Verplanck could be applied to the reticent, shy Virginian who preferred to be remembered for only three things: the *Declaration of Independence*; the *Statute of The Freedom of Religion*; and the founding of the University of Virginia.

Without a doubt, neither Thomas Jefferson nor Verplanck were guilty of hubris, as suggested below.

After reading Bryant's long essay about Verplanck's immense capacity for languages and abiding love of literature, it can be safely said that he read Aeschylus' plays, page by page.

Apparently, like Jefferson before him, Verplanck pursued

knowledge from books, but he differed in that his one passion was writing books—a task Jefferson described as "drudgery." And like the gentleman from the Commonwealth of Virginia, Verplanck distinguished himself as a reputable lawyer and politician in his own state of New York, but it was his monumental work as a humanitarian that earned him a place in history with Thomas Jefferson and other noteworthy Americans who sought to better our nation for all.

By Verplanck's time at the turn of the 19th century, there were ordinary people with extraordinary talents who accomplished impressive things, for they had the liberty to do so when opportunities arose. G. C. Verplanck's humanitarian work numbered him among those unexpected geniuses: the farmer, John Deere, who tired of walking behind a plow and so invented a mechanized plow; Henry Wells and William Fargo who crisscrossed America with stagecoaches; and Henry Ford who one-upped Wells Fargo by building vehicles that needed no horses, but who so disliked bouncing along on wooden wheels that he collaborated with Harvey Firestone to invent rubberized wheels.

Verplanck and those others had the freedom of opportunity without government rules and restrictions. There were no barriers in their path to the American Dream; they could accomplish anything they set their minds to.

Can the same be said today?

~Barry

Step XI

The Cosmic Transfer

. . . it occurred to me that I had not yet touched a single book; had not yet tested my Theory of Cosmic Transfer—my premise that in touching something Thomas Jefferson had touched, his staggering intellect would transfer, instantly, from his brain to mine.

~Barry

In December of 2012, the much anticipated telephone call came from Gerry Cataldo—the restoration of Jefferson's books had been completed; all seven were waiting in his shop for my inspection. At the first opportunity, I drove to Chestertown.

When I walked through Gerry's door, it occurred to me that I had not yet touched a single book; had not yet tested my Theory of Cosmic Transfer—my premise that in touching something Thomas Jefferson had touched, his staggering intellect would transfer, instantly, from his brain to mine.

Gerry mentioned that Jan Ross had stopped in to see the restored books, but he felt that I should have the first privilege of seeing and handling the books, a courtesy that pleased me enormously.

He placed the slipcase box that holds the 8 individual clamshell boxes on the counter before us. From an earlier conversation I knew the purpose behind the cases: to preserve the integrity of the books.

Removing one of the 8 boxes, he showed me how to open it, and took out the volume. The restored book was what I had expected—a small, handsomely bound leather volume, but what

The eight clamshell boxes housed in a separate slipcase (the books and reproductions of Mayo's tools). One clamshell box is open and laying flat to display its interior. *Courtesy of Cat Tail Run Hand Bookbing.*

struck me with awe was that it had the appearance of having just been pulled from a shelf in Jefferson's Library.

Gerry extended the volume towards me. It doesn't matter which book was being handed to me; what did matter was that I was about to touch one of Jefferson's books for the first time. I reached towards it, but hesitated . . . I felt the need to explain my Theory of Cosmic Transfer, so that when I touched the book Gerry would not step out front to intercept the transfer of Jefferson's vast knowledge to me. He understood. Next I made the request that he stand back even further since I had no idea how the cosmic transfer might manifest itself, or if it would harm him or others. I prepared myself. I can't recall the use of gloves, but I handled that book, and then the others and . . .

Nothing remarkable happened. Then again, something as complex as the transfer of high intelligence must surely take time . . .

Jill did a masterful job of strengthening the bindings, and restoring the books to their original quality. The books are now works of art in themselves, but more importantly, they are reminders that Thomas Jefferson was a very real person, and though one of our nation's greats, he did ordinary things like sinking down into a comfortable chair, and reading until his eyes closed.

~Barry

An Email Exchange Between Maureen and Jill Deiss

Hi Jill,

Yesterday was my first opportunity to examine the volumes. They are smaller than previously expected, but they're certainly not delicate—there's a masculine quality about them—their solidness and weight, their rich, brown leather and simple, unembellished lines—the kind of books one would expect Jefferson to own and treasure. I read quite a few pages of the Prometheus volume (the English translation), and can honestly say that the entire time I felt an awareness of Thomas Jefferson, a strong impression of his presence as if he sat beside me looking over my shoulder, pleased that his book was being read, once more.

To your great credit, Jill, you have returned fragile, aged books to their original strength and beauty. Mr. Jefferson would have been pleased by your workmanship; Mr. Buckley is very pleased, but in your opinion, did you meet your end-goals?

M.

Hello Maureen,

We did. The goal of this treatment was to make the books sound for handling and to make them appear as if they had never needed treatment in the first place.

Jill

Please outline the steps in the restoration process, Jill, from beginning to end.

M.

Gladly, Maureen. First we evaluated the bindings and photographed them so we'd have documentary photos to refer to. Treatment began with removing the covers . . . many were close to being detached. Susan McCabe and our apprentice Keith Boi prepared the spines of the texts . . . to go back into the covers once restored. Meanwhile, I spent time with the original covers, slightly lifting the original leather in some places to allow us to bring in materials to support the weak areas of the bindings, specifically in the joints of the covers. Amy M. Jackson pared calfskin for the bindings where original leather was no longer present, and then brought the covers and texts back together. She and I worked in tandem to replace the missing tooling to the spines and we did the final polishing of the set. Dee Evetts then created the clamshell boxes and slipcase.

Jill

Jill, it's my understanding that none of the interior pages of the 7 volumes were damaged—is that accurate?

M.

That is accurate, Maureen. The pages were still in the bindings when we started, but the joints of the bindings were cracked and broken and portions of the original spines were missing on a number of the bindings.

The original sewing that held the texts together was still in wonderful condition, so the pages were never taken apart from one another. In several cases the original sewn endbands exhibited breaks, and Susan McCabe used similarly colored thread to support and repair them.

Jill

Jill, how did you go about restoring the spines?

M.

The restoration of each spine was accomplished with a leather reback, which is a technique that repairs broken joints, and which also brings leather to areas of the spine . . . to replace missing leather. Calfskin . . . was brought in under the original materials [that] were lifted up gently to provide a place for the new material. The rebacking leather was pared thinly in those locations where its presence would have been apparent.

The spines of these books displayed two distinctive gold-tooled elements of an abstract floral nature along with . . . supporting elements, such as gold-tooled lines. [The] gold tooling was sometimes missing . . . given Mr. Buckley's vision for the set, replacing the missing tooling was the better option. All of the replacement tooling is on those areas of the spine where there is new leather; none of the replacement tooling is atop the original leather.

Jill

Is that the point at which the tools, the ones made in England, fit into your work?

M.

That's right, Maureen. Mayo had used distinctive tool designs, so the work to restore the spines would have looked unfinished if the missing tooled elements had not been replaced. The tools were made of the most beautiful brass . . . they heated to perfect evenness and stamped the most perfect gold. Nothing could have worked better!

Jill

How were the books' covers restored?

M.

Rebacking was done to restore the covers—the front and back boards of the covers were breaking away from the shoulders of the text. Rebacking brought new leather to these weak and broken joints.

When a reback is performed, Maureen, the leather utilized for the process attaches to the spine of the text, thereby attaching the text back into the cover. The replacement of the pages, once the covers and spines were in order, was part of the reback process.

Jill

The clamshell boxes are beautifully designed; the dark color and simple lines convey a wonderful sense of formality, elegance. Jill, what's the full purpose of the boxes?

M.

Believe me, they have vital purpose, Maureen. Clamshell boxes afford superior protection, protecting them from light, dust, and buffering them from changes in the surrounding environment.

Jill

Jill, what elements or thoughts went into your design of the housing?

M.

The housing was designed with Jefferson in mind. As a nod to his love of classical architecture, the slipcase bears a proscenium in the manner of Roman and U.S. buildings. Jefferson seemed partial to a touch of mystery, so the identity of the set is somewhat veiled, except to the observant soul who notices something tooled along the proscenium and connects the dots.

And the fleur-de-lis motif (across the spines of the clamshell boxes) hints at Jefferson's connection to France, love of things French, and his fluency in French language and literature.

Jill

As a final question: Is hand bookbinding a lost art?

M.

No, Maureen, not at all. As our country ages, there is greater interest in and need for the conservation and restoration of books. The Aeschylus set is a fine example of such interest by collectors like Mr. Buckley.

Jill

Step XII

David Bloom,

Freeman's, Philadelphia

. . . by preserving our national treasures we are safeguarding concrete reminders that the founding fathers were real people who pledged their fame, fortune and lives to the creation of our nation, the greatest, longest-lived republic in the history of the world.

~Barry

As detailed at the beginning of this memoir, Jefferson's books were in fragile condition at the time of Barry's acquisition. On Gerry Cataldo's advice, the notable bookbinder Jill Deiss was commissioned to restore the entire set of 7 volumes. Once completed, Barry was highly appreciative of Jill's exceptional skills as a binder, but at odd moments he harbored misgivings about the restoration—his primary concern was that the historical integrity of Thomas Jefferson's books had been impugned. In January 2013 all of his concerns were resolved after a lengthy conversation with David Bloom.

Since 1983, David has served as a Vice President & Department Head for Books, Maps & Manuscripts at Freeman's, the prominent auction house in Philadelphia duly recognized as America's first auction house (1805). A family owned business for 7 generations, Freeman's has made its presence known, nationally, in the "Auction Culture" through historically significant sales of jewelry, fine art, furniture, and antiques on behalf of private collections, estates, and museums.

A specialist in rare books, manuscripts, maps, ephemera, and antiquarian documents, David's wealth of knowledge and mercurial sense of humor has gained him a loyal following among collectors and connoisseurs of vintage books and ephemera. A gracious man, he has unlimited patience--an admirable trait noted by Barry as he came to his final question: *did the restoration process diminish the historical integrity of Thomas Jefferson's books?*

Before answering, David asked about the initial appraisal of the books' state of repair. In summary, Barry relayed Jill Deiss' report that the endpapers, marbled flyleaves and pastedowns of Jefferson's books were complete across the set, that none of the pages were torn, and that no problems existed with any of the text sewing. In her professional opinion, only the bindings had needed restoration.

With a smile, David gave his assurance that the integrity of Jefferson's books has not been diminished. He stressed that the most essential element of a book is its interior: the author's words and illustrations on the printed pages. He emphasized that professionals in the field of historical artifacts often recommend restorations of books with weakened bindings--a strong, well-bound book safeguards the quality of the interior pages; therefore, since no alterations were made to the interiors, the historical value of Jefferson's books has been preserved for time untold.

As the story of the journey of the Seven evolved into multiple drafts and the content expanded, I was puzzled by Maureen's emphasis on the restoration process until I remembered a conversation with the co-author about the responsibilities of stewardship of historical artifacts. She believes, strongly, that both my investigation into the advantages and disadvantages of restoring the 7 volumes, and my eventual contract with Jill Deiss will stand as examples to others who acquire historical objects.

I came to agree with my co-author. If I had ignored my responsibility as a steward of Jefferson's books, I would have failed to preserve the integrity of his property and may have deprived others of a tangible piece of American history.

So, upon reflection, another tip of my hat to the brilliant restoration by Jill Deiss, and also a tip of my hat to Maureen who persuaded me that duct tape was not a viable restoration technique.

As my final remark regarding all this: by preserving our national treasures we are safeguarding concrete reminders that the founding fathers were flesh-and-blood people who pledged their fame, fortune and lives to the creation of our nation, the greatest, longest-lived republic in the history of the world.

~Barry

The *Seven* in their cases to the right of Sowerby's Catalogue.

Step XIII

Bridget Hassan, Architectural Artist

Like Thomas Jefferson, Bridget was drawn to the architectural philosophy of the Ancient Romans and Greeks . . .
Maureen

A photograph of the library at Monticello was first suggested for inclusion in this book, but that idea was dismissed—a photograph would impart a modern feel to this book about historical artifacts.

A rendering of Jefferson's Library was then suggested and a watercolorist specializing in architectural artwork was sought out and found in Bridget Hassan, who had acquired that specialty through her major, architecture, at the University of Notre Dame in Indiana. Notre Dame is one of only two schools in the United States still offering programs of classical architecture. Like Thomas Jefferson, Bridget was drawn to the architectural philosophy of the Ancient Romans and Greeks, therefore Notre Dame's classical approach appealed to her from an early age.

Heavily recruited by other colleges for her advanced abilities in math and physics she was determined to study at Notre Dame, although "forewarned" of the program's intensive course work that includes fluency in Italian, and a yearlong residency in Rome to master the finer techniques of architectural sketches and watercolor renderings. Bridget's talent spoke for itself. In her fifth year she won the coveted Senior Prize (judged by three "outside" architects from Chicago) for her design of a harness racetrack and clubhouse. Later, only months after graduation, she won first place in a statewide competition for a house design during a brief period with a firm in Raleigh,

North Carolina. Now, the mother of two small children, Anna and David, she works on watercolor commissions from her home studio.

Learning that Bridget had been drawn to the architectural philosophy of the Ancient Romans and Greeks like Thomas Jefferson before her, Barry enlarged his original idea. He engaged her to make a watercolor rendering of Jefferson's library for his collection of wall-art, a rendering that could be incorporated into the design of this book.

Several months later a framed painting arrived at his home, and on April 7, 2013, he wrote:

Dear Bridget,

The 24 by 36 inch framed watercolor of Thomas Jefferson's Library at Monticello painted by you arrived safe and sound yesterday, and not only does it fit the intended space perfectly but the art work itself greatly exceeds my expectations. It is simply magnificent. Thom. Jefferson would be pleased . . . with your wonderful work.

The contract also speaks to two pencil drafts and while I didn't receive them I would like to have them as for me it personalizes the work and allows me to better appreciate the painstaking work that precedes that which you delivered.

I have also requested the opportunity to meet, which I typically request on commissioned work, and at the meeting I usually ask the artist to sign the work. Since the picture is already signed by you, I will request that you sign and remark one of the drafts that I have requested above.

Sincerely yours,
~Barry Buckley

A reply arrived in July 2013.

Dear Mr. Buckley,

Let me start by saying I apologize for the delay of my response—it does not reflect how I feel. I really appreciate having had the opportunity to complete this painting for you.

My mother has been giving me updates about the book and I am thrilled to be part of it. My Mom pours her heart into everything she does, so I know it will turn out wonderfully. Thank you also for reminding me of the love I have for architecture and watercolor. This project renewed this love!

I don't have any process drawings. I just worked on the one 24 x 36 sheet. I did take pictures of the watercolor sheet, as I was working on it. I can send those to you.

We are coming to Chestertown sometime in August or September and I would love to meet with you. Thanks again, and I look forward to seeing the finished book.

Sincerely,

Bridget Hassan

An Aside

From beginning to end this project has been a pleasure—it introduced me to the genius of Thomas Jefferson, it allowed me the opportunity to teach Barry the fundamentals of putting a book together from outline to finished draft, and it gave me another chance to work professionally with Bridget—all in all, an unforgettable and wonderful experience.

Maureen

Step XIV

Charlottesville, Virginia

. . . people didn't flock to Monticello to see buffalo robes, antlers and maps; they went there to meet Mr. Jefferson; to speak with him; to learn. ~*Barry*

In August 2013, Susan Stein and Endrina Tay, colleagues at The Robert H. Smith International Center for Jefferson Studies, invited the co-authors of this book to lunch at the Jefferson Library near Charlottesville. Acceptance opened up the opportunity to complete the research process for this memoir through tours of the University of Virginia, and Monticello atop its spectacular rise of wooded hill.

Mr. Jefferson's University

As mentioned earlier in *Step VIII*, Jefferson distinguished himself as the only American president to have founded a university, but he served beyond that measure as both architect and educator. His success in those fields was in evidence during our slow walk through UVA's landscaped grounds and historic buildings.

As architect, first and foremost, he designed an ideal, classical setting for his "academical village: the community of scholars." To experience his mastery of Ancient Greek and Roman designs, one need only pass through the colonnaded walkways and portico of the Pantheon-inspired Rotunda, or cross The Lawn (central quad) dividing brick and white-trimmed buildings edged by serpentine walls. It is a place of dignified beauty.

As Educator, a role he assumed with equal importance, Thomas Jefferson positioned the library as the university's cornerstone of knowledge, and stubbornly implemented a "radical" curriculum that laid the foundation of UVA's prestigious schools of law, medicine, mathematics, science, and art.

It's worth mentioning that the university came about because of a lost battle. For more than a half century Jefferson had espoused his belief that the greatest enemy of our new and fragile nation was an uneducated, uninformed citizenry. A free school system, he argued, would preserve the republic's future. In simple terms he explained: "It is safer to have the whole people respectably enlightened than a few in a high state of science and the many in ignorance."

His words fell on deaf ears; having lost his battle to convince the Virginia General Assembly to fund a public school system he turned defeat into victory by devoting his final years to the establishment of a public school: the University of Virginia, or as some refer to this school, *Mr. Jefferson's University.*

Mr. Jefferson's Home

For almost 40 years Jefferson built and rebuilt Monticello, but by the end of his second presidential term (1809), each and every project had been completed to his satisfaction—that is, until he sat down with paper and ink to draw up new and better ideas. He once said, "Architecture is my delight and putting up and pulling down, one of my favorite amusements" (1824).

A visitor to his home made the offhand remark that: "[Mr. Jefferson's newest projects to improve his] habitation of philosophy and virtue . . . would take a younger man a lifetime to complete . . . But he seems to have transposed his hopes and anticipations into the existence of his children . . . It is in them he lives, and I believe he finds as much delight in the idea that they will enjoy the fruit of his present labours, as if he hoped it for himself."

For Jefferson's admirers, Monticello is a testament to his brilliance as a self-taught architect, but there was more than one house or one school in his portfolio of drawings—he drafted hundreds of architectural renderings, and fittingly, his proficiency has not been overlooked. The renown art historian and architect, Fiske Kimball (1888-1955) named Thomas Jefferson the *Father of our National Architecture* for the role he assumed in the design and planning of the first federal buildings in Washington, D. C. And on the 250th anniversary of Jefferson's birth (1993), the American Institute of Architects granted him, posthumously, its Gold Medal for "a lifetime of distinguished achievement and significant contributions to architecture and the human environment."

Thomas Jefferson would have appreciated those honors. He once wrote: "Architecture is among the most important arts . . ." (1788).

The story of the "Seven" could not have been told without a comprehensive tour of Monticello and its environs. As we walked towards Mr. Jefferson's home, I tried to remember if I was about to take my 132nd tour or my 142nd, but that didn't matter. Of more importance was that on this final leg of this journey of books we were immersing ourselves in all things having to do with Thomas Jefferson.

Several options had been discussed in respect to the type of tour that would provide the best opportunity for research. Tours range from hiring a personal guide, to backstairs visits of the seldom-viewed rooms on the upper floor of Monticello, or walks through the slave quarters and gardens. Upon the advice of Endrina Tay and with Maureen's concurrence, I selected the tour that would provide the best touch-every-artifact-possible-in-spite-of-the-warnings opportunity. That meant we would take potluck with a regular tour, and it was sheer good luck that the docent we were assigned had patience for our many questions. Armed with encyclopedic knowledge, he drew us and all his listeners back in time to Monticello of centuries past, until it seemed Thomas Jefferson, himself, would appear around the corner.

The lesson learned from my 2013 tour (my 168th, perhaps) was that you never stop learning new things about Jefferson—the man, his life and times. A case in point came about when the docent stressed the importance Jefferson placed on Monticello's treasure-filled Entrance Hall—an unfamiliar line of thought for me. From previous tours I had heard he customarily kept his guests waiting while he attended to matters of his estate, but the docent of this tour added an intriguing detail: Jefferson's visitors often waited 2 or 3 or more hours. To ease their boredom of long waits in his front hall, he had the walls decked out with globes and maps of the known world, the heads, horns and antlers of wild creatures, and the "tokens of friendship" from 40 Indian tribes.

Granted, Jefferson's visitors were visually entertained while waiting, but what did they talk about until he made his appearance?

My guess would be anything and everything. Conversations would have centered upon everyday successes and failures, and upon ideas and approaches to ordinary and extraordinary challenges. And finally, when Jefferson did arrive, how often did he enter into ongoing conversations, and how often did he take someone into his library to consult books about the subjects under discussion? It's safe to say that within the confines of Monticello's front hall, knowledge was shared between neighbors, friends, and former strangers without the Internet, Home Depot, or government officials telling them what to think or do; those exchanges of knowledge were the real treasures of Monticello.

Just as each visit there has given me a fresh perspective about the life and times of Thomas Jefferson, I came away from my 2013 tour (surely my 256th) with this one thought: that people didn't flock to Monticello to see buffalo robes, antlers and maps; they went there to meet Mr. Jefferson; to speak with him; to learn.

~Barry

The Jefferson Library

The tour of Thomas Jefferson's estate was followed by the luncheon meeting with Endrina Tay and Susan Stein at the Jefferson Library, a handsome, wood and glass building that stands in a clearing of woods a quarter of a mile from Monticello.

Endrina's gracious welcome was followed by a brief but thoroughly

Jefferson Library. *Courtesy of the Thomas Jefferson Foundation.*

interesting tour of the building, which incorporates many of Monticello's architectural features such as skylights that supply an abundance of natural light. Surely, Jefferson would be humbled by the library's purpose, in part with the Robert H. Smith International Center for Jefferson Studies (ICJS), a private, multidisciplinary research center. Founded in 1994, ICJS fosters "Thomas Jefferson scholarship and disseminates findings through research and education."

As the Associate Foundation Librarian for Technical Services at the Jefferson Library, Endrina's professional career has ascended from a Bachelor of Business Administration degree from the National University of Singapore (1988) to a Masters of Science in Library Science from the University of North Carolina at Chapel Hill (2002). A leading researcher, since 2004 she has been the project manager for Thomas Jefferson's Libraries, a collaborative effort with LibraryThing.com to build a comprehensive and publicly accessible inventory of Jefferson's libraries, the books he owned, read, and recommended to others.

Over the past several years she has been engaged in two research projects under the Thomas Jefferson Foundation: "The Little Collection of Books Necessary for my Future Amusement: Thomas

Jefferson's Retirement Library," and "The Auction Sale of Jefferson's Library in 1829." Because the Aeschylus volumes claimed a place in both the Retirement Library and Poor's Auction in 1829, Endrina has been of the greatest assistance in the writing of this book. Time and again she proved her expertise through clear answers to our research questions, but above that, her patience was deeply appreciated.

After Susan Stein arrived, we sat down to lunch in a side-room with tall windows that overlooked the Roosevelt Cottage, built specially by Major General Edwin M. Watson between 1940-1941 for President Franklin Delano Roosevelt's visits (Roosevelt stayed there on only one occasion, preferring the social activity of the main house at Kenwood).

The conversation turned to Susan's background. Currently the Richard Gilder Senior Curator and Vice President for Museum Programs at the Thomas Jefferson Foundation, she completed her undergraduate studies at Beaver College in Pennsylvania before earning a Masters at the University of Chicago. She is the author of the commended book, *Worlds of Thomas Jefferson at Monticello* (1993), about which a national reviewer wrote: "Monticello's . . . eclectic collection, fully illustrated and detailed in this stunning volume, has been gathered together for the first time since the contents of Monticello were dispersed to mark the 250th anniversary of Jefferson's birth . . . An insightful essay by Stein places the objects within the context of Jefferson's multifaceted life."

The final words of Stein's book review caught our attention, for they echo one of the purposes behind this small book: to place particular objects, the *Seven*, "within the context of Jefferson's multifaceted life."

After Susan's introduction, much of the discussion centered upon Barry's acquisition of the Aeschylus volumes. The highlight came when Susan stood to better examine the two clamshell boxes that had been brought to the meeting.

Somewhat amused by the boxes' wrappings in *East Hampton* tee-shirts inside a paper bag, she put aside the clamshell box containing the handle tools and picked up the box holding the first volume of the Aeschylus set. Curiosity showed in her facial expression and voice, as she lifted the lid and withdrew the tragedy, *Prometheus*. She first made note of the superb quality of the book's bindings before asking the expected question.

"Yes," she was assured by Barry, "the other books in the Aeschylus set are as handsome, and in the same excellent condition as the *Prometheus* volume."

Next, Susan opened the book with a deferential hand and found, in short order, the sunburst ticket added by Jefferson's bookbinder, F. A. Mayo, the 1829 inscription about Poor's Auction written by G. C. Verplanck, and lastly the ownership markings inked by Thomas Jefferson.

Seemingly satisfied with the historical significance of the book, and the other unseen volumes, Susan asked Barry to consider donating the set to the Jefferson Library, but he explained that the books belonged to his two sons, as well, and so were not his to give away.

She then asked that he consider digitizing his collection through the University of Virginia. The purpose behind digitization, she explained, would be to provide researchers worldwide, electronic-access to Jefferson's conflation of Aeschylus' dramas.

As the luncheon drew to a close, Susan viewed Bridget Hassan's watercolor rendering of Jefferson's Book Room, the library at Monticello, calling it a "beautiful" piece of architectural artwork.

Digitizing the 7

Although unconvinced that digitization was a direction he wanted to take with the *Seven,* Barry contacted David R. Whitesell, the Curator of the Albert and Shirley Small Special Collections Library, at the University of Virginia.

Mr. Whitesell replied in the form of a lengthy letter that detailed the process of digitization. His conclusion stated: "Jefferson is famous for his conflated editions of various works. I assume that he did not annotate [your] set (Jefferson rarely annotated his books). Even if he did not, [your] volumes are highly significant as artifacts created by Jefferson and bound for him. Because the volumes remain in [large part in] their 'Jefferson' bindings, they should be protected from any possible damage . . . The digitizing process usually is a gentle one . . .

but damage is always possible . . . Also, because the conflated editions typically required Jefferson's binder to bind together a collection of single leaves, the resulting binding structure may be tight and not open easily—if so, the pressure needed to open the volume sufficiently for each digital image could cause significant damage to the binding structure, which may only be repairable by rebinding the volume . . . Digitizing all 7 volumes would require a significant amount of time . . . and could easily run to several thousand dollars."

The probability that digitization might damage the books dissuaded Barry from pursuing the process. His more pressing concern was an unsolved "mystery," and so he turned his attention to that.

> *Since the beginning of this project, there has been conjecture about who may have stepped into the Retirement Library between the years 1820-1826, the period of time the 7 Aeschylus volumes sat on Jefferson's shelves. After all, it wasn't unusual for him to take his guests into his library, to point out a particular book or to loan one with his recommendation. Of course, there is no possibility of knowing which of his guests may have picked up an Aeschylus volume to read at length, but our imaginations wandered at will as we strove to solve this mystery of sorts.*
>
> *We reasoned there has to be a list of visitors. Jefferson was scrupulous in recording even the most insignificant facts with respect to the operation of Monticello, to the point of identifying the cost of a nail or a bag of seed in his financial records; therefore, it seemed illogical that he would have been remiss in recording the names of his visitors. If a guestbook could be found, we could then speculate as to which of his visitors may have had the occasion to read one of the seven volumes—that is, we could speculate without definite proof.*
>
> *As our research deepened we came upon the scholarly work, Visitors to Monticello, edited by Merrill D. Peterson. This excellent reference book gives the particulars about Mr. Jefferson's guests between 1820 and 1826, the very years in question. Such guests included UVA professor George Long, the constitutional scholar and statesman Daniel Webster, the bookseller Samuel*

Whitcomb, Jr., and Duke Bernhard of Saxe-Weimar-Eisenach. From the docent of our tour we had learned that Lafayette stayed at Monticello for 10 days in November of 1824, during which time he was honored at a "grand dinner" at the University of Virginia, and that James Monroe was a constant visitor, since his estate, Highland, was only 2 miles from Monticello.

Through other historical sources we then uncovered Jefferson's practice of keeping 28 Windsor chairs in his Entrance Hall to accommodate the unending parades of daily visitors to his home. He met and spoke with the vast majority in his hall, but some were invited to stay on as houseguests for days, weeks or months. His daughter recalled occasions when over 50 guests would be lodged in the house—they ranged from young professionals like Francis Calley Gray who stayed a full month, to Jefferson's contemporaries like James and Dolley Madison who stayed so often that their bedroom came to be known as the Madison Room. Of immense amusement to me was the discovery that Jefferson would take to the saddle to escape the noise of his over-populated home. More often than not, he'd hide himself away at Poplar Forest, his "reading retreat" nearly 75 miles from Monticello—I'll say it again, he was a brilliant man.

In the end our investigation came down to this: in all likelihood Jefferson didn't keep a guestbook because there were too many visitors to track on paper. It's easier to rule out those who didn't step into Jefferson's library—George and Martha Washington, John and Abigail Adams, Dr. Benjamin Rush and his son Richard, General Kosciuszko, and John Quincy Adams. They stayed in close contact with Jefferson through correspondence, but never visited the "remote outpost" of Monticello. In that era, Jefferson's home seemed worlds away from the more civilized cities of Washington, Philadelphia, New York and Boston (it took 4 days of arduous travel to reach the White House from Jefferson's door).

Admittedly, we may never solve the mystery about which of Jefferson's guests read an Aeschylus volume, but our imaginations will continue to wander.

~Barry

Step XV
Parting Thoughts

I had rather be shut up in a very modest cottage with my books, my family, and a few old friends, dining on simple bacon and letting the world roll on as it liked, than to occupy the most splendid post, which any human power can give.

Thomas Jefferson
(Letter to Alexander Donald Paris, February 7, 1788.)

There's a very pleasant room in a white-bricked house on a lovely curve of land and water, a room that brings to mind the distant past of the American Revolution. Perhaps it's the aged-wood rafters, or the wide stone hearth with its iron kettle, or the Arnold Friberg paintings of Washington at Valley Forge that remind us of our nation's birth—then again, perhaps it's the tangible presence of Thomas Jefferson through his small, leather books that are consigned to this room for a moment in time.

The hutch that once held Kitty's china stands in a corner of the room: a worn, painted hutch that Barry and his eldest son converted into a "library" of three narrow, uneven shelves, each lined with the scholarly works of the Revolutionary Period. None of the books are distinguished by burnished leather or gold-embossed pages, but rather by the extraordinary talents of their authors—historians of the highest merit: David McCullough, Joseph Ellis, Dumas Malone, Alan Pell Crawford, E. Millicent Sowerby, and of course, Aeschylus, who was a historian in every sense of the word, for his tragedies retell Ancient Greece's emergence as the world's first powerful and stable democracy. Read Aeschylus' dramas, and perhaps you will discover for yourself the analogies that Jefferson drew upon to illuminate the struggles he and his compatriots undertook in the pursuit of liberty.

As this journey ends, we remain convinced that Thomas Jefferson and Aeschylus were kindred spirits of like mind and purpose, bonded through the ages through the timeless words of rebellion, independence, and patriotism.

Maureen

I've always known my father's fondness for American history, and particularly for Thomas Jefferson. When he first broached the subject of these books and the potential acquisition, he was already feeling post-purchase syndrome. I'm sure he was thinking this was excessive and somewhat frivolous, but these books are a true piece of American history.

My father found the acquisition and restoration process very rewarding—he and all of us consider these books a family treasure. The Seven will always hold sentimental value for us, and I know my father's story about Jefferson's books will be told to generations to come.

Barry K. Buckley

So much time and effort has been put into researching the journey of Jefferson's books from his library to the Cove, I often wonder what the journey will be like for the books going forward. I certainly know that they'll spend at least a few generations safe and secure in the cove room.

When I finally had a chance to see the books for the first time . . . along with my children Nicole and Sebastian, we were all awestruck. (Don't worry Dad, I think Seb washed his hands.) It was and is an indescribable feeling to hold the same books that were once paged through by one of our founding fathers. I hope that Nicole and Sebastian's children and their children will be equally inspired.

This journey began in Jefferson's library. We now know where the books have traveled during the past two hundred years, but only the future will know where they will be two hundred years from now.

Dekker M. Buckley

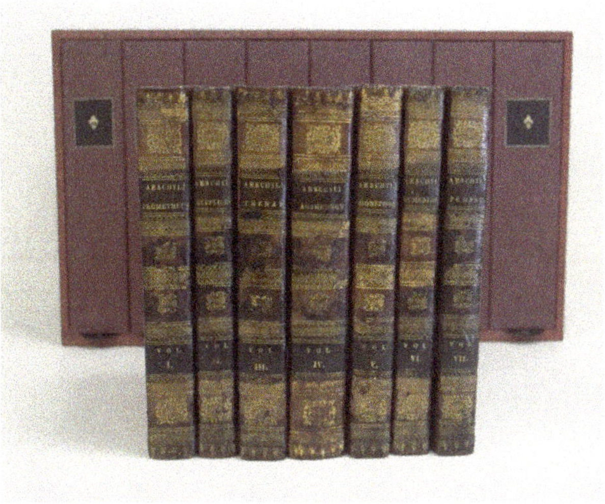

The *Seven* restored, with their new cases. *Photo Courtesy of Cat Tail Run Hand Bookbinding.*

My continued fascination with all things Thomas Jefferson is not only rooted in my years at the University of Virginia, but in my respect and admiration for the man, himself, and his boundless intellect. When the opportunity was presented to acquire something owned, cherished and touched by Jefferson, the choice was easy.

What was not so easy was the compelling back-story about books that came from Jefferson's hands to mine, hence the journey of the Seven. I wanted the path travelled to be accurate, interesting, and enjoyable to read. For the task I chose the gifted author, Maureen, but what I got without realizing it at the time was a world-class research talent who has made this story more than I ever imagined it could be.

Along with the more somber facts of this manuscript, I wanted a book that would be fun to read, and thus you may have found my attempts at humor and mirth, consistent with the granting of my request to serve as the Project O.I.

From the very beginning of this journey I have viewed the Seven as concrete evidence of Jefferson, a connection to the man who shaped the formation of this country. To touch that evidence, as he did, keeps me connected with an important part of history. At any time I can walk into the cove and pick up one of his books knowing at some point in the past that volume had been in Thomas Jefferson's hands. And every time I hold one, it serves to remind me of how far our country has migrated from the basic principles set forth by Jefferson and the Founding Fathers of this great nation.

I cannot help but add this: if one person reads this book about Jefferson's 7 books, and then reads our founding documents, and teaches one child the history of our nation, and explains to that child the significance of the Declaration of Independence and the Constitution of the United States, I will believe I have acted with responsibility as the steward of Jefferson's volumes.

By the way, I'm still waiting for the transfer . . . still waiting.

~C. Barry Buckley

Barry, Dekker and Barry
on the East Hampton.

Authors' Notes

To comply with the original premise to write a small book in 5 months, the initial research was restricted to Jefferson's libraries and the later years of his life since the 7 Aeschylus volumes were acquired for his Retirement Library. Douglas Wilson's *Jefferson's Books*, and Alan Pell Crawford's *Twilight at Monticello: The Final Years of Thomas Jefferson* were excellent sources, for both are readable, authoritative works.

Still later, as the scope of this project evolved, time remained at a premium and for that reason, the indexes of works by David McCullough, E. Millicent Sowerby, Dumas Malone, Hannah D. French, Willard Sterne Randall and other historians were only grazed for references to the historical figures and events found in this manuscript, particularly in Step VIII.

In a larger way, the Internet became an indispensible research tool through its information-rich websites such as: www.monticello.org; www.whitehouse.gov; http://classics.mit.edu/Browse/browse-Aeschylus.html; www.mountgulian.org; www.polishamericancenter.org/Kosciuszko; http://classics.mit.edu/Browse/browse-Aeschylus.html; www.masshist.org; www.librarycompany.org; and www.smithsonian.com.

Each draft of Step VIII was carefully reviewed by Barry; a noted Jeffersonian, his insightful comments led to productive discussions that resulted in a final version that combines our interpretations of historical facts without the clutter of footnotes, citations, or claims of academic research.

Perhaps Endrina Tay of the Jefferson Library at Monticello best explains the informal treatment in the writing of this book when she said: "It strikes me that what you have [written] is essentially a memoir."

The Search for the Missing Letter

Jefferson's letter to Mayo (April 10, 1820) regarding the interleaving of several Aeschylus editions into the *Seven* cannot be located.

Endrina Tay, the associate librarian in the Jefferson Library in Monticello, offered the only clues about the content of that letter. She wrote: "TJ had his Richmond bookbinder, Frederick A. Mayo, break apart [at least] four versions and interleave them into seven vols. We know this from Mayo's bookbinder's [ticket] found on the front inside covers. There is a missing letter that TJ writes to Mayo dated April 10, 1820, which probably contains binding instructions for this set, but we don't know for sure since we don't have the letter; and it's unclear from correspondence when exactly Mayo sent the finished bound vols. to TJ."

The search for the lost letter involved the Massachusetts Historical Society. Founded in Boston in 1791, M. H. S. is recognized as America's oldest historical society. At present, this society holds the second largest collection of the approximately 50,000 Jeffersonian manuscripts that are extant.

Liz Francis, an assistant librarian at the society, searched their files for a copy of the missing letter, but without results. She wrote: "[In regards to Endrina Tay's] reference to a "missing" April 10, 1820 letter, I was hoping it would be in our collection. I looked at . . . Jefferson's correspondence, 1819-1820 and also his unbound manuscripts, 1776-1827 and found no correspondence between Jefferson and Mayo in either April or May 1820."

Later, by telephone, Liz explained that the Jefferson-Mayo letter could be in any one of several other collections of Thomas Jefferson's manuscripts--the Coolidge Collection at MHS is just the tip of the iceberg. Although some manuscripts are in the hands of private collectors, thirteen major repositories hold the bulk of his writings. Those repositories include:

i. The Massachusetts Historical Society (ca. 9,500 documents and letters), which contains Jefferson's correspondence (nearly 8,800 pages of both incoming correspondence and Jefferson's retained copies of outgoing correspondence), manuscript volumes (the Farm and Garden Books), almanacs, law treatises, accounting books, and a manuscript volume that lists all of the books in Jefferson's Retirement Library.

ii. The Library of Congress (ca. 25,000 items, bound in 236 volumes), which contains the largest single collection of Jeffersonian manuscripts, including his correspondence and documents from 1763-1826, most notably his "public" papers, a draft of the *Constitution of Virginia,* letters about the University of Virginia, and several memorandum books.

iii. The National Archives (number of items unknown), which contains mostly transcripts of official correspondence dealing with the Continental and Confederation Congresses and the Constitutional Convention.

iv. The University of Virginia (ca. 1,400 items), which contains the Edgehill-Randolph papers, the Carr and Cary papers, and the Maury deposit. Many documents and letters concern the University; there are 62 architectural drawings of the University (there is a published calendar of this collection).

v. The Missouri Historical Society (ca. 1,100 items), which contains the Bixby-Jefferson collection.

vi. The Henry E. Huntington Library, San Marino, California (ca. 800 items), which contains papers from the years 1764-1826. Included are the estate papers of Jefferson's father, Peter, and documents regarding Jefferson's legal career.

vii. The New York Historical Society (ca. 700 items), which contains letters from the years 1779-1826 with highlights that include Jefferson's correspondence with General Von Steuben and Secretary of the Treasury Albert Gallatin.

viii. The College of William and Mary (ca. 300 items, part photocopies), which contains approximately 600 additional Jeffersonian items in the Tucker-Coleman papers.

ix. The Historical Society of Pennsylvania (ca. 650 items), which contains Jefferson's incoming and outgoing correspondence.

x. The American Philosophical Society, Philadelphia (several hundred items), which contains papers from the years 1775-1826: five boxes of miscellaneous letters and writings, and some official papers of the American Philosophical Society when Jefferson served as the society's president.

xi. The Virginia Historical Society (80 items), which contains papers from the years 1771-1826: Jefferson's letters are included in several collections.

xii. The Virginia State Library (55 items), which contains papers that cover the period in which Jefferson served as a state legislator and governor: drafts of bills and resolutions, land grants, patents, and tax rolls are also included.

xiii. The University of Michigan (45 items), which contains letters received by Jefferson.

xiv. There are other small repositories of Jefferson's manuscripts at the New Jersey Historical Society, the Princeton University Library, the University of South Carolina's Library, and the South Carolina Historical Society.

And, as a final note of explanation about the art of bookbinding and Jefferson's unique practice of marking his books, reference was made to Gerry Cataldo's noteworthy book, T*he Passion for Books* (2010). Gerry wrote: "A leaf is a single sheet of paper appearing as a page in a book. A gathering is the group of leaves resulting from the large parent printing sheet being folded to the correct size of the book. (Picture a very large sheet of paper, perhaps 19 inches by 24 inches. Fold the sheet once in half lengthwise, then fold one more time in half widthwise. The result is four leaves of about 10 inches by 12 inches. That's the size of the book, and those four leaves are called a gathering. Therefore this book is said to be gathered in fours.) When looking at a bound book from the top, or head, of the spine, you can usually see where the separate gatherings attach to the spine. A gathering is also known as a quire or section, and today is often referred to as a signature. However, a signature is properly, if archaically, a letter or numerical notation at the tail of the first leaf, or subsequent leaves, of a gathering serving as a notation for the binder (such as 'B4' or 'D'). Such signatures are visible on many antiquarian books . . . Jefferson would write his initial (either 'T' or 'J') beside the appropriately lettered signature."

References

Bibliography:

Crawford, Alan Pell. (2008). *Twilight at Monticello: The Final Years of Thomas Jefferson.* New York, NY, Random House.

Dumas, Malone. (1948-1981). *Jefferson and His Time: Volumes 1-6.* New York, NY, Little, Brown and Co.

Fischer, David Hackett. (2005). *Washington's Crossing: Pivotal Moments in American History.* New York, NY, Oxford University Press.

French, Hannah D. (1986). *Bookbinding in Early America: Seven Essays on Masters and Methods.* Worcester, MA, American Antiquarian Society.

Jefferson, Thomas (1989). *The Jefferson Bible: The Life & Morals of Jesus of Nazareth.* T. Jefferson (Ed.). Boston, MA, Beacon Press.

Jefferson, Thomas (2012). *The Papers of Thomas Jefferson, Retirement Series: Volume 8: 1 October 1814 to 31 August 1815.* (J. J. Looney, Ed.). Princeton, NJ, Princeton University Press.

Randall, Willard Sterne. (1993). *Thomas Jefferson: A Life.* New York, NY, Henry Holt and Company, Inc.

Sowerby, E. Millicent. (1952-1959). *Catalogue of the Library of Thomas Jefferson: Volumes I-V.* (E. M. Sowerby, Ed.). Washington, D.C, Library of Congress.

Sterne, Laurence. (1946). *The Life and Opinions of Tristram Shandy, Gentleman, London, UK,* J. M. Dent & Sons, Ltd.

Wilson, Douglas L. (2002). *Jefferson's Books.* Monticello, VA, Thomas Jefferson Memorial Foundation.

Internet Sources (in order of appearance):

Step IV: Descendancy of the Seven

VERPLANCK, Gulian Crommelin-Biographical Information. (n.d.). Retrieved from http://bioguide.congress.gov/scripts/biodisplay.pl?index=V000089

Step V: Mark Dimunation, Library of Congress

Chesapeake Campaign & The War of 1812 Marker. (n.d.). Retrieved from http://www.hmdb.org/marker.asp?marker=61039

Children's Reading | Thomas Jefferson's Monticello. (n.d.). Retrieved from http://www.monticello.org/site/research-and-collections/childrens-reading

Step VII: The Modern Relevancy of Mr. Jefferson

Thomas Jefferson Work Experience-Shmoop:HomeworkHelp. . . (n.d.). Retrieved from http://www.shmoop.com/thomas-jefferson/work-experience.html

Thomas Jefferson Collection, 1780-1881. (n.d.). Retrieved from http://quod.lib.umich.edu/c/clementsmss/umich-wcl-M-230jef?view=text

The life and morals of Jesus ofNazareth, extracted textually . . . (n.d.). Retrieved from https://archive.org/details/lifemoralsofJesus04jeff

Step VIII: Kindred Spirits: Thomas Jefferson & Aeschylus

ThinkExist.com. (n.d.). Retrieved from http://thinkexist.com/quoteation/my-father-gave-me-the-greatest-gift-anyone-could

Thomas Jefferson's Advice to His Teenage Grandson | The Bully . . .(n.d.). Retrieved from http://jrbenjamin.com/2013/10/14/thomasjeffersons-advice-to-his-teenage-grandson

Full Text of "Jefferson and His Time" - Internet Archive. (n.d.). Retrieved fromhttp://archive.org/stream/jeffersonhistime)!malo/jeffersonhis

Where did Thomas Jefferson go to college - answers - com (n.d.). Retrieved from http://www.answers.com/Q/Where-did-Thomas-Jefferson-go-

William Small - Wikipedia, the free encyclopedia. (n.d.). Retrieved from http://en.wikipedia.org/wiki/William_Small

William & Mary - Professor William Small 1734-1775. (n.d.). Retrieved from http://www.wm.edu/as/physics/about_physics/williamsmall/ind

British raised taxes on the colonies of North America . . .(n.d.). Retrieved from https://answers.yahoo.com.questionindex?qid=20100927140248^^ESPF3

James Brieg, Deism: One Nation Under A Clockwork God? (n.d.). Retrieved from http://learning. hccs.edu/faculty/

Lord Bolingbroke Quotes. S. Austin Allibone, comp. 1880 . . . (n.d.). Retrieved from http://www.bartleby.com/349/authors/21.html

Full Text of "Sources of the Roman Civil Law" - An Introduction . . . (n.d.). Retrieved from http://archive.org/stream/sourcesromanciv

Selected Writings of Sir Edward Coke, vol. II - Online . . . (n.d.). Retrieved from http://oll.libertyfund.org/titles/912

Thomas Jefferson's Reading Lists - John Uebersax. (n.d.). Retrieved from http://www.john-uebersax.com/plato/reading2.html

Thomas Jefferson's Recommended Reading | The Art of Manliness. (n.d.). Retrieved from http://www.artofmanliness.com/2014/10/08/the-libraries-of-famous-men-Thomas-Jeff

Full Text of "The Life of Thomas Jefferson" - Internet Archive. (n.d.). Retrieved from http://www.archive.org/stream/lifethomasjeffe09randgoog/life

Thomas Jefferson to John Minor, 30 August 1814, including . . . (n.d.). Retrieved from http://founders.archives.gov/documents/Jefferson/03-07-02-0455

Full Text of "The Education Works of Thomas Jefferson". (n.d.). Retrieved from http://www.archive.org/stream/educationalwork.012284mbp/

UNIT VI -Terence. (n.d.). Retrieved from http://college.holycross.edu/faculty/wziobro/ClassicalAmerica/

Jefferson Amid the Ruins | France Today. (n.d.). Retrieved from http://www.francetoday.com/articles/2012/09/09/jefferson_an

THE BEAUTIES OF STERNE.: amazon.co.uk: No author: Books. (n.d.). Retrieved from http://www.amazon.co.uk/THEBEAUTIESOFSTERNE-author/dp/BOODB09K26

The Life and Opinions of Tristram Shandy, Gentleman . . . (n.d.). Retrieved from http://en.wikipedia.org/wiki/The-Life-and-Opionions-of-Tristram

Extract from Thomas Jefferson to James Madison, 30 Aug. 1823 . . . (n.d.). Retrieved from http://tjrs.monticello.org/letter/1419

Declaration of Independence - Text Transcript. (n.d.). Retrieved from http://www.

archives.gov/exhibits/charters/declaration_transcript

Letter to Henry Lee | Teaching American History. (n.d.). Retrieved from http://teachingamericanhistory.org/library/document/letter-to-henry-lee/

From Thomas Jefferson to William Gordon, 16 July 1788. (n.d.). Retrieved from http://founders.archives.gov/documents/Jefferson/01-13-02-0266

J. L. Bell's blog/American Revolution. (n.d.) Retrieved from http://www.boston1775.blogspot.com

Martha Wayles Skelton Jefferson - Thomas Jefferson Encyclopedia. (n. d.). Retrieved from http://wiki.monticello.org/mediawiki/index.php?

The History Book Club - PRESIDENTIAL SERIES: 4. AMERICAN . . . (n.d.). Retrieved from http://www.goodreads.com/topic/show/294532-4-american-sphinx-chapter-2-75---106-

A Place of Reading: Personal Libraries - Jefferson. (n.d.). Retrieved from http://www.americanantiquarian.org/Exhibitions/Reading/Jeffe

uc004885.jpg. The Library of Congress. (n.d.). Retrieved from http://www.loc.gov/teachers/classroommaterial/lessons/Jeffer

PBS Thomas Jefferson: Head vs. Heart Letter. (n.d.). Retrieved from http://www.pbs.org/jefferson/archives/documetns/ih195811.h

Jefferson Letter to Madison - Archiving Early America. (n.d.). Retrieved from http://www.earlyamerica.com/early-america-review/volume-1/jefferson-letter-madis

Envisaging the West: Thomas Jefferson and the Roots of Lewis . . . (n.d.). Retrieved from http://jeffersonswest.unl.edu/archive/view-doc.php?id=jef.00042

From Thomas Jefferson to Joseph Priestley, 27 January 1800. (n.d.). Retrieved from http://founders.archives.gov/documents/Jefferson/01-31-02-0289

State of the Union Address | Thomas Jefferson | December 8. 1801. (n.d.). Retrieved from http://stateoftheunion.onetwothree.net/texts/18011208.html

Battle of Derne: U.S. Marines Spearhead Capture of Barbary . . . (n.d.). Retrieved from http://burnpit.legion.org/2012/04/battle-derne-us-mariens-spearhead-capture-barb

Searching for Nelson's Quote-USN/News. (n.d.). Retrieved from http://news.usni.org/2012/07/22/searching-nelsons-quote

Jefferson the Violinist | Discovering Lewis & Clark. (n.d.). Retrieved from http://www.lewis-clark.org/article/1241
Reply to the Response to the Minority Report | Thomas . . . (n.d.). Retrieved from http://www.monticello.org/site/plantation-and-slavery/reply-to-response-to-minor

Activities Xtros - National Geographic Education. (n.d.). Retrieved from http://educationnatoinalgeographic.com/archive/pedition/ac

The Lewis and Clark Expedition | The Federalist Papers. (n.d.). Retrieved from http://www.the federalistpapers.org/ebooks/the-lewis-and-clark-expedition

I have sworn upon the altar of god, eternal hostility against . . . (n.d.). Retrieved from http://www.brainyquote.com/quotes/quotes/t/thomasjeff

THOMAS JEFFERSON QUOTES III - Notable Quotes. (n.d.). Retrieved from http://www.notablequotes.com/j/jefferson_thomas_iii.html

Memoir, Correspondence, and Miscellanies. From the Papers of . . . (n.d.). Retrieved from http://www.bookrags.com/ebooks/16784/16.html

Sanctum sanctorum (Quotation) | Thomas Jefferson's Monticello. (n.d.). Retrieved from http://www.monticello.org/site/jefferson/sanctum-sanctuorum-quotation

Library (Book Room) - Thomas Jefferson Encyclopedia. (n.d.). Retrieved from http://wiki.monticello.org/mediawiki/index.php?

Search | Jefferson Quotes & Family Letters. (n.d.). Retrieved from http://tprs.monticello.org/archive/search/quotes

Knowing the God above god, Francis Bacon: The Faculties of . . .(n.d.). Retrieved from http://knowgnosis.tumblr.com/post/22146061136/francis-bacon-the-faculties-of-the

The War of 1812 | History Today. (n.d.). Retrieved from http://www.historytoday.com/jeremy-black-war-1812

O Say Does That Star-Spangled Banner Yet Wave: The Defense of . . . (n.d.). Retrieved from http://www.shtf.plan.com/headline-news/o-say-does-that-star-spangled-banner-yet-w

Oremus Hymnal: O say can you see, by the dawn's early light. (n.d.). Retrieved from http://www.oremus.org/hymnal/0/0570.html

The Blog of 1812: Thomas Jefferson's Letters re: Burning of . . . (n.d.). Retrieved from http://www.blogof1812.com/2014/09/thomas-jefferson-letter-reburning-of.html

Lesson Plans from Monticello: I cannot live without book. (n.d.). Retrieved from http://classroom.monticello.org/teachers/lessons/I-cannot-live-without

Thomas Jefferson's Library | US House of Representatives . . . (n.d.). Retrieved from http://history.house.gov/Historical-Highlight/1800-1850/Thomas-Jefferson-s-libr

Reason - Thomas Jefferson's Library | Exhibitions-Library . . . (n.d.). Retrieved from http://www.loc.gov/exhibits/thomas-jeffersons-library/reason.html

Thomas Jefferson letters 1815 January 5 - June 11. . . (n.d.). Retrieved from http://www.yamaguchy.com/library/jefferson/1815.html

Full Text of "History of the Library of Congress. Volume 1 . . . (n.d.). Retrieved from http://www.archive.org/stream/hsitoryoflibrary01johnuoft/hist

Jefferson's Formal Education - Thomas Jefferson Encyclopedia. (n.d.). Retrieved from http://wiki.monticello.org/mediawik/index.php?title=Jefferson%27s_Formal_Educat

Letter to Nathaniel Burwell | Teaching American History. (n.d.). Retrieved from http://teachingamericanhistory.org.library/document/letter-to-nathaniel-burwell/

History of the Quote: "I cannot live without book", (n.d.). Retrieved from http://blog.monticelloshop.org/?p=2030

The Conservation of the Jefferson Bible at the National . . . (n.d.). Retrieved from http://cool.conservation-us.org/coolaic/sg/bpg/annual/v31/bp31-05.pdf

From Thomas Jefferson to Frederick A. Mayo, 9 April 1819. (n.d.). Retrieved from http://founders.archives.gov/documents/Jefferson/98-01-02-0318

From Thomas Jefferson to John Laval, 27 March 1820. (n.d.). Retrieved from http://founders.archives.gov/documents/Jefferson/98-01-02-1179

Aeschylus - Wikipedia, the free encyclopedia. (n.d.). Retrieved from http://en.wikipedia.org/wiki/Aeschylus

Quotes about Greatness (668 quotes). (n.d.). Retrieved from http://www.goodreads.com/quotes/tag/greatness

H-SC | Thomas Jefferson on Why Study Classics | Hamden . . . (n.d.). Retrieved from http://www.hsc.edu/Academics/Academic-Majors/Classics/Why-Classics/Thomas-Jeffer

Agamemnon-Shmoop. (n.d.).Retrieved from http://www.shmoop.com/agamemnon/

Mythology - Spark Notes. (n.d.). Retrieved from http://sparkcharts.sparknotes.com/lit/mythology

Aeschylus and His Tragedies - TheatreHistory.com. (n.d.). Retrieved from http://www.theatrehistory.com/ancient/aeschylus001.html

Children's Reading | Thomas Jefferson's Monticello. (n.d.). Retrieved from http://www.monticello.org/site/research-and-collections/childrens-reading

Quotations on Reading - Thomas Jefferson Encyclopedia. (n.d.). Retrieved from http;://wiki.monticello.org/mediawiki/index.php?title=Quotations_on_Readubg&p

Quotes - Thomas Jefferson's Libraries. (n.d.). Retrieved from http://jlibraries.monticello.org/tjandreading/quotes.html

The Declaration of Independence - US History. (n.d.). Retrieved from http://www.ushistory.org/Declaration/document/

Step IX: Poor's Auction, Washington, D. C., 1829

From Thomas Jefferson to Richard Rush, 22 June 1819. (n.d.). Retrieved from http://founders.archives.gov/documents/Jefferson/901-02-0521

Step X: Gulian Crommelin Verplanck, Humanitarian

A Discourse on the Life, Character and Writings of Gulian . . . (n.d.). Retrieved from http://www.amazon.com/Discourse-Character-WRitings-Cromelin-Verplanck/dp/128605

A Discourse on the Life, Character and Writings of Gulian . . . (n.d.). Retrieved from http://www.barnesandnoble.com/w/discourse-on-the-life-character-and-writings-of Verplanck-Welcome to Mount Gulian Historic Site! (n.d.). Retrieved from http://mountgulian.org/verplanck.html

The Tory Trio: Judith Verplanck, Betsey Loring and Gen . . . (n.d.). Retrieved from http://maddiesancestorsearch.blogspot.com/2011/crommelin-wasborn-16-s

A Discourse on the Life, Character and Writings of Gulian . . . (n.d.). Retrieved from http://www.gutenberg.org> . . . >byWilliamCullenBryant

A Discourse on the Life, Character and Writings of Gulian . . . (n.d.). Retrieved from http://www.pub22.net/view.php?d=12&id-10141

Step XIV: Charlottesville, Virginia

by Susan R. Stein . . . (n.d.). Retrieved from http://www.barnesandnoble.com/w/worlds-of-thomas-jefferson-at-monticello-susan-r

Authors' Notes

Coolidge Collection of Thomas Jefferson Manuscripts, 1705-1827. (n.d.). Retrieved from http://www.masshist.org/collection-guides/view/fa0031

As a final note, we are deeply grateful to Katie Witek for her editorial comments, and to the many who shared their knowledge, experience and time—their contributions enriched this "journey" from Ancient Greece to the Eastern Shore of Maryland. We especially appreciate the publishers Gerry Cataldo and James Dissette—in their added roles, Gerry served as the Editor, and Jim changed our words into a book through his beautiful designs of the cover and interior pages.

★

We appreciate, too, those who are as committed as Barry to the preservation of our national treasures. Of note is the owner, president and general manager of the Dallas Cowboys, Jerry Jones, and his wife, Gene, who donated a fund for the acquisition of books for the reconstruction project of Jefferson's Library on the second floor of the Library of Congress. Those acquisitions are exact copies of Jefferson's original books, the ones destroyed by the Christmas Eve fire in the Capitol in 1851.

In speaking about the fund, Jerry Jones wrote: "Thomas Jefferson's contributions to our society were as diverse as they were important. His influence made an impact on many different aspects of American life, and that is a noble path to follow. . . I am honored. . . to turn back the pages of time, while also ensuring that a very important part of our country's legacy will be secure, fruitful, and a source of inspiration for hundreds of years to come."

Jones' sentiment echoes Barry's strong conviction that in the "preservation of our national treasures, we are safeguarding concrete reminders that the founding fathers were real people who pledged their fame, fortune and lives to the creation of our nation, the greatest, longest-lived republic in the history of the world."

★